THE KNOWLEDGE OF GOOD & EVIL

BOOKS BY GLENN KLEIER

The Last Day
The Knowledge of Good & Evil

GLENN KLEIER

THE KNOWLEDGE OF GOOD & EVIL

A TOM DOHERTY ASSOCIATES BOOK • NEW YORK

This is a work of fiction. All of the characters, organizations, and events portrayed in this novel are either products of the author's imagination or are used fictitiously.

THE KNOWLEDGE OF GOOD & EVIL

A Tor Book
Published by Tom Doherty Associates, LLC
175 Fifth Avenue
New York, NY 10010

www.tor-forge.com

ISBN 978-0-7653-2377-4

First Edition: July 2011

Printed in the United States of America

0 9 8 7 6 5 4 3 2 1

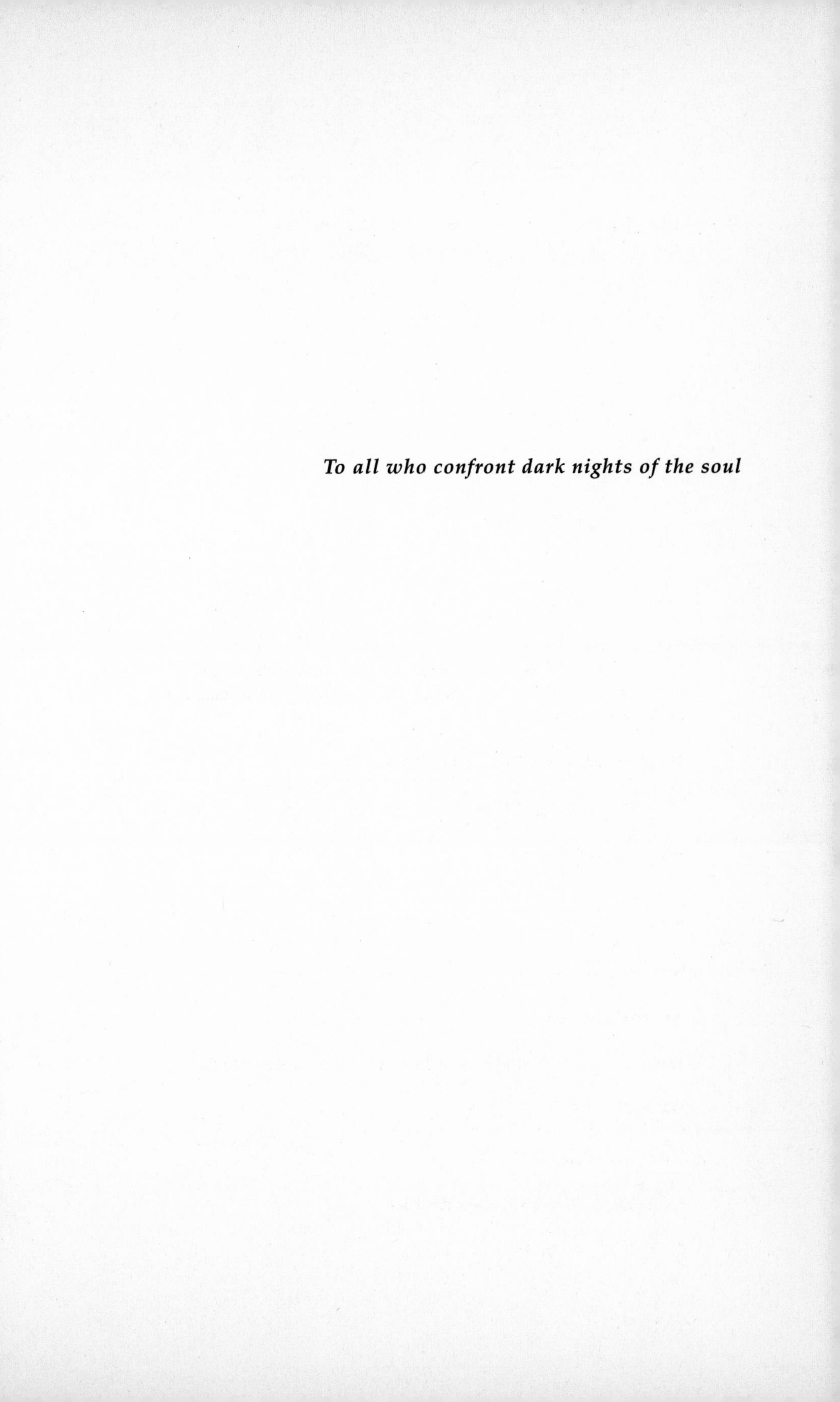

To all who confront dark nights of the soul

ACKNOWLEDGMENTS

This little allegory and I owe much to many people . . .

Foremost, Albert Zuckerman, senior agent and founder of Writers House. Al is the compleat literary agent. A mentor and sounding board, with more than thirty illustrious years in this industry. An editor, with vast expertise as a playwright, professor of dramatic literature at Yale, and author of TV shows, novels, and nonfiction. And a tireless, enthusiastic advocate. His keen, comprehensive advice was invaluable to me. Moreover, Al is a true gentleman and all-around nice guy. Thank you, my friend.

I'm grateful to another legend in publishing, executive editor at Macmillan/Tor/Forge, Robert Gleason. Bob has a substantial and distinguished biography himself, having edited many award-winning, bestselling books of fiction and nonfiction. He's also an accomplished writer in his own right, with a dozen-plus novels to his credit. *Knowledge* benefited greatly from his experience and dedication.

I'd like to recognize, too, Bob's remarkable assistant, Ashley Cardiff. Ashley was an integral part of the process at Macmillan from start to finish—both administratively and editorially—helping to fine-tune many aspects of *Knowledge.* Mark her name, she has a bright future.

Special thanks to longtime friends, Jean Amick and Dick Aylor of Kentucky Country Day School. Jean, Chair of the Foreign Language Department, and Dick, a Latin savant, assisted me with my French and Latin translations respectively, kindly polishing my rusty efforts—and without snickering!

I wish to thank the dozens of good people around the globe who helped supply images for *Knowledge.* Their splendid contributions and credits can be viewed collectively at kleier.com/images.

I also want to remember my dear mother, Mary Rose Kleier, whom I lost during the writing of this book. My eternal love. And my warm thanks to my father, Gene Kleier, and sons Ryan and Sean, who took time to read early drafts and offer helpful thoughts—as did my friend Dr. Ken Hodge.

My most heartfelt appreciation I save for my loving wife. Thank you for serving as first reader, Pam, your perspective was indispensable. You are my muse.

How fortunate I am to have the assistance of all these brilliant and generous people. What a fulfilling experience this has been.

My love to all of you, always,

GLENN

NOTE TO READERS

Originally, *The Knowledge of Good & Evil* was intended to include a number of color and black-and-white photos, paintings, and illustrations embedded within the text of the story. In the final analysis, however, many proved too large and detailed to reproduce well in print.

It was decided that a better way to present the images would be via a web page online, where each could be viewed at proper size. Replacing the images in the text now are corresponding numbers in superscript ([1], [2], [3] . . .). A legend is provided at the back of the book with a web address, kleier.com/images, where all can be viewed. To realize the full effects of the story, it's recommended not to view the images prematurely.

Although *The Knowledge of Good & Evil* is a work of fiction, the story centers around many actual events, people, and places. Much research went into the development of those aspects, and for those interested, more information and a bibliography are available at the web page kleier.com.

We hope this collection of photos, paintings, illustrations, and additional background will enrich your reading experience.

And the Lord God commanded the man, "Of every tree in the garden you shall eat, but of the Tree of the Knowledge of Good and Evil you shall not eat; for the day you eat of it, surely you shall die."

Genesis, 2:16–17

And the serpent said unto the woman, "Nay, you shall not die. For in the day you eat thereof, your eyes shall be opened and you shall be as God, knowing Good and Evil."

Genesis, 3:4–5

THE KNOWLEDGE OF GOOD & EVIL

PROLOGUE

(Based on official police records, eyewitness testimony, journal records, and facts in evidence)

COTTAGE #2, RED CROSS INTERNATIONAL CONFERENCE CENTER, BANGKOK, THAILAND, DECEMBER 10, 1968, AFTERNOON

World-famous theologian Father Thomas Merton, 53, stepped from the shower toweling his rugged face and gray crescent of hair that rimmed his head, blue eyes aglow with the fervor of his Great Secret. He hummed a Christmas carol the choir had sung for him at Mass this morning—"Angels We Have Heard on High."

If only they knew how fitting their selection was!

One week ago while visiting a sacred cave in Ceylon, Father had stumbled into something he suspected no soul now living had ever seen. Surely something no living soul was meant to see. He'd entered Heaven through a back door, looked into the very Mind of God, and escaped with a revelation so powerful it would change all humanity. Bring wars to a standstill. End forever the age-old hatreds between races, creeds, and cultures.

Even more earthshaking, unlike revelations of scripture, his vision did *not* stand on Faith alone. Anyone daring to follow Father's path could steal into Heaven and see for himself. For the first time in history, to the utter negation of all nonbelievers—*proof of God and the Afterlife!*

The Secret burned in Father's soul and he couldn't wait to present it to the world. But a revelation of this magnitude demanded a proper forum, and to that end he was biding his time until tonight. As guest of honor at an international religious conference, he was to give closing remarks. And what a finale he would make it! Hundreds of spiritual leaders and media in attendance from all over the globe, none with a clue to the bombshell he was about to drop.

The forum was hours off, however, and Father needed rest. Hooking his towel on the door he retired to the bedroom, padding naked across the terrazzo to where his pallet sat by an electric fan.

Moments later he lay dead.

But his Great Secret did not die with him. Father Merton left behind a journal . . .

ONE

The Near Future

CBS AFFILIATE, CHANNEL 6 TV, LOS ANGELES, MORNING

Grinning, Charles Dunn bustled into the little screening room, clicking on lights with a remote, feeling like he'd just won the Super Lotto. He checked his Rolex. Angela would be here soon, always punctual as a church bell.

He lumbered down to the center row, shuffled to a seat, and plopped, smoothing his suit. *Next week, the diet,* he vowed. Impossible now with winter production racing to a close. He'd been gulping coffee and donuts for hours to keep his energy. Insane business, this, creating local TV programs to compete with national broadcast and cable—and at a fraction the budget. Living Nielsen-to-Nielsen not knowing if the shows you'd birthed and nurtured lovingly as a parent would endure.

But it was moments like the one pending that made all the heartburn worth it. Charles had spoken to the home network in New York this morning, and he had *incredible* news for Angela. She'd no clue what awaited, joining him here simply to preview new footage for their series.

"And to think," he sighed, running a hand through his thinning hair, "I nearly let her slip through my fingers . . ."

It was scarcely a year ago that Angela had come to his attention, a talk show host for an obscure LA radio station at the time. Just another tongue clamoring to be heard on the crowded, late-night airwaves. Charles always kept an ear cocked for radio shows with TV potential, and he'd heard buzz about a new program catching on with area college students—often a bellwether of the next hot thing.

But tuning in, he'd quickly tuned out. *Probing the Paranormal.* A weekly news-type format investigating things supernatural. Ghosts, clairvoyants, mediums, and such. Old hat. Cable TV had been working that shtick for years with lukewarm success.

Nor was he that impressed with Angela, first blush. Fresh out of grad school, his sources told him, PhD in psychology, no previous broadcast experience. Hardly a springboard to TV. Not that she wasn't talented. A silky, arresting voice. And clever the way she applied science and reason to topics seldom handled intelligently. But *too much* science and reason. More PBS than CBS.

"Damn, did I whiff that one!"

Two months later he was kicking himself in his big, professional ass. Driving to work one morning, glancing out his window at a billboard, he did such a double take he nearly pulled a muscle in his neck. Towering before him, the image of a stunning young woman with dark hair, arms folded, leaning against the call letters of her radio station. Bold words proclaimed:

LA's #1 Late-Nite Talk Show!
PROBING the PARANORMAL
with Dr. Angela Weber

He'd almost skidded off the road. Grabbing his cell, he'd arranged a hasty meeting, only to confirm how wrong his first impression had been. Angela was *amazing*. Poised, personable, quick-witted. And uncommonly attractive. Large, hazel-green eyes that changed like a kaleidoscope with her mood—light when she laughed, dark when serious. Charles knew screen presence when he saw it.

Of course by then other producers were circling, too, and he had to pay top dollar and make tough concessions to get her. Granting her creative control of the show, allowing her to pick her own cohost—

He was interrupted by the sound of the door. Turning, he saw a lithe figure in a dark dress suit glissading down the steps toward him, walnut hair shimmering and bouncing on shoulders square as a carpenter's level. Oval face. Ivory skin. Intelligent brow.

But her smile was just a brief flash today, eyes dark.

No matter. Once she heard, he'd have her beaming . . .

Angela felt swallowed up in Charles's bearish arms, his trim, red beard scratching her cheek. As a rule, she didn't like the "Hollywood hug," but

Charles she didn't mind. He'd been wonderful to her and Ian as they'd plunged into this mind-boggling business. Seasoned and wise.

His deep voice rumbled in her ear, "Ready for Ian's solo debut?"

She hesitated, pulling back. "When he called last night, he mentioned they'd had problems. Didn't go into it, he says the video will speak for itself."

Charles motioned her to a seat.

It wasn't Ian's video that worried her. Over the course of their season he'd sharpened his investigative skills, able now to cut through the knottiest paranormal puzzle on his own. It was the way he'd jumped on this East Coast case despite her objections, despite having ample material here at home—just none that suited his tastes. It hurt that she couldn't talk him out of it, that her refusal to join him didn't matter. He'd even stayed on to do the editing, sending ahead the finished MPEG.

Charles clicked a remote to dim the lights, and the screen below came to life. Angela found herself wishing Ian's video would fail. And felt miserable for it.

A five-second countdown, then a tall, athletically slim man appeared on-screen in the light of flood lamps, standing in front of a Cape Cod–style home, patches of dirty snow dotting the yard. Handsome in a navy-blue cashmere topcoat, puffs of breath escaping into the night. Angela's heart kicked the way it always did when they'd been separated for a time.

The camera zoomed in to reveal vivid blue eyes. *So serious.* Little clue to the warmth she knew lay beneath. Dark hair neatly combed, a few unruly locks flittering like pennants in the breeze. She wanted to reach out and smooth them. A font on the screen read:

PTP Investigator, Ian Baringer

He gave that little smile of his and gestured toward the house, a hint of boyishness in his bearing. That strange, innocent quality Angela had noticed first time she'd laid eyes on him five years ago. As if he'd been plucked out of some quaint, bygone era, still adjusting to the twenty-first century. Which, in many ways, was true.

"The Devil's Due," he announced his episode, refined northeastern accent filling the theater. Her heart quickened.

The scene cut to daytime footage, same house, a middle-age man shoveling the walkway. Ian continued, *"This is Mr. Andrew Kavoski. Accountant, husband of Bernice Kavoski, father of two children away in college."*

The view widened to take in a heavyset woman with heavily coiffed brown hair, bringing Andrew a hot drink.

"Andrew starts each week a normal, healthy, typical resident of suburban Hackensack, New Jersey . . . But on the seventh day of each week, the Lord's Day, Andrew transforms like Jekyll and Hyde into this *manic creature—"*

Abruptly the video cut to a scene of the same man, almost unrecognizable, strapped to a bed, writhing, growling. Angela drew her legs under her seat.

"Victim of a severe, if passing, psychosis, Andrew has endured seizures like this every Sunday for months. Medical experts were at a loss to help, unable even to diagnose his condition."

The video switched to shots of a church.

"It seems the onset of his ailment coincided with the end of an affair he was having. His liaisons had taken place in this church basement each Sunday while he was supposed to be at Mass."

Angela glanced at Charles to see a smile on his lips.

"Andrew was finally caught in the act by his wife"—the view cut to a scene of Bernice being consoled by her pastor—*"and a week later, Andrew's strange affliction began. That Sunday morning, about the time he usually left for Mass, he suffered a seizure. Bernice called her brother, a neurologist living nearby, who rushed to their aid."*

The image of a burly, fiftyish man in a white coat came up on-screen, along with shots of Andrew undergoing a physical and brain scans.

"Andrew was hospitalized in his brother-in-law's care, but after tests, there seemed no explanation for his attack. He recovered quickly, however, without complications, and was discharged. Only to suffer another seizure the following Sunday—and again every Sunday thereafter.

"When more tests and treatments yielded no answers, Andrew—and most of his church parish—came to believe he was the victim of demonic possession. His pastor put him in touch with a priest experienced in such matters."

Angela saw the photo of a smiling, avuncular, gray-haired man in dark shirt with reverse collar.

"Father Peter Riggs and I have been friends for years, and with the Kavoskis' permission, he invited me to document the event. But sadly, the exorcism did not go well."

Jerky video ricocheted around the screen—Andrew, crazed and loose from an armstrap, attacking Father Pete with a bloodied shard of glass. Angela shrank in her seat, shocked. Never had their shows displayed such violence. She was even more appalled to see Ian take on the psychotic Kavoski, wrestling him back into his bindings.

"Whoa!" Charles gushed. "Viewers will eat this up!"

The melee ended and Ian's face materialized on-screen.

"Fortunately, Father's injuries weren't serious. He's expected to make a full recovery. And despite the setback, this story has a happy ending. Inspecting the room after the attack, I discovered something. Though I'd carefully supervised the breakfast Andrew was served in bed that day, I'd overlooked a salt shaker he'd used to season his eggs."

Impressed, Angela saw video of a medical research facility with technicians examining liquids in vials.

"Lab analysis revealed a foreign substance in the salt—phencyclidine—an animal medication. Also known by the street name 'angel dust,' phencyclidine causes hallucinations and psychosis in humans . . ."

The camera cornered a shamefaced Mrs. Kavoski.

"Bernice is a veterinarian's assistant, and confronted with the evidence, she confessed to spiking the salt. Her brother was in on it, falsifying Andrew's medical tests. Bernice's motive was to punish her husband while saving face, wanting her neighbors to think his infidelity the work of the Devil, not their failing marriage. Her plan was to teach Andrew a lesson, then 'cure' him with an exorcism. In the end, the only demons she exposed were her own . . ."

Ian appeared once more in front of the house.

"I'm pleased to report, Andrew is now symptom-free, and he and his wife are in counseling. He's declined to press charges against his brother-in-law . . ."

The video ended, the lights came up, and Angela sat back. She could hear that little voice again, nagging about the way Ian's choice of topics was slanting the show.

But Charles's focus was ratings. "Great stuff! Except, no more splitting the team. I like the sparks you two throw off." He grinned. "We're gonna need those male demos you pull—now that we're expanding to new markets!"

Angela blinked. "Syndication? *So soon?"*

His broad face glowed. "Syndication, hell. The network's taken notice, and they *like* what they see. They're flyin' in end of the month to talk *national rollout."*

Stunned, all she could do was gape at him.

"Not a done deal, of course. But when the brass come to you, it's a damn good sign."

His cell phone went off and he fished it from a pocket. Angela recognized his secretary's face on its screen.

"Your ten o'clock is here."

"I'm on my way." He hung up, looking at Angela. "Ian gets in tonight?"

"Yes." She was still reeling.

"Well, don't stay out late celebrating. I've got you two meeting with those picketers tomorrow, first thing . . ."

A small, if vocal, group of demonstrators had been protesting their show the last several weeks.

"Can't have that crap while the network's here. Work your charms on those kooks, get rid of 'em."

That little voice in her head rose another decibel.

TWO

LOS ANGELES INTERNATIONAL AIRPORT, SAME DAY, NIGHT

Angela stood at the security gate amid a small crowd. Ian wasn't expecting her, but she missed him so, this the longest they'd been apart since reconciling last fall. Her mother and sisters had given her so much grief for taking him back. But as usual, she'd ignored them.

People began to stir as passengers filtered toward the gate, and Angela could see Ian approaching in that long, easy stride, making her heart jump. He looked *so* good. Clean-cut in his button-down shirt and pleated slacks, eyes bright and alert despite the long flight.

Two young women flanked him. Pretty, in sandals, jeans, T-shirts, and ball caps. College kids, they looked. Ian was toting what appeared to be their carry-ons.

Angela came forward, catching his eye, and he broke into a surprised grin. Bidding his companions and their bags good-bye, he rushed to sweep her up. It felt wonderful, wringing the fatigue right out of her. She inhaled his scent—like the fresh-charged atmosphere before a storm.

"What are you doing here?" he cried, setting her down, kissing her.

The two young women passed, eyeing Angela, and she whispered in his ear, "Fans?"

He paid them a parting smile and wave. "No, actually. They never even heard of the show." He wrapped an arm around her, ushering her to baggage claim. "Philosophy majors at UCLA. Made for an interesting flight."

"I'll bet." She said it without sarcasm. Though she'd felt a twinge of jealousy, she knew that if the coeds had been flirting, and if they'd exercised any degree of subtlety, Ian would have missed their signals. Just as he'd missed hers when first they'd met.

He collected his suitcase and they rolled out of the terminal arm-in-arm to their car, Ian taking the wheel, heading for Santa Monica.

"I've got some interesting news," Angela told him. "Charles heard from the network yesterday. They may want *PTP.* They're coming out to talk."

His face lit up. "*No!* Incredible! When?"

"End of the month."

"Who would have thought!" He gave her a squeeze. "Now if only the ratings hold. How's the fan mail?"

"Strong. Though the poison pens are still scribbling." She decided not to go into it now. "By the way, you got some more marriage proposals."

"Have I caught up to you?"

"Close. I may get my skirts shortened."

He laughed, and she felt his warm hand on her knee, sending a thrill up her spine. Then his voice grew soft.

"So . . . what did you think of it?"

"Of what?"

"The Hackensack case, of course."

She knew; she was stalling.

He added, "I was damned lucky, I nearly lost Pete."

"Not to mention your *own* life."

"Everything was falling apart," he admitted. "But then I tried to think like you, and the answer finally came." He moved his hand to hers. "I missed you."

"Then why didn't you come home to do the editing?"

He paused. "I thought the raw footage would upset you. I wanted to clean things up first. And anyway, I had business in New York, some papers to sign for the trust."

The inheritance his late parents had left him.

"Well," she said, "you'll be happy to know, Charles loves it. And I'm sure CBS will, too."

"Good, because I've got us another one. On the flight in, I was fishing online and came across a 'miracle' at a public high school in Kansas. There's this retaining wall where a Christlike image appears. The school paints it out, but it comes right back. Believers think it's a sign from God supporting Intelligent Design. Drawing huge crowds."

Angela flinched. "And what do *you* think it is?"

"Something a little less heavenly . . . I checked the area, there's a plastics plant nearby. If my hunch is right, it's I.D., all right—Industrial Discharge . . ."

She sat back, watching him as he prattled on. He certainly looked the epitome of the normal, healthy, all-American male. Anyone seeing him now would be hard-pressed to believe he was once an obsessive-compulsive neurotic. Angela had worked so hard to help him break free of its grip. But to her trained eye, the old claws were encircling again. And she wasn't sure how to stop them.

THREE

CBS AFFILIATE CHANNEL 6 TV, LOS ANGELES, NEXT MORNING

Sun streamed into the conference room through gaps in the blinds, casting lines across an oil painting on the wall. An abstract, it reminded Angela of the floor of a bird cage. Beneath the painting was a bookcase filled with trophies—"Beldings," local advertising awards—and next to that, a large lump of ragged metal on a pedestal, plaque reading, "Woman's Head No. 7, bronze/1973/Willem de Kooning."

More meteorite than anatomy.

Sitting opposite Angela and Ian at the table were three delegates representing the demonstrators outside.

A minister from a nearby church; white, male, hefty, sixtyish, beige suit, slicked-back gray hair.

To his left, a black female reporter for an LA-based evangelical newspaper; trim, thirties, gray suit.

And next to her, a Latino woman; rail-thin, forties, brown dress, dark hair, no stated profession. But there was something about her eyes. Especially when she trained them on Ian. Smoldering. And not in an amorous way.

The three had come prepared, minister with a set of handwritten file cards, reporter with briefcase and note pad, Latino woman with a bulky purse. Angela trusted that the metal detectors at CBS's doors were working.

Let's not get paranoid.

The minister had been doing all the talking, reporter taking notes, Latino woman staring at her knotted hands.

". . . your show's agenda," the man was saying, "the way it targets spirituality—you're hostile to Christian beliefs."

Angela was staying out of it, religion Ian's forte. He'd gotten them into this, and hopefully he could get them out.

Ian responded politely, "As we state each episode, our mission is to probe the paranormal—wherever we find it."

"Yet all you ever focus on are *religious* phenomena." Donning glasses, the man read from a file card: "Weeping statues, faith healings, stigmata, the effects of prayer on—"

"Frauds, mostly. People being duped, if not bilked."

"You can find no fraud in *non*-Christian phenomena? Psychics? Fortune tellers? Scientology?"

Now the Latino woman jumped in.

"And what about your cases where there *is no* fraud?" She spoke with a mild Spanish accent, voice edgy. "The *harm* you do to people's faith! Your episode in El Centro with the widow . . . the Voice she heard in church . . ."

Angela remembered it well. An elderly woman who'd thought her dead husband spoke to her at evening services. Angela and Ian had shown it to be a radio signal skewed by the church's metal structure, playing through a filling in the woman's tooth.

"That lady," the Latino woman said, eyes tearing, "she is my *mamá*. You took away her Voice. Her comfort. Now she has *nothing*."

Ian looked moved. But he held his ground.

"She has *the truth*."

The woman snapped, "Who are you to decide which is more important?"

Suddenly she reached for her purse, and Angela froze. But it was only to get a magazine. She tossed it on the table and Angela recognized it instantly.

A two-year-old issue of *TIME*. Ian in black cassock, standing on a dock before a rusted freighter, crying black child in his arms. It always melted her. Eyes so serious. Jaw bold and clenched, Roman nose assertive as the blade of an ax. The headline read:

The Fighting Friar of Abidjan

The woman said softly, "Once you were a *hero* to people of Faith. A *priest*. Now you take our Faith away."

The reporter stopped writing and regarded Ian closely.

He sighed. "That isn't my intent. I'm simply trying to find *substance* in Faith. If God's Hand is truly behind these claims people make, *let's see the Fingerprints*."

The reporter snapped, "Isn't that the whole point of Faith? Believing in things you *can't* prove?"

Ian turned to her. "The Bible says God walks among us. That He hears our prayers, and answers them. I've spent my life trying to hold on to that belief. But what I've seen of the world, there's no God in it. If He's truly here, *show me*."

Opening her briefcase, the reporter said, "I think there's a bit more to your motives than that." She removed a thick, bound document. "Your show isn't about the truth, Mr. Baringer. It's simply cover for an old grudge. You're not trying to find God, you're trying to get *back* at Him."

She slid the document across the table and it came to rest squarely in front of Ian.

Angela felt the blood drain from her face. A copy of an NTSB Aircraft Accident Report, decades old. Though she'd never seen it before, she knew what it contained, raising angry eyes to the reporter.

"Where'd you get this!"

"Freedom of Information Act." The woman leveled accusing eyes at Ian. "Traumatic, losing your parents as a child, right in front of you like that. Knowing they gave their lives to save yours."

Angela placed a hand on Ian's arm—like a bundle of cables under load. He stared at the report as if it were the pox, full of details he surely didn't know, shouldn't know.

The reporter pressed, "You blame God for taking your parents. It's eaten at you your whole life, and now it's consumed you. So you strike back the only way you can—by destroying others' Faith in Him."

Ian was no longer listening, Angela could see. Heart sinking, she watched him rise, take the report in trembling fingers, and melt out the door without a word.

She jumped up. "That's it, everyone. Thanks for coming. We'll take your suggestions under advisement . . ."

Racing after him, she caught up in the lobby where he was on his way out the building, NTSB report in hand.

"Where are you going!"

"Cab. Home."

He wanted to be alone when he read it.

"Sweetheart, *please*," she begged. "Haven't you suffered enough?"

But there was that awful distance in his eyes again. The old claws had closed. How tight remained to be seen.

FOUR

SANTA MONICA FREEWAY, SAME DAY, LATE AFTERNOON

It took all her will, but Angela didn't leave the office until end of day, didn't even call home. To do otherwise would have told Ian she'd no confidence he could bear up to this challenge. Which was exactly right.

Punching the pedal, she weaved through traffic, fearing what lay ahead. Had their efforts together over the years toughened him enough for the ugliness in that report? Or would reliving the experience send him crashing again?

Her mind flew back to the mess of a man she'd met in grad school years ago . . .

At the time, she was taking an elective class outside her field of study, on a whim: Extrasensory Perception Theory. It was about the third day in when this new guy showed up as a late enrollee. Never seen him before, overdressed in pinpoint oxford shirt and pleated slacks, sitting alone. Handsome, with an odd air of detachment.

Each day thereafter he'd arrive at the last second, sitting apart, jotting in a journal that appeared totally unrelated to the course. Angela had thought him preppy, snooty. And to her dismay, she got paired with him as lab partners.

She did her best to make friends, but he remained aloof. Literally. He would actually shrink from her when she came close. And God forbid she brush against him—he'd recoil like he'd been bitten by a snake! Not a reaction she was accustomed to from the opposite sex.

But it wasn't long before she came to recognize his eccentricities for what they really were. Ian Baringer, she discovered to her amazement, was *phobic.* In fact, he harbored a whole host of phobias. Haptephobia, fear of touch. Gynophobia, fear of women (more precisely, fear of being *touched* by women). Aviophobia, fear of flying. Amnesiphobia, fear of memory loss. And more.

An intriguing case study for an aspiring psychologist. Angela started to pay close attention, working to earn his trust, and slowly she extracted his sad story.

Poor Ian had lost his parents as a child in a terrible accident, and it had left him with severe emotional wounds. Compounding the tragedy were unfortunate events that sent him to an orphanage in upstate New York where his trauma went all but untreated. From there he went to a seminary, remaining till adulthood, ordained a priest—a vocation that helped obscure his peculiar phobias. But then attending grad school at Berkeley, as he took his first steps into the secular world, his inhibitions had become conspicuous.

Angela, however, saw past his problems to the brilliant, honest, compassionate man beneath. Ian looked at life unlike anyone she'd ever met, through such open eyes—almost childlike in his sweetness and innocence. And the more she was with him, the more she wanted to be, falling in love, ultimately resolving to free him from his phobias.

So naïve!

She shook her head at herself in the rearview mirror, recalling the long, difficult process. Yet in time her dedication had paid off. Ian did finally break free of his aversion to women, falling in love with her, too. And so began the most rewarding relationship of her life.

Unfortunately, Ian's recovery was not complete, and not without setbacks. Including one that led to a long separation. The painful memories gave Angela good reason to fear this report, the biggest test Ian had faced since the accident, capable of undoing their countless hours of psychoanalysis, hypnotherapy, behavior modification . . .

By the time she reached their building she'd built things up, so she was thankful to be alone on the elevator, pacing as it rose, racing to their apartment, struggling to fit key into lock.

Quiet and dim inside . . . Rays of sunset sneaking across the hooked rug of their living room, Chelsea sofa, barrister bookcase. New England décor. She'd wanted him to feel at home here.

"Ian . . . ? Honey . . . ?"

No reply. Hopefully he was resting.

She slipped in, releasing a pent-up breath to spy him out on the balcony, leaning against the rail, staring across the Bay. She hurried to join him—only to halt.

On the coffee table lay the report, open to a spread of black and white photos. *Scenes of the accident.*

Skid marks on a runway. Nasty gouges in rain-soaked earth. Shattered fence. Smoldering wreckage.

Also, a separate photograph of a dashing young couple and mischievous-looking boy, his hair dark like theirs, eyes light like the woman's.

And finally, two black body bags. Large, and small.

Swearing, she rushed to his side. He failed to acknowledge her, but didn't shrink away. *A good sign.* Couldn't be as bad as she'd feared . . . She wrapped an arm around him. Like embracing a statue, his face dark granite.

"Ian?"

At length he inhaled, eyes never leaving the Bay.

"I . . . I thought I could handle it." His voice was hollow, numbed. "But it's no good, sweetheart. I'm not past this thing. I don't know that I ever will be."

Her heart shuddered and she squeezed him with both arms. "But you've come so *far.* We'll work it out together—like always."

He sighed, eyes fatalistic. "There's nothing you can do. This time, the problem's not in my head."

FIVE

ANGELA AND IAN'S APARTMENT, SANTA MONICA, WEEKS LATER, NIGHT

Angela awoke in the sweat of a nightmare. Same one that had been haunting her lately—Ian leaving her for the priesthood again. For good.

Not that he'd said anything, but all the signs were there. The harshness of that report had plunged him back into the pensive, reclusive, obsessive-compulsive Ian of old—shades of his last defection. And despite all her reasoning and logic, he persisted in the belief that this time, his agony came not from the psyche, but the *soul.*

"They were so young," he moaned. "So much to live for. It's killing me to think I'll never see them again!"

In his mind, the only remedy for such a pain was Faith. Faith that he might be reunited with his parents someday in the hereafter. His on-again, off-again affair with religion was on again. Or at least, under serious consideration. The past weeks, all he'd done was sit home poring over books of theology.

Angela had to admit, he was right about one thing. When it came to religion, she was no help. She and her two sisters had been raised unchurched by a mom who dismissed religion as superstition. Science was Angela's god, and until now she'd presumed Ian a convert, given their track record discrediting spiritual phenomena. But it seemed his Faith was as tenacious as his neurosis.

"I just need space to work things out," he'd told her.

Stupid male bromide!

She rolled on her side, wiping her brow on the sheet, careful not to wake him; he'd been having nightmares, too.

Fortunately their show was at season end, able to spare him, and Angela had kept her distance working on their CBS presentation—a sure disaster if Ian didn't shape up.

He looked terrible. Anxious, exhausted, obsessed with his doctors of divinity—Paul, Augustine, Gregory, and on. Spiritual snake-oil salesmen, in Angela's view. Dour old stoics heaping imaginary sins onto imaginary souls, looking down on women from ivory towers of celibacy. Were they gaining Ian's ear, calling him back to the priesthood?

She inched toward him, seeking the comfort of his scent—surprised to find him gone, a light under the door.

Rising, she tiptoed over in her nightshirt, peeking out to see him in his overstuffed chair. Awake, dressed, head in hand, shadow of a beard lending his features uncharacteristic roughness. A book lay facedown on the coffee table.

He glanced up as she entered, a look of grim conviction in his eyes, whispering soberly, "I know now what I have to do . . ."

His words were an auger to her heart, floor ice to her feet. He took her hands, pulling her onto his lap. She avoided his gaze.

"First, I want you to know how much I love you. How grateful I am for all you've done."

The balm before the bomb.

"Nothing will ever change that. But this thing inside me . . . I know our life will never be right the way I am."

"We can fix this, we just have to keep working at it!"

She didn't sound credible even to herself.

"We've tried everything in your medicine bag. It's time to move on . . ."

Her gut tightened.

"I know you put no stock in non-scientific methods, but years ago, before psychiatry and Prozac, people took problems like mine to monasteries. They found inner peace through the arts of asceticism and meditation. There are still a few places like that; I'm hoping one could help me."

Of course Angela knew of these places and practices. Little more than escapism and self-hypnosis. Her eyes flitted to the book on the table.

The Seven Storey Mountain. Autobiography of the famous monk, Thomas Merton. She felt her heart sink.

Back to the priesthood.

As if reading her mind, Ian hastened to add, "Trust me, I'm done with the clergy. I love you far too much to ever give you up."

All the same, he'd left her before.

She watched him pull a small box from his pocket, taking her hand, staring into her eyes. "Maybe this will convince you . . ."

Removing the lid, he revealed a huge diamond solitaire, afire in the light of the lamp. "Say you'll marry me, and I swear I'll come back with all this behind us."

She was stunned. Engagement was out of the question under the circumstances. And yet, it was possibly the only anchor they had left to weather this storm.

Nodding, she wrapped herself in his arms, ignoring the little voice that told her he wasn't coming back.

SIX

CBS AFFILIATE, CHANNEL 6 TV, LOS ANGELES, MORNING

Angela sat in her office, door closed, arms crossed, mind a jumble. Since Ian left for that monastery, the days had slipped into weeks, weeks into a month, letters growing steadily shorter and less frequent. Now it seemed they'd stopped altogether.

She'd tried his cell repeatedly, getting no answer, expecting none, since electronic devices were prohibited at the abbey. And what letters she'd gotten were maddeningly lacking in detail. Vague assurances he was making progress, pledges of undying love, how much he missed her.

But now, no word in a week. Exactly how things had gone last time he'd returned to his Church.

She felt confused, betrayed, sitting here twisting his ring, diamond having lost its luster for her. Thanks to Charles's adroit negotiations, their deal with CBS had been inked without Ian, demonstrators notwithstanding. A mind-boggling deal—but with the proviso that Ian sign upon return from "a family emergency."

Angela was just working up the courage to face Charles when her intercom broke in.

"Ms. Weber, a Father Lucien Gant on line eight, long distance, collect. Says he's a friend of Mr. Baringer's. Says it's urgent . . ."

Heart pounding, Angela watched the light on her phone blink. She recognized the name. Ian had written about his elderly mentor at the abbey. Now it appeared he'd put the monk up to a "Dear Jane."

She punched the button, snapping, "He hasn't the guts to tell me himself?"

The voice was barely audible. Anxious.

"Please, Ms. Weber, Ian needs your help! He's in St. Maarten, in the Caribbean."

"St. Maarten?" Ian had no connection there she was aware of.

"I swore not to tell you, but there's no one else!"

"What? How long has he been there?"

"Three weeks. He was sending you his letters through me—I used the abbey postmark so you wouldn't find out. But he stopped writing, and knowing what he was up to, I'm very worried!"

Flabbergasted, furious, she started to ask another question, hearing the man cry hoarsely, *"Someone's coming! Quick, take this address: 119 Southwharf, 3rd floor, Eastcoast, St. Maarten. Please go right away! You've got to stop him before it's too late!"*

She scribbled the information on a pad. "Stop him?"

"Stop him before he kills himself!"

And he hung up.

SEVEN

PRINCESS JULIANA INTERNATIONAL AIRPORT, ST. MAARTEN ISLAND, CARIBBEAN, NEXT MORNING

Angela raced out of the little terminal, hailing a cab. The driver stowed her bag, she slid into the back seat, and they rattled off.

She handed up a scribbled address, no idea where on the island it was, unable to locate it on Google Earth. The cabbie shook his head, dreadlocks waggling, eyes meeting hers in the mirror.

"No-no, M'um. Pretty missy like you don wanna go *dere*."

"Just take me, please. *And hurry.*"

All she wanted was to grab Ian and go.

She'd tried to phone Father Lucien back yesterday, only to get an answering machine telling her she'd reached "a monastery where quiet is valued and silence a virtue." Invited to leave a message, she hadn't. And though convinced she was making a fool of herself, she'd done as the frantic monk had begged, red-eyeing to Miami, island-hopping here. She'd told Charles Dunn and her family she was joining Ian for a long-overdue vacation.

Her cab exited the airport down a narrow peninsula, crossing a causeway to the main island. White sand beaches lined with palmettos, scent of salt off the breakers, puffy clouds in a bright, balmy, sapphire sky.

How she would have *loved* a vacation here. Never been much of anywhere outside California. No money when she was younger, putting herself through school after Dad took off. No time lately. She swore under her breath.

They passed through a seaside tourist trap into the island's interior, reggae playing low on the radio. Hills, scrub brush, sedge grass, small trees, cacti, sheep, goats, the occasional shack. As Angela recalled from a brochure on the plane, St. Maarten was a tiny place. Forty square miles divided in two, France controlling north, Holland south. And not a single running river.

Topping a hill, she saw below a picturesque town of pastel-colored clapboard houses and stores squeezed onto a bridge of land between ocean and large lagoon. PHILLIPSBURG, a sign read. Her driver threaded its narrow streets and they headed back inland.

What was Ian up to that could be so dangerous? Had he sneaked away here to avoid her? Or to chase some new spiritual phenomenon? Probably both. She swore again.

Shacks began to appear along the roadside, cobbled together of rusted, corrugated metal and warped plywood. The inhabitants, all black, milled about barefoot in ragged clothes. Worse by far than anything East LA had to offer. Angela's heart went out to them. She could just imagine how upsetting this must have been for the sensitive Ian.

The cab slowed and the driver switched off the radio, turning nervous eyes to her.

"*Bad place,* M'um. You *sure* you wan be doin' dis?"

She hadn't come all this way to turn back.

Mumbling, the man exited the highway and they jostled down a gravel road strewn with trash, scaring off seagulls and other scavengers. Angela assumed they'd reached the far side of the island, and soon they arrived at what looked to be an old industrial quarter. Corroded storage tanks, warehouses, and other buildings bleached chalky in the sun.

The cab halted in front of two warehouses that abutted one another. An address on the door of the first matched the one Lucien had given her, no signs of habitation but a few cars parked near the second warehouse. Angela swallowed, gave her driver a hundred dollar bill, and told him to wait.

Concealed behind a third-floor window of the second warehouse stood a black man in jeans and ink-stained T-shirt, 9mm Uzi in hand. He grew agitated at the sight of the cab, alerting men operating machinery behind him.

Suddenly the cab door opened and out stepped a most beautiful woman! Slender, in blouse and skirt.

The man gasped. Two associates appeared at his side, one also with a gun. Their jaws dropped, too.

"Você tá zoando?" the unarmed man murmured. Then scowling, he motioned to a stairwell, and the two armed men rushed down.

Angela held close to the cab as she surveyed the dismal surroundings, all quiet, no movement.

What has he gotten himself into this time?

But she was determined to see it through. She started for the warehouse—stopped by a loud screech. A door to the adjoining warehouse flew open, discharging two black men with guns, faces menacing.

"Mas quem é que vocês são?" one snarled at her.

She didn't understand, but it wasn't French or Dutch.

The sound of crunching gravel made her turn, and she panicked to see her cab speed off, showering her suitcase with dust.

You're a psychologist, she reminded herself, *you know how to deal with intimidation . . .*

Grabbing her bag, she called over to the men, "I'm late for a meeting, they're expecting me." And hurried on.

They shouted back, *"Pare!"*

She ignored them, willing the door open. It was, and she slammed it behind her, finding herself in a dingy, ill-lit stairwell. She climbed, relieved to hear no pursuit.

At the top was a windowless door, no sign, number, or bell. She placed an ear to it. Strange beeping and voices. Not Ian's, no one she recognized. Two men and a woman speaking English, each with a different accent. Asian? Russian? French? She could make out only phrases.

"Seven degrees . . . Eee-ee-gee zero . . . Cardio zero . . ."

She tried the knob. Locked. Then gave the door a rap, and the voices ceased as the beeping continued. But no answer. She banged her fist, shouting with authority, "I'm here to see Ian Baringer! *Let me in!"*

A pause, and she heard the Asian-sounding man at the door, voice tense. *"Private property. You trespass. Go!"*

"I know he's here—let me in or I'm calling the police!"

Muffled talk, argumentative. Then the Russian accent said, *"That's it—terminate!"*

More argument. Finally the door cracked, a man of slight build peering out. Asian, late thirties, medical gown, surgical mask dangling around his neck, eyes squints of fear.

"Who you?"

"Ian's fiancée."

Farther back in the room, the woman's voice said, "Luc Dow, *you idiot*! What ze hell you do?"

The Asian turned and Angela took advantage, plowing past into a large, open space. Bare, save for a nucleus of electronic equipment and pole lights clustered around an operating table, bundles of duct-taped cables snaking across the floor. Haloed in the lights was an older man with a beard. Sixties, perhaps. Beside him, a younger woman, light hair pulled back in a braid. Both wore medical gowns, staring at Angela from behind surgical masks.

She approached them, spying on the table a body wrapped in blue plastic pads dripping condensation, IV tubes everywhere. A male form, skin morbid gray, dotted with electrodes that hooked into a wall of monitors—heart, respiration, EEG—none registering activity.

Not an operation. Autopsy.

And then she saw the dead man's face . . .

Hysterical, she rushed the table, but sturdy hands grabbed her from behind.

"You want see him alive?" the Asian warned. *"Stay back!"*

She tried to swing around, claw out his eyes—but his grip was too strong.

"You've murdered him!"

"He is not dead," the older man said. *"Yet.* But you mustn't interfere."

Disbelieving, Angela looked to Ian. Serene and pale like some toppled Greek statue.

She'd seen death before.

"You're lying!"

But if they weren't . . .

The man and woman stood waiting. Desperate, Angela saw no choice, giving in, and the Asian released her. He regarded her warily for a moment, then joined his comrades, and they began to remove Ian's wraps.

"Refrigerant pads," the Russian told her, flipping a switch to set a nearby apparatus humming. She saw a transparent tube filled with blood exiting the region of Ian's groin, connecting to the machine and re-entering his body at the same point. "Heart-lung pump. As we circulate his blood we warm it, adding pure oxygen."

On one of the monitors a temperature gage began to edge up—*8 degrees centigrade, 9, 10 . . .*

The woman injected Ian with various fluids via the IVs. "Stimulants," she said.

Angela observed all in riveted horror.

Once the temperature reached twenty-seven, the Russian withdrew electrical paddles from the front of another machine, rubbing them together. The woman removed electrodes from Ian's chest, applied a lubricant, and the man positioned the paddles near Ian's heart, calling, "Clear!"

Angela held her breath and cringed.

Boom!

It was as if the current entered *her.* She jolted, too, grimacing as his body arced on the table only to collapse into stillness. Moaning, she watched the man recharge the paddles to send another volt surging. Again Ian bucked—this time a blip appearing on the monitor's flat line. Then another! Another! Quickly followed by stronger spikes!

Angela breathed again, feeling faint.

"He has the constitution of a horse," the Russian said, taking a handkerchief to his brow. "Mark five minutes, twenty-three seconds."

The woman recorded in a logbook, and Angela brushed past, sobbing, dropping to Ian's side, taking his hand in hers. It felt deathly cold. He was still unconscious, but she thrilled to see color return to his face.

The strange team continued its work, checking vital signs, administering unknown substances through IVs, and Angela glared up at them.

"What the hell is going on!"

The Asian replied, "NDE."

Near-death experience. Angela was familiar with the phenomenon, though she'd never investigated it. Not uncommon in cases where individuals seemingly die, life functions ceasing, only to revive a short time later. She presumed Ian's intent was to sneak through death's door to confirm the existence of the Afterlife, expecting to be resuscitated before it closed permanently.

The damned fool. No wonder he hid it from me!

Stifling her outrage, she spoke to him soothingly, squeezing his hand, feeling it grow warmer. He remained unresponsive—though he groaned when the woman removed the tubes from the vessel in his groin. And again when she closed the incision with a few stitches. Angela found the intimacy of the procedure repugnant.

"Who's in charge here?"

The older man dropped his surgical mask. He had an intelligent bearing.

Average height; gray, bushy hair and beard; fair complexion; eyes dark and close-set.

"Dr. Emil Josten," he said, "formerly of the Kharkov Institute for Cryobiological Studies. These are my colleagues, Dr. Yvette Garonne, Université Pierre et Marie Curie. And Dr. Luc Dow Hodaka, Universität Würzburg. We specialize in the science of suspended animation."

Angela felt a flush of anger. "You call this *science*? Experimenting with a man's life? This is criminal! This is, is—*Mengelean*!"

Josten remained calm. "I assure you, our work is perfectly legal here."

"And that makes it right? What about brain damage! *What about Ian's mind!*"

"Ze risks not so great," Garonne said. Angela turned to see her scribing figures on a chart. "Even outside ze lab, sometime people survive death forty minute, no complication."

Josten added, "Frigid-water drownings, for example. We've simply taken a natural occurrence and refined it. Improved the odds."

"Much improve," Hodaka said, gesturing to the array of equipment and pharmaceuticals. "Thanks to Meester Baringer."

Angela was no less appalled. "How many times has he done this!"

"Once before," Josten said. "A three-minute test earlier this week. We were prepared for ten today—before you interrupted."

"And you can be damn thankful I did. You could all be facing murder charges!"

Garonne snatched Ian's hand from her, checking his pulse. "No. More ze assisted suicide. *Also* legal here. Regardless, he sign ze paper for liability."

"Did he waive your medical ethics, too?"

The French woman turned to her, raising a brow. Light blue eyes, golden skin. Pretty. And she held herself as if aware of it. "Under ze circumstances, eet would be unethical *not* to help heem. He was determined to do zis, no idea how. If he deed not find us, he would have keeled himself. And thanks to heem, we advance our technique. What we learn weel save lives."

"Not at the expense of his," Angela snapped. "Once he's recovered, I'm taking him home!"

Garonne bent close to Ian's face, drawing back his eyelids, flashing a penlight. Then with a wry smile, she sniffed, "Not zis man. Not after what he claim to see . . ."

EIGHT

AN OCEANSIDE VILLA, GENEVA BAY, ST. MAARTEN ISLAND, SAME DAY, AFTERNOON

Ian and the "team" were staying at a private resort not far away, Angela learned, and soon as he could be moved, she demanded he be taken there. He remained semiconscious during the ride in a van, seemingly unaware of Angela as she sat holding his hand.

His was a one-story white-stucco villa, red tile roof, scant yards from a broad and sandy crescent of beach. New and well-appointed. Living room, dining room, equipped kitchen, bedroom and bath in back. Charming, perhaps, had Angela been in a better frame of mind.

She helped settle Ian in bed, then left him to his team, fetching her suitcase from the van. Ian was in no condition to be leaving before tomorrow, earliest. Nor was she, after this ghastly shock.

Still trembling, she took a chair in the living room. She could hear Ian coming around, responding to the "doctors" as they conducted exams. He sounded weak, but in possession of his faculties, thankfully—if that could be said of a man who treated death as some sort of excursion.

She heard Josten say, "By the way, Ian, your fiancée is here."

"Angela? *Angela's here?*" Then quiet.

Soon Josten emerged. "He's doing well, Ms. Weber. He'll be fatigued a while, probably sleep the day—more from medications than procedure." He held up several plastic bottles of pills. "Once he's fully awake, give him these—directions are on the labels. My cell phone number, too, if you need. He can shower, but keep his incision dry. And get him to eat something."

Angela bristled, feeling like she'd been made into an accomplice.

Josten added, "You can go in now if you wish."

But she remained in her chair until the doctors left. Then taking a breath, she rose, entering to find him propped up on pillows. He looked pitiful. Ashen, exhausted, tense.

"Angela . . ." he mumbled, staring past her.

She stood glaring at him, hands on hips.

"What the hell are you doing?"

No answer, brow furrowed, gaze distant.

"Of all the stupid, insane . . . *What were you thinking?"*

His answer was so soft she could scarcely hear. "H-how long was I under?"

"Under?" She blinked. "Ian, you were *dead*! Five minutes! If I hadn't come when I did!"

"Not long enough . . ." He wilted back into his pillow, eyes glassy. "I saw it, Angela. I saw the Other Side. And I learned something horrible . . . *Devastating . . .*"

He looked overcome, and closing his eyes, he drifted off.

She was dumbstruck.

He thinks he's seen the Afterlife! He is *brain damaged!*

Swearing, she drew up a chair, confused, worried, angry. The way he'd deceived her, run off, risked his fool neck, no thought but for himself.

He slept as she kept watch. Fitful at times, moaning.

But at length he settled, and she thought it safe to take a break. She trudged to the kitchen for a drink. Nothing in the fridge but remnants of takeout meals. Grabbing a glass of water she went to the table, flopping, head in hand.

His laptop sat next to her, online. He'd been researching near-death experiences, she saw, several case studies open. Also bulletins from a Catholic news service he subscribed to. She closed out the bulletins, and skimmed the NDEs. Standard out-of-body/tunnel-of-light stuff.

About to shut down, she had a thought, and calling up Google, she entered "Emil Josten"—the one doctor whose name she felt able to spell. Dozens of pages appeared. No direct hits, merely random associations with either name. But drilling down, she uncovered a "Dr. Emil Jostenberg," following a link to a four-year-old news article.

Jostenberg, it said, had been a cryobiologist at Kharkov University in Ukraine, studying the effects of hypothermia on human physiology. He'd left to set up a private research facility in Vilnius, Lithuania, which was later shut down after experiments caused the death of one man and brain injury to another. A photo left no doubt, Josten and Jostenberg were one and the same.

"I knew it! A quack!"

She was tempted to call the police, but all she really wanted was to get Ian home as fast as possible.

He'd slept long enough; it was time for answers.

Returning to his room she sat on the bed beside him, patting his hand until his eyes flitted open. Despite her anger she felt a stirring warmth. He looked distraught still, but stronger, able to sit on his own. She gave him water, seeing his hand shake as he accepted the glass, lips blue.

"How do you feel?"

"Like a m-mule kicked m-me in the head."

He seemed cogent enough, though she realized her questions would have to wait.

"A hot shower is what you need. Can you walk?"

She helped him up. His legs were wobbly, and she escorted him to the bath with an arm around his waist, noting how thin he'd become. His incision made him limp, and she felt a pang of sympathy. But seeing him okay, she left with a curt, "Don't get your dressing wet!"

While he showered she called the resort restaurant to have supper delivered. She was planning a showdown, and she wanted Ian rested, fed, and fully alert . . .

An hour later they were dining on the veranda, overlooking the ocean, sun dipping behind the hills. A romantic setting, wasted. Their conversation continued strained. Ian acted preoccupied, poking at his salad, eyes lost and sad. At length Angela's patience wore out.

"Will you tell me what's going on? Setting up that phony retreat so you could sneak off on another odyssey!"

He avoided her gaze. "How did you find out?"

"Your confederate, Lucien. He was worried about you—rightly so."

"I didn't set out to mislead you." At last she heard remorse. "I went for exactly the reasons I said, I swear. I gave it my all, but I wasn't getting anywhere. And then I stumbled across something. Something *amazing.* Not just a way to control my problem, a way to *cure* it."

"What, by ending it all?"

He reached across the table and took her hands. "I know how crazy it must look, but this time—" He broke off, staring down at her fingers. *"Your ring."*

In her pocket. She'd taken it off after Lucien's call.

His eyes shot back to hers. "Don't give up on me now. Once you hear, you'll understand . . ."

NINE

THE TRAPPIST MONASTERY OF GETHSEMANI, BARDSTOWN, KENTUCKY, FIVE WEEKS AGO, EARLY MORNING

Ian picked up the letter he was writing—longhand, no computers allowed—and left the desk of his spartan cell, moving to the window, gazing out over a rural serenity that extended to the horizon. Magenta foothills tipped in frost, backlit by dawn, brush-stroked in drifts of pink and lavender mist. Peaceful as Eden. Yet he felt no peace.

Two thousand miles he'd traveled to this isolated little community, and while outside a new season was budding, in his heart it was the dead of winter. Only a week, and already he feared he wouldn't find here what he was looking for. But if not at this world-renowned abbey, *where?*

The monastery was run by the Trappist Order of Cistercians, a sect dating to 1098, France, noted for its austere agrarian lifestyle and vow of silence. More than two hundred such monasteries had once dotted the globe, now hardly a score. Gethsemani was the oldest Cistercian abbey in the U.S., home to fifty-one monks and four novices. A fraction of its former numbers. Two thousand acres of rolling farmland and a dozen buildings clustered along a winding country road.[1]

From his window Ian could see the white masonry chapel with stone bell spire, red-roofed meeting hall, work facilities for producing the abbey's renowned cheese, fudge, and jam. He was lodging in the general quarters, a plain, four-story, white cinderblock dorm.

His cellmate and mentor, Father Lucien Gant, was sitting across the room in white frock with black hood and drape, reading the Bible. Small-framed, lean and spry, white hair, thin face, beaked nose, rimless spectacles. A resident here for six decades, he'd long ago mastered the monastic disciplines, still in sharp command of his faculties.

Whether meditating, working in the kitchens pressing whey, or stirring branch-water bourbon into vats of bubbling fudge, Lucien seemed to embody the inner peace Ian sought. Despite a life of labor and deprivation he was ever cheerful. And though permitted to give Ian only an hour of verbal instruction daily, he hadn't let that retard their lessons. He used a repertoire of pantomime to communicate, his animated expressions, gestures and sense of humor a delight. Harpo Marx in a robe, with halo.

Perhaps feeling Ian's eyes, the monk paused and looked up, pointing to the letter in Ian's hand, touching fingers to heart, shrugging and grinning. He'd correctly guessed that the letter was to Angela.

Ian smiled, and Lucien winked and returned to his Bible. Ian had mentioned Angela only in passing, speaking little of his personal life—though admitting he'd once been a priest. But Lucien wasn't one to pry.

Outside, the chapel tower tolled six bells. Canonical hour of observance known as *Prime,* ushering in the workday and the one hour when speaking was permitted.

Lucien closed his Bible around a finger, approaching Ian at the window, observing, "Gorgeous morning."

Nodding, Ian said, "Reminds me of when I was a boy. I grew up in the country."

"So what are you thinking as you behold God's majesty today?"

Ian pointed to a swath of scarred forest along a hillside. "I'm wondering what happened to mar that majesty."

Lucien's smile faded. "Ah, yes . . . The footprint of a tornado from last fall. Cost the lives of a Bardstown family, I'm sorry to say." He crossed himself.

Reflecting a moment, Ian suggested, "Shall we begin?"

They took their chairs to the center of the room and sat facing each other.

Lucien opened his Bible again. "I've been thinking about a verse for today. Something from the Book of Job . . . You're familiar with Job's story?"

Ian nodded. The tale of a man who remained loyal to God despite losing everyone and everything he loved. A triumph of Faith over the Devil.

"If you recall," Lucien said, referring to his Bible, "there was a point in Job's ordeal where he grew weak and began to doubt God . . .

"God said unto Job, 'Who is this that questions my Will without Knowledge?' And ashamed, Job answered, 'I have said things about which I did not understand; things too mysterious for me to Know . . . ' "

Lucien explained, "As Job learned, even in our darkest despair we must trust God, for we cannot Know His Plan."

"And what was God's Plan putting Job through such agony?"

"Why, He was testing Job's Faith, of course."

"But if God Knows all things, He Knew Job would stay loyal. Why abuse him like that? Other than to show up the Devil, which makes God seem rather petty, if you ask me."

"As God told Job, Man hasn't the Knowledge to question God's Will."

"So however harsh and long our hardships, we simply assume God is testing us, and endure?"

"We must have Faith in God. Like Job."

"Yes, I suppose if God spoke to me personally like He did Job, I'd have Job's Faith, too."

"But He *does* speak to you." Lucien thrummed the pages of his book.

Ian sighed. "I know you put great stock in the Bible, Father, but that can't be the sole source of your strength. You seem so contented, so at peace. What's your secret?"

The monk chuckled. "It's no secret, my boy. The answer is to stop searching for worldly solutions to spiritual questions. Put aside your issues, throw your doubts out the window, clear your mind, and just Believe. You'll be amazed how it lightens the burdens. *That's* the source of my strength."

Ian sat back. The path to peace of mind was to live one's life mindlessly? To ignore those deep whispers of the heart? He felt so frustrated, so spiritually bereft.

For a time nothing interrupted the men's thoughts, then the chapel tower sounded seven bells, reimposing silence on the abbey. Ian sighed again, and ignoring the rule, rose to ask, "Father, I need a favor."

TEN

THE GROUNDS OF GETHSEMANI MONASTERY, BARDSTOWN, KENTUCKY, FIVE WEEKS AGO, MORNING

His entire adult life Ian had resisted the concept of blind Faith, unable to ignore his questions. But not finding the peace he'd come to Gethsemani for, longing to return to Angela, weary to the depths of his soul, finally he'd decided to do as Lucien advised. He would cast aside his doubts and embrace his religion again. It seemed his only hope.

Before he could be readmitted to the Church's fold, however, he'd have to make amends to God, which required confessing his sins to a priest. Lucien had graciously agreed to lend his services. The sacrament of Confession was one occasion for which the rule of silence might be lifted, and seeking permission from the abbey's strict dom first, Ian and Lucien left for the orchards, Ian hoping its serenity would ease this uncomfortable task.

"I don't know where to begin," he said as they strode a footpath, kicking through pockets of mist, shoes wet in the low sun. The thought of the pain he must relive brought a tightness to his chest.

"Start wherever your soul needs," Lucien suggested, breath a white cloud in the chill. "We've all the time in the world. Can you recall when your problems with your Faith first began?"

"One night when I was nine . . ."

The monk frowned up at him, adding more lines to his weathered face.

"I was traveling with my parents in a small plane. We crashed in a storm, but somehow we survived."

"God was watching over you!"

"Not for long. We were unharmed, but my legs were pinned. Dad couldn't free me, and the fuel ignited." The old man's eyes widened. "My parents wouldn't leave. They wrapped themselves around me and held tight. And when fire rescue arrived, that's how they found us. Huddled, unconscious. Because I was shielded from the smoke, they were able to revive me . . ."

Lucien crossed himself. "You poor child! You must have been traumatized!"

"Didn't speak for a year. Complete amnesia. I grew up not recalling who I was or what had happened, all of it suppressed."

He paused, swallowing. "But *always* I felt the loss. Intensely. Every day. The way I beat it back was with the promise the Church made me—that someday I'd be with my parents again. Know them and feel their love again."

"After the accident, you had family to take you in?"

"No, no surviving relatives. My parents' will placed me in the care of a trusted friend, a priest, Father Ben Reinhold. Father Ben had taken charge of an orphanage shortly before the accident, and I went there as his ward. St. Lawrence Boys Haven, upstate New York. Stayed there until I entered the seminary at seventeen."

"I can't believe you were never adopted."

Ian felt his temples throb. "I remember once sitting in Catechism class—no more than eleven—staring out the window to see yet another boy drive off with new parents. Off to a *real* life, a *real* home. While I listened to a lecture on God's infinite Mercy.

"I thought I was passed over because I wasn't worthy. If only I were a better person, prayed harder, worked harder. So I put my heart and soul into it, trying to make myself perfect, pledging myself to the priesthood. And *still* others were chosen."

Lucian placed a hand on Ian's back. "You thought God had abandoned you."

"He *had* abandoned me!" Ian could feel the words spit out his mouth. "My knees wore a spot on the floor by my bed, but God never heard my prayers. Or if He did, He never answered."

They resumed their walk in silence. Then Lucien offered, "Your alienation from God, it reminds me of Mother Theresa's."

Ian snorted. "I never had Mother's strength. I needed more than the Bible to believe in God. I needed proof. And I was determined to find it."

The monk's face knotted. "But how? Where could you possibly hope to find such proof?"

"Somewhere among the miracles of the Church. I felt if I could confirm the existence of miracles, I'd have evidence of God and a spiritual world."

Lucien appeared troubled, but said nothing.

"I got my chance when the seminary sent me to study in Rome. In my spare time I traveled all over, searching out all the famous miracles—Lourdes, Fatima, Brancaleone—but I never once saw compelling evidence of God's Hand.

"Still, I went ahead with my ordination, and then the Church sent me back to the States. That interrupted things. As you know, there are few documented miracles here. So rather than give up, I turned my attentions to paranormal phenomena."

"Where there are ghosts there is Afterlife, and where there is Afterlife there is God."

Ian nodded. "I was reassigned to the same New York Archdiocese where I grew up, under the same archbishop who'd supervised Father Ben and the orphanage. I went around to various parishes helping fill in for the shortage of priests. My work took me all over New England. Fertile haunting grounds—plenty of opportunities for supernatural sleuthing. And I must say, some of the phenomena I investigated were persuasive. But I had no way to analyze them objectively—that takes special training and equipment, and I had no money. I couldn't ask the archbishop, he'd have hung me up by my collar if he'd known what I was doing.

"I was at a loss for a time. Then out of the blue, a 'miracle.'" He paused, catching the monk's uneasy eyes.

"You want to know the *real* reason I was never adopted? My parents, it turned out, were very wealthy. They'd left me a big inheritance, in trust, which I knew nothing about until my twenty-fifth birthday. By then I was a priest. Exactly what I'd been groomed to be. Exactly where Father Ben and the archbishop wanted me. Bound by my vows of poverty, chastity, and obedience."

"*Good Lord.* They kept you from adoption so they could appropriate your money!"

"That was the plan—not that I fell for it!"

Lucien looked stricken. "*What's become of my Church!* Another form of child abuse! And it cost you your Faith."

Ian shook his head. "Not yet. I had too much riding on my Faith to give it up so easily. It was my only hope to see my parents again. All the same, I was deeply hurt. So I took my money and left for San Francisco. To Berkeley, to study parapsychology."

"Where at last you found some peace, I trust. With Angela."

Reaching for his wallet, Ian unfurled a row of photos, watching the monk's face light up.

"My goodness, *she's an angel*!"

Ian smiled proudly. "Loyal, loving, and honest to a fault. And free-thinking. She draws her values from life, Lucien, not the Bible. If ever there was proof goodness can exist independent of religion, it's Angela.

"Back then, she was pursuing her master's in psychology, and she had a far deeper background in science than I could ever hope for. I asked her help on some local paranormal cases that had me stumped, and she was amazing. Debunked every one of them. Sherlock Holmes of the supernatural. Working with her was a joy, the happiest I'd ever been. . . ."

He exhaled. "But I had to go and mess it up. I let my Faith come between us, and I ended up returning to the priesthood . . . I wasn't welcomed back with open arms. They made me put my money in trust and shipped me off to Africa. And *that's* where my Faith took a beating."

The monk's head bobbed. "I know of the horrors you experienced. I recognized you when we were introduced. The Fighting Friar."

"It was appalling. Those poor children. My childhood was paradise in comparison. I ask you, where was God in all that misery?"

"He was there . . . He was there *in you*."

Ian scoffed. "Then he was poorly represented. I was a finger in a crumbling dike. An entire generation lost, nothing short of divine intervention could have saved them—*and it never came*. I decided, either there is no God, or He's simply indifferent. Like He was to my plight growing up. How can a Being Who is all Good abide such Evil in the world? The Divine Paradox!"

His words echoed off the hillsides, and noting how loud he'd gotten, he grumbled and stuffed his hands in his pockets. Lucien had no answer for him, and Ian had expected none. The Divine Paradox was a conundrum that had challenged theologians since biblical times. Not even the great St. Augustine could resolve it.

Lucien seemed taken aback. "So it was then you gave up on God?"

"Not yet. I gave Him a last chance to prove Himself."

"*Prove* Himself?"

"I've another sin to confess, Father. Worse than any of the others. Worst of my life." From the look in Lucien's eyes, Ian wasn't sure the monk was up to hearing it. But having gone this far, Ian was determined to purge his soul of its greatest burden.

"From Africa, the Church sent me back to New York. That was eight months ago, and I had a hard time of it. I wasn't over Africa *or* Angela. I felt confused, depressed. But I got no peace. I was given another tough assignment, Attica State Prison, to minister to a man on death row. A psychopath, Zachary Niemand."

Lucien recoiled. "The monster who strangled those poor boys!"

It had been all over the national news.

"Zack Niemand was from *my* orphanage. I'd actually known him. A few years younger, also never adopted. Strange boy . . .

"I spent his last weeks with him, tried to salvage his soul. I did my best. Up to a point . . . But then I gave in to a temptation that, that still shames me."

He lowered his head. "You have to understand, with everything I'd been through, to face the vile things Niemand had done, my Faith was all but gone. I couldn't take any more. I *had* to Know if there was an Afterlife to make right all this injustice. And Niemand was my means.

"Over time, as we got reacquainted, I convinced him to try a relaxation technique that Angela had once used on me. Hypnosis. And with practice I was able to coax him into a deep trance. Then one day while he was under, I gave him a command . . ." An anxious look crossed Lucien's face, breaths escaping in little white puffs. "I, I ordered him to return to me after his death."

The monk slowed, then stopped altogether.

"Oh my God! My God!"

Ian stopped, too, feeling wretched. To interfere with a soul's journey to its Judgment was a heinous sin. A sacrilege violating God's absolute authority over the spirit.

Lucien gaped at him, lips moving soundlessly for a moment before words came out. "And . . . *and did he return?"*

"After the execution, I went back to visit where Niemand and I grew up. Old St. Lawrence. And strange things began to happen. I heard voices when no one was there. Felt the presence of something I couldn't explain. I was attacked in the dark by a force I couldn't identify. No doubt in my mind it was Niemand's ghost, come to wreak vengeance on me for marooning his soul.

"The attacks continued, more violent. I feared for the lives of everyone at St. L., so I evacuated the place and turned to the only person I felt could help. I'd learned that Angela was doing paranormal investigations as a profession now—had her own radio show back in L.A. And despite how I'd ended things, bless her heart, she came.

"We worked together as before, but this was like no case we'd ever seen. The situation grew worse and worse, until finally there was an explosion and fire that nearly took my life. And when the smoke cleared, Angela had solved the mystery. *There was no ghost.*"

He looked away. "The man who raised me, Father Ben, the man I loved like a *real* father, *he* was behind it all. He'd come back to scare me off, to destroy records of how he and the archbishop had schemed to steal my inheritance . . ."

Lucien gasped.

"The shock of it broke me free of my amnesia. All the suppressed memories of my childhood came flooding back, the precious memories of my parents. I was overcome. At last, I thought, I was rid of my trauma."

"So you left the priesthood again and returned to L.A. with Angela?"

"Yes. She took me back, God knows why. Her radio show moved to TV, and she was generous enough to invite me to join her. We've been working together ever since."

They resumed their walk in silence. Lucien appeared pensive. After a time he looked up at Ian. "Assuming that revelation about Father Ben cost you your Faith, why have you come to Gethsemani?"

Ian sighed. "I lost my Faith, but not my trauma. I suffered a relapse recently. I came here seeking the peace you seem to have found."

"Forgive me, my son, but how can you hope to be at peace in your heart when you're so angry with God?"

Reflecting, Ian gestured toward the scarred hillside in the distance. "Why does a God Who creates the majesty of nature allow it to be destroyed by a tornado? Why create the miracle of human life, then allow it to be cruelly snuffed out?"

"These are unanswerable questions, best left unasked."

"But if it's impudent to ask, why give me the mind to question? *God makes no sense!*"

The monk shook his head. "You remind me of another restless soul I once knew. Another priest driven to Know the Unknowable." He paused. "Are you familiar with Thomas Merton?"[2]

ELEVEN

THE VERANDA OF AN OCEANSIDE VILLA, GENEVA BAY, ST. MAARTEN ISLAND, CURRENT DAY, TWILIGHT

The sun dipped into the hills, casting Ian in shadow as their meals sat unfinished and cold. This was the first Angela had heard of him rejoining his Faith. Another step back onto that slippery slope. She could tell by his fidgeting fingers he had more to divulge, and she had a bad feeling about it.

At length he continued, "Lucien told me something in confidence. Something *incredible.* And since he saw fit to bring you into all this, I think you have a right to know . . ."

Ian was a great admirer of Thomas Merton. It was the monk's books, written at Gethsemani, that had inspired Ian to come here, and he told Lucien so.

"I suspected as much," Lucien said. "His grave is on the grounds, would you care to see?"

They cut across fields toward the chapel, next to which lay the abbey's cemetery.

"You had the privilege of knowing Merton?" Ian assumed, intrigued.

"Many years ago. I was just a novitiate. Can't say I knew him well, but as well as most here, I suspect. A bit of a loner. Hermit in his later years—though you'd hardly know it by the steady stream of visitors he got. He was a darling of the literati."

The irony of a reclusive monk being thrust into the limelight made Ian smile.

"What was he like?"

Lucien's eyes turned inward. "A most interesting fellow. Voracious curiosity about God and the mysteries of Faith. Always probing, pushing the spiritual envelope."

"I find his writings progressive. Brave, given how reactionary the Church was in the sixties."

"He was a risk-taker, all right. Often on thin ice with the Church. Many opposed him as too liberal and ecumenical."

The monk's voice filled with awe. "Once during a moment of candor, he confided something I thought astounding. He told me he believed God's spiritual mysteries were no less attainable than His physical ones. In other words, just as the secrets of God's natural universe surrender stubbornly to science, Merton was convinced God's supernatural Secrets would yield to the persistent intellect . . ."

Ian was fascinated.

"That seemed folly to me. As the Bible states, some things Man is not meant to Know. Not until death, anyway. But like most liberal theologians, Merton saw the Bible as more allegorical than literal. It was only later, near the end of his life, that I learned how determined he was to acquire those Secrets."

They arrived at Merton's grave. Like the others nearby, it was marked by a small Coptic cross, distinguished only by a plastic wreath draped over one arm, and a vase with a few cut flowers. A simple plaque read:

FR. LOUIS MERTON
DIED DEC. 10, 1968

"Louis?" Ian wondered.

"The religious appellation he chose for himself when he was ordained."

"How old when he died?"

"Just fifty-three. Happened in Bangkok, victim of an electric fan with bad wiring. The news swept through Gethsemani like a tidal wave."

Next to them the chapel tower tolled nine bells, marking the hour of *Terce.* They bowed their heads over the grave, then left for their quarters.

"So," Ian asked as they went, "did Merton ever pry loose any of God's forbidden Secrets?" He could recall nothing Merton had written to that effect.

The monk pursed his lips. "Possibly. At least, he claimed he did. And he wrote about it, too." Glancing around, he added, "Let's wait . . ."

Once inside their cell, Lucien closed the door.

"What I'm about to tell you," he cautioned softly with an uplifted finger, "must *never* get back to Dom Girardeau."

Ian was surprised that Lucien would speak behind the back of his abbey's director. But agreeing, he pulled up his chair and they sat, heads close.

"The day Merton died," Lucien continued in a hush, "before word of his death reached us, a letter arrived, postmarked Ceylon. It was addressed to the entire abbey, scribbled with obvious excitement, almost illegible, every sentence an exclamation. In it, Merton said he'd discovered something extraordinary. Something he called the *Ultimate Reality . . .*"

Ian felt the hairs rise on his neck.

"I'll never forget how he described it." Lucien's eyes glowed. "He likened the Ultimate Reality to the Unified Field Theory. A spiritual formula to unite all religions. To unite *the world*."

As Ian recalled from high school physics, the Unified Field Theory was science's Holy Grail, a yet-to-be-discovered mathematical equation to wed the known forces of the universe—nuclear, gravitational, electromagnetic. Einstein spent his last thirty years searching for it, failing, as had all others since. To imagine Merton discovering the spiritual equivalent left Ian breathless.

"Holy supersymmetry!"

Lucien smiled. "Indeed. Merton claimed the Ultimate Reality held the power to uplift all Humanity. He said it would bring wars to an end, heal all animosities between races, creeds, cultures. Even said he could *prove* it divine. But sadly, just before he was to break the news, he died."

"He left notes, right? He was a writer."

"Yes. In his letter he said he'd recorded everything in a journal and made two copies of the entry, mailing both to colleagues. One to a Protestant theologian he corresponded with, the Reverend Karl Barth, the other to an unknown person he called simply 'My Valentine.' He promised to send the abbey a copy, too, but never got the chance."

Pausing, he sobered. "I've often wondered if God didn't punish Merton for trespassing His Kingdom."

"Trespassing His Kingdom?"

"Merton claimed he discovered the Reality in Heaven. That he found an unguarded gateway into Paradise where he'd witnessed firsthand the legions of the holy departed."

Ian's mind was turning cartwheels. If in fact Merton's experience was verifiable, it was the Answer Ian had been seeking his whole life. It would confirm the Afterlife! More important, if a living being could actually visit Heaven, Ian had hope to see his parents again—and in *this* lifetime. Forget blind Faith, here was a way to heal his soul *and* learn a Great Secret!

"The journal," he pressed. "What became of it?"

"It was eventually published as *The Asian Journal.* An account of Merton's meandering journey to the Far East. Except there was no mention of any side trip to Heaven. Or the Ultimate Reality. All edited out."

"Edited out?" Ian cried.

The monk raised a finger to his lips. "I assume the Vatican looked into his claim and thought it bogus. The product of too much wine, perhaps. Merton did enjoy his libations—some say he even smoked marijuana on occasion."

Ian gripped the old man's wiry arm. "But what do *you* say? You knew Merton. Do you believe he discovered the Ultimate Reality?"

Lucien inhaled, staring down at his hands. Then nodding slowly, he replied, "Yes. Yes I do."

Electrified, Ian begged, "The copies he sent Karl Barth and Valentine—what became of them?"

"We never heard any more of either. Perhaps the Church tracked them down and confiscated them, too."

"Maybe Barth left notes!"

"I suspect he hadn't time. He died the same day as Merton. Heart attack. Perhaps hearing the awful news."

"And you've no idea what the Ultimate Reality says?"

Again the monk paused, Ian hanging on, watching the man's gaze go distant.

"I've had many decades to ponder that question, Ian. And while I've no idea what the Reality says, I *have* come to a conclusion about what it is . . ."

Ian leaned close.

"If, as Merton claims, the Reality can unite all religions and change the world, then it must speak an important Truth. A Message to enlighten us, to open our eyes to what God wants of us."

"A wondrous Revelation of some kind!"

Lucien shook his head. "A Revelation implies something we've no prior awareness of, and I can't believe God plays hide-and-seek with His

Truth. No, in my opinion the Reality must be Knowledge God has already attempted to communicate to us through Christ and the prophets, but which Man has misunderstood. Or ignored."

"A clarification, then."

"Yes. A Great Clarification. I believe that when we die and reach the Afterlife, its Knowledge will suddenly be made clear, and seem obvious. We'll slap ourselves on our spirit foreheads and say, *How could we have been so blind?"*

Ian nodded. His instincts told him the same. "But one thing I don't understand. If Merton sent an open letter to the monastery, why all the secrecy?"

"Not long after it came, we got orders from Rome to keep silent about it. The letter vanished, and until you, I've never spoken of it."

Having worked at the Vatican, Ian knew the Church's penchant for secrecy. It was not only guarded about its internal workings, but about aspects of its theology, too, restricting certain ancient texts and Scriptures to the eyes of a few. Ian felt grateful for Lucien's confidence.

"What made you break your silence now?"

"I don't know, exactly. Something told me I should pass word along before all who read the letter are gone. In many ways, you remind me of Merton. It just seemed fitting."

"Merton's *Asian Journal*—was it edited here or in Rome?" If the manuscript was edited here, maybe he could find it. But if it had fallen into the ecclesiastical abysses of the Vatican . . .

"Rome," Lucien said, sinking Ian's hopes. "The Curia always vetted Merton's writings prior to publication because of his unorthodox views. He was forever giving them heartburn. Like the time he took a lover."

Ian gaped at the monk, seeing him break into a grin.

"1966. Merton was fifty-one, at a hospital in Louisville for back surgery. Old sports injury—he was quite the athlete in his youth. While recuperating he met and fell in love with a student nurse less than half his age. Wrote about her in another of his journals, called her simply 'M.'

"Wasn't his first, either. Growing up in Europe he'd attended Cambridge where he got a girl pregnant, then abandoned her to come to the States. Mother and child died in the Blitzkrieg, it's said, but Merton never confirmed that. Wouldn't discuss that chapter of his life. Guilt, I figure."

"And Merton's mistress in Louisville?"

"The dom eventually found out and confronted Merton, and that ended it. Merton wasn't about to destroy his career over a romance. See, 'M' wasn't the only girl whose heart he broke as a monk."

Ian was speechless. One of the world's preeminent theologians, a philanderer!

"I used to work in our post office distributing mail. The bulk was always for Merton, from all over the world. Fan mail mostly. But also letters from famous people—Coretta Scott King, Bobby Kennedy, the Dalai Lama . . .

"On occasion Merton would receive a letter postmarked from Paris, no return address, written in a woman's hand, always labeled 'personal'—which barred the dom from opening it. Merton would get very emotional over them. Once I saw him in the garden reading one, tears rolling down his cheeks. When he finished he burned it with his cigarette lighter. Whoever the woman was, she wrote him regularly—up to the time he left on his fateful trip."

"Did Merton ever write back?"

"If he did, he didn't send them through our post office for fear of the dom. But he could easily have mailed them in town. That's what he did with nurse 'M' in Louisville. After the scandal, he continued to get letters from her. Asked me to hide them when they came, said she was his spiritual soul mate."

"Do you think she was the Valentine he sent a copy of his Reality to?"

"That was always my presumption."

They fell quiet, then Lucien asked, "Well now, are you ready to receive Absolution?"

Ian gave him a sideways look. "Not yet. I may have more to confess . . ."

TWELVE

THE RURAL ROADS OF CENTRAL KENTUCKY, FIVE WEEKS AGO

First thing the next day, Ian took a bus twelve miles to Bardstown and rented a car, driving north along a twisty, rolling, two-lane highway, ignoring the speed limit. He was determined to track down "M," Merton's Louisville lover from decades before, hoping she still had the journal pages of the Ultimate Reality. Lucien had armed him with the only other clue he had—the whereabouts of the hospital where "M" had served her nursing residency in 1966. St. Joseph's Infirmary, just south of the city.

But when Ian got to the address he'd plugged into his phone's GPS, he saw only a high-rise apartment complex.

He flagged down a passerby who apprised him that "St. Joe's" had been torn down in the eighties, replaced by a new healthcare facility not far away. Taking directions, fingers crossed that the old records had moved, too, he drove on.

Soon he arrived at Audubon Hospital, relieved to learn that St. Joe's records were indeed here. An archivist was able to supply the names of student nurses from the target months—five with first or last names beginning with M, all Louisville natives. Privacy rules, however, allowed no further personal data.

Ian found a phonebook and prepared to call all listings with the five surnames. "M" was likely married now, he realized, her last name changed, but he hoped to stumble across a relative, at least, who could help narrow his search.

Thank God this isn't LA . . .

Less than an hour later he came across the brother of a woman on the list. "Mary Delt" her name in sixty-six, since married, now "Mary Howard." With some polite cajoling he got her number, whispering a prayer as he dialed, thinking how long it had been since last he'd prayed.

And then he heard the voice of an elderly female.

"Hello?"

"Ms. Howard?"

"Yes?"

"My name's Ian Baringer. Sorry to disturb you, I'm hoping you can help me. I'm trying to locate a nurse who interned with you at St. Joe's back in sixty-six. All I know is, one of her patients was the theologian, Thomas Merton."

"Goodness, her name's no secret."

"Excuse me?"

"Marjorie Jones. The famous Ms. 'M'. They exposed her years ago."

One of the names on Ian's list! "Who exposed her?"

"Reporters. After Merton's journal mentioning their affair."

His hand shook as he took notes. "Can you tell me where to find her?"

"If it's about Merton, you're wasting your time. She won't talk about him. Hasn't in all these years. Turned down lots *of money, too."*

"Please, I *must* talk to her."

The woman grunted, *"Hold on . . ."*

When she returned, Ian asked, "Marjorie Jones goes by her given name? She never married?"

"She goes by Sister *Marjorie. After Merton died, she became a Carmelite nun."*

Ian sighed. Hearing that Marjorie Jones had refused money to talk was less discouraging than this news. Carmelites were a contemplative order famous for guarding their privacy . . .

Thanking Ms. Howard, he followed her directions to a secluded institution on the southern edge of town. Much like his old orphanage, enclosed by high walls of faded red brick. It gave him an odd sense of déjà vu.

He announced himself into an intercom at a gate and was buzzed through to the front door, met by a pair of squinty eyes behind a speakeasy-like trapdoor. Then the little door shut, the big door opened, and he was admitted into a dim foyer.

"Sister Marjorie, please," he said, smiling down at an elderly woman in the somber black habit and white bib of the Carmelites.

"Wait here," she snapped, and vanished around a corner.

He could hear her shuffle down a hall, and moments later came the clopping echo of leather soles, followed by a pale, gray-haired, gray-eyed, frail-looking woman with round glasses. Also in a Carmelite habit, she held herself slightly hunched, as if in the early stages of osteoporosis.

"Sister Marjorie? Sister Marjorie Jones?"

She stared up at him, brow suspicious, voice tentative. "Yes?"

"Sorry to trouble you. I'm here about a man I believe you once knew. Thomas Merton."

Her eyes flashed and she moved past him to the door, opening it wide. *"Please leave!"*

"I'm not a reporter. This is a personal matter."

"Now!"

Reluctantly he did as told, turning for a last try.

"It's not about Merton. I'm here about the Ultimate Reality . . ."

He was outside, door swinging shut, when it came to a stop. Slowly it reopened to reveal a look of cautious wonderment on the woman's face.

"The—the Ultimate Reality? You know of it?"

"Yes."

Blinking, she stared past him, then stepped aside.

"Not here," she said, lowering her voice, motioning him toward an unoccupied drawing room. They headed for a corner sofa. "The Reality—what do you know of it?"

"Very little, actually." He didn't want to compromise Lucien's confidence.

They settled in, and she studied him.

"Who *are* you?"

"No one. A lost soul in search of some answers."

Her eyes narrowed. "I *know* you . . . I've seen you before . . ." Suddenly she brightened. "It's *you*! The priest from Africa! I *knew* it! I saw you on TV, testifying to Congress! I never forget a face!"

It seemed her life wasn't so cloistered after all.

"That was years ago. I'm no longer a priest."

She folded her arms, studying him again.

"Do you have family, Mr. Baringer?"

"Just my fiancée. I lost my parents when I was young, an only child."

"And where is your fiancée?"

"Los Angeles."

"You men and your quests! What do you want of me?"

"Merton's Reality. I *have* to find it . . ."

She wagged her head. "You think it holds the answers to all your problems, don't you? People still looking to Tom for guidance after all these years! The irony is, he was as lost as everybody else! That's what drove him to the Far East, you know, searching the ends of the earth for answers."

"And apparently, he found them."

"If you'll forgive a platitude, Mr. Baringer, beware what you seek . . . Before today, I thought I was the only one who knew of the Reality—outside a few Church officials, perhaps. Tom planned to reveal it at a conference in Bangkok. He alluded to it in his last session that morning, his last public statement." She closed her eyes.

" 'Mankind is on the threshold of a wondrous new beginning, a period of unprecedented hope and peace. Soon, a Great Truth will be made Known to the world—the Ultimate Reality.' "

Exhaling, she stood. "Wait here . . ."

Ian tensed, watching her disappear down the hall. Minutes later she returned with a yellowed envelope and hardcover book, handing him the envelope.

"All these years, I've never shown another soul . . ."

Hands clumsy with excitement, Ian fumbled out a letter. Longhand scrawl, dated the day before Merton died:

Mon. Dec, 9, 1968
My dearest Margie,

Pardon my scratching, I write with such haste, with the greatest sense of triumph ever a man could feel! My sweet Lord, I have found It! The Answer! I have witnessed at last what I've searched for all my life, heart and soul!

But let me start at the beginning . . . Last month I met with the Dalai Lama to discuss our mutual interest in the Tantric arts. Namely, that of the Buddhist Nyingmapa sect, whose forms of special meditation foster bodhicitta*—perfect emptiness—the path to divine enlightenment. I'd been practicing intensely and felt I was near a breakthrough.*

Then last week at the ruins of Polonnaruwa, ancient ghost city of Ceylon, I was meditating on a statue of Buddha in a sacred cave, steadily slowing my heart rate, and I achieved it! Bodhicitta! *A vision of God's own Truth!*

Incredible as it sounds, my heart stopped, my soul left my body, and I entered Heaven itself! I beheld divine enlightenment—the Ultimate Reality! And if not for my guides discovering me and snatching back my life with artificial respiration, I wouldn't be here to share it with the world! I've recorded all in my journal and will announce it tomorrow! Proof of God! Knowledge to uplift the most despondent soul!

Margie, you will rejoice at this Truth! Our questions about God and religion and the meaning of life are ended! Indeed, with what I learned, theology itself is obsolete!

At last, we Know the Mind of God!!

With all my heart,
Tom

Ian was breathless. "*Please,* may I see the Reality?"

Sister Marjorie lowered her eyes. "That's all I know of it. When Tom's journal was finally published, there was no mention. I wrote Church officials time and again, but they ignored me. My relationship with Tom, I suppose . . ."

It seemed Sister Marjorie *wasn't* Merton's Valentine after all. Ian felt crushed.

"The Church denied you, despite becoming a nun?"

"Whatever the Vatican knows of Tom's vision, it won't say. But there are tantalizing clues."

She held up the book.

The Asian Journal of Thomas Merton.

Opening to a dog-eared page, she said, "Let me read from an entry dated December 4, 1968. It's supposed to cover Tom's epiphany in the cave of the Buddha:

"Suddenly I slipped free of this existence into a realm of utter joy and enlightenment. No more uncertainty, no more anxiety, the dust of my confusions gone as I gazed upon the most beautiful and now-obvious Truth.

"At last I've found what I was searching for—a spiritual Knowledge long lost to Man, with the Wisdom to reconcile all doubts and fears.

"What else need I Know? It says all!"

It said nothing . . .

Sister Marjorie paid Ian a sympathetic look.

"I've come to believe the Ultimate Reality isn't a Truth Man can live with. Whatever it was Tom learned in that ancient city of the dead, it was something long hidden from the world, a forbidden fruit. A Knowledge I suspect Tom stole, and God reclaimed. Perhaps his death should serve as warning to those who would see into the Mind of God."

Ian was hardly listening. Merton's experience was either a hallucination or he'd truly expired during his meditation and seen the Hereafter, only to be resuscitated. Ian had to know which. And he had an audacious idea how to do so.

THIRTEEN

THE VERANDA OF AN OCEANSIDE VILLA, GENEVA BAY, ST. MAARTEN ISLAND, CURRENT DAY, EVENING

Angela could see where all this was going, but she let Ian finish.

"Merton's vision was the product of a meditation that slows the heartbeat," he said, voice fervent. "Only he took it too far, he stopped his heart altogether! *That's* how he saw Heaven, he had an NDE! *Bodhicitta,* he called it."

"So you thought you'd finally found a way to prove the Afterlife."

"More than that—a way to see my parents again. In *this* lifetime."

"It's not enough to believe you'll see them in the next?"

He leaned forward, taking her hands. "You've got to understand. I know deep down inside, if ever I'm going to heal this hole I *have* to see them. My plan was to do it quickly with an NDE and get home to you, all our troubles finally behind us."

"But the risk!"

"Not so great as you think. Unlike Merton, we built in safeguards."

"*Safeguards?* Ian, you *kill* yourself!"

His eyes searched a moment, then he asked, "Have you ever heard of an extreme water sport called free-diving?"

"*What?*"

"Skin-diving performed in the open ocean—but without a breathing device. Divers attach to a lifeline and heavy weight, and descend to incredible depths on a single gulp of air. Five-hundred feet or more, reeled up before they pass out. That's how I see my NDEs. 'Spiritual' free-diving, backed by the best team and equipment in the world."

Angela groaned. "Josten's no expert, he's a quack! *A criminal.* He killed a man doing this stuff! And your other 'doctors' wouldn't be here either if they were legitimate."

"I know all about it, Emil told me everything. It wasn't incompetence, it was equipment failure. But you're missing the point." He squeezed her hands. "Angela, *I found it.* I have *proof*!"

Then the light left his eyes and he lowered his gaze, voice, too. "Just not the proof I expected . . ."

The last rays of sun withdrew behind the hills, Angela's spirits sinking with them. How many times had she and Ian pursued these "proofs" of his?

He released her hands and sank back in his chair, tone growing sober. "We scheduled my first NDE for three minutes," he continued. "A test, to see how I'd weather it. All my vitals were suspended—heart, brain, respiration. But the incredible thing is, *I was still conscious.* Dreamlike, but *not* a dream. I actually felt my spirit separate from my body, though I could tell I was still tethered to it, like some ethereal umbilical cord.

"I found myself floating above the table, the team oblivious. I could see their every move, all in slow motion. Up through the ceiling I floated, into daylight, warehouse receding below, ocean waves undulating to shore like the backs of great, green snakes—all so vivid.

"Then suddenly I was drawn into the middle of this huge, sloping tunnel of cloud. Dark at the bottom, bright at the top. I somehow began moving toward the light, feeling wonderful pulses of warmth and peace pass through me. As I neared the end I couldn't see beyond, too brilliant, but I heard the most glorious choir.

"And then I halted. Like my soul had stuck on a snag. I felt a pull and began to slide back. I didn't want to go, fighting like a fish on a line. But it was too strong. Last I heard, a voice was calling. Distant. Male. Not my father, but familiar somehow. Ghostly.

"And suddenly I realized where it was coming from, and I felt this terrible rush of dread! The *dark* end of the tunnel . . ."

A full moon had risen over the ocean, painting Ian's face in a phantasmal glow. It gave Angela gooseflesh.

"Before I could identify the voice, I awoke on the table, staring up at my team. Words can't describe how I felt." His eyes glistened in the silver light. "All these years of searching, the failures, frustrations . . . and now—*proof.*"

She allowed him a moment, then said, "So, you're a Believer again."

He looked at her as if *she* were crazy. "Angela, I saw an existence beyond life! I Know now—there *is* a God!"

"Sweetheart, what you experienced wasn't proof. It sounds no different than any other NDE. Tunnels of light, euphoria, heavenly choirs—all common claims."

"Exactly. It *validates* those claims."

"Look, I'm no expert on NDEs, but I know there are *non*-supernatural explanations. Loss of oxygen is a well-known cause of hallucinations."

"Hallucinations that just happen to follow the NDE paradigm? Millions of people over the years, all hallucinating on the same wavelength?"

"Millions *predisposed* to the same wavelength. We all know the standard NDE tunnel drill, Ian. Everyone has notions of the Afterlife, whether we Believe or not. Even atheists. In the throes of death, slipping into delusion, the mind draws on what it knows. What else is there?"

"There's the *un*known. And what I learned from my second NDE—the one you interrupted—science be damned, I *know* it didn't come from me!"

FOURTEEN

AN OCEANSIDE VILLA, GENEVA BAY, ST. MAARTEN ISLAND, SAME EVENING

Ian shoved aside his dinner, observing Angela in the pale light. *Angela the realist, the skeptic.*

Yes, in the past he'd given her reason to question his judgment—if not his sanity. But this was different. These were *no* hallucinations. He had indeed been to the Other Side—twice now. And after what he'd learned there this last trip, he desperately needed Angela's support.

He watched her sitting with head cocked, porcelain complexion aglow under the moon, sculpted beauty marred only by the furrows of her brow. It was imperative that he be calm and rational now as he explained what happened next, knowing his words would sound anything but . . .

Inhaling, he pressed on. "I suffered no ill effects from my first NDE, and after a few days rest we undertook a second. Ten minutes. Time enough, I trusted, to find my parents.

"It began as before. I felt my soul leave my body, attached by the ethereal leash, rising into the sky, entering the cylinder of cloud—that wonderful sense of tranquility.

"And then almost immediately I heard my name called out. That same, eerie-familiar voice again, as if expecting me. I turned toward it, and before I realized, I was drifting down into a warm veil of fog. I smelled something odd, like frying bacon, and it dawned on me that I seemed to possess all my senses. Maybe a sixth—I felt keenly *intuitive.*

"I looked down at myself and was surprised to be in a dingy-white robe, no weight to it, my skin ghostly translucent. I went to touch the cloth and my hand passed through—and right through *me*—without sensation."

Angela arched a brow, but he ignored it.

"As I descended the voice grew louder, sing-songish—*'Eeee-uhnn, Eeee-uhnn.*

"Then the tunnel darkened, my feelings of peace gave way to dread, and suddenly I emptied out onto a vast, gloomy plain. Dim, endless, perfectly flat. Blanketed in thick smog, tinged orange by the glow of a distant sunset.

"I saw a shape ahead in the haze. Slim. Male. Pale-skinned. Spectral. Features hard to make out. Robe like mine, only gray.

"As I drew closer I recognized him, and I was stunned. *Hurt.* The one person waiting for me on the Other Side wasn't my parents, or a departed friend or teacher. It was that psychopath from my orphanage, Zack Niemand . . ."

Angela looked uncomfortable, shifting in her seat.

"I asked him, 'Am I in Hell?' And he said, 'Neither Hell nor Heaven—Limbo.' Limbo, where unchristened innocents go. But knowing Niemand's sins, I couldn't believe he wasn't damned.

"I asked, 'Why are you here, weren't you baptized?' And he said, 'In life I lost my faculties. I wasn't to blame for my deeds, but I'm not deserving of Heaven, so I exist in-between.' He spoke whistling his S's—the same impediment that had caused him such bullying at St. L.

" 'Are you suffering?' I asked, and he said, 'We feel nothing here. No pain, no pleasure . . .'

"I'd so many questions, but I couldn't linger. I backed toward the tunnel entrance, excusing myself to find my parents. But Niemand shook his head and said, 'They don't want you to find them.' I asked, 'You know my parents?' He said, 'From the night of the fire at St. L. They were sent to acquire the soul of Father Ben, and since my soul was stranded there, to collect my wandering spirit.'

"Apparently Niemand didn't know *I* was responsible for stranding his soul, so I kept that to myself, ashamed. But his news of my parents stopped me, and he explained, 'Sometimes the Angel of Death calls on Nether spirits to do Her work. And while your parents were at St. L that night, they rescued you from the fire.' "

Ian felt his heart falter, having to muster his composure to finish.

"*Twice* now my parents have saved me from flames! I felt overcome, and I rushed for the tunnel—but Niemand called out, 'You won't find them up there.'

"I didn't understand, and I turned to see him point toward the glowing horizon.

" 'Your parents dwell below,' he said. "In the Pit.'

"And before I could ask more, I felt a pull on my lifeline, heading back . . ."

FIFTEEN

AN OCEANSIDE VILLA, GENEVA BAY, ST. MAARTEN ISLAND, SAME EVENING

Angela stared at Ian, dumbfounded. This was no run-of-the-mill NDE. At least, not like any she'd ever heard. The detail, the continuity spanning both accounts. Not that she was persuaded. Ian's visions, though intriguing, were the figments of an expiring mind, nothing more.

But that being the case, it begged a disturbing question. What was the root of his hallucinations? Given they came from within, what subconscious pain inspired them?

Angela could see the torment he was suffering. What could possibly make a kind and just man like Ian want to remit the homicidal Niemand to Limbo while damning his beloved parents to the bottom rung of Hell? Had his parents done something that warranted punishment? Some long-buried incident? Physical abuse? Sexual abuse? She would have to raise these points carefully . . .

"I don't understand. Your parents were heroic. They gave their lives to protect you. Why do you think God would damn them?"

Ian lowered his eyes. "What do you know about the concept of mortal sin?"

"Very little."

"In the Catholic Faith there are two classes of sin. Venial and mortal. People who die with either on their souls—meaning they haven't purged themselves first through Confession or sincere contrition—will be punished in the next life.

"Venial sins are minor offenses, atoned for after death in Purgatory, a place of temporary suffering. Once the soul is purified, it's allowed into Heaven.

"Mortal sins are grave offenses that cannot be atoned for after death.

Mortal sins deprive the soul of all sanctifying grace and condemn it to eternal damnation."

"But weren't your parents devout? If they'd sinned, wouldn't they have gone to Confession? How could *both* have died with mortal sins on their souls?"

A shadow passed over Ian's face. "Of all sins, there is one Confession can't absolve, an act of despair that defies God's authority over the life He's created. *Suicide.* Suicide is the ultimate rejection of God, unforgivable because only a *living* soul can be cleansed of mortal sin. So serious, it's punished in the deepest Pit of Hell."

"Your parent's didn't commit suicide; they were protecting you!"

"If Niemand was telling the truth and my parents *are* damned to the Pit, it means their death must have been an act of despair. Faced with my death, they lost Faith in God and chose to die with me. In God's eyes, that's suicide."

"What God would condemn parents for refusing to abandon their child?"

Ian slumped. "Who Knows the Mind of God?"

Angela was incredulous. "You believe God damned your parents for one bad decision—made under unbearable stress—and let a serial killer off with a slap on the wrist?"

"I don't know what to believe. I've got to go back; I need more time."

She could no longer keep the façade. "I'm *not* letting you throw your life away over a fantasy! What you experienced were fragments of memories your subconscious strung together like a bad dream. Guilt for what you did to Niemand; the fire at the orphanage. *That's* your Hell, Ian!"

He turned aside. "If my parents *are* damned it's because of me. And unless I'm damned, too, an NDE is my only chance ever to see them again. I've no choice."

She studied his face in the moonlight. Did he have a death wish? Her little voice cried out for her to flee. But she had no choice, either. She was all that stood between him and his self-destruction.

SIXTEEN

AN OCEANSIDE VILLA, GENEVA BAY, ST. MAARTEN ISLAND, NEXT MORNING

Angela spent a fitful night on the living-room couch, in her street clothes, sun well up when she heard a knock at the front door. Rising stiffly, she shuffled over, opening on Emil Josten and Yvette Garonne, medical bags and bakery rolls in hand.

"We're here for a follow-up," Josten said.

Garonne eyed Angela's crumpled blouse and skirt, and Angela felt her face flush. She snatched the blanket from the couch and went for Ian.

It was an effort to wake him, and he was groggy on his feet as she led him out in his pajamas. He greeted the doctors through a stifled yawn, then gave Angela a kiss on the cheek. She made sure Garonne saw.

While the doctors conducted their physical, Angela withdrew to the kitchen for coffee.

"Well, Ian," she heard Garonne purr, "you zeem no worse for ze wear."

Looking, Angela saw her unbutton his top, roaming with a stethoscope, calling out numbers for Josten to record. The woman's familiarity grated—especially when she had Ian drop his bottoms to inspect his sutures. "Zis might teekle," she trilled, and Angela had to turn away.

Josten asked Ian about his NDE, and Ian gave only a cursory response. Neither doctor recorded it, Angela was pleased to note, their interest clearly physiological, not spiritual. Satisfied that they weren't encouraging his "visions," she downed her coffee and slipped off to shower.

When she returned in fresh clothes, they'd finished.

"No complications," Josten was telling Ian. "You're a 'go' for Friday morning."

Ian showed the doctors out, and then excusing himself to shower, he left Angela nibbling a roll.

Three days to change his mind. But not a clue how . . .

There came another knock, Angela opening this time on an elderly man in the dark suit and reverse collar of a priest. No one she recognized. Short, white-haired, slim.

He smiled shyly, eyes bright, admiring.

"You're even lovelier than your pictures!" he said, taking her hand warmly in his. "Father Lucien Gant."

Surprised, she invited him in.

"I'm so relieved to find you here," he said. "Sorry for not coming sooner, I'd no passport. We Trappists don't get out much, you know . . . Tell me, how is Ian?"

She offered him a seat on the couch. "Okay. For now."

"Thank God you reached him in time!"

"Yes. Thank God."

She brought coffee, and Ian soon entered in a short-sleeved shirt and slacks, breaking into a wide grin. He gave the monk a hug and a clap on the back.

"I thought I heard a familiar voice! How are you, Lucien?"

"Good, thank you. But more important, how are *you*? You've lost weight!"

"I'm fine now that Angela's here," he replied as they settled around the coffee table. "I can't believe the dom let you out."

"First trip in twenty years. And first time abroad . . ."

He lost his smile. "But I must tell you, I wasn't exactly 'let out.' I'm afraid I was sent. The dom is very concerned about you, my boy. We're *both* concerned."

Ian sobered, too. "The dom knows?"

"Forgive me, it came out during my Confession. But God's Hand was surely in it—it led me to an important enlightenment."

His face turned sheepish.

"I'm sorry to say, Ian, I used poor judgment telling you about Merton's Reality. As I now know, your experiments not only risk your life, they risk your soul. You must give them up."

Ian blinked. "Give them up? But I've succeeded."

Lucien paled. "God help us! *You've been to the Other Side!*"

"As far as Limbo. I spoke with a spirit there."

The monk waived his hands in the air. "Say no more! It's *forbidden*! Whatever you've seen, you *mustn't* tell!"

"Forbidden?"

"To trespass the Afterlife is a sacrilege! A *grievous* sin! God will punish those who pry into His Mysteries!"

Angela sat back, pleased at the tack things were taking.

Ian was at a loss. Lucien's position on the Afterlife had hardened considerably since last they'd discussed it. Never had he seen the monk upset, much less distraught like this.

"I don't understand, Father. You once told me that the Mysteries of the Afterlife are based on Truths God has already given us. 'Great Clarifications.' How can it be a sin to shed light on Knowledge we should already have?"

"There are *two* kinds of divine Knowledge, son. *Revealed* and *hidden.* Revealed Knowledge is Truth God chooses to share. Hidden Knowledge is Truth He withholds for His Own Purposes. God has always kept specific Knowledge of Heaven and Hell hidden from Man. Merton's Reality, it appears, contains hidden Knowledge of Heaven—for which he paid with his life."

"But the Bible itself speaks freely of Heaven and Hell."

"Look again. The Bible speaks only in *general* terms. No details, no physical descriptions. In fact, as the dom pointed out, the Bible *forbids* prying into God's Secrets."

"I know of no such Scripture."

"Deuteronomy, for one. Chapter 18, verses 10–12: '*There shall not be found among you anyone who conjures spells or calls up the dead or consults with mediums or soothsayers or spiritists or sorcerers. For all who do these things are an abomination to the Lord.*' "

Ian shook his head. "I'm not conjuring spells or spirits; I'm using *science.*"

"However it's done, to obtain such Knowledge outside of death defies God's Will. Only rarely has God made exceptions. Look to the New Testament—Second Corinthians, where God favors St. Paul with a glimpse of Heaven: '*I know a person in Christ who was lifted up to the Third Heaven—whether in the body or out of the body I do not know; God knows. And he was admitted into Paradise to learn things that are not to be told; that no mortal is permitted to tell.*' "

Lucien reiterated, "Things not to be told; that no mortal is permitted to tell. Surely you see, beyond God's chosen few, Knowledge of the Afterlife is not meant for the living. It's one thing to be invited into the House of God and gifted with its Secrets. It's quite another to sneak through a back door and steal them! Such a thief must pay with his life, if not his soul."

"Two obscure passages!"

"No, Ian. God makes this clear from the very first Book of Genesis. I was unaware too until the dom opened my eyes. If you recall, before Adam and Eve's fall from grace they lived in a worldly Paradise, in union with God but separated from His Heavenly Realm. They lived in unrestricted bliss—but for one thing."

"God forbade them to eat from the Tree of the Knowledge of Good and Evil."

"Yes. And then the serpent came to Eve, tempting her with the promise that if she and Adam ate the Tree's fruit, they would Know what God Knows. So they ate and were cast out of Eden. But have you ever stopped to consider what, exactly, the Knowledge of Good and Evil is?"

Ian shrugged. "An understanding of what is right and wrong, surely."

"More than that."

A sudden awareness stole over Ian, and he whispered, *"Knowledge of Heaven and Hell."*

"Precisely! The *full* Knowledge of Heaven and Hell. Not just an Understanding of Good and Evil, but the divine reasoning behind it—*insight into the Mind of God Himself!"*

The monk blotted his brow with a handkerchief. "Knowledge that underpins not only the workings of Heaven and Hell, but the entire Universe! A Knowledge so profound, Man cannot possess it in life. Only in death, only as a spirit—something we *also* Know from the Book of Genesis. After Adam and Eve ate of the Tree of Knowledge, God said, 3:22–24: *'Behold, man is become as God, Knowing Good and Evil. And now he must not put forth his hand and take also of the Tree of Life and eat, and live forever.'* "

Ian turned to Angela. "After Adam and Eve's Sin, God declared another Tree off-limits to Man, the Tree of Life. He stationed an angel with a flaming sword to guard it."

Lucien added, "From that time forward, God has hidden Himself and His spiritual world from Man. But He left us with the promise of Scripture that if we Believe in Him, we'll one day share in Eternal Life.

"So you see now, if Man reveals Knowledge that is meant to be hidden, and it verifies the existence of God and the spiritual world, it will nullify God's Plan for our salvation. It's our Faith, Ian, that earns us our Heavenly reward. Faith in God, in the absence of proof."

"And failing Faith," Ian added darkly, thinking of his parents, "we suffer His Wrath."

Lucien nodded. "Indeed, God can be wrathful. After Adam and Eve ate of the Tree, God uprooted it and cleaved it in two, dividing Good from Evil. He planted the Good half in Heaven, the Evil half in Hell, and now the only way for us to obtain either Knowledge is to die."

Ian squinted at him. "I've never heard that aspect of the Creation Story."

"Also something I learned from Dom Girardeau—privileged information you mustn't repeat."

"Privileged? How did the dom hear of it?"

"It goes back to Thomas Merton and that last letter he sent the abbey."

"Of course. The Secret Merton discovered in Heaven was the Knowledge of Good. The Ultimate Reality is the Knowledge of Good!"

Lucien held up a hand. "While it seems so, I caution about second-guessing God. There are many Mysteries to Heaven, and it's unclear from Merton's letter what the Ultimate Reality is. Regardless, the story of God splitting the Tree didn't come from Merton. Not directly, anyway. Dom Girardeau learned of it years after Merton's death, after he became dom of Gethsemani.

"One day while cleaning out old files, Girardeau came across the papers of Father Flavian Burns—the dom during Merton's final year. The papers contained notes of a phone conversation between Burns and the CDF in 1969—conversations about Merton's Reality."

Angela interrupted, "Who is the CDF?"

She'd been silent until now, but Ian could see it hadn't been for lack of interest. He answered for Lucien, "The Congregation for the Doctrine of the Faith. Ancient office of the Vatican responsible for safeguarding Catholic theology. A 'heresy watchdog,' so to speak. You'd know it by its original name, 'The Congregation of the Inquisition.' " He saw her brow crease.

Lucien added, "The CDF decides what doctrine is—and isn't—appropriate for the Faithful to Believe. And Merton's Reality was deemed inappropriate. The CDF ordered Burns to destroy Merton's letter, but Burns resisted. Like most of us at the abbey, Burns believed Merton's vision must have been beatific, and he yearned to know what the Ultimate Reality was.

"So to gain Burns's cooperation quickly before news of the Reality's existence could spread, the CDF gave him the warnings I just gave you, and shared with him the privileged Scripture about God dividing the Tree.

"Like you, Burns concluded that the Reality was the Knowledge of Good, and seeing how Merton and Karl Barth died after coming in contact with it, Burns was persuaded that God wanted the Knowledge to remain hidden. He then destroyed Merton's letter and swore the abbey to silence. All the same, he took notes, which Dom Girardeau later came across. And when the dom learned of your plans to trespass the Afterlife, fearing for your soul, he sent me to warn you."

Lucien paused, looking uneasy. "I regret to add, the dom also sends an ultimatum. If you persist on this path, you risk Excommunication. Further, he says that there are forces in the world beyond the Church's purview—*powerful* forces—committed to stopping such sacrilege."

"Forces? What forces?"

"The dom couldn't say."

Ian fell silent, and Lucien turned hopeful eyes to him.

"So now, in light of what you've heard, you're ready to give up this ungodly business?"

"I've seen nothing yet of Heaven or Hell—barely a glimpse of Limbo. And if that's a sin, I've already been punished for it—I learned my parents are damned!"

Lucien recoiled, crossing himself. "Even now it may not be too late for you! Hopefully you haven't reached the point of no return—hopefully God sent me in time!"

Ian thought of the plane crash, the explosion at the orphanage. "*Twice* my parents saved me from fire—how can I abandon them to Eternal Fire?"

"But there's nothing you can do for them. Damnation is forever!"

Angela touched his arm. "You've got to listen."

He stood. "If God is as Merciful as you say, Lucien, He'll forgive me my trespass."

The monk stood also, making the sign of the cross over Ian. "I pray for you, my friend. If Merton stole the Knowledge of Good and paid with his life, *what price will you pay for the Knowledge of Evil?"*

SEVENTEEN

AN OCEANSIDE VILLA, ST. MAARTEN ISLAND, THREE DAYS LATER, EARLY MORNING

Angela spent another restless night on the couch. Just before dawn she rose and stole to Ian's door in her nightshirt, seeing him in bed, uncovered and shirtless in the moonlight, face peaceful, breaths long and relaxed.

How does he do it? Scheduled to die in a few hours, he slept like a child in his mother's arms. Angela wanted to grab him, shake him. *Why do I love this madman?*

She knew why. . . . Going to the kitchen table, she opened Ian's laptop, calling up YouTube and a two-year-old video. A newscast with tens of millions of viewer hits. Same newscast she'd used to torture herself those years she and Ian were apart. Fast-forwarding, she hit play.

The image came up ghostly dark with eerie-green tint. Night-vision camera. It gave her the same chill now as when she first saw it on national TV. Desolate dockyard. Boat husks, salvage scrap, rusted derricks, dilapidated buildings, broken windows. Fog swept past as the camera moved herky-jerky to the sounds of footsteps and panting.

Suddenly the view blurred, the blockish face of a man ballooning close. Mid-thirties. Forehead, cheeks, and chin smeared with soot, eyes anxious. He was holding the camera, pointing it back at himself as he hurried along, whispering tensely, *"We're at the old industrial wharfs of Lagune Ebrié, the waterway separating the port of Abidjan from the Gulf of Guinea. It's several hours before dawn."*

He panned the camera to reveal six men ahead, black clothing and stocking hats, treading stealthily in single file. All bore rifles save a tall, slim individual.

"If we're caught by the wrong people it could mean our lives. But Antonio Ponti and Father Baringer have this planned to the last detail . . ."

Antonio Ponti, Director of Security at the Vatican, Angela knew. An acquaintance of Ian's from his days there who'd come to his aid in this crisis.

"Ahead lies a warehouse where scores of children are being held. Les petits riens, *as they're known here—'the little nothings.' Orphans of AIDS and poverty. Among them is eight-year-old Anya, a student of Father's mission school, who was snatched from the playground two weeks ago."*

The camera shifted and Angela saw the silhouette of a warehouse. Quiet, dark but for a dim light glinting through filthy windows.

"Each month slavers come here to smuggle boys off to mines, farms, fishing boats where they labor eighteen hours a day, seven day a week for the rest of their lives. Girls end up in factories, as domestics, or prostitutes. But with luck, not today . . ."

The troop gathered behind a large, corrugated shipping container, and Ian came into view. Lean face blackened almost unrecognizable, eyes grave, determined.

Angela inhaled. All the times she'd seen this, she still felt a rush. Ian in a simple cassock, no body armor, no weapons like his comrades. Next to him, a burly, wide-shouldered man, early fifties, dark hair, the bearing of a leader. Antonio Ponti. He whispered in Italian-accented English, *"Eight of them, all asleep in front, no sentries. Children in a back room. We mustn't risk gunfire. When I signal, move fast."* He placed a hand on Ian's shoulder, looking to him and the cameraman. *"Wait here until we secure the building, then come get your pictures."*

Another man had Ian's opposite shoulder. Josef Varga, Ponti's first deputy and a close friend of Ian's then. Face hardly discernable under his paint, he appeared Slavic—strong cheekbones, wide jaw. His accent confirmed it: *"Don't worry,* mój bracie," he assured Ian, *"Christ's Sword is with us."*

Ponti and his men moved out, stealing to the warehouse, flattening against its walls, readying equipment. On Ponti's order they broke open the door with a mighty crash, storming through.

Despite orders, Ian followed, Angela biting her lip as the cameraman muttered, *"Oh damn! Oh damn!"* chasing after. The image went erratic, sounds of panicked shouts in a language Angela didn't recognize, Ponti's men switching on spotlights, briefly blinding the camera. When the picture returned it was of the building's interior, color normal. Makeshift living quarters along the front wall, eight black men rousted from a row of cots, blocking the glare with their hands.

One fumbled a gun from a table, was quickly disarmed and pinned.

Then Angela heard Josef shout and she held her breath as she always did at this point. The camera jolted to a man pulling a pistol from under a pillow, aiming at Ian. Angela winced to see Josef throw himself in front, absorbing three bursts to the chest before the gunman was subdued. Thankfully the brave Josef was only stunned, protected by a Kevlar vest.

Six slavers brought in check now, the last two breaking for the far side of the building. Angela tensed again as Ian gave chase and quickly overtook them, hauling them up short. When they resisted, he cracked their skulls together, dropping them in a crumple. All under control, he rushed to a back room, forcing its door, met by a stampede of kids. One frail-looking little girl cried out to him in a pipsqueak voice, and he swept her up to the cheers of his team.

Angela felt a familiar warm glow, and luxuriated in that for a minute. Then she jumped the video ahead, stopping at the front office of a police station. Black men in green uniforms and red berets receiving the eight captives.

An official behind the counter regarded Ian over a pair of half-rim glasses, noting in a French accent, *"You realize, Father, these men have the politicos in their pockets. They will all be back on the streets tomorrow, up to their old tricks again."*

Ian seemed taken aback. He snapped, *"I've Faith in God!"*

The official made a face. *"I'm afraid God turned his back on this place a long time ago."*

Pausing, Ian turned to the cameraman, eyes impassioned, begging, *"Take your story, tell the world. Maybe* somebody *out there will care!"*

Angela froze the image. Indeed, once this documentary aired, Anya and the plight of *les petits riens* received worldwide attention, Ian becoming a reluctant celebrity. He appeared before the U.S. Senate Subcommittee on Foreign Relations, then the UN General Assembly. It led to international sanctions against Cote d'Ivoire, and a case was brought before the World Court. Before it was over, prominent European businessmen were indicted and jailed.

And another gratifying sidebar. Donations streamed into the Catholic mission in Abidjan. Angela made a contribution herself. Anonymously.

Yes, she knew why she loved this madman.

EIGHTEEN

A BACK HIGHWAY OF ST. MAARTEN ISLAND, LATER THAT MORNING

Ian sat silent in the driver's seat, stealing a glance at an equally silent Angela next to him. She looked exhausted, bright hazel eyes gone dull. Beyond the stress she was obviously feeling, she couldn't be sleeping well on the couch, stubbornly insisting, *Let's just get this done and go home*—then *we'll talk!*

Her anxiety was all the worse, certainly, because she thought his trips to the Other Side delusional. Even Lucien, who *did* believe him, rejected the idea that Ian could find his parents in the vastness of the Abyss—much less ease their suffering. But how could the monk be so sure when no one had ever attempted it?

Not that Ian was making light. Raised on fire and brimstone, he was terrified at the prospect of entering Hell's Gate, life dangling by a slender, ethereal tether on his soul. But it was either attempt the unthinkable or abandon his parents to eternal torment—after they'd given both lives *and* souls for him.

He took a hand from the steering wheel, reaching between the front buttons of his shirt to touch the scapular Lucien had left him. Scapulars were sacred amulets of the Catholic Faith, two iconic cloth badges the size of large postage stamps, connected by shoulder bands and worn under the shirt on chest and back. Each badge held the image of a saint whose special powers protected the wearer.

Ian's scapular bore the plastic-laminated images of St. Christopher, patron saint of travelers, and St. Jude, saint of the impossible. According to Lucien, it had been brought back from Rome by Dom Girardeau years ago, blessed by the late Pope Benedict XVI. *Where you're going,* Lucien had told him, *you'll need all the protection you can get.* Ian had accepted it gratefully, promising to wear it until he and Lucien met again. Albeit, he knew the monk held no expectations for a reunion. Either in this life, or the next.

Angela watched Ian finger his good-luck charm. *Religious superstitions.* Nothing good in their relationship had ever come of religion, and she wondered how normal, how *happy* their lives together might be if only he'd been spared his Faith. Still, it seemed to give him strength now. He was surprisingly calm for a man about to face death for the third time.

Well, Angela had her own Faith, and that's where she turned now for *her* strength. To the Science of Psychology, which offered her a possible solution to this nightmare.

In cases of unresolved childhood trauma like Ian's, it wasn't unusual to see the damaged psyche heal itself. The mind was a resilient, resourceful organ, drawing on such things as flashbacks and hallucinations to mend old injuries. And judging from the accounts Ian had given of his NDEs, that's what was happening here.

His subconscious, it seemed, was seeking closure, trying to reunite him with his parents in the Afterlife. Now if only the reunion would take place today, perhaps Ian could finally put his demons to rest. That was Angela's hope, anyway, as their car rolled up to the warehouse.

They exited under the scowls of the watchmen at the windows next door, Angela whispering nervously to Ian, "Who are they?"

"Brazilians, I think, they speak Portuguese. No idea what they're up to, they've hassled us since day one. But if we keep to ourselves, they let us be."

Drugs! She shivered as they walked the gauntlet of glares, hurrying in, climbing the stairs.

The doctors greeted them cordially, matter-of-factly. As if Ian were here for nothing more than a flu shot.

Angela felt Ian's hand around hers and she looked up into the steel blue of his eyes, realizing this could be the last time she'd ever do so. Leaning in, she squeezed him long and hard until she'd regained control.

"Go, find your parents," she told him. *"And come back to me!"*

He promised. Then kissing her, giving her a smile she was unable to return, he slipped off behind a curtain.

She watched his shadow strip, and soon he emerged in only boxer shorts and scapular. Luc Dow Hodaka began fitting him with electrodes,

Angela looking on anxiously. This would be her first time enduring one of his NDEs from the start. His longest. Ten interminable minutes . . .

The doctors stretched him out on the table and Angela winced as they pierced his arms with IVs for what appeared to be a transfusion.

"Red cell packing," Josten told her. "Familiar with it?"

She shook her head.

"Similar to the blood-doping techniques some athletes use to increase endurance. Over the past weeks we've drawn several liters of Ian's blood and separated out the red cells. Now we transfuse them to boost his blood-oxygen capacity. Protects his organs during suspension."

Angela winced again as Yvette Garonne made an incision in Ian's upper leg, opposite side this time, inserting a large tube in a vein. Machines began switching on, beeping, buzzing, whirring.

"Do you use anesthesia?" she asked.

"No," Garonne said, clipping a tube to Ian's nose. "Not even sedative. He wants to be lucid for ze experience. We give oxygen first, then hydrogen sulfide."

"Poisonous gas!"

"A preservative," Josten said. "Ensures cell viability during stasis." He gestured to other IVs now dispensing liquids into Ian's arms. "He gets a cocktail of medicines, helps his organs weather the stress."

Meanwhile, Hodaka wrapped Ian in blue plastic pads connected to a nearby machine via hoses. When finished, he flipped a switch and blue fluid began circulating.

Josten said, "We gradually lower his temperature—internally with a heart/lung machine, externally with cooling pads—down to seven degrees centigrade." He injected a substance into an IV through a syringe. "Muscle relaxant. Keeps him from shivering."

"You follow progress here," Hodaka told Angela, pointing to monitors near the table. "Heart, temp, breath."

Josten gestured to a flat screen display, adding, "Also, this EBAIR . . ." Angela saw several tracks of colored lines zigzagging across a grid. "EEG Bispectral Algorithm Index Recorder. Gauges brain activity and levels of consciousness. As his vitals slow, the lines drop. Once his heartbeat arrests, we switch off the heart-lung, wait for the EBAIR to register zero, then start the clock—a ten-minute procedure today."

Procedure. He made Ian's death sound so clinical. Yet Angela had to admit she was impressed. Josten seemed a veteran of this bizarre fringe science. Conscientious, mindful of details. Hodaka, too, who performed his duties smoothly and affably, giving Ian a smile or kindly pat, apologizing for the discomfort he put him through.

Less so Garonne. Her approach was more perfunctory, as if her interests lay elsewhere and this were a chore. But Angela couldn't fault her apparent expertise.

The temperature readings edged down. Thirty-three Celsius, thirty-two, thirty-one . . . Ian's heart and respiration readings slowed with it, Angela's heart aching as he slipped into unconsciousness. When the temperature sank to seven, Josten added another fluid to an IV.

"Hypothermic potassium solution . . . Last step."

In moments Ian's respiration halted, then his heart, and one-by-one the monitors flatlined.

"Cardiac arrest," Josten announced, idling the heart-lung machine.

Trembling, Angela felt her heart seize, too.

The darting spikes of the EBAIR soon diminished, grew irregular, and then smoothed completely as Ian's brain functions ceased.

"Time," Josten said, starting a digital clock.

Angela held her breath, eyes moist as Ian entered the realm of the dead once again.

NINETEEN

AN OLD WAREHOUSE, EASTCOAST, ST. MAARTEN ISLAND, SAME MORNING

Feeling his soul slip free of his body once more, Ian rose above the table, looking down to see his team busy with their instruments. Angela sat off by herself in a chair, legs drawn up, arms wrapping her knees, his ring still missing from her finger.

"Have Faith," he told her, though he knew she couldn't hear. He would find his parents this trip. How, he didn't yet know . . .

He passed through the ceiling into sky, urging his soul on, finding he could control his velocity by simple force of will. Quickly he shot into the tunnel of light, banking left, descending through bands of yellow-brown cloud, exiting to arrive once again at the threshold of Limbo.

Immense, murky, fog-covered flatland, broken only by drifting drapes of smog. Eternal twilight, cast orange in the flush of smoldering horizon.

Through the haze appeared the wispy spirit of Zachary Niemand, looking surprised. "I felt you coming," he cried, "but I couldn't believe it. *Three times."*

As before, he spoke with that wet-whistle impediment, slurring his S's as though his tongue had a hole in it.

"I'm back to see my parents," Ian replied, fog scattering beneath him as he settled onto black firmament. It felt warm and damp to his bare feet, like compacted mud. "I need you to take me."

Niemand's face turned even paler. "I can't! Neither of us can go; the Dark Angels would get us. They hate souls—'specially undamned souls like us."

"How do you know I'm not damned?"

"Your robe."

Ian held up an off-white sleeve, lighter in shade than Niemand's. Niemand explained, "Robes are the rap sheet of the soul. Darker the color, worse the sins. Souls bound for below come here first. If they don't return to life, they harden, and the weight of their sins drags 'em down to the level of punishment fitting their crimes. Robes of the damned are charcoal, black even. But by the looks of yours, all you'll need is a quick pass through the Mill to cleanse you."

"Dark Angels—devils?"

"Just like they taught at St. L. Rebel angels, cast out of Heaven eons ago, condemned to run Hell. Bitter, vicious brutes. They hate souls. 'Specially newly molted ones, like you. New souls take time to harden—though you're never really solid . . ."

He demonstrated, poking a hand through himself. Ian did likewise to his own soul.

"What's frustrating is, you can't feel yourself or other souls. Everything *else* you feel—'specially the wrath of the Dark Angels if they get you! But don't worry, you're safe long as you stay here. No Angels, White or Dark, have powers in Limbo."

No intentions of staying, Ian asked, "What can you tell me about my mom and dad?"

"Only time I saw 'em was that night at St. L, and they never spoke. But I could see in their eyes they were suffering the torment of the Pit. Even when sent out on a task, the spirit moves but the soul never leaves."

Ian didn't understand the distinction between spirit and soul, but he had more urgent questions.

"Has anyone ever escaped Hell?"

"Purgatory, never Hell. And certainly not the Pit—that's the deepest Realm. There are stories of newly molted souls stealing a look at Purgatory—prophets and zealots from olden times. But forget finding your parents, it's a labyrinth down there. You'd get lost if not caught, no way back."

Unless you have a lifeline. "How many Realms?"

"Seven—not counting Limbo and Purgatory."

"Like Dante says."

Niemand snorted. "Dante's a joke here! He was a transient like you; he never saw past Purgatory. His *Inferno* is half-assed. Little more than rumors he picked up in Limbo."

"But how do you know if you've never been to Hell?"

"Dark Angels. I do favors for 'em sometimes, I overhear things." His voice turned defensive. "Most Limboans won't associate with demons, afraid it'll bar 'em from Heaven come Judgment Day. See, we got snobs here just like at St. L. But I find demons interesting. Anything to pass the time. The Infernal time . . ."

Reminded of time, Ian pressed, "What more can you tell me of Hell?"

Niemand turned to the glowing orange horizon. "The Dark Angels say it's all part of the same universe as Heaven and Earth. Like a vast egg. Earth the yolk, Heaven above, Hell below. They say Heaven and Hell have actual boundaries, impenetrable walls called *Golgotha*."

"What of Hell's Seven Realms?" Ian wondered if he'd have to travel through them all.

"They fall along a continuous path of descent, I'm told, each more terrible than the last.

"First comes *Hades of the Sereb,* just past Hell's Gate. It's where the slothful go. As they're lazy, they haven't far to travel. Next is *Hades of the Inner Chamber,* where the lustful get their passions driven out of 'em . . ."

Ian watched a smirk cross Niemand's pale lips, wondering how God could spare a ruthless monster the horrors of Hell but not his parents.

"Beneath that is *Hades of the Sub Chamber,* for gluttons. Then *Hades of the Messen* for the jealous, *Hades of the Meten* for the selfish and greedy, and *Hades of the Metal Oblong Gate* for those damned by foul tempers.

"And finally, for the prideful, the seventh and vilest Hades of all—where your parents lie—the *Pit.* Where those who put themselves above God are humbled."

Distraught, Ian wanted to begin the descent immediately. But he had a last, crucial question. "What about time? Does it pass here at the same rate as on Earth?" It didn't seem so, based on Ian's previous experiences.

Niemand shrugged his ghostly shoulders. "No way to know. No days, nights, clocks."

Ian thought for a moment. "How long would you estimate it's been since I was last here—in Earthly time?"

The spirit ruminated. "A month, I guess. At least."

"Three days," Ian told him, heartened. "Your best guess—how long would it take me to reach the Pit?"

"I told you, the Dark Ones will get you before you make it past Purgatory! And beyond that, you'd never find your way; your soul will harden first. The Abyss is too vast!"

"How long?"

"Impossible to say!"

"Hours? A day?"

"A day maybe—if you knew the way. But on your own, you'd be lost. *For eternity.*"

Grateful for the help, heedless of the warning, Ian thanked Niemand and turned toward the smoldering orange glow. Instead of advancing, however, he found himself yanked back toward the mouth of the tunnel.

He cried out to Niemand and the spirit reached for him, but their hands passed through each other.

TWENTY

DOWNTOWN PRAGUE, CZECH REPUBLIC, SAME DAY, EVENING

A dark limousine with opaque windows slipped out of traffic and halted at the curb of a busy intersection, sidewalks choked with people on their way to restaurants, clubs, and theaters.

The rear door swung wide, streetlamps revealing a man in a dark suit and tie, sixties, silver hair, deep-set eyes, prominent nose and high cheekbones. As he held the door, a ring on his index finger flashed in the light, gold with a Coptic cross of black onyx.

Observing from the sidewalk, Josef Varga took a last puff of cigarette and tossed it, hustling to the car, slipping inside, and it sped off.

He found himself in a spacious passenger compartment, separated from the driver by soundproof Plexiglas. Opposite was his superior, Cyril, of the High Council. Cyril extended his hand and Josef bent to kiss its ring.

"Fidelis Tantum Deo," Cyril intoned.

"Potius Mori Quam Foedari," Josef answered.

Switching to Czech, Cyril said, "You look tired."

Josef stared at his reflection in the Plexiglas, seeing a sober-eyed man a few weeks shy of his thirtieth birthday. He had his *táta*'s blocky jaw and thick nose, his *matka*'s shock of brushy hair.

Once he'd seen himself playing *futbol* for the UEFA, married to a nice Catholic girl he would have met at *Univerzita Karlova,* children, all the comforts of family. But that was back when he was a callow teen, before *Matka* sent him to the Cameldolite monastery in Bielany. There his eyes had been opened to the Lord's Work, and in the years since, he'd dedicated himself to defending the Faith wherever his sacred vows took him.

Cyril removed a large envelope from an attaché. "I don't like disrupting your task in Moldova, but we have a more pressing issue. A new name has been added to the Book."

Expecting as much, Josef held out his hand.

Cyril held on to the envelope. "A more troubling situation than usual. An old problem has resurfaced. It appears someone has developed the means to cross over to the spiritual side and return again. Repeatedly . . ."

Josef was dumbfounded. He'd heard of such practices occurring centuries ago, but nothing in recent times. An offense he'd certainly never confronted.

"Worse, the perpetrator works for an American TV network, for a program that investigates the supernatural. Only a matter of time before he broadcasts his activities, and I don't have to tell you what that could mean."

Josef's heart quickened. "Who?"

"An old acquaintance of yours. The priest whose life you saved during that African business. A *fallen* priest now. Ian Baringer."

The words struck like bullets. *"No!"*

"I'm afraid so . . ."

Josef felt the envelope slip into his hand, and Cyril hit a button on the console, telling the driver to take them back.

Not Ian. They'd been like brothers. Ian's Faith may have been troubled, yes, the man's doubts had surfaced at times during their days in Rome. But Josef also knew him to be a person of great compassion. However grievous his trespass, surely it was out of ignorance.

"If I could just speak to him, sir. Ian is an honorable man, I can make him listen."

Cyril shook his head. "He was given the chance, and failed. He's been to the Other Side three times now, Josef. He Knows too much. His name is in the Book."

Josef's heart sank. He'd never before had to purge anyone he knew personally, much less someone he loved and respected. And though sworn to defend his Faith against all threats, God help him, he had no stomach for this.

As the car pulled to the curb, he asked, "Please, let me give this to another."

"Inexpedient. Baringer knows you, he won't suspect."

Josef lowered his head, feeling Cyril's eyes. Then at length he heard a reluctant grunt.

"All right, send another if you must. *But I hold you responsible."*

TWENTY-ONE

EASTCOAST, ST. MAARTEN ISLAND, THREE DAYS LATER, MORNING

Ian sat in his car in front of the warehouse, engine off, fingers drumming the wheel. He'd arrived early, awaiting his team in anticipation of what he trusted would be his fourth and final journey into the Beyond. But at the moment his thoughts weren't on the ordeal ahead.

Angela had left him this morning. After he'd survived his third NDE three days ago, still failing to find his parents, he'd scheduled a last attempt. It was more than she could bear. They'd had an awful scene earlier and she'd rushed off in a cab for the airport.

He'd tried to reason with her. "If this were all in my head," he'd argued, "what I experienced on the Other Side would have to come from things I already know. How do you account for the other stuff?"

She'd countered, "Your 'Seven Realms of Hell'? Simply the Seven Deadly Sins, with a little Dante tossed in."

"What about the *names* of the Hells? Sereb, Inner Chamber, Sub Chamber, Meten, Mesen, Metal Oblong Gate . . . That's not Dante!"

"Who knows where your subconscious picked it up—*Faustus,* the Syfy channel—"

"I've no choice, I'm going back. And I'll need the maximum time Emil can give me."

She'd fixed fearful eyes on him until he came clean, telling her, "An hour." And then she'd gone livid.

"Are you nuts! He's done an hour before? On who?"

"Primates."

That's when she burst into tears and packed her bag.

Her parting words still haunted him. "If you *really* believe there's an Angel of Death," she'd sobbed, storming past him to her cab, "how many times can you cheat Him?"

He had no idea, but it didn't change what he had to do.

His thoughts were broken by the sound of tires crunching gravel, and he looked to see Josten, Hodaka, and Garonne pulling up. Only then did he realize that the hoodlums who'd been menacing them for so long were nowhere to be seen.

He took it for a good omen.

The team greeted him with smiles, if sober eyes. He could feel their tension. Earlier, Josten had balked at the length of today's procedure.

"An hour is too extreme, Ian. Assuming you survive, it will stress your organs *permanently*. One way or the other, this will be the last of it!"

Ian was girding for more resistance, but it didn't come. A few awkward pleasantries, then up the stairs to the lab, silent as a funeral procession. Until they opened the door.

"Holy shit!" Hodaka cried.

The place was in ruins. Tables overturned, equipment smashed. Ian ignored Josten's warning, rushing in to find the vandals gone. All that seemed to have escaped the rampage was a fridge, overlooked in a corner.

"Who would do this?" Ian moaned. "And why?"

He suspected the thugs next door.

The doctors entered tentatively, poking among the wreckage. Minutes later Hodaka yelled again, and Ian saw him crouched beside a toppled cabinet.

Rushing to his side, Ian was stunned to see a *body*. Faceup on the floor in a pool of blood. A man. No one he'd ever seen. Sixty, perhaps. Fair complexion, medium build, gray hair, dark clothing, eyes open and glazed. Obviously dead.

Ian moved closer as the others gathered, seeing an apparent bullet wound in the left temple.

"Anyone recognize him?"

No one did.

Garonne took her cell to the stairwell, calling the police, while a white-faced Josten searched the man's pockets for identification, coming up empty.

"A gunshot, all right," he said, pointing out powder burns in the man's hair. "Close range."

The right arm was stretched out, palm open, and Josten called everyone's attention to what it held. Two hollow, lozenge-sized glass cylinders. Taking one, he grunted and went to the wrecked defibrillator unit, bending down.

"It came from here," he declared, rising to show an identical-looking cylinder from a circuit panel. "Fuses!"

Ian and the others approached, and Josten displayed the two side-by-side between thumb and forefinger.

"But see the difference," he pointed out. "The fuse from the defibrillator is *defective*."

Indeed, its filament was burnt in two.

Josten reached back into the panel to withdraw another fuse with the same problem, turning to Ian.

"I suspect our visitor here switched them out, intending the unit to fail when we jumpstarted you today. Were the lab not destroyed, you'd have died of equipment malfunction, no one the wiser."

Ian shook his head, mystified. "He was trying to kill me? Then someone kills *him*? *And* wrecks our equipment? It makes no sense!"

Advising they not touch anything else, Ian herded everyone to the front of the room. Soon, several uniformed police arrived led by a man in a dark suit and tie.

"Inspector Jan van de Veld," he announced himself, a black man speaking Dutch-accented English. Early fifties. Average height, salt-and-pepper hair, eyes brown and stolid as a poker player's.

Ian made introductions and gave an overview as the inspector took notes. When Ian finished, the man asked, "Any idea who is behind this?"

Hodaka pointed to the wall separating them from the adjoining warehouse. "Hoods next door. They got guns."

Van de Veld had two men go check. Then ordering Ian and the doctors not to leave, he went to examine the body.

A short time later the two officers returned, spoke with van de Veld, and the inspector approached Ian again.

"You're in charge?"

"Yes."

"And you've no explanation for this? No idea who the victim was?"

"None. As I said, it was like this when we got here. And we never saw this man before."

The others nodded.

Ian felt the inspector's eyes, and the man snapped, "For your information, the space next door is empty. Assuming there *were* tenants, why would they attempt to run you off if they themselves were leaving?"

Ian had no answer, and Josten stepped forward.

"I have something you may find helpful." He offered up the fuses and his sabotage theory.

Van de Veld listened, frowning, accepting the fuses into a handkerchief. When Josten finished he barked, "You know no better than to disturb a crime scene? What else did you tamper with?"

Josten went red, shook his head, and stepped back, and the inspector turned to Ian.

"What is it you do here?"

"Research."

"What kind of research?"

"Experiments . . . Suspended animation."

Van de Veld looked around.

"I see no cages. No mice. No rabbits. What do you conduct your experiments on?"

Ian blinked.

"Me."

TWENTY-TWO

GENEVA BAY, ST. MAARTEN ISLAND, SAME DAY, AFTERNOON

Ian stood in the doorway of his villa, watching a police car roll up and discharge a numb-looking Angela and her suitcase. Inhaling, he hastened to meet her, taking her bag, escorting her inside. She said nothing, but once the door closed, she turned to him, eyes horrified.

"A man killed in your lab! An attempt on your life! I told you those quacks were criminals!"

"No, sweetheart, they're as shaken as we are. It's all some terrible mistake."

He watched her wilt, and she cried, "I was boarding when they pulled me out of line. *I thought you were dead.* They took me down to their station and grilled me like some—some—*terrorist.* Now I can't leave the island!"

"Someone brought your name up when they questioned us."

"Yvette Garrone!"

"I'm sorry. Soon as this is cleared up, I'll get you on the first plane home, I promise."

"Both of us."

He shook his head. "I've got unfinished business."

"Ian, you're *out* of business! Your lab's a shambles! The only way those 'doctors' are going to stick around is if they're in jail."

When he failed to respond she let out a wail, snatched her bag, and brushed past to the bedroom, calling back, "This time *you're* sleeping on the couch!"

She emerged minutes later in sports top and shorts and went out the door, leaving him speechless.

⁂

Marching down to the beach, Angela kicked off her sandals and broke into a jog. She weaved through a patchwork of blankets and sunbathers, hoping the fresh air would clear her head. Nearby, cabana boys ferried food and drink to guests reclining under umbrellas, and she muttered, *"There but for the grace of Ian's God!"*

His damned obsession had now run him afoul of thugs and murderers, and Angela was at a loss how to help him, how to get their life back . . .

The day was cloudless, pleasant breeze, sun and sand warm on her skin, though it failed to soothe. She soon escaped the congestion, heading for the solitude of some sand dunes.

And then lumbering up a crest, she happened upon a lone female sunbather. Topless on a blanket, paging through a fashion magazine.

Yvette Garonne.

Of all the luck!

It took restraint not to run her over. But Angela refused to be put off stride, and lowering her head she plowed past, stealing a sideways glance, receiving the same.

She had to admit Garonne *was* beautiful. *Although,* she thought, *her breasts sag—and so does her ass!*

It wasn't like her to be petty, but something about this woman. And still feeling her eyes, Angela thrust out her chest and added a triumphant jaunt to her step . . .

The miles melted away, anger too, and by time Angela returned, Garonne was gone. She retrieved her sandals and headed for the villa, hungry. But as she neared, she heard a familiar voice through a window.

Garonne again!

The tramp had doubled back to make a play for Ian!

What composure she'd recouped was gone in a huff, and primed for battle, Angela blew through the door—only to come to a sweaty, sputtering halt.

Sitting with Ian was not just Garonne, but Josten, Hodaka, and the man who'd interrogated her at the police station this morning, Inspector van de Veld. On the coffee table, drinks and a platter of sandwiches.

The room went quiet, everyone turning as Angela felt the fire in her eyes spread into blush.

"Good timing," Ian told her. "There's been a break in the case."

As the inspector waited with arms folded, she took a seat on the couch next to Ian, forcing Garonne to make room, working to compose herself.

Once she'd settled, van de Veld cleared his throat.

"The parties responsible for the murder and damage to your lab have been caught," he announced. "It was indeed the men in the warehouse next door. A counterfeiting ring from Brazil."

The room let out a sigh, and Ian congratulated him. But the inspector held up a hand.

"The credit goes to your government. Your Secret Service was monitoring the ring, and it seems the ring was monitoring you. For reasons still unclear to me, these men felt you would discover their activities—some voodoo notion about astral travel. They moved out and destroyed your lab as a parting shot. Your Coast Guard intercepted their boat."

Ian frowned. "So the dead man was a counterfeiter? They killed one of their own?"

"That was my presumption, too. But according to the Secret Service, no. He was someone the ring found hiding inside your lab and silenced as a witness."

"Then who was he?" Josten asked.

"And why he sabotage us?" Hodaka added.

Van de Veld replied, "We've yet to identify him, but it's unlikely he was from this area. Pale skin, no tan lines. Neither your government nor Interpol has records of his face or prints. All we have to go on are the fuses he tampered with. And this . . ."

He removed a five-by-seven color photo from his coat, placing it on the coffee table for all to see. A close-up of a man's chest, shaved to reveal a four-inch, multicolored tattoo over the heart.

A crest of some kind, Angela saw, featuring a sword, point down, tip piercing the head of a coiled snake. Stretched over the crossguard and blade was the figure of Christ, as if crucified on the weapon. And arcing above and below the image, two Latin phrases. Ian translated, "*Fidelis Tantum Deo,* Loyal Only to God; *Potius Mori Quam Foedari,* Death Before Dishonor."

"Your Latin is better than mine," van de Veld said. "You've seen this before, then?"

Ian shook his head.

"Anybody?"

Angela certainly hadn't.

Getting only blank stares, the inspector said, "Obviously a coat of arms, but we've no record of it, nor does Interpol."

"Perhaps ze mark of a rival gang," Garonne suggested.

"Perhaps . . ." He turned to Ian. "The attempt on your life was sophisticated. Professional. Any enemies?"

"Years ago, maybe. But I've no idea why anyone would try to kill me now."

Van de Veld sniffed. "Yes, why bother when you're so intent on it yourself? Who else knows of your activities?"

Ian looked to his team. "Have you discussed our experiments with anyone?"

They shook their heads.

"There's Lucien," Angela offered. "And the dom."

The inspector raised an eyebrow.

"Father Lucien Gant," Ian said dismissively. "A monk at a monastery I visited in the states. Jonas Girardeau is abbot. They're priests, for Christ's sake. In their eighties."

"The tattoo appears religious," van de Veld pointed out.

"And they oppose your experiments," Angela added.

Ian scoffed. "You met Lucien. You honestly think he's behind this?"

She had to agree. But then she recalled, "The dom told Lucien there were 'forces' that would try to stop you."

"A scare tactic," Ian said, waving her off. He turned to the inspector. "Neither man is suspect, I'd stake my life on it."

"You *are* staking your life on it," the inspector snapped. Taking information on both priests he prepared to go, adding, "Forensics is finished with your lab. You're free to return to it or leave the island, as you wish. But if you want my advice, you will leave. I have your number, I'll call with developments. And for tonight at least, I'll post men at your villas."

He retrieved his photo of the tattoo, and Ian asked, "Can I get a copy?"

Van de Veld handed it off. "I have others." Then bidding them goodbye, he left.

No sooner had the door closed than Ian turned to the doctors. "How bad is the lab?"

Angela was incredulous.

Josten gasped, "You can't be serious!"

"One last trip, that's all I ask."

He was met by sober silence, to Angela's relief. But then he played that ace he always had up his sleeve.

"Double. *Triple.* I'll pay you triple. And we'll move to another country, under cover. Set up a secure compound with a troop of guards . . ."

Another round of silence. But this time the team exchanged glances, and Angela's heart sank.

Garonne offered, "I know a meelitary hospital in Capetown weeth a unused wing. *Very* secure."

They began to discuss the feasibility, and against Angela's protests, finally accepted the deal. With proviso that their plans be implemented in strict confidence.

"How long till we're up and running?" Ian asked.

"We'll need all-new equipment," Josten said. "We can salvage our records hopefully, your blood cell packs from the fridge, but that's the extent . . . Three weeks, earliest."

"If money's no object?"

Josten scrunched his face. "Two weeks, *maybe.* Impossible to say yet."

The team left to recover what they could from the lab, and Angela went to the couch. Ian joined her, and she plucked the photo from his hand.

"Who was this man? What's this symbol mean?"

"I don't know, but I know who might. Antonio. The Vatican has a huge archive of heraldry."

Antonio Ponti. Vatican security director.

Ian glanced at his watch. "Too late to call. Let's get some sleep and try tomorrow."

But Angela had little hope of sleep.

TWENTY-THREE

AN OCEANSIDE VILLA, GENEVA BAY, ST. MAARTEN ISLAND, NEXT MORNING

Ian cleared the breakfast dishes, yawning. He'd not fared well on the couch last night, appreciating what Angela had been putting up with. But she didn't appear to have slept any better. Grumpy, quiet, elbows on the table, chin in hand, drooped over her third coffee. Between sips she studied the photo of the strange tattoo.

"Can we try Antonio now?"

It was lunchtime in Rome, but Ian chanced it, holding his phone where he could see its video screen. After a few rings there appeared the image of a serene-looking man, broad-faced, fiftyish, dark hair and dark, expressive eyes, napkin tucked under chin.

"Sorry, Antonio, I caught you at a bad time—"

"No-no, Ian," came his deep, commanding voice, Italian-accented. *"I've always time for you, my friend. How's my favorite revolutionary?"*

"Revolting as ever. You?"

"Good. It's been a long time . . ." His eyes narrowed. *"But this isn't a social call, is it?"*

"I'm down in St. Maarten with a friend. I'm afraid I got us into a bit of a scrape."

"A scrape, eh? That's my Ian. How may I help?"

"I've got an odd request. I'm trying to identify someone. All I have to go on is a tattoo—a religious crest of some sort. I thought, with your resources . . ."

"Show me."

Angela handed over the photo and Ian held it to the phone, hearing Antonio swear in Italian.

"The tattoo is over his heart?"

"Yes, but how—"

"Ian, listen to me very carefully." His voice was calm but deathly serious. *"You and your friend must get off the island immediately. Drop everything, hire a plane, and fly straight to me!"*

"What's going on?"

"Don't ask, go. Tell no one. Hurry, you're in grave danger. I'll explain when you get here."

TWENTY-FOUR

A BASEMENT FLAT IN AN OLD TENEMENT, PRAGUE 8, CZECH REPUBLIC, SAME DAY, EVENING

Alone in his apartment, Josef Varga hunched over a table, tinkering on a small plastic and metal device. He shielded his fingerprints with latex gloves, his only light a gooseneck lamp at his elbow. His creation was nearly finished, and he saw by the clock of a computer monitor that he was well ahead of deadline.

He took a break to light a cigarette. *"Hernajz,"* he muttered, smoke escaping with the oath. But his dark mood had nothing to do with this project—routine and mindless work. It was the news he'd received earlier . . .

The lamp cast his silhouette against the wall, unruly hair, sharp jaw and cheekbone, light shining through beakers and vials and swirling smoke to create a bizarre image. Like some mad alchemist. A disturbing thought for a man who regarded alchemy as the Devil's work.

His gaze shifted to his flat. A hovel compared to his old quarters in Rome. After his transfer and promotion to Sword three years ago, he'd been forced to disappear. And where better to hide than in plain sight, living in a *panelák*?

Paneláks—featureless, soulless concrete high-rises—thrown up by the hundreds during the Soviet Great Push, an enduring insult to Prague's magnificent architecture. Yet over time the citizens had grown inured, much the way the eye overlooks mars and cracks in an ancient piece of art. Perfect for Josef's purposes.

The flat he occupied was tucked into a windowless basement corner, with a sunken entrance from a back alley. To further discourage intrusions, he'd co-opted the Communist reputation for construction, replacing the address on his door with a DANGER/ELECTRIC sign. And now, apart from the occasional drunk who stumbled down his stairs, he performed his work undisturbed.

His attention returned to the device in his hand. A facsimile of a hypodermic syringe, but with two needles, each five centimeters long, set three centimeters apart. Heavy gauge, like those used by large-animal veterinarians. The shafts were curved in the manner of small claws, fed from a reservoir tube with fill markings, operated by a single plunger.

He raised the device to the light of the lamp. *Not quite.* Holding one needle over a Bunsen burner until it glowed red, he adjusted its angle with surgical tweezers. Then he removed and set aside the plunger, and turned to his computer. He skimmed an article from the English SSAR *Journal of Herpetology*, slowing to read with a Czech accent, " '*Naja haje*. Average yield per bite of lyophilized venom: sixty milliliters.' "

Among the vials on Josef's table was a small pharmaceutical bottle of clear fluid. He picked it up and broke its seal, carefully pouring sixty milliliters into the syringe reservoir, adding twenty more for good measure.

"An especially *large* asp . . ."

Reinserting the plunger, he inverted the syringe and forced air through the needles, catching overflow drops on a cotton swab. He was about to cork the tips and box the device when he was startled by a knock at his door.

An overhead monitor displayed a large man in the pale glow of a streetlamp, face obscured by a snap-brim hat, tipped low.

Josef swore, recognizing an associate. Hastening over, he unfastened the deadbolt, opening to the length of a chain, revealing a tall, brawny form in a dark jacket. The alley appeared otherwise deserted, thank God.

He undid the chain, hurrying his visitor inside. The man moved like a ghost, removing his hat to bare a thatch of long blond hair, face expressionless, square and pug-nosed, eyes light-colored.

Josef snapped, "What the hell are you doing, Quintus! Hand-off is at ten, Heydrich's Corner!"

This was not just bad form, it was bad luck. Heydrich's Corner held special meaning for Josef, the intersection where Nazi *Oberführer* Reinhard Heydrich—Hitler's heir apparent, the infamous "Butcher of Prague"—was assassinated in 1942. Josef was named after one of the resistance fighters responsible. He often chose the Corner for his deliveries, seeking its special blessings.[3]

Beyond that, Quintus had broken a rule. *Ordo* protocol required transfers to be made in passing, with minimal contact—certainly not at a Brother's lair. Josef respected the rules, which was why he'd leapfrogged in rank over the more senior Quintus, who sometimes bent them.

"New timetable," Quintus said, accent German. "I leave for Damascus in vun hour."

"Then you should have phoned."

The man shrugged his big shoulders. "You vere on my vay to airport."

Josef wasn't buying it, they could have easily met at the Corner. Quintus had dropped in to gloat. These past few years the two men had often been paired on assignments, to Josef's dismay. The feeling was obviously mutual, though neither ever crossed the line to state it. Their styles clashed. And recently, with Josef's promotion to Whetstone, the tension had mounted.

Still, Josef had to admit there was no Sword more capable. In Quintus's eight years he'd never failed a mission. An *extraordinary* feat. Usually succeeding first attempt, sometimes at great peril to his life. If his methods were questionable, his skill and courage weren't, and the Council cut him slack, tapping him for crucial missions—which increasingly involved Josef.

While Josef was able to overlook most of Quintus's foibles, one he could not. A trait that offended Josef to the heart of his Christian sensibilities. Quintus *enjoyed* his work. Josef could see it in his eyes, if no one else could. Times when they were on assignment, disposing of someone whose name had been added to the Book, Quintus's pilot light would flare. What others took for pious fervor, Josef knew to be bloodlust—the true reason Quintus proved so accomplished. It violated a most sacred tenet of the Order: *There shall be no pleasure in the taking of human life.* Swords were instruments of God, carrying out a somber duty in response to the moral failing of the life sacrificed. And as Scripture taught, to derive pleasure from the suffering of others—however evil their sin—was itself a sin.

Josef just wanted to be done with the man. Going to the table he stuffed the syringe in a box, packed it with cotton, and sealed the lid with tape.

Quintus, however, would not be denied.

"Bad news, Reynolds," he needled. "First Brother lost since John Paul II. Brazilian cartel, I hear. Who could habe foreseen?"

"*I* should have foreseen," Josef admitted, thinking that might satisfy him. "I sent Reynolds, I should have checked the area for subversives."

"So de target escapes. To vhere?"

"Rome, if his plane keeps its flight plan."

"God moves him closer fur you."

Josef bristled. "Maybe for once God could twitch a Finger and solve the problem Himself!"

Quintus laughed. "*Ve* are His Fingers, Brother. *Und* a sure Finger does not twitch."

Thrusting the box into Quintus's hands, Josef ushered him to the door. "Use this only in the Middle East or North Africa. A rural location, ideally."

"Response time?"

"Seconds, if you catch a vein. Otherwise, five, six minutes for a man of ninety kilos."

"Painful?"

"Excruciating."

Josef opened the door, and in the light of the streetlamp he saw a smile cross the man's face.

TWENTY-FIVE

SOMEWHERE OVER THE MID-ATLANTIC, SAME DAY, EVENING

As the little six-seater jetted across the ocean, Ian worked on a laptop, using onboard satellite Wi-Fi to search for clues to the mysterious tattoo. Nothing, so far.

He paused to observe Angela curled next to him under a blanket, eyes closed but not sleeping, brow knit. Beautiful in the glow of the overhead, complexion flawless, tinged with a blush of Caribbean sun. They were alone in the cabin, all quiet save for the thrum of the engines.

It was the first small plane Ian had flown since a child, since that fateful night. Exceedingly more difficult for him than he'd let on to Angela. But he had no choice. Having worked with the redoubtable Antonio Ponti before, he knew that when the security director spoke, if you were wise you listened. So he'd chartered the fastest jet available and he and Angela had left that afternoon for Rome.

Though he didn't think Angela at risk, he'd done as told, insisting she come. She'd offered no resistance, too frightened. He'd ordered his medical team out, too, and after they'd salvaged what they could from the lab, they'd flown off in separate directions to round up more equipment and arrange for a new facility.

Angela shifted, and Ian retucked the blanket around her. He felt wretched involving her in this nightmare. She'd had little to say since leaving the island. How badly he'd damaged their relationship he didn't know, but he was determined to repair it, make it more than before, everything it should have been to begin with. Everything this wonderful woman deserved . . .

It was late by the time they touched down at Ciampino International, plane taxiing to a remote apron.

Angela shivered as they deplaned, air much cooler here than the islands. She accepted Ian's warm arm around her, if still chafing over his behavior in St. Maarten. Before she could work on that huge problem, however, there was now this even larger issue of assassins. And forget how all of this might affect Charles Dunn and CBS . . .

They were met on the tarmac by a sober-looking man in a dark suit and tie. Antonio Ponti, Angela knew, though they'd never met. Average height, powerful build, face broad, hair dark and graying at the temples, eyes brown and expressive as a spaniel's. He had an earnest, intelligent air.

"Thank God you made it," he greeted, voice deep and rich with an Italian accent. But he gave them no chance to reply, ushering them away, using his authority to expedite customs, then out to a chauffeured car. Only when they were inside, driving off, did he pause to give Ian a hug.

Ian responded with a rare smile. "Wonderful to see you, Antonio. You look great."

He laughed. "I look old. Carla and I are grandparents now, Nikki had a little boy last week."

Ian congratulated him, and Angela watched the man's eyes turn to her, heavy brows rising.

"And now tell me, who *is* this lovely lady?"

"This is my fian—my associate, Angela Weber. We work on a TV show she has in LA . . . Angela, Antonio . . ."

The director took her hand in both of his. Large, warm and strong. "A delight, *signora,*" he said. "My apologies for the hasty reception."

She smiled, seeing a calm and confidence in his eyes that she much appreciated right now.

"What type of TV show?" he asked.

"We investigate paranormal phenomena."

Ian broke in, "Please, Antonio—what's going on? Why the fire alarm?"

The director exhaled. "I will get to that. But first, tell me about St. Maarten. And spare no detail."

"It started *before* St. Maarten," Angela said, wanting Ian to include Lucien and the dom.

Ian obliged, beginning with Gethsemani, explaining how he'd gone there hoping to reconcile his lifelong heartache over the loss of his parents—a loss Antonio seemed aware of, Angela noted. But when Ian reached the part where he'd learned of Thomas Merton's vision and the Church's moves to suppress it, she saw the director frown.

"That's the first I've heard of this Ultimate Reality. Not that the Curia would bring it to my attention unless it was a security issue. God knows what Secrets they sit on!"

He listened again stoically until Ian reached his NDE experiments, then grimaced. "*Buon Dio!* Surely there's a less dangerous way to heal your soul!"

"You haven't heard the half of it," Angela warned.

Ian pressed on. He spoke next of how his experiments led him to the threshold of Hell, where he'd learned of his parents' fate in the Pit. And how he was resolved to cross that threshold to find them.

Antonio's face grew ashen, and he crossed himself. "You have my deepest sympathy for your poor parents, my friend. But this idea to breach the Gates of Hell, this is madness! *You go too far!*"

Angela was pleased to have the director on her side, if amazed he'd accepted Ian's story so readily. She had to remind herself, the Vatican was a spiritual kingdom where the Afterlife was viewed as fact. Not surprising that Antonio was a Believer.

Ian finished with an account of the counterfeiters. "They wrecked my lab and killed an intruder they found hiding there. Turns out the dead man had sabotaged my equipment. Had I gone under again it would have been for the last time. We've no idea who he was. No ID or jewelry. No distinguishing marks—other than that tattoo."

Antonio asked, "Aside from your medical team, who knew of your experiments?"

"Just the two monks from Gethsemani, but—"

"What order?"

"Cistercian Trappists."

The director's eyes puzzled. "A very ancient order . . ."

The men fell quiet, and Angela turned to the window, having seen little of the city so far. They'd just crossed a bridge over what she assumed was the Tiber, a castle gleaming across the waters. Ahead were towering citadel walls. Then rounding a corner, she was thrilled to see the great piazza of St. Peter suddenly beside them, its colossal Basilica aglow. It loomed far larger and more magnificent in reality than ever it had in her imagination.[4] Behind was Vatican City sparkling in soft lights against the night.

Ian had described the tiny, 109-acre kingdom as both a physical and spiritual bastion, and Angela so hoped he was right. A quiet harbor for the weary traveler . . .

They zoomed past the Square and headed for a tunnel in the massive walls. A sign read *PORTA SANT ANNA*/ST. ANNE'S GATE. There they were met by Swiss guards in bright orange, yellow, and blue uniforms who lowered halberds. Antonio dropped his window and the guards saluted him with a snap to attention. Antonio mumbled commands, one man went to a phone, and the car sped on.

Exiting the tunnel, they rumbled across cobblestone courtyards onto a wide boulevard, *Via del Governatorato,* and again Angela had a breathtaking view of the basilica. Then passing through the city to the rear grounds, they approached a regal, five-story, yellow-brick building.

"The *Palazzo del Governatorato,*" Ian told her. "Seat of Vatican temporal authority."[5]

She felt like a child in a fairyland. But it was all familiar to Ian, who returned to the matter at hand.

"That's everything I know about the saboteur," he told Antonio. "This is all some terrible misunderstanding. I just want to fix it and get back to my work."

Their car pulled into a space marked *PERSONALI DI AUTORIZED,* and Antonio turned to Ian, lowering his eyes.

"I'm sorry," he replied softly, "but I'm afraid there's no going back . . ."

TWENTY-SIX

PALAZZO DEL GOVERNATORATO, VATICAN CITY, ROME, SAME NIGHT

The director's words had shaken Angela, and as the three exited his car she looked to Ian for an explanation, receiving only a confused wag of the head in return.

Abruptly two police vehicles roared up next to them and armed gendarmes jumped out. They spoke to Antonio in Italian, then bolted into the Palazzo.

Ian leaned into Angela, voice a nervous whisper, "He's posting guards at the entrances!"

She took his hand, heart racing as Antonio led them up a broad flight of steps, across a courtyard and through the tall front doors of the Palazzo. They passed into a foyer of white marble floors bedecked with statues of what Angela presumed were saints. A spectacular sight, had she the presence of mind to enjoy it. Up a grand staircase, crossing more marble floors to a door flanked by two gendarmes.

Antonio opened it with a key, and a guard went inside while they waited. Moments later he returned to announce, *"Tutto il sicuro."*

"Grazie," the director said, and the guard resumed his post as Antonio escorted his guests inside, closing the door.

The office appeared very old, stately, with a musky mahogany scent Angela found reassuring, somehow. High ceiling, crystal chandelier, tall windows closed off by red velvet drapes.

The walls were paneled halfway up in dark, intricately carved wood, and above, not quite encircling the room, were portraits of sober-looking men. Hundreds. First, crude drawings, then progressively more artistic, ending in sharply detailed likenesses, each named and numbered.

A chronology of popes through the ages, Angela recognized.

Antonio seated them in front of his desk, large and covered with documents meticulously arranged. Going to a cabinet, he removed a bottle of Courvoisier and poured snifters for all, toasting solemnly, *"Vita lunga."*

The director drained his glass in one gulp, sitting back, taking a long breath. Generally he sipped his brandy to savor its oaken flavor, but tonight he drank for warmth. To take the chill off the night and the news he'd just received from his unsuspecting young friends.

He observed them through heavy eyes. *Such a handsome couple. Such a tragedy.*

Never had he known anyone more decent than Ian Baringer. A priest, risking his life to take on ruthless slavers, unarmed. Antonio had led many a man in combat during his younger days, but few as heroic.

And this stunning young woman. So lovely. So innocent. *Angelo dolce e prezioso.*

He stared into his empty glass, unsure where to begin or how much to reveal. He didn't want to frighten them into paralysis, but he couldn't mislead them. The sad truth was, despite his best efforts to hide and protect them, their odds of survival were next to none . . .

Meeting their anxious eyes, he began, "I don't know if what you do is sinful or not, these experiments of yours with Death and Hell. I'm a soldier, not a theologian, I leave the moral calls to God. But there are some who see such things as grave violations of God's Will. And unfortunately, they take it upon themselves to intervene."

Ian nodded. "The man with the tattoo was a religious extremist. Do you know who he was?"

"Not who. *What* . . . I must ask your oath not to repeat what I tell you."

They gave their words.

"This tattoo, it's the symbol of a very old sect. A brotherhood of militants cast off from the Church centuries ago, known as *Ordo Arma Christi.*"

Ian translated, "The Order of the Weapon of Christ."

"Yes. Christ's Weapon. *Ordo Arma Christi* dates to medieval times. There's virtually no history of it outside the *Bibliotheca Secreta*"—he clarified for Angela—"the Vatican Secret Archives. And once you hear its checkered past, you'll see why the Church keeps silent."

He gazed at the portraits that lined his walls, eyes coming to rest on number 180. A profile of a dour-looking old man in an ornate, high-collared cape and domed "beehive" tiara. Eyes bugged; nose prominent and acutely pointed over a fleshy, upturned chin; mouth small, lips pinched as if holding in secrets.[6]

"It goes back to the reign of Pope Innocent IV, in 1245. At that time, Innocent was mired in a nasty power struggle with Holy Roman Emperor Frederick II of Germany. Innocent wanted to expand his papal states into Frederick's territory, claiming the right as the Emperor's spiritual authority. Frederick saw otherwise, so Innocent excommunicated him. In turn, Frederick tried to depose Innocent. It led to war, the pope's forces were defeated, and he was driven into exile.

"But Innocent was proud and cunning, and determined to avenge himself. And he had a powerful organization to help him, too. The Office of the Inquisition."

Antonio watched his guests' eyes widen.

"The Office had been in existence for years, with a network of spies across Europe keeping watch on heresy and other threats to the Faith. So Innocent took advantage. He appropriated its spies and wed them to a select corps of knights and crusaders—men handpicked for their allegiance to the Church, sworn to obey without question or hesitation. A 'spiritual CIA,' if you will. And to make it official, he issued a secret decree. A papal Bull, *In Tutamine Cathedrae.* In Defense of the Chair—the pope's throne. The Bull had three provisions:

"First, it created a new ecclesiastical Order, *Arma Christi,* designating it 'Holy Protector,' responsible for safeguarding the Church against all threats.

"Second, in the event Frederick succeeded in deposing Innocent, the Bull charged the Order with restoring the true papal succession, however long it took, by whatever means.

"And third, to protect *Arma Christi* from an antipope Frederick might install, the Bull proclaimed the Order secret and self-governing for all time, setting up strict rules under which it was to operate. If only we knew those rules, but the Bull has long been lost.

"In the end, Innocent survived Frederick, who was poisoned—*Arma Christi,* I suspect—and unfortunately the Order survived Innocent. It lives on to this day in the shadows, a power and authority all to itself. Lying low until it feels the Faith threatened, then rising up like an invisible loose cannon; a destroyed career here, a mysterious death there. Masters of the tragic accident . . ."

Antonio expected a response, but the two simply sat gaping at him, drinks untouched.

He continued, "The Order is said to be presided over by a council of twelve—who, no one knows. Its spies are called 'Eyes & Ears,' but it's unclear how widespread they are. E&Es gather intelligence for the Council, which makes pronouncements on those it considers threats to the Faith. Once a threat is declared, the Council dispatches operatives called 'Swords' to remove the threat. Swords are known to wear the Order's emblem tattooed over their hearts."

Ian exclaimed, "Spies! Assassins! I've never even heard the name *Ordo Arma Christi*! You mean in all this time the Church has done nothing to end it?"

"Oh, She's tried many times. In 1609 Paul V repealed Innocent's Bull and dissolved the Order. But because *Arma Christi* considers itself permanent and self-governing, it ignored him. Other popes tried to infiltrate the Order with their own spies and assassins, in vain. How do you penetrate what you cannot see?

"And on the rare occasions members were found out, they never talked—despite facing torture and death. They would kill themselves first. In their minds, death in service to the Order, including suicide, is martyrdom in God's Eyes, guaranteeing Salvation."

Face pale, Angela asked, "Have . . . have *you* ever had dealings with them?"

"I've no way to know. I suspect the Order attempts to infiltrate Church operations, and as security director I must prevent that. I've studied everything the Archives offer. But I confess, in all my years I've never identified a single E&E for certain."

"Assassins for Christ?" she cried. "But Christ was a pacifist! How can they justify that?"

Antonio spread his hands. "Same as the fanatic who blows up the abortion clinic. Or the bishop who protects the pedophile priest. There's no Faith like blind Faith, Angela. It anesthetizes the conscience. To *Arma Christi*, there's no sin for actions in defense of the Faith."

"What does any of that have to do with us? Why *Ian*?"

"To close the door he's opened on the Spiritual World. Remember, the Order considers itself Protector of the Faith—a Faith which can exist only if the Secrets of the Afterlife remain hidden. In the Order's view, if Man were to learn these Secrets, God's existence would be indisputable. Man would no longer be dependent on Scripture to Believe, he would *Know*. Such a thing would cancel God's Test of Faith, barring Man from Heaven forevermore."

"But how did the Order learn of Ian's NDEs?"

"I've no idea, but it's obviously worried his story will get out and others will follow. A repeat of what happened in the Middle Ages."

Ian blinked, shaking his head as if his ears had tricked him. *"Middle Ages?"*

"Oh yes, my friend. You see, what you're doing is nothing new. As long as fourteen hundred years ago people were trespassing the Afterlife."

Everything Antonio had said sounded incredible, but this last was inconceivable to Ian.

"I've never heard of such a thing!"

"In fact," the director said, "history is full of accounts. Mostly about Purgatory and Hell, not so much Heaven. Beginning in the sixth century . . . Stories like *The Dialogues of Gregory the Great* and *Furseus's Vision.*

"Some accounts are very explicit. *The Vision of Wetti,* for example, tells of a monk who died of fever October 30, 824 on the island of Reichenau, Germany. Wetti's soul goes to Hell and witnesses tortures of a very graphic and sexual nature. He returns to life only long enough to tell his tale. I could go on—*Drythelm's Vision, Charles the Fat's Vision, St. Brendan's Voyage*—"

"Folklore!" Angela said.

"Perhaps. But what happened after the year 1348 is not so easily dismissed. Prior to that time, most Christians were simply too occupied with surviving this life to worry much with the next. Then overnight all that changed."

Ian knew. "The Black Death."

"Yes. It struck Europe like a hammer. Up to half the population wiped out. Horrific. People thought it the Wrath of God, and faced with death, they were desperate to know what lay beyond—especially to know what Damnation held in store. Hell became all the rage. The stuff of sermons, literature, paintings. And as the Plague worsened, the obsession grew, driving some to cheat Death to learn its Secrets."

Ian couldn't imagine people attempting NDEs without benefit of his technologies, eager to hear more. But looking to Angela, he saw her wilting.

"Enough," Antonio said. "We'll continue tomorrow over breakfast."

As Ian helped Angela to her feet she trembled in his arms, and Antonio approached to place his hands on their shoulders.

"You'll be safe tonight," he promised, fingers firm, voice assuring. "I have quarters for you, you'll be under constant guard. Get some rest, we'll need all our wits to deal with this . . ."

He turned away, and Ian thought he heard, ". . . if not a miracle."

Under protection of two plainclothesmen, Ian and Angela were escorted to a private sector of the Vatican and provided separate apartments, given they were unmarried. Side-by-side. Angela was upset with the arrangement, but there was no choice.

Their guards entered first, ensuring the rooms were secure and windows locked, lighting space heaters to take off the chill. Then they assumed watch at the doors as Ian and Angela were made to kiss good night in the hallway like two teenagers.

TWENTY-SEVEN

PRIVATE GUEST APARTMENTS, PALAZZO DEL SAN CHARLES, VATICAN CITY, NEXT MORNING

Angela awoke early from a fitful sleep, daylight leaking through the drapes. For a moment she was heartened to think Antonio's account last night simply a nightmare. But then head clearing, reality elbowing in, she slid from bed and shuffled hurriedly to the door in her nightshirt.

Peeking out, she saw only one guard.

"Is Mr. Baringer up?" she asked, wincing in the light.

"Si, signora. He is meeting Direttore Ponti at the *Governatorato* for breakfast. He asks that you join him when convenient."

Not happy to be left behind, she quickly showered and dressed in a skirt and blouse, leaving with the gendarme for the short walk. The weather was overcast and cool, and he lent her his coat.

They entered by a side door, down a corridor to a small dining hall where she spied Ian at a table reading a newspaper. His gendarme stood guard near another door through which Antonio was just arriving. The director approached her with a smile, kissing both cheeks.

"You look lovely this morning," he told her.

He was being kind, she'd seen the circles under her eyes.

Her gendarme went to join his partner, and Ian greeted her with a kiss on the lips, assisting her into the chair next to his. He looked worse than she, she thought. As if he hadn't slept at all.

Once they'd settled, Antonio turned to Ian. "I wanted to ask before we begin, what do you hear from our old friend, Josef Varga?"

Ian sighed. "Nothing. Last we talked was shortly after Africa. Next I knew, he'd joined a monastery in Poland somewhere. I sent several letters, but never heard back."

The director nodded. "He was a noviate at that monastery before he came to us. All the same, his decision to go back was a surprise to me. Do you suppose it had to do with Africa?"

"I wonder. I know he was upset by what he saw there. Morning after the rescue, I found him in the mission chapel, alone. He'd been there all night . . . Josef had a complicated Faith."

"That he did. I pray the monastery brings him peace."

"Amen."

Angela knew Josef only as the courageous man who'd saved Ian's life, and that his friendship had meant a great deal to Ian. She also knew how hurt Ian was by Josef's abrupt departure for the monastic life, not even a word of farewell. It showed in his face now.

A server came with a pot of coffee. But when he went to pour, Antonio intervened, summoning a gendarme to switch out the pot with one from another table.

"Is that really necessary?" Angela asked, heart jumping.

"A precaution. Your meals are being specially prepared, as well."

She felt Ian's hand on her arm, and placed her hand atop his.

Once the gendarme had resumed his post out of earshot, Antonio asked, "Now, where were we last night?"

Ian was quick to respond. "The Middle Ages—people cheating Death."

The director stirred his coffee, staring into its blackness. For a moment Angela wasn't sure he'd heard, but as if coming out of a thought, he raised his eyes, speaking softly, "As I was saying, Ian, you are not first to trespass the Afterlife. Or to run afoul of *Arma Christi* for doing so. Going back to the time of the Plague, many people were risking their lives to learn Death's Secrets. Secrets of the Underworld, anyway, it seems Vatican Archives contain no accounts of Heavenly experiences. I assume because cheating Death is more a Hellish activity. In any event, according to available records there were three methods used, each condemned by the Church . . ."

Ian leaned forward.

". . . The most common method was by means of supernatural 'gateways.' Actual, physical entrances into the Underworld. A dozen such places existed across Europe and Scandinavia, most among temple ruins and odd geologic formations. People frequented them since ancient times. England's Glastonbury Tor is a famous one. Cone-shaped hill with a tower atop, said to have guarded a window to Hell—till Henry VIII razed it in 1539.

"But the most notorious by far was St. Patrick's Cave of Purgatory, in

Ireland. It was believed that souls of sinners were punished in its depths, and people traveled from all over to see—the most popular pilgrimage in the West before the Church closed it in 1497. Popular even though many who entered failed to return alive. Mortality was upwards of one in twelve.

"Dangerous as gateways were, there was a riskier route. A mysterious German brew known by various names, including 'Devil's Tears.' It caused a condition of temporary death, enabling the soul to pass over to the Underworld and back. At least for those who survived. An estimated twenty percent died in the attempt."

"The Age of Enlightenment," Angela noted dryly.

"Indeed. The Church condemned the use of Devil's Tears as witchcraft, and its ingredients have been lost. But Archive records claim that Dante's *Divine Comedy* was inspired by it. And are you familiar with the medieval painter, Hieronymus Bosch?"

Ian nodded, but Angela had only a vague awareness of the man's bizarre works.

"Bosch lived during the late 1400s," Antonio said, "in the Hapsburg region of Germany. Prolific painter, turned out hundreds of Afterlife scenes, in great demand. Especially his works of the Underworld, which were very graphic. The Archives say he used Devil's Tears to create them. True or not, the suspicion led to a terrible tragedy."

The director paused as covered plates of food were delivered by another gendarme—opened to reveal scrambled eggs, sausage and pastries. They looked delicious, but Angela's appetite had waned. The gendarme left, and Ian urged Antonio back to his story.

"Another 'Innocent' was pope at the time. Innocent VIII. He'd seen some of Bosch's paintings of Hell, and he found them shocking—all the nakedness and depravity. He was convinced it was the work of Devil's Tears, and in December 1484 he ordered the Inquisition into Germany to purge it of witchcraft. So began the tortures and burnings that ravaged Europe for hundreds of years, costing hundreds of thousands of lives."

The director fell quiet, and they made an attempt at their meals.

At length, Ian asked, "So, what became of Mr. Bosch?"

"Poisoned in 1516. *Arma Christi,* most likely. Afterward the Order began a relentless hunt for his paintings. It managed to destroy most of them over the centuries, but for some reason in the mid 1800s, it suddenly gave up. Why is a mystery, but about two-dozen Bosch works still survive—including several the Order tried hardest to get. Very unlike it."

Ian pressed, "And the third route to the Afterlife?"

"The Black Art of Necromancy. Summoning spirits via gramarye and alchemic formulas."

Angela nearly choked on her eggs. But the director looked entirely serious, adding, "The practice was flagrant sorcery, to be sure. It never came into widespread use. By the 1600s, with the help of *Arma Christi*, the Inquisition had all but rooted it out, burning the necromancers and their formulas on the same fires. The Plague had also run its course by then, so with the gateways closed, and Devil's Tears and Necromancy purged, the madness faded. It took more than three centuries, but the Order successfully defended the Faith."

Antonio went quiet again, and Angela studied him.

Finally she had to ask, "You don't *really* believe it was the Afterlife people were seeing?"

"It's immaterial what I think, the Order obviously believed it. It waged constant war to end the practice, hunting down, destroying all evidence of it. And judging from your experience in St. Maarten, the war is still on."

She reached across the table and placed her hand on his, searching his eyes.

"But Ian's lab is destroyed! Isn't that enough for them?"

"Knowing the Order, if its intent was only to stop Ian's NDEs, I don't believe it would have tried to harm him. You must understand, *Arma Christi* is a fanatical sect. Once it identifies a threat, it doesn't quit until that threat is eliminated. Or it's convinced there's no longer anything to be gained trying. The question we must answer now is, does the Order still consider Ian a threat?"

She felt Ian's fingers tighten on her arm.

"What about Angela?" he said. "She'd nothing to do with this—surely they wouldn't harm her!"

The director paused. "Given she wasn't a target before, I'm hopeful that's the case. The Order may be extreme, but it's governed by a strict code. Its guiding principle is seen in its crest—a sword cutting off the head of a snake. It doesn't kill indiscriminately, not even for vengeance. Still, if it considers Angela a threat to reveal your NDEs on her program, she's in danger. The prudent thing is to safeguard you both until we know."

"But *how* will we know?" Angela asked, despairing. "And *when*?"

Antonio couldn't bear the poor woman's eyes. If in fact her and Ian's names had been entered in the Order's fearsome *Liber de Damnatis*, another Sword was surely on his way.

"There's little chance the Order is unaware of your presence here," he admitted. "It may not be the powerful force it once was, but I don't underestimate its spies. If it still considers you a threat, I suspect it will act soon—within a week or so. My advice is to stay calm and remain here under my protection. Let's see if it makes a move."

He wished he had more time for them, but he was already late for an important meeting.

"My deepest apologies," he said, rising, meal unfinished. "I will be tied up today, but I place you in excellent hands. *Never* leave their company. I recommend you pass the day in one of the *musei riservati,* they're quite secure. We'll breakfast tomorrow, and should you need me for any reason, don't hesitate to call."

And he phoned his department, ordering up two additional guards.

TWENTY-EIGHT

VATICAN CITY, ROME, SAME DAY, LATER THAT MORNING

Numbed by Antonio's words, Angela and Ian took his advice, retiring to one of the Vatican's *musei riservati*—private museums off-limits to the general public. Four gendarmes watched over them now, Angela holding tight to Ian's hand. Though there were few other patrons, she felt uneasy in these musty halls. On display were papal documents from the Middle Ages, and she wondered what their authors may have known of the enigmatic *Ordo Arma Christi.*

Neither she nor Ian had broached the weighty subject on their minds, and at length she leaned in to whisper, "You have to call Emil and cancel the lab!"

His response was to point to one of the exhibits.

"Look . . . A papal Bull from Innocent IV."

Angela shivered, recognizing the name of the pope who'd created *Arma Christi.* Displayed under glass was a wrinkled brown document the size of a small poster. Lengthy text of faded, florid Latin script, embellished with fancy rubrics, red wax seal at the bottom. She grew excited.

"The secret Bull Antonio spoke of!"

"No, but no less abhorrent. *Ad Exstirpanda.* Until Eradication. The notorious Bull that gave the Inquisition its power to torture."

She shivered again. "Torture! Murder! I don't understand! You believe in a God who lets His Church do these things?"

Ian sighed and shook his head. "The Divine Paradox."

"The *what?*"

"Ancient theological riddle: 'How can a God Who is all-Good and all-Powerful allow Evil?' I've wrestled that question my whole life."

"I never heard you mention it."

"I learned my lesson. There *is* no satisfactory answer. And arguing it only upsets Believers. It got me in trouble with Father Ben at the orphanage, and it got me pulled on the carpet at the seminary. Even my old friend, Josef Varga—the only time he ever blew up at me."

Angela was surprised to hear him mention Josef, a sensitive subject he generally avoided. Perhaps on his mind now after Antonio raised the topic at breakfast . . .

Ian missed his old friend. Josef was the closest he'd ever come, probably ever would come, to a brother. Their years in Rome were good ones, particularly their time on the Vatican soccer squad. Josef had been a fierce competitor, far more gifted than Ian, taking him under his wing so selflessly. A man of strong moral convictions, unflagging courage, and loyalty. Ian looked up to him.

Yet in all their time together, Ian never really felt he understood him. A private man. Serious to the point of brooding at times. But highly intelligent. Educated at a monastery in the Czech Republic. And that was about all the history Ian had of him. Except that Josef must have come from fine Catholic stock, given what it took to pass Vatican security's rigorous screening.

In fact Josef was one of the most devout men Ian had ever known, and not even of the cloth. Ian had come to realize, however, that good friend though Josef was, confiding in him as such was a bad idea. At least where thorny issues of Faith were concerned.

Ian would never forget that afternoon of the Paradox. They'd just dropped a tough *futbol* match to archrival Naples—despite receiving a special blessing that morning from the pope himself. Battered, ailing, he and Josef had retired to a café off St. Peter's to bathe their aches in some chianti. And feeling his tongue loosed, Ian had quipped, "It doesn't seem God heard Papa's blessing today."

Josef was quick to reply, "God doesn't lend His Heart to trivial matters."

That had surprised Ian, knowing how seriously Josef took their games. Nearby, a TV was airing a news report. A bus had skidded off a rain-slicked road in the Apennines, thirty disabled elderly on a pilgrimage to St. Pellegrino abbey, killed. In that sad drama Ian saw a perfect example of the Paradox. God's insensitivity.

He drew Josef's attention to the story as survivors told of their harrowing plunge off the mountainside, victims begging God's mercy, to no avail. Heartrending. Ian had watched Josef's angular face grow dark, expecting a comment. But getting none, he'd pressed, "So what, then, does it take to touch God's Heart?"

Suddenly Josef rose, eyes blazing.

"It's not our place to question God!" he bellowed. "We must accept His Will—unconditionally! *How can you hope to serve God as a priest if you distrust Him?"*

And he stormed out.

Ian had never seen Josef so upset. The man was more orthodox even than Father Ben! Stung, feeling terribly deficient, Ian decided never to argue the Paradox again . . .

A hand on his arm snapped him back to the present.

"The lab," Angela urged. "You've got to call it off!"

Finally she got his attention.

"I spoke with Emil last night," Ian replied. "Don't worry, we're taking extra precautions to cover our tracks."

"Precautions?" Had he heard nothing Antonio said?

"I can't get into it now. Just trust me, I'll tell you when the time comes."

She persisted, but got nowhere, shut out again. It seemed he had no regard for her, only for himself and his absurd, dangerous obsession. Hurt, feeling marginalized, she grew angrier by the passing hour.

They were hardly speaking by the time they returned to the *Governatorato* for supper, guards delivering their meals again. Afterward they were escorted back to their rooms, weather continuing cool, rain in the air. Ian placed an arm around her, but she shrugged it off.

As before, the guards checked out the rooms, lighting the space heaters, giving the all-clear.

Two guards left as two stood watch, and once again Ian placed his arm around her, moving to kiss her goodnight. Again she ducked him, slipping inside, locking the door.

She headed straight to the desk and phoned an airline, booking an early flight to LA. Then finding stationery in a drawer, she scribbled a note she could scarcely read through her mist.

Ian—I can't take it anymore. If you don't care enough to spare me this pain, we have no future. Give up the madness now or it's over. A

Placing his ring atop it, she set the alarm, shucked her clothes, threw on her nightshirt, and buried her sorrow under her bedcovers.

TWENTY-NINE

PRIVATE GUEST APARTMENTS, PALAZZO DEL SAN CHARLES, VATICAN CITY, NEXT MORNING, PREDAWN

Angela awoke with a start, heart thumping.

Another nightmare. This time, Ian burned at the stake by the Inquisition as she looked on, helpless!

Her wits were slow to return, and she struggled to sit, strangely dizzy and disoriented. Her head throbbed, her nightshirt was soaked, throat parched.

Throwing back her covers she slid from bed for a glass of water—only to reel, legs buckling, and she crashed hard to the floor, pain shocking her mind clear.

Something was *very* wrong. Her lungs burned.

Terrified, wheezing, she crawled for the door, limbs sluggish, blinding ache behind her eyes. She feared she wouldn't make it, finally grasping the knob, too weak to turn it, close to passing out, terrified of the consequences. Summoning all her will she put her last strength to it, and tumbled out into the hall . . .

She lay on her back sucking in delicious air. Above, the faces of the guards swirled, mouths agape. In her sweat-soaked nightshirt, she realized, she was virtually naked.

The men scrambled to help, averting their eyes as they hoisted her to her feet.

"Ian," she huffed, "where?"

"His room, *signora,*" one man responded, the other wrapping her in his coat.

"Get him! *Hurry!*"

But they had no key. Leaving Angela braced against the wall, they pounded on Ian's door, wrenching at the knob. She called out for him. No answer.

"Break it down!" she cried.

They kicked together, bursting in, and she saw Ian through a haze lying in bed, eyes closed, in his pajamas. Before the guards could reach him, however, they staggered to their knees, coughing.

Angela screamed to Ian, no response, and inhaling deep, burying her nose under the coat, she charged in. But with her next breath she went woozy, too, dropping to the floor.

Frantic, she willed herself past the guards, grabbing Ian's hand, tugging.

Too heavy!

Then a guard managed to reach her side, latching on to Ian, and together they dragged him into the hall.

THIRTY

PRIVATE GUEST APARTMENTS, PALAZZO DEL SAN CHARLES, VATICAN, SAME DAY, DAWN

Angela and Ian sat in her room at the end of her bed, changed into street clothes, blankets over their shoulders, window and door open despite the chill outside.

They'd recovered quickly in the fresh air, suffering only headaches. A Vatican physician had pronounced them and the guards fit—space heaters the apparent source of the problem.

Antonio was on his way, and while Angela and Ian waited, she'd insisted Ian stay with her, protocol be damned. But she'd thought to remove her note and ring from the desk. Three new gendarmes were standing guard, and a fourth had been inspecting Ian's space heater. He appeared now at their door to report,

"*Scusi.* I find the trouble . . ."

Approaching, he opened a handkerchief to display what appeared to be bits of old, shredded rag. Angela hadn't a clue, but Ian took out a pen, poking through the debris.

"Mice," he said. "Nesting material. We used to find it in the barns at the orphanage. Look close, droppings."

Angela took his word for it, just thankful to hear their scare had been the work of mice, not men. But when the guard left, she asked Ian, "What are the odds this would happen now? And to *both* of us?"

"No greater than the odds of you waking in time to save us," he reasoned, placing an arm around her. This time she didn't pull away.

Antonio was greatly relieved to see his guests safe, entering their room with a prayer of thanks, giving Angela a kiss, Ian a hug, apologizing repeatedly.

"I fail to protect you inside my own gates! Under my very nose!"

Angela smiled graciously. "Protect us from mice?"

He hated to spoil their illusion. "Not mice, I fear."

Her smile melted, and Ian said, "But the nests . . ."

"Vintage *Ordo.* The heaters were operating perfectly the first night, were they not? Suddenly the vents clog? Both rooms? I examined the cloth—as easily shredded by tools as teeth. Infused with a poisonous chemical, I suspect. I've sent samples to the lab."

"The droppings . . ." Angela persisted.

"Judging by their uniform color and texture, the residue of commercial food pellets, collected from the bottom of a cage . . . I'm sorry, my friends, this was no accident."

Angela whispered, "Then we have our answer."

"Yes, the Order made its move. And we have another unfortunate answer as well. I've been infiltrated."

Ian gaped at him. "An *inside* job?"

"Your quarters were known only to my security force. This building is restricted. Yet the assassin knew exactly where you were, no trouble gaining access, fully informed about the heating systems. Information no doubt gained with the help of a spy. Yes, the Order is here."

Antonio withheld the full extent of his worry. With a mole in his ranks now, every level of Vatican security was compromised—the pope himself was at risk.

"You are welcome to stay as long as you wish. I'll do my utmost to protect you. But I must confess, for all I know the very guards I assign you are spies."

Angela trembled. "But their tattoos—the crests! You can identify them!"

"Regrettably, only Swords bear crests, and I'm afraid the one who did this is long gone. Swords are too valuable for the Order to embed, they're reserved solely for missions. No, I have an Eye & Ear on my force. And at this point, I know of no way to expose him."

Feeling their despair, he offered, "If you wish, I can place you in the care of an ally in another country. Someone with strong defenses. I have several I trust."

Ian looked uncertain. "For how long?"

"Indefinitely, I'm afraid. You must understand, wherever you go now, whatever you do, the threat is not apt to go away."

"Live under lock and key?" Angela cried. "Prisoners the rest of our lives? I'd rather be dead!"

Ian agreed, and the director admitted, "To be frank, it's doubtful anyplace I send you will prove safe for long. In time, the Order will penetrate it."

"There's got to be a way to appease them!" Ian said. "I'll give up my NDEs, buy them off!"

"How would we even contact them to negotiate? Not that I have faith they would listen."

"But why Angela? She's totally innocent!"

"Yes, but to whom do we plead her case? I'm sorry to be so blunt, but if there's any hope for you, you must understand the gravity."

A soft hand touched his arm, and he looked down into Angela's pitiful hazel pools.

"What would *you* do if you were us?"

He placed his hand on hers. "As distasteful as it sounds, I would run. Get out in front, keep moving. Change my looks, assume new identities. At least you wouldn't be confined to one place like a prisoner. And maybe, with God's help, you could elude them."

He watched them exchange anxious looks. But there was nothing more he could say. The decision was theirs, and as badly as he felt for them, he had other very weighty obligations.

"I'll leave you to discuss matters. Call me whatever you decide, I'll help any way I can."

They thanked him and he departed with a heavy heart, leaving them in the care of a half dozen gendarmes—as much for the guards to guard each other.

Angela had never felt so dejected, sitting with hands in a knot, watching Ian pace the room. The future that Antonio had painted for them was near hopeless. Regardless, she wasn't just going to languish here waiting for the inevitable.

"Antonio's right. We have to leave. Right away."

"But if it's not safe under his wing, *where*?" Ian looked like he was about to lose it. "This is *my* fault! I brought this down on us! *If anything happens to you . . .*"

Angela stood and took him by the shoulders, bringing him to a halt, forcing his eyes to hers. "Listen to me. Down in St. Maarten, when I saw you lying on that table lifeless—and tonight, thinking I'd lost you again—I realize, no other man could *ever* mean as much to me . . ."

His brow knitted.

"Okay, you're a pain in the ass sometimes. Half nuts *all* the time. But for some reason I'll never understand, *I love you.* I always will. We're in this together, and together, somehow, we're going to find a way out!"

She let go, reaching into her pocket for his ring, slipping it on.

He blinked. "You're taking me back?"

"On one condition—and I'm holding you to it. From here on, no more closing me out. Because I swear, Ian, if I take off this ring again, *it's for the last time.*"

His blue eyes steeled, he gave his word, and they wrapped themselves in each other's arms.

"Well," she said, "do we run or do we stay?"

She felt his broad shoulders shrug.

"We run."

THIRTY-ONE

SOMEWHERE IN THE SKIES OVER WESTERN FRANCE, SAME DAY, LATE AFTERNOON

Angela's dark hair was much shorter now, cut with loose bangs, casual and carefree. Ian's was blond, and he had the beginnings of a mustache. They both wore jeans and sweatshirts, only passengers in their small jet, Ian working on his laptop, Angela reclining, resting.

She'd spent most of the flight asleep, exhausted after last night's travails and today's hurried preparations. Stirring now, she gazed out her window on a spectacular sunset—a field of cloud stretching unbroken to the horizon, plowed up in serene furrows of crimson, orange, and purple.

If we could just stay up here, she thought dreamily. *Float above our problems for a while . . .*

Ian's choice of destination did nothing to entice her head from the clouds, either. To ensure the Order wouldn't second-guess them, he'd picked the most unusual, unappealing first leg she could imagine. A cold, craggy, mist-swept isle on a desolate lake . . .

Going on the lam, as Angela learned, was far more complicated than simply packing and fleeing. After they'd apprised Antonio of their intentions, he'd seen to it they were properly equipped.

First, new identities. Several sets. They would need to reinvent themselves periodically, and Antonio had used the influence of his office to furnish them a series of false names and matching U.S. social security numbers, passports, and driver's licenses. Also credit cards—funded through one of Ian's accounts via the Vatican Bank.

"Always keep your IDs handy," Antonio had advised. "You never know when you'll need a quick switch."

He'd also furnished them new videophones, and more important, detailed instructions on how to use them safely. Angela was amazed how problematic phones could be.

"These days," Antonio had warned, "cells can be more danger than they're worth. When they're switched on they broadcast a traceable frequency."

Angela had asked, "But if we use new phones and numbers, how could they tell it's us?"

"There's now voice recognition technology that can sort through millions of transmissions to spot an individual. Each voice, even disguised or encrypted, has a distinct wave pattern, unique as a fingerprint. All the Order needs is a sample snippet of you speaking—say from your TV show—and it can match it to your phone in seconds, fix your location anywhere in the world."

"What about text messages and tweets?" Ian asked.

"Only good until you make a voice call. Then your cover is blown and they have your frequency. Land lines are better—assuming you can find one when you need it. It gives you a longer window. But sooner or later they're traceable, too."

He'd handed Ian a slip of paper. "Whenever feasible, use e-mail with secured addresses. This is mine. But there are times you can use your cell safely. In the middle of a flight, for example. If the Order gets a read, it can't reach you, and if you keep your conversation short, it isn't likely to know your direction. Same for a call from a train or car—though obviously, you're more vulnerable on land."

He'd offered them bodyguards, but unable to guarantee the integrity of his force now, he recommended against it, and Ian and Angela concurred.

With the director's help, they were ready by mid-afternoon. He'd put them in ball caps and sunglasses, sneaked them into a car with darkened windows, and drove them to the airport himself. Using his connections again, he'd skirted them past customs and out to a little jet—a different charter than their inbound flight, with a new pilot.

Their farewell had been sad and anxious. Angela could still feel the man's powerful arms. Like being in the embrace of a gentle gorilla. He'd insisted they keep him apprised of their situation, promising them aid anytime, anywhere. But he'd declined to know their destination.

"Never tell anyone except your pilot. And wherever you go, stay one night only. Change your mode of travel. Plane, car, train. Keep them guessing . . ."

Angela had seen the worry in his eyes, and it lingered with her as their jet droned along on a northwesterly course. She snugged up to Ian, inhaling the security of his scent, and he patted her arm. For a time she stared lazily at his face, watching his gaze flit back and forth across his screen. Then with a yawn, she asked, "What are you reading?"

"Dante. Want to see something interesting?"

He angled his laptop to show her an illustration of Dante's seven levels of Hell.

She shrugged. "I thought Zack Niemand said Dante got it wrong."

"He said you have to separate the wheat from the chaff. I'm taking it all in and I'll sort it out when the time comes."

It took her a second to blink away the haze, then she bolted upright. "Wait a minute! You said you were giving up your NDEs!"

"I said I'd be *willing to* to appease the Order. But it's too late for that, there's no point."

"No point? How about to not kill yourself? How about to appease *me*?"

He looked puzzled. "Sweetheart, I thought we had an understanding. I'm finished living my life half nuts. One last trip, long enough to see my parents. *I have to.*"

There was no arguing with him, and she understood now the *real* reason he'd chosen this first, godforsaken whistle stop. He was seeking clues to what awaited him in the Underworld.

The pilot broke in to announce final descent, and quickly they plunged into cloud . . .

It was dark when they touched down in the coastal town of Donegal, Ireland. Rainy and cold, the region still subject to the North Atlantic's foul temperament this time of year. Wearing jackets Antonio had supplied, toting overnight bags, they darted across the tarmac to a small terminal. The rest of their luggage they left on the plane, Ian having paid their pilot well to remain on standby.

After customs, they rented a car and headed inland for the town of Pettigo, twenty kilometers south on the shores of Lough Derg. Their ultimate destination was Station Island, somewhere in the center of the lake, site of the legendary gateway to Purgatory, St. Patrick's Cave.

THIRTY-TWO

A SMALL MOTOR INN, PETTIGO, IRELAND, NEXT MORNING

The night passed uneventfully, but Angela hadn't slept well, hearing Ian up frequently at the windows to check outside. Finally at first light they both rose for good, showered, and left, stealing from their room into clammy mizzle and fog.

With the weather last evening Angela had seen little of the area, and it didn't appear visibility would improve much today. Adding to the gloom was her belief that this was all a wild-goose chase. She viewed St. Patrick's Purgatory in the same light as another murky legend of these North Isles—the Loch Ness Monster. And once Ian had stowed their bags in the car, she asked, "You *really* believe this cave is a gateway to the Underworld?"

He paused. "I believe there are some things out there that science can't explain. All those pilgrims over the centuries had to be seeing *something* down in that cave. I want to know what it was."

"Assuming we can get inside. Didn't Antonio say the Church closed it up?"

"Five hundred years ago. But I read online, in 1790 they built a cathedral over the cave and allowed pilgrimages again. Into the church, anyway, not the cave."

"And you think they'll make an exception for you."

Few barriers, it seemed, could withstand Ian's wallet. Nevertheless, Angela saw a possible silver vein in this cave. If, as she believed, Ian's subconscious was attempting to reunite him with his parents, perhaps it would allow him to do so here. A far-safer venue than another NDE . . .

Their inn sat at the intersection of two country roads across from several stone buildings. One, a café with awnings over steamed windows, lights on inside. Down the roads in any direction, however, civilization vanished, disappearing into bleak, misty moors. Like something out of *The Hound of the Baskervilles.* It made Angela jittery.

Ian nodded toward the café. "The coast looks clear. How about breakfast?"

She hesitated, but the aroma of fresh-brewed coffee tipped the balance.

The place was small. Four booths, four tables, counter with stools, grill manned by a middle-aged woman in a stained apron. Just three patrons. An older couple eating at a table, and a studious-looking, fortyish man in a corner booth, reading a book. Benign locals all, it appeared.

Ian ordered at the counter, waffles, juice, and a pot of coffee. Nearby were racks of tourist miscellanea, and Ian picked out a booklet, *True Tales of St. Patrick's Purgatory,* skimming. When their order came, he had the woman add it to the bill.

"Listen to this," he said as they settled at a table. "First written account of the Cave, by a Benedictine monk, Henry of Saltry:

> "In the days of King Stephen of England, in the year of Our Lord 1153, a certain knight Sir Owain Miles came to regret the misdeeds of his life. And fearing for his soul, he sought atonement.
>
> "Therefore did he journey by boat and steed to the end of the earth, to the land of spirits and cloud, to the Isle of the Saint and the Cave of Purgatory. A fortnight spent he in fast and prayer, then into the depths by dusk he went, saying that should he not come forth by dawn, to presume him taken by the Devil.
>
> "Scarce had he entered than he came upon the sentinel Cornu, part heron, part man, without wings or feathers. The beast uttered a cry like the blowing of a clarion, causing demons to fall upon Owain and assail him most grievous.
>
> "Yet the brave knight pressed forward, through flaming pits of stench, wherein he saw devils nail souls of naked sinners to fiery wheels, basting with molten metal, flogging and impaling, rolling them ever on to ply the filth. But ne'er did Owain falter, proceeding to the very gates of Hell to behold visages so foul they cannot be told.
>
> "Nigh expired, Owain called upon the Lord, and at sunrise was delivered from his torment to the mouth of the cave. No more had he to fear the wages of sin, for Owain's soul had been cleansed in Purgatory."

Angela heard a chuckle—the studious-looking man in the corner. Average build, brown hair, bright-green eyes, gray mustache, cardigan sweater.

He called over in thick brogue, "There's more history ta that isle out there than all the rest o' Ireland combined."

Grinning, he closed his book and approached.

"Donald O'Farrell," he said, "Dublin University, here studyin' the monastery."

He seemed harmless, but Angela thought it best to keep to themselves. All the same, Ian rose to shake hands.

"Sue and Phil Baker," he introduced, using the first set of names Antonio had provided.

"I've done breakfast," O'Farrell said, "but fer a cup o' coffee, I'll share ya some stories."

Angela started to decline but Ian was too quick. The man pulled up a chair, setting down his book. *Cemetery Records of Station Island.*

"First trip ta the north regions?" he asked.

"Yes," Ian said. "Weather takes some getting used to."

O'Farrell laughed. "God-fersaken place, t'isn't it? Had that repute since ancient times. Romans called it *Ultima Thule*—World's End. Realm o' the Dead."

Ian filled the man's mug from their pot, and as he lectured, they ate.

"Back then, people thought when ya died yer soul followed the settin' sun ta the edge of the world, where it rose ta Heaven or fell off ta Hell. Ireland bein' the western-most of the known lands, 'twas the Great Divide, and Europeans steered clear. But then St. Patrick come along in 430 to convert the Celts. Indiana Jones of 'is day, 'e was. Tales of 'is feats spread all o'er the Continent. Ever hear o' *Legenda Aurea*?"

Ian translated, " 'The Golden Legend.' No."

"Thick book from the 1200s, all the old myths. Tells 'ow Patrick chased a giant snake out ta that isle an' slew it. Last o' the snakes 'e rid from Ireland. Blood give the water its rusty hue, 'ence the name, Lough Derg—Lake Red."

Screening his mouth with a hand, he added softly, "*Real* cause is seepage from the peat bogs, but don't let the locals hear ya say it!"

Ian and Angela laughed. The professor was interesting, charming. But Angela still preferred they not get chummy.

"Seems slayin' the snake 'twasn't enough ta convert the Celts though, so Patrick gathered 'em out on the isle an' scribed a big circle in the earth with 'is staff. Straight away a 'ole opened into Purgatory, swallowin' up the worst sinners, causin' the rest ta see the light. An' ta make sure 'is converts didn't backslide, 'e left the cave open, a reminder of the perils o' sin."

Finding an opening herself, Angela rose and thanked O'Farrell, Ian getting the message.

But the professor accompanied them to the counter, and as they paid, he asked Ian, "Ya been out ta the isle, then?"

"We're heading to the ferry now."

The woman behind the counter snickered as she handed Ian his change. "Gonna have a bit o' a wait there, laddie. Ferry don't run in the off season."

Angela winced to hear O'Farrell say, "I've chartered a boat, if ya'd care ta share expenses."

THIRTY-THREE

LOUGH DERG, IRELAND, SAME DAY, LATER THAT MORNING

The fog had lifted somewhat by the time Angela, Ian, and their new acquaintance, Professor O'Farrell, left the café. On the short stroll to the docks, Angela could finally make out the lake through the haze. Large, it appeared. Mist-swept, shrouded in low-hanging clouds, bounded by jagged shoreline of rock and pine-forested bluffs. Apt setting for an entrance to the Underworld. She zipped her jacket.

O'Farrell led them onto a wharf past a dozen boats, including a big, flat-bottom vessel where men were scraping paint from the hull. Angela assumed it the ferry. Nearby sat a weathered old cabin cruiser, inboard engine gurgling oily smoke out the back, scent of diesel in the air.

"That's us," O'Farrell said, waving to an elderly man coiling rope on deck.

The man responded with a gap-toothed grin. On the boat's stern, faded letters read SAFE SHEOLS. Angela was *not* reassured, and she flashed Ian a concerned look. He missed, but O'Farrell caught it.

"Not ta worry, my dear, I checked 'er out. Tub's seen better days, but she's sound."

He extended his arm to Angela, and still uncertain, she allowed him to escort her aboard.

Once on deck, O'Farrell turned to face the ruddy waters. Eyes glowing, he intoned:

". . . by that dim Lake
Where sinful souls their farewell take
Of this vain world, and halfway lie
In death's cold shadow, ere they died . . .

"Sir Thomas More," he said. " 'E wrote that after a pilgrimage 'ere in 1534. Very next year, 'Enry VIII lopped off 'is head!" Chuckling, he added, "Let's 'ope 'is visit ta the Cave saved 'im time in Purgatory."

They stepped into the cabin, finding seats, soon departing across still waters with no crew but the old captain. Ian turned to O'Farrell.

"Thomas More was here?"

"A fact. Lots o' famous people. Kings, noblemen, knights, clergy. Men only back then, the Cave was considered too dangerous fer womenfolk. 'Twas a warnin' posted at its entrance, written in blood: *'Multos Purgatorium Ingressos Nunquam Redivisse.'* "

Ian said, " 'Many Who Enter Purgatory Never Return.' "

"Ya know yer Latin. The warnin' was fer real. Tradition was ta spend the night in the Cave, and lots who did were found dead as a stone next mornin'. Hundreds o' graves on that isle. That's what I'm 'ere researchin'. Need to check a few last headstones, an' I'm done."

It sounded like O'Farrell was a Believer.

Angela asked, "How did the people die?"

"Unknown. Most were discovered lyin' on the cave floor, faces contorted, no visible injuries. As if evil spirits 'ad carried off their souls."

"So is Sir Owain's story typical of what people saw?"

"Truth be told, most came away seein' nothin' a'tall. But of the few favored with a vision—or cursed, if ya prefer—the majority o' stories tended toward the lurid . . ."

Glancing out a window, Angela gasped to see a tall, angular conflation of stone suddenly emerge from the mists, looming toward them like the prow of a dreadnought.

THIRTY-FOUR

THE PAPAL APARTMENTS, APOSTOLIC PALACE, VATICAN CITY, SAME DAY, MORNING

Antonio Ponti's heart raced as he passed through the *Sala del Tronetto,* last of three throne rooms before the red-draped door of the papal library. Not since the Germans bombed the Vatican in '43 had a pontiff been made to confront security matters. The director felt shamed by this duty, but there was no choice. In his tenure here he'd never faced a graver crisis. Papa had to be apprised of the danger and of the steps being taken to safeguard him and his college of cardinals.

In addition to this unfortunate disclosure, however, Antonio had another ticklish issue. A special favor to ask. He needed to know if perhaps somewhere within the confines of the *Volta Papale*—the pope's private vault—there might exist secret information on *Arma Christi.* In particular, the ancient Bull that created the Order, said to contain the rules by which *Arma Christi* governed itself. It could help Antonio identify his spy. Maybe even offer clues to help poor Ian and Angela.

But Antonio had never heard of anyone making such an audacious request of a pope, no idea how His Holiness would respond. Yes, Julius IV was kindhearted, good-natured, and an extraordinarily pious man. But he was also supreme spiritual leader of one billion people, a sovereign of strength and conviction who placed great stock in protocol. And he was known to have a temper. . . .

Standing at the library door was the papal chamberlain, who greeted Antonio in Italian. Antonio replied in kind, and the man excused himself to enter the room, returning shortly to say, "Go right in. Papa's finishing some work, if you don't mind waiting."

The director thanked him and proceeded into the *Biblioteca Papale,* the hall where Julius conducted much of his less-official business.

Antonio knew it well. Spacious, high-ceilinged, tall windows, walls lined with glass bookcases and a thousand ancient tomes. Above the cases, paintings of exotic animals; in the center of the room, a long mahogany table. Beyond was the pope's large, if plain, wood desk where Julius was now seated signing papers.

Young for a pope. Sixty-six. Full head of silver hair, parted and combed neatly as a choirboy's. Face long, as was his nose. Lips thin and elegant, eyes bright and intelligent under rimless spectacles, sparkling in the light of a crystal chandelier. He wore a full-length, all-white, button-up simar, gold crucifix on a gold-link chain around his neck, tucked in the gap between two buttons.

The director felt enormous affection and respect. And as always, a sense of awe.

Julius was attended on his left by his *Camerlengo*—head secretary—and on his right by three nuns. At his side, portfolio in hand, stood a smallish man of slight build who nevertheless held himself with authority. Grayhair; thin face; arching nose; active, birdlike eyes. And black cassock with the scarlet piping and fascia of high rank.

Pietro Cardinal della Roca, Prefect of the Congregation for the Doctrine of the Faith, the office responsible for safeguarding Church dogma.

At fifty-seven, Cardinal della Roca was also young for his position, an esteemed theologian and close spiritual advisor to the pope. Antonio had known him for years, but not well. In the tradition of Curia prelates, della Roca played his cards close to the vest—if not shy about peeking at other hands. And he was a tenacious protector of his turf. More than once Antonio had sought his cooperation in security matters, not getting it.

Approaching, Antonio watched a nun set a document in front of the pope, indicating where to sign. Julius dashed off his signature, a second nun removed the document and passed it down the line to a third, who then added it to a stack, and the process repeated.

The pope glanced up at the sound of Antonio's footsteps, bidding him cheerily in Italian, "Morning, Tony. How's my favorite guardian angel today?"

Antonio smiled and replied, "Well, Papa. And you?"

The pope returned to his papers. "I'd be better without this weather. The damp does my arthritis no good." He gestured to his attendants. "They wait for rainy days to bring me these tasks!"

Tittering, the nuns and the *Camerlengo* also exchanged greetings with Antonio. Della Roca nodded.

"And how is your mother?" Antonio asked.

"Better, thank you. At her age it's always something, but she seems between ailments. God wants her here to keep an eye on me, I think." He looked up over his glasses. "I understand you have business of some urgency?"

"Yes, Papa. But it's best I wait till you have a free moment."

"Ah . . . Very well, I'm ready for a break. Let me finish Pietro's papers so he can be on his way."

He affixed his signature to more documents, the nun gave them to della Roca, who placed them in his portfolio, thanked the pope, and left. Then the nuns gathered the remaining items and departed with the *Camerlengo* by a side door.

Julius motioned Antonio to a chair across his desk.

"How is the family? And that beautiful grandson?"

Antonio felt a warm glow. "Fine, Holiness. It meant so much your favoring us with the baptism. Carla can't stop talking about it. She thinks little Vittorio a saint already."

The pope chuckled. "I must do my part to uphold our ranks; God knows we need every soul these days. But tell me, what's on your mind?"

Sobering, the director lowered his eyes. "I'm sorry to trouble you, Papa, but we have a security issue. A *serious* one. Two days ago I gave sanctuary here to a young man and woman under assault from an old nemesis of ours. The man is the priest I assisted in Côte d'Ivoire several years ago, you may recall."

"The child slavery affair," the pope said, nodding gravely. "The American missionary. So brave. But I trust he isn't drawing you into any more such adventures."

"No, Papa, I respect your wishes. Nevertheless, the young man—who I'm sorry to say has taken a hiatus from his vows—he seems to have a penchant for trouble. This time he's crossed paths with . . . with *Ordo Arma Christi.*"

Blinking, the pope removed his spectacles.

"God help him."

"Yes, Papa. And God help *us*. I regret to tell you, despite my diligence it appears the Order has infiltrated us. I fear I have an Eye & Ear on my force."

The pope sank in his chair. "We'd no problem for so long, I'd put it out of my mind . . . *Are you certain?"*

"Yes, Papa. Yesterday a Sword made an attempt on the lives of the man and woman. The heaters in their rooms were sabotaged, made to look like the work of mice."

"But how do you know it wasn't mice?"

"Mice with a knowledge of chemistry—poisonous substances were involved. I'm concerned for your safety. I've assigned my most senior men to the Noble Guard and I am conducting a thorough investigation, running new background checks on all."

The pope mumbled what sounded like a prayer, and Antonio mustered his nerve to ask, "Papa, I hesitate to trouble you with this, but given the gravity . . . By any chance, might there be information in the *Volta* to shed light on *Arma Christi*? Clues how to contact it? Something to help me learn—"

He watched Julius go white and rise.

"Never! You must *never* ask that! The contents of the *Volta* are for no eyes but the pope's!"

Antonio stood also, face reflected in the pope's bookcase, red as a cardinal's fascia.

"Deepest apologies, Holiness!" he panted. "Forgive me, please, a foolish mistake. It won't happen again!"

The pope scowled and looked away, pursing his lips. Then his gaze softened, and calmer, he said, "No, Tony, forgive *me*. The pressures of this office sometimes exceed my restraint . . . I pray your concerns are ill-founded, but I appreciate them. Investigate your force if you must. But, please, let's not make a to-do. The last thing the City needs is a witch hunt."

Burning with humiliation, Antonio assured, "You can rely on my discretion. And I will take every precaution for your safety."

Julius waved him off. "With you, God, *and* Mama watching over, what have I to fear?"

Antonio left, heart heavier than ever.

Though he'd come away without the help he sought, he realized now he should have expected no better. Men of the cloth, whether priests or popes, were innately trusting. The religious mentality was to see the good in mankind, head in the sand about ugly matters of spies and assassins.

His job, however, was to assume the worst in men. Antonio had a sacred obligation to safeguard the papacy, the Vatican, and his Church.

Even if he had to work around the pope to do it . . .

THIRTY-FIVE

THE WATERS OF LOUGH DERG, IRELAND, SAME DAY, MORNING

Hearing Angela utter a hushed cry, Ian followed her eyes, spellbound to see a massive stone fortress materializing before them, floating atop the waters like the last stop at the end of the world.

STATION ISLAND, a sign read.

Home to infamous St. Patrick's Purgatory.[7]

Not a fortress, Ian realized as the boat drew closer, but a small city emerging from the fog. A tiny isle of few acres packed to the shoreline with three- and four-story structures of somber gray stone. And rising above all, an imposing, castlelike basilica with copper-capped octagonal dome.

The boat maneuvered to a dock where few other vessels were moored, and as the captain tied off, Ian, Angela, and Professor O'Farrell disembarked. No one to greet them, not a soul anywhere that Ian could see. But the professor needed no guide. Pointing to a paved road that hugged the shore, he declared, "Thataway."

They soon passed beneath a stone-and-metal archway that spanned the road, across which was splayed the Latin phrase, *Purgatorium Sancti Patricii.*[8]

O'Farrell said, "A bit dreary this time o' year, but ya should see it in season—no more beautiful a place in all Ireland."

Ian turned to gaze up at the basilica, pulse quickening. "So the Cave is in the church?"

"Under it."

"And the Cave's entrance?"

O'Farrell gave him an odd look. "*Entrance?* There's no entrance, me boy. The Church 'ad the Cave filled in centuries ago. Cathedral 'twas built o'er it. Ya didn't know that?"

Ian came to a halt, stricken. "*Filled in?* For God's sake, *why?*"

"Ta end the sacrilege. The things seen in that 'ole were so vile, the Church had ta put a stop to it."

They resumed walking, Ian despondent as O'Farrell explained, "In 1497 they banned all pilgrimages. Didn't work though, people kept comin'. By the 1600s, even women. Led ta all sorts of debauchery. Got so bad they razed ever' buildin' on the isle, imposed fines an' public whippin's on trespassers. *Still* they came. Finally in 1790 they filled up the Cave, built the basilica atop, an' allowed pilgrimages once more. Popular, but never again the rage it once was."

Ian felt robbed, foolish. And angry he hadn't been more thorough. He'd devoted most of his research to the visions seen in the Cave, not the Cave itself. And he'd seen no mention on the Purgatory website about the Cave being destroyed.

He fell silent, Angela carrying the conversation.

O'Farrell led them inside the basilica to view an array of dazzling stained-glass windows, pointing out one in particular. St. Patrick standing before his Cave with upraised staff. Beneath, a quote Ian recognized:

Hamlet, Act I, Scene 5:
Yes, by Saint Patrick . . . Touching this vision here . . .
Never make known what you have seen tonight.

"Ya see," O'Farrell whispered proudly, "even Shakespeare knew o' St. Patrick's Purgatory."

Outside again, they passed a cemetery and the professor reminded them how many pilgrims had never left the isle. Excusing himself, he went to finish his research.

Ian turned to Angela.

"Sorry for the wasted trip. I feel like an idiot."

She took his hand. "Antonio told us to keep the Order guessing, and you've certainly done that. But next time, someplace not so damp."

He already had a destination in mind. One he knew she'd love . . .

When O'Farrell returned, they headed for the boat. On the way, he asked Ian, "So what was it ya were 'opin' ta find in the Cave, anyways?"

"I don't know. An insight into the Afterlife, maybe."

The professor smiled. "Ta paraphrase an ol' Dublin playwright, Sean O'Casey: 'The more ya learn o' the next world, the less ya know 'o this 'un!' "

Ian did not find that enlightening.

As the boat departed, he watched the basilica disappear back into the mists, frustrated to be denied the mysteries that lay buried beneath, no less determined to keep looking. Angela rested her head on his shoulder, dozing as O'Farrell scribbled in his journal. Then midpoint, the professor excused himself to go on deck, and moments later the engine throttled back.

THIRTY-SIX

THE WATERS OF LOUGH DERG, IRELAND, SAME DAY, NOON

Dozing on the return trip, Angela felt the boat roll to a stop, opening her eyes to ask Ian, "Are we there already?"

In answer, the cabin door swung wide and a stranger stepped through, stopping just inside, face flushed, one hand in his coat. He paid them a peculiar look and they rose to their feet.

"There is only *one* path to the Afterlife," he rasped, "and now in God's Name, *I'll show you.*"

Angela was stunned to realize it was O'Farrell! Accent Slavic now, no mustache, eyes gray, demeanor transformed from milksop to monster. He pulled a strange instrument from his coat, pointing it at Ian, and Angela let out a cry.

She heard a click, seeing a small projectile dart out trailing a thread-thin wire. Too fast for Ian to duck, it struck his upraised arm, glancing off the crystal of his watch.

A tazer! The kind used to control violent psychotics, Angela recognized. Had the dart pierced Ian's skin, he'd be on the floor now, convulsing.

"Srać," O'Farrell growled, discarding the spent weapon, fumbling out a fresh one.

Angela felt Ian's strong hands sweep her behind him, and he backed her away, plucking a life preserver from the wall for a shield.

"Going to make this difficult, are we?" O'Farrell snorted, taking more careful aim.

Before he could get the shot off, Ian's arm lashed out like a cobra, life preserver striking the tazer, knocking it to the floor, and Ian was on him in a bear hug. Angela lunged for the weapon but O'Farrell crushed it underfoot, then bent, whipped Ian over his back, and slammed him to the deck.

Angela saw with sinking heart, a former priest was no match for a trained assassin. O'Farrell unleashed vicious kicks, Ian grunting as Angela shrieked for the captain and attacked O'Farrell with wild, desperate, puny swings—she'd never been in a fight!

But she distracted the man enough for Ian to stagger to his feet. He raised his fists, and the two squared off.

"So," O'Farrell said with cool confidence, "we do this the old fashioned way." He put up his fists, too. *"Vincere aut mori."*

"Ne cede malis," Ian replied, eyes determined.

Frantic, Angela searched for something to use as a weapon, in vain, watching the assassin close in on Ian. Suddenly O'Farrell let loose a ferocious punch, and Angela grimaced—only to see Ian slip it, dancing sideways! O'Farrell swung again and Ian dodged again, this time returning a solid blow to the jaw. The man reeled, shook it off, charged once more, same results.

Angela was flabbergasted.

But O'Farrell changed tactics. Approaching more warily now, he lashed out with a foot, catching Ian hard in the midsection. Ian winced, recoiled, and O'Farrell pressed his advantage, leg pummeling like a jackhammer. Angela saw with despair that Ian had backed himself into a corner, about to go down as she stood by helpless.

And then as if dreaming it, she saw Ian plant a foot against the wall and shoot out, surprising O'Farrell, landing a powerful right to his head. The man went flat-footed and Ian followed with blinding combinations until the man's knees folded and he went crashing to the floor, out cold.

Angela rushed to Ian, trembling, hesitant to touch him for fear of his injuries. *"My God,"* she cried, "are you okay?"

He nodded, bent over huffing, hands on knees, and she gushed, "Where the heck did you learn *that*?"

"St. L . . . priest . . . ex-boxer . . . Quick, check the captain."

She hurried to the pilothouse to find the captain sprawled on his side, unconscious. Heart and respiration steady, thankfully, though too heavy to move. Reporting back to Ian, she saw O'Farrell slumped in a chair now, stirring, hands bound behind with wire from the discharged tazer.

"I found these on him," Ian said, holding up a set of rental-car keys. "No identification. And this—" He pressed something into her hand. A third tazer. "Stand guard, I'll get the captain."

Angela kept nervous watch while Ian limped topside, returning with the man over a shoulder, resting him in a chair, covering him with his jacket. O'Farrell was awake now, staring darkly out the window, face bloodied.

"Who are you?" Ian demanded. "Your *real* name."

Silence.

"We may not know who he is," Angela snapped, "but we know *what* he is."

She grabbed the front of his shirt and sweater, ripping them open, buttons scattering across the deck. There on his chest, the telltale tattoo. He growled and pulled away.

"Tazers leave little mark," she said. "His plan was to stun us and dump us overboard to drown—make it look like a boating accident. Cold-blooded murder."

The man turned to her with strange calm.

"Not cold-blooded, my dear. Believe it or not, in our short time together I've actually grown quite fond of you both. I wanted your deaths quick and painless."

Ian gave a snort, and O'Farrell responded, "I take no pleasure in my work, I simply do God's Will. Just as Abraham obeyed when told to sacrifice his son."

Angela cried, "God has you kill innocent people?"

His eyes went indignant. "*Innocent?* You are *thieves.* You've broken Faith with God! You would steal His darkest Secrets! Lock the Gates of Heaven, open the Gates of Hell!" He glared at Ian. "And you, *a priest.* You dare pry into the Mind of God? I warn you, chase your parents to Hell and you'll unleash the Knowledge of Evil on the world. *You'll doom us all!*"

"Whatever your quarrel with me," Ian snapped, "Angela has nothing to do with it!"

O'Farrell scoffed. "She will broadcast your blasphemy. Her name is in the *Liber de Damnatis* next to yours."

Ian grabbed him roughly by the collar but the man didn't flinch, snarling, "There is no escape for you. My Brothers will amend my failure."

Ian swore with disgust and released him, and O'Farrell closed his eyes, composing himself. It seemed to Angela he was praying. After a time he stopped to take a long look around, then whispered serenely, *"As Christ gave His life for me, I offer Him no less . . ."*

Abruptly he leaped from his chair, racing for the hatch, hands still bound behind. Ian and Angela were taken by surprise, charging after. But he was too quick, crashing through the door, stumbling for the side of the boat. Then with a last glance back, smile on his lips, he turned and jackknifed over the rail.

Angela clung to Ian in disbelief as the man plunged into the frigid water, dolphin-kicking downward, disappearing into the rusty gloom.

THIRTY-SEVEN

THE WATERS OF LOUGH DERG, IRELAND, SAME DAY, AFTERNOON

Still shaking, Angela tended to the unconscious captain as Ian took the boat's wheel, heading for home port fast as the old engines would go. She could hear the pistons knocking, black smoke trailing in the water, and she feared they wouldn't make it. But finally they sputtered into dock, placing the captain in the care of fellow boatmen, someone calling an ambulance.

A small crowd gathered, and Angela watched Ian slip a wad of large bills into the captain's pocket. Then grabbing her hand, he edged her away, limping.

She whispered to him, "We can't just leave like this!"

"No choice, O'Farrell could have an accomplice . . ."

Her pulse jumped again. She held tight as they retraced their steps to the inn, every man they passed a potential assassin. Though their car looked untouched, Ian gave it careful inspection, then soon they were speeding back to Donegal, keeping nervous watch behind.

Angela's trembling grew worse, aftershock, and once they hit open road she blurted, "How did they find us! They know all about your NDEs! Your plans! They know *everything*! And what the hell is a *Liber de Damnatis*?"

Ian exhaled. "Latin. *Book of the Condemned*."

"But we did everything Antonio told us—stayed off our phones, used fake IDs . . ."

She watched Ian chew his lip, and then he swore.

"Our flight plan."

"What?"

"Planes have to file flight plans before takeoff. Air-traffic controllers get the data, maybe the Order's Eyes & Ears have access. Once they saw Donegal, knowing my interests, the rest would be obvious."

He flipped his phone on, and she grabbed his hand.

"They'll trace the signal!"

"They already know we're here . . ."

He reached their pilot, ordering a return flight to Rome. When he hung up, Angela grabbed his hand again.

"But now they'll be waiting in Rome for us!"

"Hopefully. Because we're going to throw them a curve." He gave her a wily look. "A flight to Rome will cross Lyon, France. Lyon has a night train to Venice, I've taken it before. We'll make a last-minute landing in Lyon, send the plane on to Rome, then catch the train to Venice. That should leave the Order scratching its head a while."

She blinked, warming to the idea of Venice.

He added, "Remember the medieval painter Antonio told us about?"

"Hieronymus Bosch?"

"I saw online, a Venice museum has an exhibit of his paintings."

"But Antonio said the Order is trying to destroy them!"

"Not since the mid 1800s, remember. It gave up. And I think I know why . . . I read that the surviving Bosch works were first photographed in 1852. Calotypes, the process was called. The paintings had been hidden away for centuries, and the photos were an instant sensation. Thousands of copies circulated all over Europe. *That's* why the Order gave up. The horse was out of the barn, they couldn't contain the forbidden images anymore."

"Maybe. But how does that help *us*?"

"I'm not sure yet, except it shows that the Order isn't some mindless terminator. Like Antonio said, it isn't motivated by vengeance, there's a limit to how far it will go to win a battle. Maybe we can learn what that limit is."

"Why Bosch? What more can his paintings tell us?"

"Things *Arma Christi* didn't want the world to know."

"You think they hold secrets to Hell. You're looking for a damned roadmap!"

"I've been studying them online," he admitted, "and they *are* amazing. Complex cryptograms. Huge—some eight-by-fifteen feet. Too large for a computer screen. I need to see them up close."

Exhausted, Angela rested her head on his shoulder, closing her eyes. They had to flee somewhere, and Venice seemed a big improvement over Lough Derg. All the same, next time *she* would choose their destination.

Assuming they survived to have a choice.

THIRTY-EIGHT

THE DEPTHS OF THE BIBLIOTHECA SECRETA, VATICAN CITY, SAME DAY, LATE AFTERNOON

"Misericordia!" Antonio grunted, moving a heavy footlocker from shelf to floor—last of two dozen such containers he'd lugged up and down. He was sweaty and grimy after two hours in this, the *Apostolic Penitentiary,* highest-security section of the Secret Archives.

Where files on *Ordo Arma Christi* were kept.

Last he was here was to perform his due diligence when first taking office. No cause to return since, the Order having lain low all these years. But now faced with a crisis, he was reexamining the files. This time at his own pace, not under the watchful eyes of some cardinal sentry. He hoped to spot things he may have missed. *Any* clue to ferret out this damned mole and help his young American friends escape their sentence.

The Secret Archives were located far beneath a Vatican courtyard, eighty-five kilometers of shelves filled with the surviving records of the Church dating to the very birth of Christianity. A warehouse of priceless artifacts, documents, and manuscripts so vast, most of the contents hadn't been viewed in centuries, much less cataloged.

Here in the Apostolic Penitentiary were stored the Church's most sensitive modern documents. One hundred thirty-five rooms, ten-by-ten-by-fifteen meters, mesh-metal doors, fluorescent fixtures, kept under lock and key. Off limits to all but the pope, select Curia cardinals, and curator monks who tended the archives like so many silent worker bees.

And Antonio Ponti. As Director of Security, Antonio had access to all corners of the Vatican. Even the pope's private *Volta Papale,* the papal vault. But with strict constraints. He was authorized to enter only for specific purposes, such as to apprehend an intruder, or on approved, official business. And regarding the latter, he was required to be in the company of a

Curial cardinal, having taken an oath to that effect—a vow of obedience and confidentiality.

Lately, however, he'd struggled with the oaths of his office. As his heart told him, within the breadth and width of God's Grand Plan, some things transcended vows. The security of his Church, for one. Human life, for another. And with *Arma Christi* penetrating his defenses, threatening both, he felt pressed to extraordinary steps.

He'd no trouble eluding the Archive gatekeepers. Everyone was aware of the turmoil in his department, Vatican grapevine what it was, and he'd used that as cover. He'd come here under pretext of a security check, changing out the regular guards, taking advantage of the shuffle to steal off here. But after hours of searching he'd shed no new light on *Ordo Arma Christi*.

"Why does God allow such Evil into His Church?" he muttered, dropping to a knee, finding the latch of this chest locked like the others. Removing a wire tool from a pocket, he easily picked it, too, throwing back the lid in a swirl of dust. He fanned the air to watch his hopes drift away with the cloud, recognizing the contents.

Files from the last-known exposure of an *Arma Christi* operative. Reign of John Paul II, 1995. The pope had been on a trip to Manila, during which Islamic terrorists plotted to attack him with a suicide bomber dressed as a priest. Thank God Philippine security received an anonymous tip, trapping the terrorists in a building, killing them in a gun battle. Among the bodies recovered was that of a man identified only by a tattoo over his heart.

Was he part of the plot? Or had *Arma Christi* penetrated the terrorist cell in an effort to thwart it? There was no way to know. Nor did the files provide a clue.

Antonio shut the lid, swearing, having learned nothing for his pains here. He hefted the case back up to the shelf, anxious to leave before he was found out. But as he balanced the chest on the shelf edge, ready to give it a last heave, his eyes fell on an odd, purselike object in the shadows behind.

He halted, straining under the weight. The object lay smashed against the rear of the shelf, an orphan of careless filing, he suspected. Nothing he recognized from his trip years ago. He lowered the case back to the floor, using it for a footstool, stretching to haul the object into the light.

A brown leather satchel, thirty by thirty centimeters, slim, with strap and buckle flap. Old-fashioned courier's pouch, like those once used to protect hand-delivered documents. No markings other than a few nasty scuffs.

He opened it to find a yellowed, letter-sized envelope stamped with the Vatican's official red receipt, dated *16 Marzo, 1939.* Addressed to:

Seine Würde, Eugène Tisserant
Vatican Stadt, Italien
Privat und Vertraulich

German. A tongue Antonio didn't read. But he recognized the name. Cardinal Eugène Tisserant, high-ranking Curia official during the reign of Pius XII, and beyond. The envelope was unsealed. Inside, a letter and a second, smaller envelope. The letter was in Latin, which Antonio knew well.

Berlin, 14 March, 1939
Your Eminence:

I do not understand the significance of the item I present to you here, but as it is of obvious importance to the Reich, I place it in your hands for appropriate disposition. I attach with it the tragic story of how it came into my possession.

Yesterday morning a young man was struck by a car as he crossed the Vosstrasse to the new Reich Chancellory. Witnessing the accident was one of our pastors, Father Bernhard Litchenberg. Father Bernard went to offer his assistance, only to see the driver of the car exit and search the victim's pockets. Moments later SS arrived and seized the driver.

As Father turned to go, he stumbled across something in the gutter. This satchel. Suspecting it belonged to the victim, he picked it up and an envelope fell out. He noted the name to which it was addressed, and tucking everything under his coat, he came immediately to me.

I have since learned that the victim died, and the driver of the car committed suicide in jail, leaving no means of identification but an odd tattoo over his heart—Christ crucified on a sword. That is all I know. I leave the envelope unopened, trusting you will make sense of this strange affair. I pray that in some small way it will benefit the cause and accelerate an end to the madness.

Yours in Christ,
Bishop Konrad Graf von Preysing,
Diocese of Berlin

Puzzled, Antonio set the letter aside to inspect the smaller envelope—and felt his heart stop.

Reichsführer-SS H. Himmler
Präsident Verein Das Ahnenerbe Forschungs-und Lehrgemeinschaft
Reichskanzlei, Berlin

Nazi SS Chief Heinrich Himmler—Hitler's second-in-command! The envelope was stamped front and back with red warnings against unauthorized eyes.

But the flap was no longer sealed, and hands trembling, Antonio shook out the contents. A parchment, thirteen centimeters square, folded. It felt very old, brittle in his fingers. Gently he pried back the edges, seeing what appeared to be a map. Crude, hand-drawn, with numerous Latin designations in washed-out, brownish ink. At the top, a French inscription identifying the document.

And Antonio felt his eyes would pop.

THIRTY-NINE

THE SKIES ABOVE FRANCE, SAME DAY, LATE AFTERNOON

As their jet traveled a return course in the direction of Rome, Ian and Angela sat working on laptops. Ian was relieved that Angela appeared recovered from their harrowing experience at Lough Derg, he fortunate to suffer no worse than a gimpy leg and sore ribs.

The past hour, he'd been reading more tales of St. Patrick's Purgatory. Fascinating. But now he was back onto the paintings of Hieronymus Bosch. And the more he delved into the hellish works, the more excited he grew. There was indeed something strange going on here.

Bosch's depictions of the Underworld were stunning. Shocking. Masterpieces of complex phantasmagoria. The recurring theme was the wages of sin, portrayed in outlandish and erotic tortures inflicted on the damned by bizarre demons.

Prior to Bosch, Ian learned, there were no images of Hell anything like these gripping panoramas. Each was a labyrinth of Christian icons, astrology, cryptic symbols, and pictograms whose meanings had long ago been lost. Ian was increasingly convinced they were drawn from eyewitness experience, laced with clues to what awaited him in his next NDE. And with luck tomorrow, he hoped to solve some of these puzzles . . .

He'd grown so absorbed he'd almost forgotten to call Antonio. He wanted to report back about Lough Derg, and needed to do so while still in flight, before Lyon. Then should the Order detect the signal, it would have no reason to suspect the plane's true destination wasn't Rome.

All the same, his call went straight to voicemail. Antonio had warned against leaving messages, so Ian was reduced to e-mail. A lengthy one, relating their unfortunate encounter with the Sword; how the Order seemed to know their every move; and how Ian suspected it was accessing their flight plans. He also advanced his theory about *Arma Christi* giving up on the Bosch paintings once the works had received wide exposure. And in conclusion, he promised to call again tomorrow, noon.

One more call before Lyon.

He reached Emil Josten in New York City, the doctor busy acquiring equipment for the new lab. Their exchange was mostly from Josten's end, and when finished, Ian reported to Angela.

"Yvette Garonne got us that new lab location in Capetown, and most of the equipment is now on order."

Seeing her frown and shrug off the news, he changed topics.

"Okay then," he said, angling his laptop toward her, "maybe you'll find *this* more interesting . . ."

Angela leaned into the screen, squinting. A complex painting, very detailed. And very disturbing. A nightmarish Alice-in-Wonderland torture chamber of naked souls assaulted by demons.[9] She wrinkled her nose.

"*That's* what you're studying, medieval pornography?"

It was more lurid even than the tales of St. Patrick's Purgatory he'd been passing along. Well, Angela had been doing some research of her own. The past hour she'd been looking into phenomena like St. Patrick's Cave, seeking a *scientific* explanation. And she was on to something that, with a little more work, she hoped would bury Ian's belief in supernatural gateways.

FORTY

A BASEMENT FLAT IN AN OLD TENEMENT, PRAGUE 8, CZECH REPUBLIC, SAME DAY, NIGHT

Josef Varga sat at a video monitor, viewing archive episodes of the American TV show, *Probing the Paranormal.* This one entitled *The Heart of St. Peter.*

On-screen was Ian Baringer with a svelte brunette, standing inside a church. Behind, on a pedestal, a life-sized, lifelike statue of a balding, haloed, bearded man in a flowing robe. The statue's right hand was upraised as if bestowing a blessing, the other at his waist, holding a set of skeleton keys. The woman was gesturing to the statue—

". . . sound and vibration tests were unable to detect the presence of any anomalies whatsoever, including the alleged heartbeat claimed by so many parishioners."

The scene cut to people in blindfolds. One by one they reached up, pressing palms first to the chest of the statue, then to that of a plaster dummy beside it. Ian's voice said, *"Those parishioners who felt a heartbeat in the statue of St. Peter also felt it in the control statue, seeming to rule out a miracle. The more likely answer, they were sensing their* own *pulses in their thumbs, which became noticeable due to elevating their arms—not to mention their expectations."*

The faces of Ian and the woman returned to the screen, and Josef froze the picture.

"Ian, Ian!" he muttered. "You *have* gone to the devil!"

On the table beside him, his cell phone sounded—ringtone of a church bell tolling. Caller ID showed his superior, Cyril, and Josef uttered a quick prayer before answering. "Any word, sir?"

"None. But we know Baringer and the woman left Ireland. We must presume Dimitri dead."

Josef closed his eyes. He had indeed underestimated his old friend.

*"Ponti's helping them. He's probably revealed our existence—*another *scoop they'll take to TV."*

"Where are they now?"

"Over France. Retreating to the Vatican, it appears. I want you to leave immediately."

His pulse quickened. "I'm too well known there!"

"Who else? Quintus is in Damascus. Everyone's on assignment."

"There's Hendric . . ."

An exasperated sigh. *"Hendric is too limited."*

"But when it comes to his forte, there's none better. The Vatican E&Es can arrange things."

"If Ponti doesn't ferret them out first!"

A pause, and an oath.

"All right, send him. But this time, in the Name of God—finish it!"

FORTY-ONE

THE PLAIN OF LOMBARDY, NORTHERN ITALY, A PRIVATE SLEEPING CAR OF A TRAIN, EARLY NEXT MORNING

Angela awoke in her curtained berth, better rested than she'd felt in days. In part, it was the soothing rock-a-bye of the coach and hypnotic click-clacking of the wheels—she'd never slept on a train before. But mostly, it was her faith in Ian's subterfuge.

He'd been very clever last night. Waiting until they'd reached Lyon airspace before instructing their pilot to land, staying off his phone after, purchasing their train tickets separately at the station using fresh credit cards and IDs. He'd thought of everything. She felt safe with him, still marveling at how he'd bested that assassin in Lough Derg.

Peeking out her curtain, she saw him up and dressed, sitting with his laptop in their compact cabin. So much nicer than a plane. Fold-up bunks, efficiency bath, dresser, drop-down table, loveseat, and broad window.

A wall clock indicated Venice still ninety minutes away, and outside, Angela saw a splendid country morning flashing by. Great rolling fields of grape arbors, brown vines tinged with green. How she wished they could stop and explore. Someday, hopefully . . .

"*Buongiorno,* beautiful," Ian greeted, setting aside his computer, patting his lap.

She slid from her bunk and climbed aboard, giving him a kiss. He tasted of cinnamon and oranges, and she noticed a tray of rolls, juice, and coffee on the table. Each roll had a little bite gone.

"Where did that come from?"

"Dining car."

Alarmed, she feared he'd not taken proper precautions. "Sweetheart, you can't just—"

But he shut her off with a kiss. Exasperated, she tried again, but he kept smothering. And when finally he pulled back, she found herself staring into a mischievous smile.

She gave up, breaking into a laugh, mussing his blond locks. *"What am I going to do with you?"*

His smile expanded to a grin. "I've got a suggestion . . ."

Kissing her again, he slipped his warm, sinewy arms under her nightshirt, encircling her, and soon they were nested on the seat, relishing a moment of tranquility to the gentle rocking of the train . . .

After breakfast and a shower, Angela sat drying her hair as Ian took his turn in the bath. His laptop lay open next to her—another tale of St. Patrick's Purgatory. She sighed.

She didn't want to spoil the pleasant start to their day, but if she had any hope of diverting him from his suicidal path, she had to chip away at these otherworldly delusions. And at least where St. Patrick's Cave was concerned, she had a chisel. Something she'd been researching online.

As he exited the bath in a towel, she began, "I see you spent your morning in Purgatory."

He grinned from under tousled hair. "With a little heavenly time off for good behavior. I've read everything about that cave I could find."

"What is it you're looking for?"

"Common elements in what people saw down there. I figure, the more alike the accounts, the more likely they are to be factual. Corroborating details. For instance, most descriptions of Purgatory I've read say it's located directly in front of Hell. Meaning that to reach Hell's Gates, I'll have to pass through Purgatory first. I'm trying to learn what that entails."

While he shaved, she asked, "What do you know about the Temple of Delphi?"

"Where ancient Greeks went to have their fortunes told?"

"Yes. If you recall, the fortunes were told by oracles—priestesses who fell into a trance and spoke in tongues. The temple priests would then interpret the babbling for patrons, claiming it prophesies of the god, Apollo."

"Your point?"

"I've been doing some reading myself, and I've come across some interesting facts. Historic records show Delphi was discovered in the eighth century BC. Shepherds were watering their flocks at a mountain spring and noticed the sheep bleating and acting strange. When the shepherds investigated, they felt dizzy, and one went into a trance and started jabbering.

"Word spread and people thought the spring mystical, so they built a temple over it. That led to the cult of the oracle, which lasted till the Church destroyed the temple in the fourth century AD. But it took till *this* century for scientists to finally learn what was behind the trances."

"Wine?"

She ignored him. "A spring still flows from the ruins, and researchers traced its source to an underground geologic fault. The fault emits natural gases—methane, ethane, ethylene—that travel up the water as bubbles. The gases are poisonous, and it's known some oracles died during trances. But the gases also cause hallucinations—or as the Greeks thought, prophecies."

Ian shook his head. "The visions at St. Patrick's Cave were too alike to be random hallucinations. I believe they were NDEs. So what if poisonous gas caused near-death experiences, there's no comparison. Delphi was about Mt. Olympus; St. Patrick's Cave, the Underworld."

"All relative. People approached both experiences primed by their expectations, whether of demons or gods. They were *predisposed* to see what they did. The power of suggestion."

A smile crossed Ian's lips. "You wait," he said. "Before the day is over, trust me, you're going to see things even *your* science can't explain."

FORTY-TWO

A BASEMENT FLAT IN AN OLD TENEMENT, PRAGUE 8, CZECH REPUBLIC, SAME DAY, MORNING

". . . Venice, it appears," Josef said in Polish, talking to his cell on the table beside him, video display switched off. His eyes were focused on a vial as he measured grams of white powder into it, pausing to glance at his wristwatch. "They're half an hour out. Where are you?"

"A-14, north of Bologna. I'm exhausted. All roads may lead to Rome, but they're all busy!"

"Apologies for the missteps, Hendric, they are clever, these two. Call me when you reach Venice, we should have a tight fix on them by then . . ."

FORTY-THREE

VENICE, ITALY, SAME DAY, MORNING

Angela and Ian rolled into *Stazione Ferroviaria Santa Lucia* without incident, packed, ready to exit the train. Ian put on sunglasses and a ball cap, Angela only sunglasses.

"Don't forget your hat," he reminded.

"But I just washed my hair!"

He grabbed a cap and stuck it on her. "No time to let our guard down. By now they know we pulled a fast one, and they've probably figured out how."

The sense of security she'd been relishing was gone . . .

They left for the station platform rolling their bags, ever watchful. Signs directed them to *Grande Canale*, where they descended a ramp to the *vaporetto* stop to catch a *motoscafo*—a water taxi. Angela was glad Ian knew both Italian and his way around. He picked out what looked to be a fast boat, struck a deal with the driver, and they clambered aboard, motoring off.

The morning was bright and warm, the sky cloudless, the canal busy as any metropolitan main street. Water buses, taxis, private boats, gondolas plying the jade-green waters. It was fronted by rows of multistoried, pastel-colored buildings with red tile roofs, interrupted by the occasional grandiose palace, restaurant, hotel, or dome-topped cathedral. Despite her worries, Angela was enthralled.

Ian pointed to an old Gothic palace, balconies and windows festooned with bright-orange and black flags.

"*Ca' Foscari*. Built in the 1400s at the height of the Renaissance . . ." He nodded toward a crowded open-air market, "The *Pesheria*. People have been selling fish there for a thousand years . . ." And on the opposite bank: "*Ca' d'Oro*. Golden House. It once had actual gold-plated walls."

Angela begged, "Can't we make time for a few?"

He squeezed her hand. "Trust me, the best is ahead . . ."

Coming into view now around a bend was the ocean, and a sight that left Angela breathless. A shimmering pink and white peninsula jutting out into the bay, gleaming like some elaborate wedding cake afloat on the sea. It featured an open plaza in the middle with tall obelisks and a giant bell tower. Behind was an ornate basilica—a cross between medieval church and Moorish temple, Angela decided. And on the right, a sprawling Gothic palace of filigree, pillars, arches, and Coptic crosses.[10]

They circled around, and Angela noticed that one wall of the palace ran flush to a tributary canal, creating a sheer, four-story cliff. Opposite was another palace of equal height, and connecting the two, a stone footbridge that spanned the canal at the third story.

Ian told her, "*Ponte dei Sospiri*—Bridge of Sighs. So named for the sounds prisoners used to make crossing from the *Ducale* courts to the gallows."

That was a bit of history Angela could have done without. She felt a shiver, reminded of the death sentence she and Ian carried—and of yesterday's ordeal on the lake. Suddenly she was on edge again.

They continued to a landing, docking among a myriad of watercraft and their tenders—any one a potential Sword. Ian seemed unconcerned, standing, eager to disembark.

We've told no one, Angela reasoned, *how could the Order possibly know? Get a grip!*

All the same, she accepted two large bottles of spring water from her driver, stuffing them in her shoulder bag, holding it by its straps like a weapon. Ian paid, tipping the man well to wait with their suitcases, and then taking Angela's arm, he helped her ashore.

It was low tide, and ahead of them a stone stair ran to the piazza, Ian leading the way. Angela tried to focus on the magnificent architecture coming into view, but that voice in her head was humming again, and as they reached the top of the stairs, it grew louder. The square was vast and crowded, and the idea of wading into its currents of strangers brought a knot to her stomach, the excitement of this wondrous place gone.

She pulled Ian to a halt, whispering nervously, "Please, let's be quick. And *discreet*."

He promised. Then giving her a kiss, tugging her hat brim lower, he picked up the pace. They'd hardly gone ten yards, however, when her inner voice turned into a siren. Among the crowd were a dozen gypsies greeting arrivals and working tourists. One stood out. A man in his late thirties, dark hair, dark clothing—juggling three long, sharp-looking knives, blades glinting in the sun. And spotting Angela and Ian, he made straight for them.

Her heart raced. Aside from him singling them out, something else didn't feel right. Unlike his fellow panhandlers, his face was clean-shaven, clothes neat and unwrinkled. And before Angela could think, he'd moved within striking distance, lips breaking into a sly smile.

She froze, pulling Ian to a halt again. He was slow on the uptake, maybe accustomed to seeing such spectacles here. But then realizing, he stepped protectively in front as the stranger called out in a bold voice, *"Goda l'atto, il mio bella?"*

Angela wasn't letting Ian take the brunt this time. Dropping to a crouch she spun out from behind, swinging her purse on its straps like a hammer-thrower, hurling it with all her might. It struck the man full in the chest and he went sprawling, knives clattering to the marble surface.

Onlookers gasped and moved back as more gypsies came charging over, followed by two policemen. The gypsies helped the fallen man to his feet, yammering heatedly at Angela and Ian. The man appeared unhurt, merely winded, gaping at Angela while the police tried to sort things out.

"He was attacking us!" Angela told one official, gypsies arguing their side, Ian attempting to arbitrate in Italian. After some back-and-forth the police returned the purse to Angela, the knives to the man, and sent both parties on their ways with an exasperated *"Vada! Vada! E non ritorni!"*

Ian hustled Angela off, gypsies still carping.

"So much for being discreet!" he grunted.

She kept watch over their exit, embarrassed and confused. "But how do we know he isn't *Arma Christi*?"

"The cops said he's worked the plaza for years. Lucky for us he's a known pickpocket, or we'd have been hauled in for assault."

"What was it he shouted at us?"

"He wanted to know if the pretty lady liked his act . . ."

They hurried on. As they passed one of many large obelisks on the plaza, Ian ducked behind, drawing Angela after. They waited, then peeked to see if they were being tailed. Nothing suspicious, gypsies or otherwise.

"Too spooked to go on?" Ian asked.

She hesitated.

He took her chin, raising her eyes to his. "If the Order *is* watching," he said with a grin, "they know better than to mess with us now!"

He dissolved her scowl with a kiss.

Before them stood the gleaming façade of the *Palazzo Ducale* museum. And if Ian was right, hidden among its artworks were five-hundred-year-old Secrets to the inner workings of Hell.

FORTY-FOUR

PALACE OF THE SANCTUM OFFICIUM, VATICAN CITY, ITALY, SAME DAY, MORNING

Pietro Cardinal della Roca, Prefect of the Congregation for the Doctrine of the Faith (CDF), sat at his desk, long face gathered in a frown, reading one of many thick reports piled before him.

His office was located in the same palazzo where Galileo was once made to defend his science, an impressive seat of authority. Spacious, with inlaid-bronze ceiling, crystal chandelier, lead-glass windows wrapped in heavy tapestry drapes, walls finished in mahogany, and built-in bookshelves sagging under ponderous tomes. His desk was sixteenth century hand-carved black oak with matching chair; floor covered in wall-to-wall silk Persian rug.

He set aside the report and removed his glasses, rubbing his eyes.

Once was a time when the job of safeguarding doctrine entailed little more than policing books and other printed matter for heretical content. The Church used to maintain a list of such prohibited materials, the *Index*. But now in this age of electronic publishing—websites, blogs, e-books, and all—the Office was overwhelmed. Everywhere, blasphemy and pseudo-theology rocked the Faith of Catholics still reeling from the Church's recent scandals.

"Il Dio li aiuta," Pietro muttered. But in his heart, he feared God wasn't listening.

A knock at the door broke off his gloomy thoughts. His secretary, a pinched-faced nun in a black-and-white habit, announcing an unscheduled visitor.

Pietro welcomed the interruption—until hearing the name. Lucio Cardinal Menzetti, Prefect for Economic Affairs—the office responsible for Vatican finances. The man's presence was no doubt bad news, as the

Vatican's finances were bad news, and Pietro had no intention of trimming his already gutted budget. He gave the nun a scowl. But not one to procrastinate, he followed it with a nod.

Menzetti entered quickly, shutting the door, floating across the carpet. Tall, gaunt, pasty complexion of a mortician. Indeed, he looked dourer than usual.

"Good morning, Lucio," Pietro greeted, adding with a straight face, "you're looking well."

Menzetti responded in kind, taking the chair offered.

"I apologize for my hasty visit. And you'll forgive me if I get directly to the point."

Pietro sat back, folding his arms. "Speak freely."

"You're aware of the unfortunate state of our finances."

"I am."

"Well, I must inform you of a distressing development. It appears our shortfall this quarter will exceed projections. We cannot meet obligations without curtailing programs further or liquidating assets—and I'm afraid Papa prefers the latter. He's instructed me to contact private museums. I'm to entertain bids on art in the *Museo Profano*!"

Pietro felt a pang. The Museum of the Profane, so named for its non-Christian artworks of antiquity, was one of the Vatican's most treasured and popular collections, a personal favorite.

The Prefect added in a stricken voice, "This is a catastrophe, Pietro! *The works are priceless!*"

"How did you respond?"

"With an alternative plan to cut some programs and a few marginal missions."

"And?"

"Papa rejected it. Instead, he *increased* funding to *all* our missions, *everywhere!*"

"Popes and their charities. Come between them at your peril."

"One program in particular I earmarked—a vague bursary—*Crumen pro Fidis Tutamine.*"

Pietro nodded. He was familiar with the Fund for the Defense of the Faith. "It's a CDF disbursement. I authorize it each year at Papa's discretion. But I know nothing about it, Papa won't discuss it. A private charitable mission, I've always assumed."

Menzetti leaned forward and lowered his voice. "Yes, it's classified a 'mission.' But I looked into it, and the records provide *no* description. The fund is handled in blind trust through a Swiss depositary. Contributions date back centuries, though some papacies let the bursary lapse—and that's precisely what our situation demands. It would save us millions! But Papa won't have it. I tell you, his largesse is breaking our back!"

Pietro sat reflecting, feeling Menzetti's eyes.

"Pietro, we can't let this happen, it can only lead to more such decisions! You have Papa's ear, speak with him! Make him see reason before our treasures are lost!"

"If I have Papa's ear—and that is arguable—it's in the realm of theology, not finance. Still, I share your concerns. I'll speak with him."

Looking a bit less burdened, Menzetti sat back. After a pause, he asked, "So, what do you hear of that recent murder attempt in the City?"

"No more than you, I'm sure."

Menzetti smiled, cocking his head. "Oh no, Pietro. You are too well connected, nothing misses your attention. Tell me, who was the intended victim?"

Pietro rolled his tongue along a cheek. Perhaps there was benefit to disclosing what he'd heard from one of his chambermaids, wife of a Vatican gendarme. Menzetti was an inveterate gossip. He would pass word along the Curial grapevine, adding to sentiments already building against Vatican Security Director Antonio Ponti—a man Pietro felt had acquired too much power in recent years.

"I tell you in confidence," he said, guaranteeing the man's loose lips. "A young couple was involved. A woman, and that American priest who got us into that brawl in Côte d'Ivoire a few years back—Ian Baringer. Except, he is no longer a priest."

Menzetti's eyes narrowed. "Maybe the murder attempt was the slavers seeking revenge."

"I suspect a fresh batch of scoundrels. It seems Baringer was up to some shady business in the Caribbean. It led to a murder, and he and his mistress fled here. Of course his old comrade-in-arms, Director Ponti, welcomed them with open arms."

"God help us, we need no more scandals!"

"We do not. Ponti behaves as if he runs the City. Yesterday he was seen prowling the Secret Archives—unsupervised. Another matter I shall take up with Papa."

"Please, Pietro, one crisis at a time! Speak to Papa of mine first." And rising, offering his thanks, he turned and floated back out the door.

Pietro sat for a while staring at the stacks of paper on his desk. Then softly he echoed, "One crisis at a time . . ."

FORTY-FIVE

PALAZZO DUCALE MUSEUM, VENICE, ITALY, SAME DAY, MORNING

After the bustle of the plaza, Angela was relieved to find attendance light inside the museum, people apparently opting to be outdoors this beautiful day. She welcomed the quiet, able to relax a notch to take in the *Ducale's* breathtaking beauty. Like one continuous work of art—luxurious halls of arched ceilings, frescoes, and statuary.

As they made their way toward the Bosch exhibit, Ian picked up a brochure, reading aloud:

> "Hieronymus Bosch was perhaps the most famous and controversial of all Early Renaissance painters. Born in 1450 in the Hapsburg town of Hertogenbosch where he took his name, he died sixty-six years later, and little is known about him in between. Like his paintings, he remains an enigma.
>
> "His works are unique among medieval artists, unlike anything that came before. Provocative, surreal, with mystical and biblical qualities reflecting the pessimism and fear of the era—a period of great social, religious, and political upheaval.
>
> "Bosch's influence has resounded over the centuries, seen in artists as diverse as William Blake and Salvador Dalí. He is best known for spectacular triptychs—large, three-panel altar pieces painted on wood . . ."

Soon a large banner proclaimed *BOSCH LOGGIA,* and they'd arrived at the gallery. Seventeen items on exhibit, it said in Italian and English, including seldom-seen works on loan from other museums around Europe. And again, few patrons—a small tour group of elderly women.

The paintings were displayed side-by-side along one immense wall, approximately ten feet apart. Ian and Angela approached the first, a seven-by-five-foot center panel of a triptych entitled *The Last Judgment.*[11]

The image was so detailed and complex, Angela could make little sense of it from a distance. But as she drew closer, she grimaced. A panorama of sadism even more grotesque and confusing than the painting Ian had shown her on his laptop yesterday.

At the very top was Christ sitting serenely in Heaven above the fray, presiding over the damnations of Hell below. Down in the Abyss, a horrific, disturbing nightmare. Swarms of demons and bizarre, part-animal/part-inanimate creatures torturing countless naked souls. The abuse was as perplexing as it was obscene.

Angela grunted, "Bosch was demented!"

Ian shook his head. "He wasn't trying to titillate. This is a visual sermon meant to frighten sinners into rectitude. The tortures reflect the nature of the sins, if only we understood . . ."

After studying it closely for a time, they moved on, Ian looking for specific works from his research, he said.

They stopped next at a flat, five-foot square of wood on which were painted five circles—a large one in the center and smaller ones of equal size in the corners. *Tondos,* Ian called them. Each was filled with images. A label read: *Tabletop of the Seven Deadly Sins and Four Last Things.*[12]

"It's a real tabletop," Ian said. "Bosch was making a visual pun, 'tabling' the Seven Deadly Sins."

He pointed to the center circle, a medieval morality play in cartoon, with examples of the deadly sins arranged in frames around God's all-seeing Eye. The Eye contained the risen Christ, under which was the Latin inscription *Cave, cave, Dominus videt.*

"Beware, beware, the Lord sees," Ian translated.

The examples of the Seven Sins also had Latin captions.

In the bottom frame, two men quarreled over a woman—*Ira,* Wrath, Ian said. Clockwise, a dog coveted a bone in his master's hand as the man stared with *Invidia,* Envy, at a rich falconer. Next, a bailiff took a bribe, *Avaritia,* Avarice; followed by a woman plying her family with food, abetting their *Gula,* Gluttony; then a napping priest being admonished by a nun for his *Accidia,* Sloth; and a couple being interrupted in a tryst, *Luxuria,* Lust. And lastly, a woman admiring herself in a mirror, the most deadly sin of all—*Superbia.* Pride.

Angela examined the smaller tondos in the corners. Upper left, *Death;* then *Judgment; Heaven;* and *Hell.*

Ian took special note of the Hell tondo—seven scenes of the damned being punished for each respective Deadly Sin.[13] He puzzled his face.

"Which sins are which? And how do the punishments relate to the crime?"

Angela pointed to an image of demons surprising a naked couple in bed. "Lust, I suppose. But I don't get the punishment. Or how it fits."

Next was a man in a tent attacked by a demon.

"Gluttony," she guessed, "only because there's food on the table. No idea what that punishment is, either . . ."

Then came hellhounds snapping at people half-buried in the earth; a demon with a knife gutting a man atop a stove; people stewing in a cauldron; another couple harassed by another demon. And in the center, a devil chef tenderizing a hapless soul.

Angela shrugged. "I don't see *any* correlations."

Ian agreed, looking vexed.

They walked back to re-examine *The Last Judgment* painting, and after a time Ian swore under his breath, dissatisfaction in his eyes. He drew Angela's attention to the left side of the massive panel, halfway up, near the very edge—the image of an angel escorting away a soul while a demon took aim with a crossbow. The figures were so tiny, they were nearly lost amid all the outrageousness.[14]

"If I hadn't viewed this up close," Ian said, "I would have missed it."

"What? A lucky soul plucked from Hell?"

"No. According to the Bible, damnation is forever. Bosch wouldn't make that mistake." He swept his hand across the macabre landscape. "This isn't a depiction of Hell—this is *Purgatory.* Notice the difference between these images and those we saw in the Hell tondo?"

She had. "These are much better drawn. More precise, more detailed. The Hell tondo was simplistic and vague."

"Because," Ian ventured, "Bosch was *guessing* at Hell. He never saw it. Like what Zack Niemand said about Dante and Milton, Bosch was afraid to go beyond Purgatory. What he Knew of Hell he got secondhand. And like Dante and Milton, he probably got most of it wrong . . . I don't know how much I can rely on these paintings."

Angela paused to let his disappointment settle, then offered gently, "Maybe you shouldn't rely on them at all. Maybe Bosch never traveled to the Afterlife. Maybe these paintings are just a bunch of silly medieval fantasies."

She was surprised to see a dry smile cross his lips.

"Oh *really*?" he said.

Taking her hand, he led her to the next Bosch artwork, stopping in front, extending his arm like Moses presenting the Israelites with the Promised Land.

"Then how," he asked, "do you explain *this*?"

Angela gasped. On the wall before her was a painting perhaps a foot and a half wide and four high. Small in size, comparatively, yet colossal in its implications. It depicted the souls of the saved rising toward a celestial tunnel, the end of which glowed with the brilliance of Paradise. Its title, *Ascent of the Blessed.*[15]

"This," Ian said, "is what people claim to see during an NDE. This is what *I* saw. And obviously Bosch saw the same thing—*over five hundred years ago.* How do you account for *that*?"

She couldn't. Nor could she escape a terrible sense of disquiet stealing over her. She wanted to leave, but Ian wasn't finished. One last enigmatic work left to see . . .

They arrived before the final item in the Bosch exhibit, and Ian gaped at it, spellbound. He'd never seen this before, no idea it even existed. Not a triptych or tabletop, a canvas. Not a painting, a drawing in pen and chalk. Large, four feet by seven. *The Woods that Hears and Sees.*[16]

Next to it on the wall was a data sheet describing the image as a working sketch for a much larger painting lost to fire long ago.

"Arson," Ian guessed, not having to suggest by whom.

In keeping with Bosch's style, the drawing was surreal—an old, withered tree, the side of its trunk missing as if blown off in a storm. It stood in a field amid seven disembodied eyes. Birds nested in its branches, an owl sat in a hollow of its trunk, and a fox curled inside a cavity at its base. Behind was a wood flanked by two giant, human ears.

"What does it mean?" Angela asked.

Ian studied it, unsure. Then suddenly he felt the blood drain from his face, and he gasped, *"I'll be damned.* Remember the Bible story Lucien told us? God splitting the Tree of Knowledge, planting the Good half in Heaven, Evil half in Hell? I think *this* is one of the halves!"

Angela squinted at the sketch. "How do you figure?"

"It fits with the medieval symbolism I've been reading about. The seven eyes in the field represent the seven Realms of Heaven and Hell. The fox is the cunning it takes to find the Tree. The owl, its Knowledge. And Bosch cast the Tree's fruit as birds—icons of elusiveness—suggesting how difficult it is to acquire the Knowledge."

"And the giant ears?"

"Symbols of wariness—Bosch warning that the pursuit of Knowledge can be dangerous."

They continued to mull the drawing, then Ian heard Angela inhale. Her face darkened and she whispered, "Maybe there's more to it. What if Bosch meant the fox to be *Arma Christi* guarding the Knowledge, and the Eyes & Ears its spies!"

Suddenly Ian had the unnerving sensation that the eyes and ears in the picture were now spying on *them*. He'd seen enough. Grabbing Angela, he hurriedly retraced their steps through the loggia.

"So," she panted, "what did we learn here?"

He turned for a last look. "I'll admit, it doesn't seem Bosch left much of a roadmap. But I can't help thinking there's a message somewhere in all this. Something important I'm missing . . ."

FORTY-SIX

VIGONZA, ITALY, SAME DAY, LATE MORNING

"There," Angela said, pointing through the windshield to a cozy little trattoria on the left. "How about that one?"

Ian pulled around behind, tucking their car into an alley, letting the engine run as they watched and waited. Since leaving the museum a few hours ago, they'd rented a car and driven west, no destination in mind, simply wanting to put the cul-de-sac confines of Venice behind. And having had but a few pastries for breakfast, they were looking for a fast, safe lunch.

The trattoria seemed a good choice to Angela. Corner of a quiet town square, full windows front and side, good visibility from within. After ten minutes of precaution, they slapped on sunglasses and hats and hustled inside.

They were early for lunch, few diners. And from the looks of them, all locals. Ian picked a table near the back door to afford a quick exit if needed, and a waiter brought menus and a bottle of chianti.

"Our nerves could use this," Ian said, pouring.

Indeed, after a few sips of wine on an empty stomach, Angela felt a welcome glow. The most relaxed she'd felt since the train.

But short-lived. They'd hardly placed their orders when in walked a heavyset, hunch-shouldered man in a white suit and wire-rim glasses. Tall, fortyish, long brown hair, face pasty-pale, nose bulbous, eyes small. He sat at the bar near the kitchen service window, ordered a Campari, and opened a newspaper, holding it close as if nearsighted. There was nothing unusual about him, aside from the fact that he was alone and didn't appear Italian—his paper was in a language Angela didn't recognize. And he never paid them so much as a glance.

All the same, Angela felt uneasy. But seeing Ian appraise and dismiss him, she said nothing, her sixth sense having embarrassed her once already today.

As their salads came, Ian glanced at his watch. *"Damn,* I nearly forgot—I told Antonio I'd call at noon." Pushing back his chair, he looked out the window.

"We're in luck—a phone booth, land line. Go ahead, I won't be long." And he was gone.

She stole another glance at the stranger. Other than to take an occasional drink, he didn't budge. And never turned a page . . . She changed chairs to where she could keep an eye on both him and Ian.

"Ciao." Antonio's voice came through. *"Am I glad to hear from you!"*

"Likewise, my friend."

"Are you calling from a safe place?"

"A land line. We're in between destinations."

"Good. I got your e-mail. Sorry I'm so hard to reach, I've been busy." He sounded stressed. *"This Lough Derg incident is very bad news. You and Angela must return here at once."*

"Thanks, but I think we finally gave them the slip."

"Then I'll send bodyguards. I've two good men I trust."

"No, changing our routes midflight seemed to work. We'll just keep moving till the lab's ready."

"Mio Dio—you're continuing your experiments?"

"One last NDE. And if it goes well, I hope to use it to get *Arma Christi* off our backs."

"You have a plan?"

"The beginnings. You recall what I wrote you about the old photos of the Bosch paintings."

"Yes. And you have a point. I know of another instance where the Order gave up on a cause it knew was lost . . . Dante."

"Dante!"

"Well, not Dante, per se—his Divine Comedy. *The Order poisoned Dante shortly after he finished the manuscript. Then like with Bosch, it focused on destroying Dante's work, believing it held Secrets about the Afterlife."*

"But it gave up?"

"Eventually. You see, Dante wrote the Comedy *a hundred years before the*

printing press, when manuscripts were hand-scribed. But it was so popular, despite the Order's efforts, copies kept appearing. One survived to be printed, and finally the hounding stopped. Who knows, if printing had been around for Dante, maybe the Order would have spared his life."

Ian felt a flash of optimism, trying to catch Angela's eye. But she seemed preoccupied.

"I assume, then, your plan is to tell your story on your TV network?"

"Yes. If what that Sword, O'Farrell, said is true, it's their big fear. Maybe if I can show the world the Afterlife is real, the Order will have no reason to silence us anymore. Why smash the bottle once the genie's out?"

"You forget, Ian, it's not just the existence of the Afterlife the Order guards. It's the Secrets. Secrets like Merton's Ultimate Reality. I daresay his death was no accident. And as long as you're alive, you're a threat to acquire more Secrets."

"For a time, maybe. But once people learn of my experiments, others will follow—like in the Middle Ages. *Arma Christi* can't stop them all. The Secrets will leak and the Order will be reduced to a bunch of zealots without a cause."

"This isn't the Middle Ages, my friend. People will demand proof before risking their lives in costly experiments. And how do you prove something spiritual? How do you prove to the world the Afterlife is real?"

Inside the trattoria Angela kept watch from behind her sunglasses, finishing her salad as the tables filled with customers. All regulars it appeared, all indifferent to the strange man at the bar. So far, nothing overtly suspicious out of him, Ian still on the phone.

But then abruptly he emptied his drink, set down his paper, and rose, Angela tensing. He turned in the direction of the restrooms, however, and she was able to breathe again. Until she saw him amble past the kitchen's service window where two steaming plates of pasta had arrived, a waiter snatching them up, delivering them to *her* table.

She stared down at the savory-looking dishes, heart thumping. They appeared perfectly fine. Plump, tempting dumplings of ravioli in thick marinara sauce, sprinkled with grated parmesan, smelling of fresh garlic, basil, oregano . . .

Ian was *still* on the phone. She motioned to him but he held up a forefinger, asking for more time. Then the stranger returned, ordered another drink, and resumed reading.

"Since you are so hell-bent on seeing your parents," Antonio continued, concern in his voice, *"I must send you something. Something I stumbled on in the Archives that may help—though I fear it will be blasphemous for you."*

"I'll take the chance."

"I feared you would. But this has to be the last of it, Ian. If I show you another route to your parents, you must abandon these suicidal NDEs of yours . . ."

Angela's eyes continued the circuit—man at the bar, Ian in the phone booth, meals congealing in tomato sauce. Until at last Ian rejoined her.

"You shouldn't have waited," he said. "Sorry I was so long, but I've got great news . . ."

Angela was scarcely listening. The stranger had just downed his drink, and she tensed again as he tossed off some bills, tucked the paper under his arm, and exited the trattoria. She hurried to the window, removing her sunglasses, watching him cross the street.

For a moment it seemed her instincts had been wrong. But then just as she began to turn away, he stopped, angling to look back, eyes meeting hers. *Cold, telling eyes.* A chill shot through her and she spun to see Ian lifting a bite of pasta to his lips.

"NO!" she cried, rushing, knocking the fork from his hand, upsetting the table. Everything crashed to the floor, wine, pasta splattering, restaurant coming to a standstill.

Ian leaped up, eyes and mouth agape. Then he pulled out his wallet, stuffed money into the stunned waiter's hand, grabbed Angela, and swept her out the door.

FORTY-SEVEN

VIGONZA, ITALY, SAME DAY, EARLY AFTERNOON

A block from the restaurant behind an abandoned building, the heavyset man with wire-rim glasses sat at the wheel of a car, speaking into a cell phone on the dash. As he talked, he carefully placed what appeared to be a little spray bottle of breath freshener into a small metal canister, closing its air-tight lid, slipping it in his coat pocket.

". . . I was able to season their meal," he said in Polish. "A rather virulent, fast-acting strain. But they didn't bite."

"They order and don't eat?" a male voice retorted.

"The woman suspected me, I could tell. I finally left, and they left right after. It's useless now, I'm compromised. Send another."

"There is no other, Hendric!"

"There is *you,* Josef . . ."

FORTY-EIGHT

A RURAL HIGHWAY, NORTH VENETO ITALY, SAME DAY, AFTERNOON

Ian and Angela sped past rolling fields of freshly plowed earth, terrain growing ever hillier, snow-crested Alps looming in the distance. Ian was at the wheel, Angela with a half-consumed sandwich in her lap, by-product of a pit stop for gas.

". . . I don't see it," Ian was saying. "How could they find us? I know we weren't followed. And that guy was there *before* my phone call."

"I don't know how, I just know . . ." She glanced behind, expecting a car to come roaring up any moment like something out of a gangster movie. But nothing, supporting Ian's belief that she'd overreacted. Again.

He wagged his head. "You're holding me to a double standard. You won't accept my NDEs, but I'm supposed to accept your sixth sense?"

"That guy at the bar was no spirit, Ian. He was a *real* person in the *real* world and he walked right by our plates!"

"You know what I mean."

She sighed. "Sixth sense may sound supernatural, but it's nothing more than subliminal awareness."

"How so?"

"There are always things going on around us that we miss but our subconscious picks up on. People give off subtle cues. A fleeting expression or eye movement. Slight change in posture, a hint of pheromones. And believe me, something about that guy back there *reeked*."

"But you don't reject the idea of a sixth sense, do you?"

She paused, troubled that she couldn't reconcile her own intuitive experiences with what she'd just said. Particularly her feelings at the museum earlier, which still left her spooked.

"I suppose not."

"Then it's not asking too much for you to keep an open mind about *my* supernatural experiences."

"Fine. But my sixth sense has no clue where you're taking us. *Now* will you tell me?"

He grinned. "How about the Alps for a little skiing?"

"*That* was Antonio's advice? You aren't serious!"

They were both skiers. He'd learned while in Europe, she in high school. And they'd spent a wonderful weekend together in Tahoe once. It sounded too good to be true.

"Not pleasure skiing, unfortunately. But what if I told you there's a way for me to see my parents again *without* another NDE?"

Again it sounded too good.

"If you recall, Antonio told us that back in the Middle Ages people had three paths to the Afterlife. Gateways, like St. Patrick's Cave; potions, like Devil's Tears; and necromancy—communing with spirits."

Now what madness am I in for?

"Gateways, potions, and NDEs all push the limits of death to take you to the Other Side and back. Necromancy works in reverse. It uses an alchemic formula to bring the dead *to you*."

She shuddered. And yet, if this harebrained alternative could keep him from another NDE, buy her more time to wrestle his neurosis . . . She asked, "But weren't all records of necromancy destroyed?"

"Maybe not. Antonio found something in the Vatican Archives."

"The formula?"

"No, but hopefully a way to recover it. A long lost map to where a copy might be. Assuming it's genuine, the map has a bizarre history. It dates back to 1639 and a French monk by the name of Polycarpe de la Riviere."

The name meant nothing to Angela.

"Polycarpe was a professor at Montpellier University, and he wrote a paper on necromancy. The practice was all but wiped out by then, and his work contained one of the last known formulas. The Inquisition got wind, so Polycarpe took his paper and fled for Vienna. But on his way through the Alps he ran into a storm and was forced to take refuge in a cave."

Angela grimaced, and Ian hastened to add, "Just a regular cave, no gateway. Two chambers. A main room adjoined by a smaller room through a narrow opening. Polycarpe knew the Inquisition was on his trail, and certain they'd destroy the formula if they caught him, he copied it on the wall of the smaller room. Then he hid the opening with rocks, and when the storm passed he set out for Vienna again.

"But the Inquisition was waiting, he was arrested, his paper burned, and he was put on trial. Despite torture, he kept the location of the cave secret. Then just before he was executed, he made a map to it and its hidden room, and passed it to a confidant."

Angela guessed, "The map ended up in the Archives."

"But how it got there is an even *stranger* story. It went missing for exactly three centuries, until the winter of 1939, when a man named Otto Rahn uncovered it in the library of a French monastery. Rahn was a Nazi in the *Ahnenerbe Büro,* the Heritage Bureau, working under Heinrich Himmler. Himmler, as you probably know, was a huge believer in the supernatural, chasing after things like the Spear of Jesus, the Sudarium, the Holy Grail."

Angela recalled that the Nazis had an infatuation with the occult. "*Raiders of the Lost Ark.*"

She meant it as a joke, but Ian didn't laugh.

"Point of fact, the underlying theme of that movie was dead-on accurate. The Nazis were seeking mystical relics and icons for their new Blood Religion. The idea was to weave them into a pseudo-history to give the religion authenticity.

"But Himmler's interest went way beyond propaganda. He wanted the items for their alleged powers. The necromantic formula, for instance. He was convinced it could be used to divine the future. And hearing Rahn found Polycarpe's map, he was ecstatic. He ordered Rahn to memorize the map and send him the original by secret courier, then find the cave and retrieve the formula.[17]

"Whether Rahn succeeded is a mystery. He died alone in the Alps of unknown causes March 13, 1939. At the hands of the Order, Antonio suspects."

"And the map?"

"It seems the Order stepped in again. The courier made it all the way to Berlin and was crossing the street to Himmler's office when he was run down by a car. His pouch with the map was knocked to the gutter, and by luck a priest found it, who gave it to his bishop, who passed it on to the Vatican."

"Antonio is sending you the map?"

"A copy, by e-mail."

"But I thought necromancy was a black art. Didn't Antonio say it's condemned by the Church?"

"It is. He's sticking his neck out for me again. But if this works, I won't have to go through another NDE. I'll be able to speak to my parents' spirits—hopefully see them."

She bit her lip. "And just where is this cave?"

"On an Austrian mountain near a ski resort. We'll pick up equipment, find a place to stay, and download the map."

They drove on, winding steadily up toward the white-tipped peaks, the sky clouding.

The view was spectacular, but Angela hardly noticed. Taking another look at the empty road behind, she pulled her jacket tighter.

Stolen Nazi booty. Ancient lost map. Formula to raise the dead.

Her sixth sense was flaring again.

FORTY-NINE

A SECLUDED CHALET IN THE TYROLEAN ALPS, MAYRHOFEN, AUSTRIA, NEXT MORNING

Angela awoke to hear Ian in the kitchen, sun streaming through the bedroom window of their little cabin. Cozy and rustic. Walls, floor, and ceiling all pinewood, Christmassy scent in the air.

It had taken them until nightfall yesterday to reach the Mayrhofen ski resort, slowed by a snowstorm. And for all Angela's fears and watchfulness, it didn't appear they'd been followed.

They'd learned of this chalet stopping to rent equipment for today's expedition. A private, fully-equipped, ski-in/ski-out villa tucked in a sparse woods on one of the resort's main peaks, Mt. Eggalm.

With the storm last night, Angela had seen little of the area, and sliding from bed she tiptoed across cold wood, parting the curtains to behold a spectacular, sunny vista. To her right, a panoramic mountain range extending in unbroken saw teeth to the horizon. Somewhere among its serrated crests, Ian believed, lay Polycarpe's cave.

To her left, picturesque Mayrhofen, a quintessential Alpine village cupped in a bowl-like valley. Stone church with steep-pitched roof and tall spike of bell tower, patchwork quilt of chalets, shops, and gingerbread-style *bier* taverns. Smoke billowed from chimneys, people up and shoveling sidewalks, plow trucks working the roads.

Maybe it was the spell of the Alps, or just the thin air, but up here the threat of *Ordo Arma Christi* felt more distant, Ian's outlandish plan to reach his parents somehow less far-fetched.

She followed the scent of coffee, finding Ian at a table with his laptop. On-screen was the image he'd downloaded from Antonio last night—yellowed parchment with jumbled lines and scribbled Latin phrases. It bore a heading in French that appeared to have been added at a later date, scripted in different ink, by a different hand: *Là où fût cachée la Gramaryé de Polycarpe.*

" 'Where Polycarpe hid his black magic,' " Ian had said.

Angela had gone to bed doubting the maze would get them anywhere but lost. This morning, however, Ian greeted her with a confident smile.

"I pinpointed the cave and plotted our route. Not far!"

Open on the table was a color trail guide of the area. Ian tapped his finger on a mountainside with a number of ski runs winding down its face like strands of spaghetti, broken by the occasional straight line of a chairlift.

"We're here," he said, "at the bottom of Mt. Eggalm." He shifted his finger to a higher peak behind that featured no marked trails or lifts. "The cave is up here, at the top of Mt. Grüblspitze. Eggalm has chairlifts front and back, but we'll have to ascend Grüblspitze on foot."

Angela judged it a trek of about a mile up steep-looking passes. Though she kept herself in shape, this was more ambitious than expected, not to mention the idea of skiing off-trail past resort boundaries where there were always hidden hazards in the snow. Nor did she relish the thought of exploring some unknown, dank cave with the possibility of *Arma Christi* lurking.

Ian read her mind. "We've had no trouble since Ireland."

"No trouble *we know of.* Do we hire a guide?"

"Grüblspitze is mostly open terrain, and Polycarp's map is clear enough. A few sticky wickets, but nothing too tough. Can't get lost, we just follow our tracks back."

"And what if we get stuck in one of those wickets?"

"Worst case, we call Mayrhofen ski patrol. I keyed their emergency number into our cells."

It seemed he'd thought of everything. Laid out in the living room was the equipment they'd acquired last night—two sets of snowshoes, all-terrain cross-country skis, boots, poles, and warm ski clothing. Also knapsacks packed with basic supplies—water, lunches, and a digital camera to record the necromantic formula, should they find it.

Ian glanced at the clock. "7:30. Chairlifts are open . . ."

Downing a quick breakfast, they made a circuit of the windows to ensure the coast was clear. Fresh snow made the job easier, *any* tracks suspicious. But there were none, and suiting up, they donned knapsacks with snowshoes attached, stepped outside into their skis, and set off.

The air was crisp, refreshing, the sky cloudless, and Angela was relieved to see few other skiers, no lines at the lifts. As planned, they rode the main chair to the summit, hopped off, and prepared to ski down the back bowl.

Angela paused, gazing across the divide at their objective. Mt. Grüblspitze was a series of broad snowfields separated by horizontal bands of shear rock. Like some haphazard layer cake. And while there appeared to be gaps through most bands, the mountain was girdled high up by an impassible-looking belt, no visible access to the crest above where the cave allegedly lay.

Ian followed her eyes. "Not to worry. Polycarp's map shows the passes he took, and I matched it to a Google Earth image of Grüblspitze."

Another thought struck her. "Christ, Ian—we'll be targets in a shooting gallery out there! A sniper this side could pick us off at will!"

He shook his head. "That's not the Order's way. Remember what Antonio said, its method is the accident."

If that distinction was mean to reassure, it didn't . . .

Behind them, riding up alone on the Eggalm chairlift was a heavyset man in white parka, skis, and backpack. He held a phone to his ear, staring over fogged glasses at a GPS device in his other hand; gloves, snowshoes, and poles on the seat next to him. He did not look happy.

"You should have taken this," he snapped in Polish. "You're the athlete. And I've no experience with these chemicals—I'm out of my element on all accounts!"

Listening to rebuttal, he twisted his face, replying, "Yes, but only a plum for me if it *is* the formula they seek. Assuming it exists! And assuming I don't break my neck!"

Angela shadowed Ian as they slalomed down the back side of Eggalm, up to their knees in powder. They had the slopes virtually to themselves, and she felt invigorated, rejuvenated, carving a fresh trail, genuflecting through the turns in their cross-country skis, alive and clear-headed in the brisk air.

They soon arrived at the base of the mountain, gliding past the return chairlift to the rope barricades that bordered the resort. Angela checked behind, not a soul. But she could see Ian was all eyes ahead, gazing up at the formidable heights of Grüblspitze. If he was to be believed, hidden somewhere among these granite clefts lay another route to his fantastic goal.

FIFTY

THE TYROLEAN ALPS, AUSTRIA, SAME DAY, MID-MORNING

Angela was exhausted. Navigating even the lower levels of Grüblspitze was proving more of a challenge than Ian had predicted. They'd switched to snowshoes, skis strapped across their backs, deep drifts requiring frequent stops in the thin air. Angela had bogged down twice, needing Ian's long arm and ski pole to haul her out.

"On the positive side," he'd panted, "we'll be able to ski down."

It was all that kept her going.

They plodded on for more than an hour. Best she could tell, no one was tailing them, though her perspective was limited by the up-and-down terrain.

She'd just turned for another look back when Ian abruptly stopped, causing her to plow into him. It nearly toppled them both, and she felt his arms steady her as she looked past into a crevasse—cliffs of ice vanishing into bottomless dark.

He inched them back.

"Was *this* on Google image?" she gasped, heart beating like a timpani. The fissure was at least ten yards wide, splitting the mountain side-to-side without apparent end.

"I, I misread it. From the aerial view I took it for a logging trail . . ." He pointed left. "But if we just follow it, there's a crossing point."

He moved on and she trailed after, legs rubbery. The chasm eventually narrowed and the snow closed over. Then thirty yards ahead Angela saw it reopen after passing a lone tower of rock, wider than before, stretching out of sight. She was relieved when Ian made no attempt to cross. But when they reached the halfway point, he stopped.

"No," she huffed, wagging her head adamantly. "Snow bridge . . . collapse under us . . ."

He removed his gloves and pulled out Polycarpe's map, pointing to one of its many abstract scribbles that made no sense to her. "This is that spire of rock over there," he said, directing her eyes to the granite tower across the divide. "It marks the spot where Polycarpe's path crosses the gorge. There's a solid ridge under the snow here, Google Earth clearly shows it."

Taking the map, she squinted at it. And looking up again, she was appalled to see Ian edge out across the snow bridge, probing with his pole. Before she could even cry out, she watched horrorstruck as he suddenly pitched forward and vanished.

She froze, no sound but her hammering heart. Then as if from the bottom of a well, a sheepish *"I'm okay, I'm okay . . ."*

Stunned, relieved, she watched him struggle to his feet, neck-deep in a drift. He tramped around like a man stomping grapes, unable to get traction, swearing, finally making his way to the other side, head-to-toe in white.

Angela just gaped at him. He looked like a snowman. A red-faced, humiliated snowman. Then for some reason—the release of pent-up stress, light-headedness from the altitude—she began to laugh. Uncontrollably.

"Ooo-hoo-hoo!" she howled, joined by a chorus of rollicking echoes. Each time she recovered enough to steal a glance at him, it sent her into another peal, and by the time she'd laughed herself out, he'd found a more level route back to her, standing hands on hips.

"Would you find it so funny," he snapped, "if I'd fallen into the crevasse?"

"Yeah," she snapped back. "And it would serve you right, too! Maybe I'm getting used to the idea of you killing yourself."

Scowling, he pulled her to him and she felt his lips wet and bracingly cold against hers.

They pushed on, and an uneventful hour later were in direct view of the summit. Only to find their way blocked by a twenty-foot plateau of granite. Too sheer to scale, it spanned the entire mountain face. Angela saw no way around.

Ian pointed across the top of the plateau to an open slope of snow. Beyond was the crest of the mountain, a ridge of immense rock slabs heaved up side-by-side like a crooked bookshelf.

"The cave's at the base of that crest," he said, excited. "Come on, there's a pass through this."

Dubious, she followed. But again he proved right. They soon came upon a near-hidden chute that cut through the plateau like a winding, white river. Thirty feet wide on average, bordered by dark, sharp-angled granite ledges and flat-topped formations like some hellish art gallery.

It was eerily silent inside, a meandering ascent through a catacomb. Rounding the first bend Angela looked back, walls seeming to close in, ledges interlocking like opposable claws. This was by far the most arduous leg of the climb yet, but with Ian's help, and using the outcrops as handrails, she finally exited the other side, puffing.

"Just a bit farther . . ." Ian encouraged.

A gentle slope now, fortunately, enabling her to regain her breath. As they neared the base of the summit, however, she saw another complication.

The cliff was riddled with crevices and cavities, the angle of the sun turning each into the potential mouth of a cave.

She grumbled, "I'd like to know how Polycarpe found it in a blizzard!"

Ian studied the map, and pointed right. "This way . . ."

They made a crag to crag search, Angela running out of energy and patience. But at last Ian gave a whoop, shedding his backpack in front of a four-foot-high aperture.

Until now Angela had put little stock in Ian's map or plan, thinking they'd gain nothing more today than blisters. But suddenly faced with the reality of this blind alley, she heard that voice again, the knot returning to her stomach.

She scrutinized the mountainside below. Desolate as ever, no trace of life, no excuse to back out.

Ian helped her shed her equipment, planting their skis and poles side-by-side at the entrance, ready to go.

"Just in case," he said. Then, handing her a flashlight, he ducked into the hole.

Angela took a last look around, then swore and followed.

FIFTY-ONE

NEAR THE SUMMIT OF MT. GRÜBLSPITZE, TYROLEAN ALPS, AUSTRIA, SAME DAY, NOON

No sooner had her eyes adjusted than Angela heard Ian groan. She saw, too. If this were indeed Polycarpe's refuge, it wasn't the lost, secret crypt they'd envisioned.

Roughly twenty feet wide and forty deep, it was littered with refuse—snack-food wrappers, beer cans, bottles, broken glass, and the blackened cinders of many a campfire. The walls were coated with graffiti in a variety of languages, the rear of the cave chest-high with heavy rocks and more garbage, wall-to-wall. The sordidness added to Angela's discomfort, and she felt certain that Polycarpe's formula, were it ever here, had long been vandalized.

Ian, however, was undeterred. Setting his light on a ledge, he rolled up his sleeves and began clearing. He concentrated on the left wall, where the map showed an opening to another chamber. Angela pitched in, anxious to finish. It was already noon, Mayrhofen chairlifts closing at 4:00, and she refused to spend the night in this dreadful place. Thankfully Ian hadn't raised the prospect.

An hour passed, Angela checking outside periodically, no signs of pursuit. They took a quick lunch, spent another weary hour, and she was close to a sit-down strike when Ian let out a cheer. In the beam of his flashlight, two feet above grade, the hint of an opening in the wall . . .

They redoubled their efforts, soon exposing a small tunnel. And at last, the remaining rubble cleared, Ian turned to her with a hopeful grin.

"The moment of Truth," he said, teeth and eyes gleaming in his dirty face like a coal miner's.

He dropped and snaked in.

"Another room, all right!" he called back excitedly. "No litter—just a layer of dust!"

Kneeling, she shined her light in, unable to see him. The atmosphere smelled stale, dank, perhaps last inhaled by human lungs nearly four hundred years ago.

I'm breathing the same air as Polycarpe! she thought with a shiver.

The image of a mad medieval monk in her head, she flattened, closed her eyes, held her breath, and wriggled in. The passage was narrow, she could feel herself clenching. But then strong hands took hold and pulled her through.

"Tight fit," Ian said, lifting her up, brushing her off.

She caught her breath, seeing his light dart around. A small chamber. Eight feet high, twice as deep and wide. No signs it had ever been disturbed. And no signs of any formula.

Until Ian directed his light back above the mouth of the tunnel . . .

Again Angela felt the air empty out of her. Starting near the ceiling and ending just above the tunnel mouth was an ominous-looking transcription. Lengthy, complicated calligraphy in what she took to be Latin. Also weird symbols she didn't recognize—sharp-angled stick letters, like a primitive alphabet.

Ian moved his light first across the top lines. "Old Latin," he said. Then across the stick letters. "And ancient Norse runes."

He began to read, words sounding like something out of *The Exorcist*. "*'A fronte praecipitium, a tergo lupi—'* "

"Not now!" she said. "Take pictures."

"Right, right . . ."

He rifled his knapsack for the digital camera. Then positioning himself where he could frame the entire formula, he aimed and clicked.

Nothing. No flash.

"Damn!" Again he tried, and failed. "It was working before we left!"

"Did you bring a pen, some paper?"

"No."

"Your cell phone—it takes pictures."

"Too risky."

"The signal can't penetrate rock."

Passing the camera to her, he pulled his phone from his jacket, flipping it on, mumbling, "I hope these are clear enough . . ." But before he could shoot, Angela got the camera working.

"You had the power switch on standby," she told him, handing it back. "Hurry—this place gives me the creeps."

This time it worked. He took shots from every angle, checking the results on-screen. Satisfied, he motioned Angela to the tunnel and they crawled out to the main cave.

She made straight for the exit only to realize she was alone, Ian back gathering stones.

"What are you doing!"

"We can't just leave the formula for anyone to find."

Groaning, she pitched in once more . . .

It was 3:30 by the time they finished. A half hour to make the chairlift, too close for comfort. They grabbed their things and scrambled outside, late afternoon sun blinding off the snow. Angela squinted as she stepped into her skis. Then she heard Ian swear, and she saw, too, heart freezing.

A *third* set of snowshoe prints trailing theirs up the mountain. The tracks stopped outside the cave, turned, and continued upslope, disappearing behind a craggy spur.

"Someone out for a hike," Ian whispered, looking around nervously.

"Traveling off-trail, and *alone*?"

He grabbed her arm. "Quick, the cave."

"No way I'm crawling back in that hole! Come on, at least make it hard for him—"

She righted her skis and launched down the hill, poling hard, dropping to a crouch. Glancing back she saw Ian follow, and sped on to the plateau before pulling up. He skidded beside and they turned to see a stout, white-clad figure lumber toward the cave, shoebox-size object in hand.

"We got out just in time," Angela panted. "Maybe he didn't see us."

"What's he doing?"

"We're not waiting to find out—*go!*"

She pushed off again, entering the chute like a downhill racer, picking up speed as she maneuvered through the curves, zigzagging past granite ledges that reached out menacingly.

"Slow down!" Ian called after her.

But the channel was steep and she was already worn out, legs quaking as she strained against the turns, narrowly avoiding the rock, skirting so close her shoulders brushed. She felt her thighs burning, cramping, she was losing control. Unable to hold her balance any longer, she caught a ski, spun, and crashed hard . . .

For a moment she was at a loss, staring up into fog, seeing it dissolve into blue sky, then into the panicked face of Ian. As if from afar she heard, *"Angela! Sweetheart!"*

He tore off his gloves, wiping snow from her cheeks. She rose up on her elbows, groggy, seeing the exit of the chute behind him. Somehow she'd made it through, escaping the rocky claws.

"I'm okay," she puffed, and he lifted her up, supporting her on her unsteady legs. She'd lost both skis, she saw, only one pole left strapped to a wrist.

How do I get down the mountain now?

But that worry gave way to a far greater one.

Suddenly the mountain rumbled underfoot and an explosion ripped the air, followed by the sound of a freight train roaring down.

She shot Ian a terrified look, and faster than she could think, he grasped her by the waist, raised her up, and sent her flying. She landed to the side of the chute just as a torrent of white burst through, snatching Ian away.

FIFTY-TWO

THE SLOPES OF MT. GRÜBLSPITZE, TYROLEAN ALPS, AUSTRIA, SAME DAY, LATE AFTERNOON

Angela lay half buried in snow, dazed, disoriented. But as her head cleared she saw nothing of Ian. Or of the person who'd brought this devastation down on them. The slope below was a trough of white ruin, no trace of life.

Panicking, she wrenched herself free, screaming for Ian. She still had her one ski pole, and tearing the disk from its tip she began frantically probing the depths, eye out for the assassin, expecting him any second.

Oh God! Oh God! Ian could be anywhere! Underfoot even, just out of reach!

Fighting to keep her wits she began plumbing her way down the hill, shouting his name. In her frenzy she'd nearly forgotten the emergency number keyed into their phones, and ripping off a glove with her teeth she fumbled out her cell, heedless now if the Order detected the signal.

A male voice responded, *"Mayrhofen skipatrouille."*

"Help!" she cried. "Avalanche!"

"Lawine?"

"Mt. Grüblspitze, south face—a man's buried—*hurry!*"

"Ja! Ja! Avalanche. Grüblspitze. Ve send rescue."

She hung up, despondent. If Ian were still alive, he had probably but minutes left . . .

And then—an epiphany! *His cell phone.*

Had he switched it off back at the cave? She couldn't recall. In the rush he might have forgotten. Finger trembling she hit his number, holding thumb over speaker, straining to hear his ringtone in the quiet . . .

But Grüblspitze held silent as a mausoleum.

He turned it off! It's smashed! He's buried too deep!

Patched into his voicemail, she hit redial, dropping to her knees, planting her ear to the snow.

Nothing.

Over and over she tried, expanding her search in an ever-widening sweep. Time ticked on, light waning as the mountain engulfed her in shadow, only her sobs to break the silence.

Where is ski rescue, goddammit!

Despairing, she thought she heard a faint bell. Distant pinging, hardly audible over her panting and the pounding of her heart.

Yes! Listening between gasps, she zeroed in, at last hearing it directly beneath. She tore into the snow bare-handed as the rings grew louder.

Only to have her excitement turn to stunned disbelief.

A lone cell phone, nothing more.

Her wail resounded off the cliffs: *"Noooooo-Noooooo-Noooooo!"*

Snatching up her pole again, unable to feel it in her frozen fists, arms aching, she probed. Again, again, again—Ahab stabbing the great White Whale.

And then she felt something . . .

Strength all but gone, she clawed into the snow once more to make out the front of a jacket. *Ian's!* Then his face! But as she scraped it free of ice, her heart sank.

He wasn't breathing. Skin white and cold as the snow.

FIFTY-THREE

THE SLOPES OF MT. GRÜBLSPITZE, TYROLEAN ALPS, AUSTRIA, SAME DAY, LATE AFTERNOON

The last conscious thing Ian remembered was being slammed by a tsunami of white, hurled backwards at incredible speed, stripped of his skis and knapsack, tumbling, helpless.

Then at some point he found himself floating in the air near a jagged summit, dazed. Mt. Grüblspitze, he recognized, gazing down on its crumpled hillside to see where Polycarpe's cave had once stood, now a pile of rubble, no sign of the assassin.

Angela!

He was relieved to see her alive and safe, groping in the snow with a pole. He called to her but she didn't hear. His body, he realized, lay somewhere in the frozen heap beneath her. Yet he had faith she would find him, save him. She wouldn't give up, he knew. But he also knew his camera with the photos was surely destroyed. And the necromantic formula, hidden in the cave all these centuries, was now buried under tons of rock.

He drifted upward, entering the tunnel of light. And again he heard the whistling call of Zachary Niemand, heading down toward the sound, soon finding himself in the murk of the Netherworld once more.

But this time as Niemand's slim, shadowy form came into view, Ian could see the spirit was not alone. Near him stood a much larger and more formidable shape. Two heads taller, three times as broad, backlit by orange glow.

The creature wore no robe, skin shiny dark and leathery. Head, neck, chest, and shoulders massive; arms rangy and muscled, angled out like a gunslinger's—forced out by the girth of its biceps. Fingers long, clawed, and curled. And supporting its bulk, a pair of pillar-thick legs set on lizard feet with nasty, hooked dewclaws.

It wore a helmet on its head, like a Viking's . . . No, *not* a helmet! Drawing closer, Ian was amazed to see horns protruding from the sides of the monster's forehead, face scarcely human, eyes large and black under a prominent brow, without pupils. Its muzzle ended in a blunt snout with scowling lips and snaggled, pointed teeth, tusks arcing from its lower jaw like a wild boar's.

Terrified, Ian knew he was in the presence of a dreaded Dark Angel.

Niemand was quick to assure, "Don't be scared, he won't harm you. Not even Heaven's Angels have powers in Limbo." Gesturing toward the creature, he announced proudly, "This is Zagan, a Lord Guardian of the Abyss."

The giant said nothing, observing Ian through seemingly empty eyes. Ian noticed movement on the black surface behind the creature—a tail! Thick, coiled, ending in a barb that twitched now and then.

Niemand said, "Zagan was here on other business, and I told him about you. How you come here, your interest in the Pit. He wants to speak to you."

Ian settled nervously on the ground. It felt warm, like packed mud beneath his bare feet. He kept Niemand between him and the beast.

Zagan shifted on his tree-trunk haunches, glowering down at Ian. Then the muscles of his jaw rolled, steam vented from his mouth, and he rasped, "What do you seek here, *soul*?"

There was contempt in his tone, voice the rumble of a rusty engine.

Ian retreated slightly. "My parents."

The demon angled his huge head to observe Ian more closely, breath stinking of rotten meat.

"And you would dare the Pit for this?"

"Unless, of course, you can bring my parents to me—"

The glassy eyes flashed. "You would have me fetch your parents *for* you? *You are the Angel of Death that I do your bidding?*"

Ian backpedaled, shrinking. "No-no! I meant, if you would *permit* them to come."

The monster turned his irritation on Niemand. "Have you told him *nothing*?"

"I tried," Niemand mewled.

Zagan blew a hot, foul plume at Ian. "Souls do not roam Hell at their leisure, fool!"

This time Ian held his ground. "My parents gave their lives for me. I *have* to see them again. Even if it means going to the Pit."

The creature regarded him with disdain. "None willingly enter the Abyss. And never a graced soul."

"I assure you, I'm not crazy."

Zagan sneered, "There is no insanity here. Madness is an escape granted only to the living. But as you prove, *ignorance* survives death. You would write over the memories of your parents with what lies in the Pit?"

Imagining his parents' anguish, Ian stepped closer. "This is all some terrible mistake! They were good people. Nothing they did could warrant damnation."

"No sin warrants damnation, yet it is so."

"There's got to be *something* I can do for them!"

"No damned soul escapes Hell. That Door was sealed after the fall of Man."

Ian blinked his transparent lids. "There was a Door?"

"For your kind, *not mine*."

Ian heard bitterness. Moving closer still, Zagan's rancid breath was scathing as Niemand explained, "In the beginning, Hell was created to imprison those who rebelled in the Angelic War—eons before the coming of Man. It was never intended for souls."

As Ian recalled from the Book of Genesis, though the angels were created first, before Mankind, God made Man in *His* image. Superior to angels, to be served by angels.

Zagan said, "When Man came to be, so came the Tree with the Knowledge to open all doors. Man would have Known its fruit, but he fell. The Knowledge was cleaved, its Evil cast into the Pit, guarded where no damned soul can go." He smirked. "All men Know well the road to Hell, *none* the way out."

"You mean, the Knowledge of Good and Evil can open Hell's Door?"

"An absurd question. No damned shall ever leave."

Desperate, Ian searched the demon's blank eyes. "What if I agree to take my parents' place?"

Niemand moaned, wagging his head. Even Zagan seemed taken aback. *"Bodhisattva!"* the monster muttered. "You are *truly* ignorant. If you knew the misery of the Pit you would not offer such a thing."

"Then at least let me go to them." Ian wondered if devils were capable of compassion. "Please, let me see them. *One last time . . .*"

Again Zagan seemed surprised, barbed tail quivering in the dull light.

At length he replied, "If granted your request, what do you offer in return?"

Ian hesitated. "I suppose you'll want my soul."

To his astonishment, Zagan threw back his head and roared a long, vile laugh. Ian and Niemand cowered as the demon came to a brusque halt, scoffing, *"Your soul?* Of what value is your soul to us? More work! Another sniveling spirit to tend!" His blank eyes narrowed and he extended a gnarled, sharp-clawed finger at Ian, his tone grave. "The fare for your passage will be *costly.*"

"How costly?"

"That is not for me to say, nor for you to negotiate."

Mulling, Ian hedged, "So long as it's understood, I won't break any of God's Commandm—"

Instantly the demon cringed, erupting in a thunderous howl, covering his pointed ears. Niemand waved frantically at Ian. *"Never* speak His Name in front of them!"

They ducked to avoid Zagan's thrashing tail, Niemand crying, "Lucky you're in Limbo, or he'd shred and eat you! No worse an agony than to be turned to demon shit!"

Terrified, Ian apologized profusely as Zagan grimaced, ranting, swearing, rubbing his ears.

But at length the fit abated and the monster rose to full height again, regarding Ian sullenly with hardened eyes. There was a surlier edge to his voice now.

"If your offer is accepted," he snarled, "whatever fare is set will place no sin on your soul. But know that you will not be told your fare until *after* you reach the Pit—though you must agree to it *beforehand* without condition. And you must pay in full after, without delay."

"I'll be able to see both my parents? Speak to them?"

"See and speak to them."

"And I'll be free to leave Hell, then?"

"If you survive. There are dangers in the Abyss beyond the control of its Guardians."

"What happens if I fail to pay?"

Zagan expelled hot vapor. "Nothing. Unless and until your soul is damned. Then you will pay *dearly.* Regardless, a penalty will be exacted upon your parents too terrible for you to imagine."

"But what—"

"*Enough!* I go to make arrangements. If you dare come again, come prepared to enter the Gate. *You will get no second chance.*"

With that he spun on his toes, kicked his tail out of his way, and stalked off into the gloom.

Ian and Niemand stood gaping at each other.

"What do you think?" Ian asked.

"I don't know! I've never heard the likes of this!"

"Can he be trusted?"

Niemand spread his hands. "After all, he *is* a devil . . ."

Before Ian could ask more, he felt himself lurch backward, drawn up into the tunnel, watching Niemand's troubled face recede into the mists.

Then he awoke in a heaven of white, an angel's lips pressed to his, breathing life back into him.

FIFTY-FOUR

KRANKENHAUS, MAYRHOFEN, AUSTRIA, SAME DAY, EVENING

"It appears, Fräulein Brown," the *hauptprüfer* told Angela, addressing her by her assumed name, "you vere, as you say, in the wrong place at the wrong time . . ."

She sat in a small conference room at the Mayrhofen hospital, wrapped in a blanket, shivering. But not from cold. Across the table was the local police inspector, a raw-boned, blustery man in his fifties, short-cropped hair, ruddy complexion.

"The terrain vas clearly marked *verboten*, yet you ignore it. Avalanches are a risk after such snowfall."

She was scarcely listening. Still in ski clothes, she was also in shock, looking past the man to a mirror and her pale reflection. Hair damp and awry; eyes swollen, red; cheeks streaked with cave dirt and tears. Not that she cared.

"The unfortunate victim," the inspector continued, opening a folder, showing her a photo, "you are certain you never saw him before?"

She glanced at it and turned away. "Positive," she lied, recognizing the man from the trattoria yesterday. "Like you said, wrong place at the wrong time."

All she wanted was to get back to Ian, who lay unconscious in bed upstairs, her efforts on the mountain to revive him successful. The Sword's death was by his own hand, blowing up the cave, bringing a rockslide down on himself—for all outward appearances, a natural accident. But Angela had to get Ian out of here fast, not knowing when the next assassin would arrive, perhaps here already.

The inspector arched his brows. "I find it odd the man carried no means of identification but his phone, unfortunately smashed beyond use.

Und that odd *Tätowierung* on his chest . . . I think it best you und your fiancé remain in town until ve sort this out."

"May I go to him now?"

He nodded, gathering his file. "Let me know vhen he vakes. I must have his statement."

She promised, and ducked out into the hall in sock feet, no shoes to replace her ski boots—only to collide with a tall man carrying a briefcase.

Cowering on the floor, she feared the worst.

He gaped at her, reaching down. *"Entschuldigung, Fräulein Brown?"* he said, jangling a set of car keys. *"Ich habe Ihr Auto für Sie."*

It took her a second. Earlier while awaiting Ian's medical tests she'd arranged for another rental car, afraid to return to their chalet . . .

With a trembling hand she signed some forms, the man handed over the keys and parking stall number, and she continued down the hall.

In addition to arranging for the car, she'd made two other calls, heedless of her phone's signal now, the Order surely knowing their whereabouts. First, Antonio. But unable to reach him, she'd left voicemail, begging him to call right away. Then an old friend back in the States, a professor from Berkeley, to ask a favor . . .

She exited an elevator onto Ian's floor, relieved to find him as before, alone in his room, asleep in bed, face bruised and swollen. Sitting beside him, she kissed his good cheek. He'd suffered a concussion, but incredibly, no internal injuries or broken bones.

Suddenly her phone rang, startling her. She'd left it on hoping to hear back from Antonio, and that's whose number she saw. His face came up onscreen and she watched him take in her disheveled appearance, frowning.

"Angela! What happened!"

"Avalanche. *Arma Christi.*"

"Are you all right?"

"Yes, but Ian's pretty banged up. I'm with him in a hospital. We lost the formula, a Sword blew up the cave."

"Ringrazi il Dio! And the Sword?"

"Killed in the explosion."

The director looked astounded. *"Surely God protects you! What now?"*

Angela felt herself tear. "I don't know, Antonio. We've tried everything to shake them."

"Well, you can't stay where you are. Can Ian travel?"

"I'm not sure, but I have a car."

"Listen to me—get him the hell out of there! Now!"

"And then what?" She could no longer hold back the tears. "How do we stop these people if we can't reason with them? We don't even know who they are!"

His eyes grew pensive and he looked away. Then turning back, he said with a strange tone of resignation, *"Don't give up hope, I've a last place to seek an answer."*

She took heart, wiping her eyes.

"Leave now," he told her. *"Put some distance between you and that place, and call me on the road tomorrow."* He paused to add, *"Do you pray, Angela?"*

"What?"

"Do you pray to God?"

"Not since I was a child." A by-product of her father.

"Try again. And pray I'm doing the right thing!"

He bid her good-bye and she switched off her phone.

She couldn't bring herself to pray, but she heeded the rest of Antonio's advice. Shaking Ian awake, she watched him roll his eyes open, slowly focusing on her, and she took his face gently in hand.

"How do you feel, sweetheart?"

He groaned, "Like I was hit by a truck."

"Do you remember anything?"

"You breathing the life back into me . . ." He managed a smile, needing help to sit. "My knapsack? Camera?"

"Gone. Do you remember the formula?"

"Only the first few lines . . ."

"I just spoke to Antonio. I'll fill you in later—we've got to go. Can you walk?"

"I don't know . . ."

Grunting, he swung his legs over the side and she went to the closet, feeding him his clothes, helping him dress. A painful process, his limbs stiff, clothes damp and cold.

But when she came to one item, she paused.

"What about this?"

"My scapular. Lucien gave it to me, remember?"

She examined it in the light. Two separate pictures, each an inch and a half square, mounted in cloth frames, connected by a loop of string. One felt thicker than the other.

"What's it for, again?"

"It brings blessings to the wearer. St. Christopher, patron saint of safe journeys; St. Jude, saint of the impossible."

"Well they've sure done you a lousy job . . ."

She began prying at the thicker frame with a fingernail, and Ian objected. But not before the picture fell out onto the bed. Along with a microchip, tiny battery, and antenna.

Ian's face, already pale, lost the rest of its color.

"My God, *not Lucien*. I don't believe it!"

"No, but what about that abbot who sent him? The one who heard his Confession?"

"The dom? Dom Girardeau—an *Arma Christi*?"

She snatched up the parts, marched to the room's john, and flushed them, scraping her hands. "There, let the Order chase us through the sewers for a while. *Now* maybe we'll have some peace!"

As she returned to Ian the door to the room opened, and a large man in a white uniform entered with a tray of food.

"Vas ist diese?" he asked, seeing Ian dressed.

"I'm checking out," Ian told him.

The man frowned. *"Nein.* Specialist come see you."

Ian ignored him, proceeding with his jacket, and the man set down his tray and left.

Hurrying, Angela wrapped an arm around Ian, helping him stand. He leaned on her and they hobbled into the hall in sock feet, away from the nurses' station, Ian moaning with every step.

Someone yelled from behind, *"Warten!"* and Angela looked back to see the orderly. She rushed Ian into a stairwell and he shifted his weight to the banister.

"Get the car," he told her. "I'll meet you in the street."

She hesitated. But seeing him able to descend on his own, she went ahead, racing down and out to the parking lot, feet wet, cold, and sliding in the snow.

The car was in its appointed slot, and she jumped in, speeding back to the stairwell to find—

No Ian. Instead, she saw the orderly and two security guards outside, searching the grounds with flashlights.

They caught him! They're looking for me!

Panicking, she braked. The men saw, and ran toward her. Then suddenly the passenger door flew open and a dark shape leaped in, shouting, *"Drive!"*

She shrieked.

"Go, go, go!" Ian cried, and she stomped it. Tires squealing, they fishtailed past the men, who chased on foot, waving their lights, hollering. Angela sped on, west out of town at breakneck pace, taking a narrow two-lane highway up into the mountains.

At length she slowed to the speed limit, eyes never long off the rearview mirror. She felt a cold hand on her arm.

"You okay?"

Unsure, she nodded. "You?"

"Achy and wet and damned tired of running. But now that you found that tracking device . . ."

She turned up the heater. "I couldn't risk going back to the chalet, I left everything. We'll stop for clothes and supplies once we get where we're going."

"And where is that?"

"Not far. Somewhere I hope will shed some light on all this Afterlife business."

He sighed. "It better be a floodlight. On the mountain, buried in the snow, I had *another* NDE . . ."

FIFTY-FIVE

OFFICE OF THE DIRECTOR OF SECURITY, PALAZZO DEL GOVERNATORATO, VATICAN CITY, SAME DAY, EVENING

Antonio sat in his office, elbows on his desk, chin in hand, mind in turmoil. A lone lamp failed to disperse the gloom around him as he searched his soul for a reassurance he could not find.

Finally muttering, *"Il Dio lo aiuta!"* he rose and grabbed his coat.

It was quiet in the hall, he likely the only occupant in the building at this hour. Descending the stairs, heels clacking against the marble, he pushed out into the courtyard. Few cars on the Via del Governatorato.

Crossing, he entered a canopy of trees. Ahead was a small church, mustard gold in the streetlamps. *Santo Stephano degli Abissini.* The sanctuary he always retreated to when wrestling problems.

Most citizens of the City favored the imposing St. Peter's for their spiritual reflections, but Antonio preferred a more intimate setting. Especially now, needing to air his conscience. He'd committed no sin, yet in his heart he felt he had. Because in the hope of safeguarding his Church and two good people, he'd decided to break a sacred vow . . .

Placing his hand against the door's familiar twelfth century carving of the Sacred Lamb and Cross, he opened onto hush. As he'd hoped, only a handful of worshipers this late, and to his relief, none he knew.

The church had a single nave flanked by rows of columns that dated to the first millennia. On one wall, a fifteenth century Roman-style fresco of Madonna and Child. Antonio paid them a respectful nod, dipped his fingers in Holy Water, crossed himself, and took a pew.

The sacrament of Penance was underway in a nearby confessional, and he waited patiently for a stall. Then entering, he knelt, clasped his moist palms together, and when at length the confessor slid back the divider screen, Antonio inhaled and whispered, "Bless me, Father, for I am about to sin . . ."

The shadow on the other side stiffened, and an elderly voice responded with a tone of surprise, *"Excuse me? You say you are* about *to sin?"*

"Yes, Father."

"My son, absolution is not something to be handed out in advance like some voucher! How can you possess sincere contrition for a sin you intend to commit?"

"I do not commit this sin for personal gain, Father. The safety of others is at stake. Lives may depend on it."

A pause, then, *"And what is this sin you feel you must commit?"*

"I cannot say."

"I see . . ." The shadow rubbed its chin. *"Tell me, which Commandment does it violate?"*

The director was unsure. "The Eighth, I suppose . . . And maybe the Seventh, too."

"You intend to bear false witness? And to steal?"

"I intend to break a sacred oath. And to steal information that is not mine. Information that could prevent great harm from coming to the Church and innocent people."

The confessor went quiet again. At length he said, *"If, after seeking the guidance of the Holy Spirit, in your heart you feel this act necessary to aid Mother Church and innocent brethren—and it will not of itself harm others—then in the eyes of God you commit no sin. You need no forgiveness. Go in peace, and may God be with you."*

Thanking him, Antonio exited the booth, leaving with the answer he'd hoped for. But he did not go in peace.

FIFTY-SIX

A HIGHWAY IN THE TYROLEAN ALPS, SAME DAY, NIGHT

Angela and Ian traveled a curvy, two-lane road high up in the mountains, having crossed into Switzerland an hour ago, Angela at the wheel. No moon, few cars, steep cliffs, road treacherous with patches of ice. It took sharp focus. Not easy for Angela after the tale she'd just heard. Ian's most implausible NDE yet.

She'd held silent, uncertain how to respond, until finally he demanded, *"Well?"*

"Christ, Ian," she sighed. "Now you're kicking around Hell with a demon tour guide?"

"Not Hell, Limbo. I haven't even seen Purgatory yet."

"And what did he call you? *Bodhisattva?"*

"A Buddhist term. An enlightened being who forgoes nirvana to save others."

Stifling a barb, she asked, "If no one's ever escaped Hell, how can you possibly hope to save your parents?"

"I don't know yet. According to Zagan, the Tree of Knowledge is the key."

"But you can't believe God would leave such Knowledge in Hell. The damned would have moved mountains to find it, they'd have all escaped eons ago."

It felt insane arguing this!

"No," Ian replied, "Zagan said the Tree is protected where no damned soul can go."

"Then why do you think *you* can go there?"

"Because my soul isn't damned . . . It's part of a plan I'm working on. A way to not only help my parents, but to get *Arma Christi* off our backs."

"Plan?"

"Antonio thinks I'm on to something about the Bosch paintings—that the Order gave up the hunt after photos started spreading. Same thing happened with Dante's *Divine Comedy.* The Order doesn't waste time on lost causes. Once the horse is out of the barn, *Arma Christi* goes away."

"So how does that help us?"

"Remember what O'Farrell said? The Order's fear is that word of my experiments will get out and others will follow, like in the Middle Ages. If I go on TV and tell the world what I Know, the Order will be overwhelmed with NDE'ers. Whack-a-mole. They'll leave us alone."

She hated to throw cold water on him. "One problem with that plan, Ian. No one's going to believe you—much less risk life and brain damage to do what you do."

To her surprise, he nodded. "Right, they'll demand proof. I've been giving that a lot of thought, and I have to admit, I was stumped . . . until today." His eyes shined. "How *do* you prove the existence of something that's completely spiritual? Heaven? Hell? God?"

"My point exactly."

"But there *is* a way. You prove it with *Divine Knowledge.* The answer is for me to bring back a Truth so compelling, everyone will Know it comes from God. Something so credible, so indisputable, people will *have* to Believe. And that Truth is the Knowledge of Evil."

Secular beliefs aside, Angela felt the blood drain from her face. "But the Knowledge of Evil is forbidden fruit. You steal it, you'll pay—like Adam and Eve!"

He shook his head. "I've already paid. We *all* have. Adam and Eve were cast out of Paradise to labor and suffer and die, and we inherited that sentence. *Original Sin.* To punish me again is double jeopardy. God may be wrathful, but He's just."

She couldn't argue theology with him.

He added, "Zagan confirmed what Lucien told us—God split the Tree and planted the Evil half in the Pit of Hell. Where my parents are. If I find its Knowledge, I can save them *and* us."

A signpost ahead said they were nearing Bern.

"Ten more kilometers," Angela breathed, exhausted, head throbbing.

"To where?"

"To acquire some knowledge," was all she would say.

Her best hope to open the steel trap of Ian's mind was to find a place that understood the science of NDEs. And she'd chosen the most renowned research center there was. The Swiss Institute of Neurological Studies.

FIFTY-SEVEN

THE APOSTOLIC PALACE, VATICAN CITY, ITALY, NEXT MORNING

The *Sala Clementina* was a reception hall within the pope's residential palace. A vast, lofty room covered floor-to-ceiling with sixteenth-century frescos and friezes. At one end was an enormous fireplace adorned by a red velvet papal coat-of-arms. In front of that, a large throne from which the pope conducted his more routine ceremonies.

This morning the pontiff was busy conferring blessings, attired in all-white simar and gold crucifix on a gold chain, flanked by Swiss guards in tricolor uniforms, black berets, white gloves, and ruff collars. Beside him stood his chamberlain in red cassock with lace-trimmed rochet.

Groups of the faithful were being ushered in through a door at the rear and directed along a velvet rope barricade to await admission before the pope. Then kneeling for a quick benediction, they would circle back out a separate door, all with assembly-line efficiency.

Watching from mid-room as he chatted with several Vatican officials was Cardinal Pietro della Roca. He'd come hoping to steal a minute with the pope, having looked to do so for days now. But Julius's tight schedule had yet to present an opportunity, and Pietro's issues, though serious, were delicate. He preferred not to betray his concern by raising them to the importance of an appointment, keeping an eye on the pope's itinerary, dropping in from time to time.

And now he saw his opening. As the last group of conferees, the Vatican *futbol* team, knelt for its blessing, Pietro excused himself and shuffled to the front, skirting the barricade, catching the pope's eye as he rose.

"Papa," he said softly, "a moment's word, please."

The papal chamberlain stepped in, clearing his throat to mention the next appointment. But the pope smiled and held up a hand. "Oh, I think we can spare our Prefect a tick of eternity." And taking Pietro by the elbow, he led him a few steps away.

"Now," he said, patting the cardinal's arm, "what's on your mind this morning?"

Pietro lowered his voice. "My suggestion, Papa, about the security department—have you had a chance to reflect?"

"I have. And while I share some of your concerns, I'm not sure I agree with your proposal. Yes, Tony exercises more independence than I would prefer at times, but his duties are demanding and we must give him the flexibility to perform them."

"Duties that would benefit, surely, from more direct spiritual oversight."

The pope shook his head. "His is a much different world than ours, Pietro, and we should be grateful we're removed from it. The more distance, the better! Regardless, your hands are full defending doctrine, let Tony worry about security."

"Papa, his judgment bringing that wayward priest and woman here. *The embarrassment.*"

"That 'wayward priest,'" the pope reminded, "is the same man who brought us such acclaim in Africa. In that one instance he did more to restore the Church's good name than I've achieved my entire reign! Perhaps with Tony's help the young man will find his way home to us."

Disappointed but knowing the pope's mind was set, Pietro hastened to add, "Another quick issue, Holiness, if you will . . ." The pontiff had already started to turn away, pausing. "Lucio came to me the other day, very upset."

The pope's demeanor soured. "My decision about the museum?"

"Yes, Holiness."

"And you question me as well?"

"No, Papa. I simply regret the weight of circumstances. If there were any other way."

"None the Lord has shown me. And certainly none at the expense of my charities!"

"Lucio mentioned a certain bursary—the Fund for the Defense of the Faith. I thought perhaps, after so many years, it might warrant review. I could look into it for you."

Immediately he regretted his words. The pope's face reddened and he snapped, "*That* is a matter for my judgment alone! *Its costs are none of your concern!*"

As quickly as he'd erupted the pope blinked, eyes and voice apologetic. "Forgive me. I, I find financial matters very stressful these days. I ask your prayers that God guides my decisions."

Deeply shaken, Pietro assured, "You are *always* in my prayers, Holiness!" And bowing, kissing the pope's ring, he shrank away.

Julius watched Pietro go, ignoring his chamberlain's watch-glancing. Then with a heavy sigh he murmured, "If God leaves me no alternative, it *must* be His Will."

FIFTY-EIGHT

THE OUTSKIRTS OF BERN, SWITZERLAND, LATER THAT MORNING

Angela and Ian left the inn where they'd overnighted, off to a slow start after yesterday's harrowing ordeal. They wore new clothes they'd bought last night at a twenty-four-hour Euro Walmart, having also replaced other essentials left behind, including new laptops and Ian's lost cell phone.

Ian was at the wheel, adamant he felt fit enough to drive, if grimacing every time he braked. He did look better today. Left cheek bruised but less swollen. And Angela liked that he'd shaved his mustache and dyed his hair back to its natural shade.

"The Order's looking for a blond now," he'd told her last night, getting her advice on hair-coloring.

Yes, she preferred the old Ian . . .

The day was sunny, if cold, and from their vantage point on a hill above town, Angela looked out on the city of Bern. More a village. Old-European. Neighborhoods of two-story houses, steep-pitched shake rooftops interspersed with church spires and clock towers.

She was in good spirits. Having rid Ian of his insidious scapular, she felt optimistic that they'd finally eluded the Order. And now navigating toward the destination she'd yet to disclose, she was hoping to disabuse him of his NDEs.

They arrived at a modern office park, pulling into a lot beside a large building of glass and brushed steel. A sign read:

DAS SCHWEIZER INSTITUT DER NEUROLOGISCHEN

Ian gave her a suspicious look. "We're here to have my head examined?"

"Tempting, but no. An old grad-school professor of mine has connections with the Institute. I called him and he set up a meeting for us. By the way, we're married. Ian and Angela Grant."

"A meeting with whom? For what?"

"Dr. Lizbeth Roentger, one of the world's foremost authorities on unconscious cognition. I want her take on your NDEs. And I want your full cooperation, okay?"

He muttered, but did not object.

Waiting to ensure they hadn't been followed, they entered the building, passing through a bright lobby with a fountain, up an elevator to the *Kognitive Forschung Abteilung*—Department of Cognitive Research.

A receptionist showed them into an airy office. Wide windows, blond wood floors, abstract paintings, bookcases filled with medical books. The doctor rose from her desk at the far end, welcoming them by their assumed names, shaking their hands. A woman of small stature but confident bearing. Sixties. Short, stylish gray hair. Intelligent eyes. The wall behind her was papered with academic diplomas, awards, and certificates.

Angela thanked her for seeing them on short notice.

"I couldn't pass up a case of multiple NDEs," the doctor replied in German-accented English, seating them across her desk in overstuffed blue and green leather chairs. *Calm, peaceful colors,* the psychologist in Angela knew. She felt in her element.

Dr. Roentger smiled. "I've known only a handful of double NDEs—never a triple."

"Quadruple," Ian updated.

"Recent skiing accident," Angela clarified.

The doctor raised an eyebrow as if unsure she weren't the victim of some prank. Then staring at Ian's bruised face, she nodded, studying him. "I congratulate you on your catlike resilience. I'd certainly like to hear more."

Ian looked hesitant, and for a moment Angela feared he was going to renege. But inhaling, he complied. He spoke in generalities for the most part, ignoring the uncomfortable fact that his first three NDEs were intentional, attributing them simply to "medical situations." And he glossed over his encounters with the mass murderer, Zack Niemand, "a dead acquaintance," and the demon, Zagan, "another spirit," emphasizing instead the realism of his experiences.

When he finished, the doctor sat back, tenting her fingers.

"I must admit, Mr. Grant, I find your story fascinating. Of the few multiple NDEs on record, *none* follow a sequential progression like yours. And I've never heard such cohesion, such detail."

Ian's eyes brightened and he shot Angela a look. Dr. Roentger's response wasn't what Angela had been expecting, and she felt her stomach tighten.

The doctor regarded them both for moment, then asked, "Do you mind telling me what it is you hope to accomplish here today?"

Angela replied, "To get a *rational* explanation for what Ian experienced."

Roentger smiled. "I thought I detected a bit of conflict. Let me say up front, I take a neutral position on NDEs. Currently, no test of science can either prove or disprove them. But if you wish, I'll share some insights our field has to offer, and you may draw your own conclusions."

Angela and Ian nodded, and the doctor continued, "The challenge is to apply objective tools to a subjective phenomenon. NDEs, whether real or imagined, are literally in the mind of the beholder. Despite all our technologies, science hasn't the means to distinguish between valid and invalid perceptions, so we must work toward an explanation indirectly.

"But first, let me correct a misconception. Most people believe that NDEs occur *after* death. There are, however, two types of death. 'Clinical death'—the temporary cessation of brain function—from which a person may recover. And 'actual death'—where the brain both ceases to function *and* loses viability.

"In point of fact, no one reporting an NDE was ever actually dead. Actual death is irreversible. Even survivors of clinical death often suffer brain damage. It follows then that people who experience NDEs are never truly dead, despite a flat EEG. Their brains remain viable enough to resume function."

Relaxing a bit, Angela watched Ian's brow furrow.

He asked, "But how can a brain register a flat EEG and still experience conscious thought?"

"Neurologically speaking, it can't. More likely, the NDE occurs either prior to, or just after, a period of clinical death—not during."

"Then how do you account for the fact that the longer I was dead, the longer my NDE?"

"To borrow from one of Bern's former residents, Albert Einstein, it may be a matter of relativity. For someone experiencing a car crash, for example, seconds can seem an eternity. Same for the unconscious mind. During dreams, a minute of 'real time' by the clock can seem far longer to the dreamer. Or far shorter. The mind, it seems, has its own chronometer."

Ian shook his head. "What I experienced was *real*. As real as us talking here right now."

Dr. Roentger nodded. "The Greeks recognized it two thousand years ago as *phantasia catalyptica*—seizures of fantasy. It's not unique to NDEs. Jet pilots report out-of-body experiences during steep dives, as do subjects of centrifuge experiments, where forces of acceleration rob the brain of blood flow.

"We know from image scans of the living brain, thought centers are wildly active during periods of oxygen loss. A state of hallucination we call *Anweisenheit*—unconscious consciousness. Similar effects can also be induced chemically, as with the so-called 'spirit drug' DMT, which can provoke intense religious visions."

Ian's jaw set in that stubborn way of his. "What about the peace and euphoria I felt? How does that square with the trauma of death?"

"Surprisingly, euphoria is a by-product of oxygen loss. Some people even exploit the effect during sex, intentionally suffocating themselves to enhance orgasm. *Asphyxiophilia,* it's called, responsible for thousands of accidental deaths each year. David Carradine, famously."

Ian appeared troubled, and the doctor offered: "It helps to look at what's going on inside the dying brain. As you know, the brain is composed of billions of neurons—pathways through which chemical messages and conscious thought flow. But when the brain is oxygen-starved, emergency measures take over.

"First, endorphins are released into the bloodstream—'feel-good' hormones to help the brain cope with the stress. That may explain the sense of peace you felt. Then other hormones move to insulate the nerve cells from damage. But these also cause the cells to misfire, which could account for the visions people claim to experience."

Ian sat in a slump as if buckled under the weight of science. But his jaw held firm.

"The tunnel of light—how do you explain so many people seeing the very same thing? Going back hundreds of years? How could we all have the *same* vision?"

The doctor smiled. "Allow me to show you . . ."

She picked up a remote, and suddenly the window blinds closed and the lights dimmed. A projector popped down from the ceiling and a screen unfurled against the wall behind the desk. On the screen appeared an image, an amorphous sphere of light-and-dark blue blotches roughly resembling a bull's-eye.[18]

"This," the doctor explained, "is a representation of the nerve receptors within the brain's visual cortex—the area that processes sight. It's wired the same in all of us. As shown here, receptors are denser in the middle, reflecting the way we see—our field of vision being sharper at the center of our eyes. Now consider what happens when the brain starts to die and these nerves begin to misfire . . ."

She pressed a button and the blotches began to flash at random, faster and faster. It created a spiraling effect, giving the illusion of traveling up a tunnel toward a bright light. Angela had to look away, dizzy, and Dr. Roentger clicked the remote again, returning the room to normal.

Ian continued to stare at the wall after the screen retracted. It seemed the doctor's points had reached him, but how deeply?

Dr. Roentger went on, "In fairness, I must now add, there are aspects of the NDE phenomenon for which science has *no* rational explanation. Documented cases where people describe things experienced during clinical death that could not otherwise have been known to them.

"A woman who saw a shoe on a ledge outside her hospital room, though it was visible only from the roof. People who describe encounters with recently deceased individuals they couldn't possibly have known were dead. Though rare, these instances cannot be dismissed."

Angela would have preferred a stronger conclusion, but was pleased overall, feeling free now of the qualms she'd carried since the Venice museum. She stood, thinking they'd taken enough of the doctor's time.

Ian stood, too, but he remained fixated on the wall behind the desk, focused on one of the framed medical degrees. Walking closer, he asked, "Dr. Roentger, your maiden name is 'Barth'?"

"Pronounced 'Bart.' Ignore the 'H.' "

"Any relation to the famous theologian, Karl Barth?"

"Why, yes. My grandfather."

A light went on in Ian's eyes. "Your grandfather used to correspond with another theologian, Thomas Merton. Do you happen to know if Merton's letters still exist?"

As Angela recalled, Barth was one of two people to whom Merton allegedly sent copies of his Ultimate Reality. She groaned inside, fearing Ian's mind hadn't budged.

The doctor replied, "That's a question for my sister; she's custodian of Grandfather's papers. She lives nearby; would you like me to arrange a visit?"

FIFTY-NINE

PETRIN PARK, PRAGUE, CZECH REPUBLIC, SAME DAY, NOON

Josef Varga sat alone on a bench high atop Petrin Hill, arms and legs crossed. He came here often when his mind was troubled. Today, to await a most distressing call . . .

Behind him stood Petrin Observation Tower, a sixty-meter replica of Paris's Eiffel Tower, built in 1891 for Prague's Jubilee Exhibition. Even from its base, Josef had a superb view of the city. Looking southeast across the Vltava, he could see the blackened stone cupola of the cathedral of Saints Cyril and Methodius. A place that held great meaning for him, and his eyes lingered.

It was to this church that Czech resistance fighters Josef Gabčik and Jan Kubis had fled after attacking *Oberführer* Reinhard Heydrich—the only attempted assassination of a high-ranking Nazi ever to succeed. The two brave fighters held off four hundred Waffen SS from the cathedral for four hours before the tragic outcome. A source of immense pride for the occupied nation. And today, countless thousands of Czechs like Josef proudly bore names honoring the heroes.

But Josef's connection to his namesake transcended most. He was also born the same day as Gabčik, April 8. And in a town that had changed its name to Gabčikova in tribute to the valiant fighter. Remarkable occurrences of Fate that Josef had always seen as an omen.

Now, however, his mind was on another omen and another hill far from Petrin. A *third* Brother lay dead in the Alps. What did it mean? Was God telling Josef to stop passing the cup of this assignment and drink it himself? Or were these deaths a sign God was protecting Ian?

His reflections were interrupted by the sound of a church bell in his pocket, like a death knell.

The call he'd been expecting—Cyril.

"Baringer must have found the tracking device," came the heated voice. *"The signal's gone dark, and he's vanished!"*

Josef swallowed. "And the formula?"

If Ian had it, Polycarpe's sorcery could be spreading across the globe this very moment, provoking more invasions of the Afterlife, out of control.

"Unknown. Most likely lost in the avalanche. With Hendric . . ."

A pause, then: *"It's time you searched your soul, Josef . . . The Cathedral, tonight, eight."*

SIXTY

A STATELY RESIDENTIAL SECTION OF BERN, SWITZERLAND, SAME DAY, EARLY AFTERNOON

Ian pulled to the curb in front of an elegant three-story home, letting the car run as he and Angela went through their surveillance drill.

The house sat on a bluff above the scenic Aare River. Built of sandstone in the Victorian style, old but well-maintained. Tall windows, shake-shingled roof, multiple chimneys. Below, a village clustered both sides of a three-arch stone bridge. Charming. Peaceful. No suspicious vehicles or activities.

Ian switched off the engine. Angela had been quiet since the Institute, and he'd been preparing. He turned to her.

"As we heard, science doesn't have all the answers."

Her eyes never left her window. "And we don't have *any* answers. We need to be looking for a way out of this mess, not chasing after Merton's Reality."

"This *is* our way out. If Merton's right, the Reality is a glimpse into the Mind of God—maybe the Knowledge of Good itself! It's the divine truth we need to prove the Afterlife to the world. Didn't Merton say it has the power to end wars, heal all wounds?"

"To make *Arma Christi* call off its jihad?"

"Why not? Or at least, powerful enough that others will want to see the Afterlife for themselves. The Order will be up to its Eyes & Ears in NDEs, it'll forget us."

"I'm sorry, I just can't see people risking NDEs over some dead monk's vision."

"You mean, like *I* did? You underestimate how far people will go to for Faith, Angela. It's what gave the Church its martyrs." He looked up at the house. "And right now, *my* Faith tells me there's something providential in all this."

Now she turned to him. *"Providential?"*

"Think about it. In St. Maarten, the counterfeiters kill that Sword and save my life. At the Vatican, you wake in time to save us both. On the boat, that dart strikes my watch. You save me from an avalanche. And now we find one of two people in the world who might have the Reality."

"Sweetheart, *fanatics are trying to kill us.* There's nothing providential in that! And you think we've got some—some *guardian angel* watching over us?"

He grinned, leaned across the seat, and kissed her cheek.

"No. Guardian *Angela* . . ."

Before she could respond, he popped out and walked around to open her door. She held back a beat, then sighed and took his hand, and he escorted her to the house.

A maid answered and they were admitted into a sunlit foyer. Moments later a smiling, sturdy-looking woman in a flower-print dress entered from the back. She introduced herself in German-accented English, Alfreda Hummel, granddaughter of Karl Barth. She'd been expecting them.

Ian guessed her to be in her early seventies. Face round and cheery, hair silver and perfectly coiffed. She seated them in a drawing room around a coffee table, maid serving tea.

"You have a beautiful home, Frau Hummel," Ian said, admiring its period furnishings—a claw-footed mahogany étagère filled with fine-cut crystal, a Grotrian-Steinweg grand piano.

"This was *Großvater* Karl's house," she replied, beaming. "He built it for his retirement. It's been in the family ever since; we've kept it just as it was."

Opening a broad, leather-bound book on the table, she showed it to them, proudly flipping through newspaper and magazine articles. "*Großvater* was the most prominent Protestant theologian of his day . . ."

Ian saw pictures of a tall, thin man with glasses and an oft-askew shock of gray hair.[19] Barth had even made the cover of *TIME*, April 20, 1962.

"A man of strong spiritual convictions, and he paid dearly for it. Exiled from Germany in 1935 for refusing to pledge allegiance to Hitler. That began the horrible decade *Großvater* called his 'Dark Night of the Soul.' He was so filled with anger that God could allow such Evil—a theological dilemma he never did reconcile."

The Divine Paradox, Ian recognized. The seeming incongruity of an all-good, all-powerful God Who nevertheless abided Evil. Even a renowned thinker like Barth couldn't fathom it.

Ian was intrigued, but he had more pressing issues.

"Frau Hummel, I understand your grandfather and Thomas Merton corresponded. Would it be possible to see Merton's letters?"

"*Großvater's* papers are all housed here," she said. "This was both home and office."

Standing, she motioned them to follow, and Ian's pulse quickened. She led them down a hall to a pair of pocket doors, opening into a stuffy room. Wood-shuttered windows, walls of dark paneling, fireplace at the far wall bordered by heavily laden bookshelves. In front of the fireplace was a large walnut desk, surface cluttered with books and documents.

"*Großvater's* study. We left it just as it was the day he passed. Same day, coincidently, that Father Merton died." She smiled. "God called them to Heaven together."

Ian suspected their deaths weren't God's call, and a glance from Angela conveyed like sentiments.

"Frau Hummel," he asked, trying to mask his excitement, "do you happen to have the last item Merton sent Dr. Barth?"

She circled the desk to its file drawers, and Ian watched intently as she began thumbing through yellowed manila folders, arriving at one marked *Merton, Vater Thomas.*

"I trust you'll settle for a photocopy," she said, offering Ian a single sheet of paper. "We handle the originals as little as possible. You can keep this if you like."

An image of a five-by-seven letter copied onto a larger sheet, handwritten in English, fold line visible in the center. Ian recognized Merton's characteristically bad script.

Dec. 5, 1968
My Dear Karl,

Forgive me for gloating, I burst with excitement to tell you—I have just found that which you never thought possible. Proof of God's Will! The Ultimate Reality!

I experienced it yesterday in the spirit, leaving this life briefly for the next to discover the reward God has prepared for all loving souls! What I learned will astonish you, fill you with the same great hope for Humanity that I now feel! It will change you as it has me! Change the world! Change everything! A new beginning!

I recorded all in my journal and am sending you a copy now, separate cover, though you may not get it before I make my announcement in Bangkok. (If only I could see the look on your face!)

In light of the Reality, I am visiting Europe after all, tending to a personal matter in Paris. Very important and long-overdue! Afterward, I will accept your invitation and visit you in Bern. I hope to bring a special companion with me.

Together, the three of us will celebrate the Reality and plan how to spread its divine Knowledge and blessings to the world! So much to discuss!

In God's boundless love,
Tom

Letter trembling in his fingers, Ian asked, "The Ultimate Reality . . . Please—*may I see it?*"

"A package arrived for *Großvater* that morning, special delivery, postmarked Ceylon. We have the receipt." She showed Ian a yellowed ticket from the desk. "Receipt, but no package. What *Großvater* did with it, we've no idea."

Ian stared at the ticket's return address:

Fr. Thomas Merton
Room 224
Galle Face Hotel
Colombo, Ceylon

SIXTY-ONE

BERN-BELP AIRPORT, SAME DAY, LATE AFTERNOON

Convinced they'd eluded the Order at last, Angela and Ian were still taking no chances. They dropped their rental car off in downtown Bern and cabbed to the airport, changing IDs, chartering a sleek little Cessna Citation.

Ian had their pilot file a flight plan to Rome, intending to change destinations in the air again. They would then overnight to Sri Lanka—formerly Ceylon—the exotic locale where Merton had experienced his extraordinary encounter with the divine. Ian's hope, to trace the monk's footsteps and uncover clues to what the Ultimate Reality was, if not the Reality itself.

Surprisingly, Angela hadn't objected, though Ian knew she had no Faith the Reality could solve their problem, much less his parents'. Perhaps it was seeing how much it meant to him. Or more likely, to keep him from taking the direct route to Merton's Reality via *another* NDE beyond the one already planned—an option he didn't dare bring up.

Once they reached altitude and changed directions for Sri Lanka, Angela settled in for a nap, and Ian opened his laptop. He found a batch of new e-mails waiting.

Dr. Emil Josten, reporting that lab preparations were on track, estimating three more days; Charles Dunn, producer at their TV station in LA, wondering why he hadn't heard from them, where they were, when they'd be back; and a worried Antonio Ponti, asking Ian to check in.

Ian sent Josten a thank you, then replied to Dunn:

Charles—Sorry. Stumbled onto huge story—HUGE! Prepare for major network-wide news release, imminent. Will keep you posted. Ian

It being safe now to use his cell, he called Antonio, the man's sober face popping on-screen.

"Ian! What a relief! Are you and Angela safe? Have you recovered from your injuries?"

"We're fine. And hopefully in the clear now. Angela found a tracking device the Order planted on me. In a scapular I got from the Cistercians."

"Mio Dio! *Spies everywhere! And I understand the Polycarpe formula is lost."*

"Afraid so. I've no choice now, I've got to make another NDE. The lab's almost ready."

The director's eyes flitted anxiously. *"Before you do, contact me again. I'm working on something else for you—something I can't discuss yet. Promise you'll call first!"*

Ian promised, and Antonio turned to someone offscreen, listening, then back again.

"Apologies, Ian, I must go. Is there anything you need? Anything more I can do?"

"You've done more than enough already. Our thanks, Antonio. Angela sends her love . . .

He hung up, feeling bad for the added burden he placed on his good friend's shoulders.

Angela stirred, mumbling, "Antonio?"

"Yes. He's working on something new for us. Wouldn't say, but I'm hopeful."

She nodded, closing her eyes again, and he went back to his e-mails.

Four from Josten's assistant, Yvette Garonne.

Yesterday evening: *Ian—Making progress. Got some questions. Call to discuss. Yve.*

This morning: *Ian—Hiring two more MDs to help out. Where are you? Yve.*

Noon: *Ian—Emil still seeking 3rd H/L bypass. Says he's talked to you. My turn. Yve.*

And minutes ago: *Ready pending arrival of Emil and bypass. Where the hell are you???*

Ian tapped his phone against his chest, thinking. Then he flipped it open and dialed.

Garonne greeted him with an irritated pout. *"Well! If eet isn't ze late Meester Baringer!"*

He smiled. "Sorry, Yvette. I've got a narrow window for calls. I save it for Emil."

"Where are you?"

"Can't say. But Emil tells me you're ready."

"Once he get me ze third bypass unit—and your blood packs. I don't know why ze holdup, I can get a unit from Pari tomorrow! He leave me with all ze grunt work!"

"He's a stickler about equipment, no quarrel there."

"So when you come down?"

"Soon as that last bypass arrives. Three days, Emil says. I'll keep you posted . . ."

Thanking her for her dedication, he begged off, watching her miffed face vanish.

At the sound of Garonne's voice Angela snapped to, hearing the news about the lab, feeling her stomach tighten. *Three days.* Little hope left that she could talk Ian out of his obsession. She didn't speak Faith, he didn't speak Reason.

And yet, something he'd said earlier *was* starting to make sense. His argument for revealing Merton's Reality to the world, that it might inspire Believers to undergo NDEs. Angela had to admit, Faith had a long legacy of inciting reckless behavior—and not just back in medieval times. Didn't people today take up deadly snakes? Refuse themselves life-saving medical treatment? Even kill and commit suicide for their beliefs? For some, religion hadn't evolved a tick since the Dark Ages. Maybe Ian was on to something after all . . .

"That letter Frau Hummel gave you," Angela said, tugging on Ian's sleeve. "The one Merton sent Karl Barth—where is it?"

He blinked, searching for it, handing it over.

She reread its clipped lines . . . No clues to what the Reality might be. Yet one thing the monk made eminently clear. Whatever he saw in that cave, he was convinced it was divine. And if a man of Merton's theological acumen was convinced, Angela had to think other believers would be, too. Enough, perhaps, to make Ian's plan work.

She found one passage particularly encouraging: *It will change you as it has me! Change the world! Change everything! A new beginning!*

A new beginning. Exactly what she and Ian needed . . .

"Okay," she told him. "I'm on board. Let's do it. Let's find the Reality."

He looked flabbergasted. "Seriously?"

"This personal matter in Paris Merton talks about," she said, tapping the letter, "the special companion he wants to bring with him to Bern. It has to be My Valentine."

Ian's eyes grew bright with enthusiasm. "My thoughts, too. Merton finally made up his mind to have a real relationship. He was leaving the priesthood for her."

"So, assuming Valentine is still alive, and still in Paris, why Sri Lanka?"

He shrugged. "We've nothing to go on in Paris. Only her first name, no address. My thought is to retrace Merton's last steps, see if we can find notes, messages he may have left behind. Who knows, maybe even a copy of the Reality."

It made sense.

Ian angled his laptop to show her a passage from a book he'd been reading.

"Merton's *Asian Journal*," he said. "The Reality is edited out, but there are intriguing hints."

> *Oct. 15, 1968, San Francisco airport:*
> I am off, heading across the Pacific to the Orient, filled with hope and a grand sense of destiny. After a lifetime of meandering uncertainty, I am at last on course, going back to the home I've never known in this life. May I not return without settling the Great Question . . .

"You see," Ian said, excited, "Merton actually *predicted* his journey to Heaven!"

Angela was on board, not overboard. "Self-fulfilling prophesy. He expected something big, and when the opportunity presented itself, his subconscious delivered. No miracle in that."

"Still, it won't hurt to walk a few miles in his shoes."

"Agreed. So where first?"

"The place where he had his vision. Polonnaruwa—City of the Dead."

SIXTY-TWO

THE CATHEDRAL OF SAINTS CYRIL AND METHODIUS, PRAGUE, CZECH REPUBLIC, SAME DAY, LATE NIGHT

A limousine crept down a quiet city street, pulling to the curb in the gloom between two lampposts. Abutting the sidewalk was a tall stone retaining wall crowned by a taller fence of wrought-iron rails and stone columns. Atop the columns were statues of saints and winged angels guarding the courtyard of a small, Baroque cathedral.

The cathedral was stone, old and tarnished with soot, and in the jaundiced light of the streetlights it had a charnel presence. Its courtyard sat high above grade, nearly hidden from the street, accessible only from the cathedral or by a double set of stairs near where the limo parked.[20]

The rear door of the vehicle popped open and a man emerged, dark trench coat, collar turned up. Glancing around, he strode to the stairs and up, opening a gate with a key, slipping through, closing it softly.

Inside, the courtyard was transformed by the streetlamps into a somber, piebald world. The man moved quickly toward a recessed area near the cathedral, face serious as he passed in and out of the harsh yellow glare.

Cyril, one of *Arma Christi*'s High Council.

Ahead in the shadows a red ember glowed, waxing to orange, subsiding as a waft of smoke escaped into the light.

"Fidelis Tantum Deo," Cyril whispered.

"Potius Mori Quam Foedari," a soft voice returned.

From out of the gloom stepped a young man in dark clothes, tossing a cigarette. Tall, athletic build, bushy hair.

Cyril extended his ring, Josef bowed to kiss it, and the two vanished into the murk.

It was for no casual reason that Cyril had chosen this location. The

Cathedral of Cyril and Methodius was dedicated to the patron saints of the Czech Republic, missionary brothers who'd converted the region a thousand years ago. But as Cyril knew, it held a more personal and poignant significance for Josef. It was here in 1942 that resistance fighter, Josef Gabčik, had perished.

Powerful backdrop for a vital task tonight . . .

The men came to a door and Cyril unlocked it. Flipping on a light, he led the way down a narrow flight through louvered doors to a catacomb, then along a hallway to a dungeonlike room illuminated by a single, low-watt bulb . . .

The room where Gabčik died.

Brick floor, outer wall of thick concrete, single slit of a recessed window high up—too high to see anything but the blackness of the sky. Under the window, in a corner of the wall near the floor, a ragged-hewn hole—the beginnings of an escape tunnel scoured by Gabčik himself.[21]

Someone had mounted a small cross of red roses inside, and around it were scattered bouquets and hundreds of cards, notes, letters. Messages from pilgrims who'd journeyed here to pay their respects, sanctity so thick in the air it was tangible. It never failed to touch Cyril. And as he'd hoped, he saw the same in Josef.

Closing the door, he laid heavy eyes on his young Sword, watching him shift his feet. He waited a full minute, then said in a voice stern but calm, "Because of my trust in you, Josef, the Order faces a grave crisis. . . ."

Josef was certainly aware that should Baringer succeed in revealing to the world the Afterlife's ineffable Secrets, Man would no longer be reliant on Scripture to Believe, Man would *Know*. God's Plan for salvation through Faith alone would end, Mankind forevermore denied the rewards of Heaven.

But there was more to it now. *Much* more.

"It's not only that Baringer will corroborate the Afterlife," Cyril said. "The Council has come to realize there's a *greater* threat."

Josef's eyes showed worry. "Greater than the end of salvation?"

"This next NDE he plans," Cyril said, feeling his throat constrict, "an hour to search for his parents—*four hours* by Underworld reckoning. He has no idea what Evils he'll expose himself to—and by extension, *the world*! A mortal, gallivanting around in the Great Below! God Knows the consequences! Why, Baringer could trigger an event of Cosmic proportions! *Unleash Hell Itself!*"

Josef paled and his brow appeared moist.

Cyril composed himself, allowing his subordinate a moment to reflect. Then he said, "Three years ago when I elevated you to Sword, some on the Council thought it unwise, your position at the Vatican too valuable. But your Faith and courage in Africa showed me something *more* valuable. Then again when I made you Whetstone over others more experienced, some questioned. Once more I believed in you . . . Yet now you cast shame on my judgment."

Despite the dimness, he saw the man's eyes glisten.

"My courage hasn't deserted me," Josef replied, voice aggrieved. "But my Faith . . . I've prayed for strength—I, I just can't bring myself to take Ian Baringer's life."

"Because you know him?"

"Because I understand him. Sir, Ian is *not* Evil. The wrong he does is out of ignorance, not malice. And if I know this, surely God knows this. Maybe that's why he escapes us. He's survived four attempts on his life—I fear God's Hand protects him."

Cyril snapped, "Hitler survived a *dozen* attempts! Was God protecting *him*? Besides, it's immaterial whether Baringer is Evil, he is a *vessel* of Evil—and that vessel must be destroyed before its poison spreads!"

Feeling his point miss, Cyril tried again. "Can't you see, son? The man's survival is no sign. It's a *test*. You were given this assignment and you shirked it. It's cost us three Brothers, and now it threatens our very salvation." He searched Josef's pained face. "You're still our best hope, the one person Baringer won't suspect, and I'm not letting you off."

He waited, got no response, and sighed. "At this juncture, even *I* doubt you . . . I've no choice, Josef. I order you to surrender your Whetstone to Quintus. You will work under him now to eliminate this threat, and you will follow his orders without question. *Do you understand?*"

Josef raised watery eyes. "*Quintus?* Sir, *not* Quintus!"

"The Council has spoken . . ."

Josef slumped against the wall, and Cyril let him hang there a while before adding, "I've something else to tell you."

Slowly Josef straightened.

Cyril began to pace, mind stretching back. "Once, years ago when I was a young Sword, I too had a crisis of Faith. The Elder whose ring I now wear was concerned, and he brought me here to this crypt. Like you, I'd heard the rumors, but he confirmed them. Josef Gabčik and Jan Kubiš were indeed *Arma Christi*."

He got the reaction he sought. Josef stiffened, eyes fixed on him.

"Most of their story you know. At the time, Europe was under Nazi control, the Faith under threat, and the names of many enemies had been entered in the Book. Among them, *Oberführer* Reinhard Heydrich. Heydrich was assigned to Kubiš, a veteran Sword, and Gabčik, a novice.

"Their plan was to attack Heydrich's car en route to his office when its driver slowed for a turn. But this you do not know. Gabčik had never taken a life before. When the moment came and he leaped into the road with his gun, he froze. Fortunately the driver stopped, enabling Kubiš to hurl the fatal grenade. Kubiš and Gabčik fled here, only to be trapped by the SS. Nevertheless, Gabčik was able to get a last message out . . ."

He pulled a yellowed scrap of paper from his pocket and placed it in Josef's trembling hands. Cyril knew its words, scribbled longhand in pencil, in Czech:

Christ forgive me. I was called to His Duty and failed. But another Test looms, and God help me, this time I will keep the Faith. Potius Mori Quam Foedari. Josef Gabčik

Josef dropped his head, and Cyril continued, "Kubiš was soon shot and killed, Gabčik left alone and running out of ammunition. But rather than surrender, he fought to the last bullet, then used it on himself. And so in the end, he kept the Faith . . ."[22]

He allowed Josef to regroup, then concluded, "You see, son, even Gabčik had his moment of weakness. He was blessed it didn't cost him his mission. God granted him a second chance; he was able to redeem himself. God has granted you *four* such chances. And now it seems, a *fifth* . . ."

The man's head lifted.

"We've learned Baringer will undertake his final NDE in three days. Until then, we believe he will hold off going public with what he Knows. A last opportunity to redeem yourself."

Josef wiped his eyes, handing back the note. But Cyril waved him off.

"It's yours to pass on," he said, and turning to go, he added, "perhaps someday when *you* wear this ring."

SIXTY-THREE

ANURADHAPURA INTERNATIONAL, ANURADHAPURA STATION, SRI LANKA, EARLY NEXT MORNING

Angela awoke with a start, jet touching down in the island nation of Sri Lanka. Out her window the sun had scarcely broken the horizon of tropical jungle. Next to her, Ian was in shorts and hiking shoes, ready to set off for the ancient ruins where Merton had experienced his "vision."

She hurried to freshen up, joining him for coffee and cold cereal, and then grabbing their bags, they bid their pilot farewell, no longer requiring his services.

The air was muggy, even inside the terminal—an old, metal-shell structure the size of a high-school gym. Immediately Angela felt conspicuous; she and Ian the only westerners she saw, everyone appearing of Indian origin and dress, Ian much taller, too.

She whispered, "Is the Order European only?"

He looked around, frowned, and took her hand.

"Just keep moving . . ."

Customs went quickly, but not so acquiring a car. One rental stand and a language barrier. But finally Ian secured an older, jeeplike vehicle, a map, and directions.

If they understood correctly, the ancient Dead City of Polonnaruwa lay seventy-five kilometers to the southeast—an hour's journey. Ian's plan was to drive on afterward, having arranged to overnight in Colombo, a city on the southwest coast. From there they'd fly on to Singapore, next stop in Merton's Asian tour.

Leaving the airport, they passed a military motorcade traveling the opposite direction. Angela saw a section of town ahead in shambles, many buildings burned-out shells, grim-looking peasants picking among the ruins.

"There's been civil war here for decades," Ian said. "Another religious conflict. Hindu Tamils fighting Buddhist Sinhalese. It's mostly over now, but it's taken a heavy toll."

The word "mostly" bothered Angela.

They took a two-lane road out of town, passing through rolling farmland of what Angela guessed was soy. Along the way they encountered bicycles, mopeds, brightly painted trucks—even oxcarts and the occasional elephant. Angela was enthralled. Then came a stretch of lush forest interspersed with small villages, seedy truck stops, and food stands. After that, signs of habitation diminished, at length melting away altogether into vine-choked jungle.

"Let me tell you about the Dead City of Polonnaruwa," Ian offered, perhaps to take her mind off their isolation. "It's a three-thousand-year-old time capsule. An Asian Pompeii. Capital of the Sinhalese empire once, and a wealthy metropolis. *Too* wealthy. India kept sacking it, and finally it was abandoned around 1200 AD. The jungle swallowed it up, and it was lost until the twentieth century. But because the structures were cut from solid rock, they're perfectly preserved. Like stepping into the ancient past, they say. A spiritual experience . . ."

The forest continued unbroken save for the occasional gravel road that wandered through. Then at length a sign directed them down one of those roads, and after a rough and winding drive, they dead-ended in a parking lot. Few other cars, City hidden by hills and a thick curtain of vegetation. It added to Angela's uneasiness, though she saw only enthusiasm in Ian's eyes.

He pulled the car to a dusty stop, hopped out, and circled to meet her.

"Talk about following in Merton's footsteps!" he said.

She forced a smile, he took her hand, and they walked a dirt path into deep, cool shadow. Quiet, but for the occasional odd cry of a bird; air thick, scent of decaying vegetation. Then rounding a bend, they emerged into hot sun again, coming to a surprised halt.

Before them, spread across a broad valley, was an array of formations hewn entirely from outcroppings of gray stone. Palaces, temples, towers, monuments, shrines. More necropolis than city—structures desolate and frozen in time like tombstones. Eerily quiet.

Ian let out a whistle. "The ancient Romans had nothing on these people!"

It looked more Aztec ruin to Angela, given the jungle.

They made their way down, Ian showing little interest in the amazing formations they passed, having a specific site in mind. Soon they reached a hillside of rock into which massive statues and a wide, rectangular opening had been carved. A sign read:

GAL VIHARA, CAVE OF THE SPIRITS OF KNOWLEDGE[23]

Another cave.

Despite the heat, Angela felt a chill. It was here, many decades ago, where Thomas Merton allegedly experienced his epiphany—just days before his mysterious death . . .

The Cave was attended by three giant stone Buddhas—reclining, standing, sitting. As this was a temple, Angela and Ian obeyed a sign to remove their shoes, hobbling across pebbles to the dark entrance. Then Angela took Ian's hand, inhaled deep, and they slipped inside.

No one else here. More grotto than cave, somewhat shallow, ceiling supported by pillars. Like a mausoleum.

As Angela's eyes adjusted she beheld yet another large Buddha chiseled into the rear wall, in the lotus position, surrounded by carvings of Disciples. But nothing to suggest the Secrets of the Ultimate Reality; no hints from the stone-faced statues. Only uncomfortable stillness.

She hung back while Ian explored. And then he searched out a spot on the floor in front of the Buddha, sat, and drew his legs under, hands palm-up in his lap, eyes shut, in perfect mimicry.

"Merton entered alone to meditate," Ian said. "He sat like this, reciting mantra, following the Tibetan rites of *nyingma*. Steadily lowering his heartbeat, working toward a state of perfect contemplation. The complete emptiness of *bodhicitta*. Pulse slower, slower, s-l-o-w-e-r."

It was too much. She went and grabbed his shoulder.

"You're scaring me."

"I'm trying to get a feel for what Merton experienced."

"Yes, and while you sit there like we've got some divine umbrella over us, a Sword could be sneaking up! I'm sorry I don't relate to this stuff, Ian, but we can't just close our eyes to the real world!"

"For once, why not open your eyes to the *spirit* world?"

She exhaled. "I've no faith in the spirit world—anymore than I do in your God protecting us."

He stood. "Four times we escaped *Arma Christi*. Luck, you say. But if it continues, even you have to admit, at *some* point we cross the line from luck to miracle, right? You tell me, *where*? Draw me that line!"

This gave her pause. She realized she had no criteria for miracles.

"I'll make you a deal," she conceded. "If we find Merton's Reality, and it has the power to stop *Arma Christi*, I'll open myself to your spirit world and miracles. But for now, I don't believe in divine intervention. And I sure as hell don't believe a miracle ever took place in this cave."

Grinning, he wrapped an arm around her and escorted her outside.

"Maybe one just did . . ."

SIXTY-FOUR

VATICAN CITY, THE PAPAL PALACE, SAME DAY, EARLY MORNING

Antonio hastened toward the ornate doors of the papal throne room, returning the salutes of his Swiss guards, trying to control the tremble in his hands. Three more such lavish rooms and he arrived at the pope's private library, door unguarded. He entered, relieved to see the pope's desk unoccupied, though he knew it would be.

Seated at a table nearby sorting papers was a lean man, late seventies, black cassock and the scarlet trim and sash of a cardinal. *Prefetturra* of the papal household. Antonio knew him well. A genteel, trusting man.

The *prefetturra* looked up, chirping, "You're early."

"Yes, I've much on my plate today."

Drawing closer, he watched the cardinal's smile wane, and the man noted, "You look pale this morning, *Direttore.* Are you ill?"

"Insomnia."

"Ah, yes. There's much to keep us awake these days. Try a glass of Barolo before retiring."

He promised he would.

"So, I understand we have a problem with the *Volta*?"

Antonio glanced out the window onto a rain-swept St. Peter's Square. "A glitch in the grid. It showed up on a monitor last night. Nothing serious, I'm sure. I thought I'd check while Papa says Mass."

"Of course."

Collecting his papers, the *prefettura* stood and ushered Antonio to a door at the back, up a set of stairs. Above were the pope's private apartments. Seven large chambers plus a small chapel and staff quarters for the papal housekeepers. And the *Volta Papale.* The pope's most private and personal repository.

Passing two austere front rooms they came to a study overlooking the

Cortile di San Damaso. Antonio had been here only once before, at the beginning of his tenure, receiving instruction from his predecessor on how to open the *Volta.* Nothing seemed changed—dark paneled walls, bookcases, reading sofa, the pope's large, private desk.

"I'll wait here," the cardinal said, going to the sofa. He held up his papers. "I trust you'll need no longer than half an hour; I must get this to the *Stamperia Segreta* by eight."

Antonio went directly to the rear of the room and faced the wall, heart pounding. *You've no choice,* he told himself for the hundredth time. *Papa's life could depend on it.* Breathing a prayer, he pressed a section of panel, seeing it swing out to expose a locked wooden door. He inserted a card in a slot in the door, which opened out onto a short hall that ended in another door—this one large and of polished steel. To its side, a keypad. Above, a security camera. He ignored the camera, having switched it off from his office, and closing the first door behind, punched a code into the pad, finger shaking.

There came the sound of metal against metal, air rushed past, and the door sprang ajar, lights flickering on.

Antonio faltered. Before him now stood the *Patrimonii Secretiti,* the most private collection of spiritual artifacts and documents in the world. The *Patrimonii* was rumored to contain sacred relics dating back to Christianity's earliest days. The sponge that had pressed wine to Christ's lips on the cross. A piece of wood from the Holy Rood. Also secret prophecies, visions, revelations, and ancient scriptural texts deemed too sensitive or disturbing for release.

The *Patrimonii* had been handed down exclusively from pope to pope over the centuries, today housed in this sophisticated vault. Though access was restricted solely to the pontiff, the Director of Vatican Security was also entrusted with the code that it might be passed on to the papal successor, and for issues of security and maintenance in the pope's absence. Antonio had taken an oath never to look upon or otherwise violate the vault's contents.

An easy oath to keep, to date, no occasion ever to visit the vault. But now, intent on safeguarding his Church and pope, and to preserve the lives of two innocents, Antonio was about to break his vow.

Somewhere within this room, he prayed, lay an eight-hundred-year-old papal Bull, *In Tutamine Cathedrae,* "In Defense of the Chair." The Bull allegedly containing the rules by which *Ordo Arma Christi* governed itself.

Antonio hoped to use it to help identify the shadowy sect and rid his Church and American friends of its menace. Given the Bull's potential to embarrass the Church, if a copy existed, it would be here, hidden among other problematic secrets.

Pulse racing, Antonio placed a hand to the cold metal. The door opened effortlessly, quietly. Inside resembled a bank vault. Stainless steel, six meters on a side, shelves circling the walls from the halfway point up.

The contents, however, were surely unlike any other vault. Filling the shelves were countless exotic, mysterious items—icons, paintings, small statuary, stone tablets, pieces of cloth, artifacts of silver, gold, and precious gems. All looked very old, categorized by cards with Roman numerals.

Beneath the shelves, butted shoulder-to-shoulder, were two dozen metal cabinets of equal depths but varying widths and drawer sizes. Two hundred drawers, Antonio estimated, each with Roman numeral and key lock. And in the center of the room, alone under the focus of a spotlight, a cabinet larger than the others. One and a half meters high, wide and deep, with a score of numbered, shallow-draft drawers, also bearing Roman numerals and key locks.

Antonio's heart sank. Searching all this could take hours, far longer than he could risk.

Surely Papa keeps an inventory. If not for himself, his successor . . .

The lone center cabinet seemed the likely place.

Donning latex gloves, he tried its drawers. Locked. But he'd come prepared. A simple wire tool easily opened the first, and holding his breath, he drew it back . . .

A large envelope, lying atop crimson felt lining. Fine white linen paper, some thirty centimeters square. Across its face was a directive written in what Antonio recognized as the pope's meticulous hand:

A successore meo confestim aperiri

"To be opened immediately by my successor."

Instructional documents, perhaps. And hopefully, an inventory. Heart hammering, he removed it with care.

Then he swore. Its flap was secured by the official papal seal, impressed in red wax. Each pope had a unique coat of arms. This, a knight's shield spanned by a cross.

Antonio replaced the envelope precisely as he'd found it and dropped to the next drawer, picking its lock.

A document between plates of glass. Broad sheet of brown papyrus scroll, title in faded brown ink:

Prohibitae Praedictiones

The Forbidden Prophecies.

Averting his eyes, Antonio moved on.

In the third drawer, four smaller documents of brown parchment also pressed between glass. Much older looking than the previous. Badly worm-eaten and tattered around the edges, ink faded nearly to the color of the paper, written in ancient Aramaic—a language Antonio recognized but could not read. Below the pages, a Latin translation, and Antonio nearly choked at the title:

Revelatio XXIII

Revelation. The book of the Bible that contained prophecies of the End Times. But the Book of Revelation Antonio knew had only *twenty-two* chapters.

Hastily he shut this drawer, too.

It seemed futile. The papal Bull, if here at all, could be anywhere. Meanwhile, the *prefetturra*'s half-hour deadline was looming.

The director's thoughts returned to the first drawer and its envelope. *Monstrous* thoughts. The papal seal presented little barrier, given time and the right tools. A simple matter to sneak the envelope back to his office and, assuming it contained the inventory list, determine the whereabouts of the Bull. Then reaffixing the seal, he could return it under pretext of making follow-up adjustments to the *Volta*, find and photograph the Bull, and be gone.

But stealing a private papal missive was a far more egregious breach than he'd bargained for. He vacillated, precious seconds ticking.

Balanced against the threat of Arma Christi, *surely a lesser evil. Surely God will forgive me!*

Reopening the drawer, he snatched the envelope, slipped it inside his coat, closed the drawer, and left.

SIXTY-FIVE

RUZYNE INTERNATIONAL AIRPORT, PRAGUE, CZECH REPUBLIC, SAME DAY, MORNING

Quintus taxied his little jet into its hangar, running his hand through his long, yellow hair. It felt greasy. He'd just returned from Baghdad after another difficult but successful mission, and all he wanted next was a shower and sleep.

Instead, he had to rush off to see Josef Varga in an attempt to clean up the man's bungled assignment. An unpleasant enough meeting made all the worse now that their roles were reversed, Quintus serving as Whetstone. And he was in no mood for Josef's thin skin.

Above his head, a speaker buzzed.

He stabbed a button on the console, snorting, *"Ja?"*

"Where are you?"

He recognized Cyril. "Ruzyne. Just landed."

"Listen to me—Josef's coming to you. You've got to leave for Rome soon as he gets there."

"But I am exhausted."

"Security at the Volta was switched off for an hour this morning. Ponti was there. God knows what he found."

Sobered, Quintus swore. "Vhat about Baringer?"

"There'll be time for that, Ponti's the greater threat now. Josef is the only one who can get to him—and we're counting on you to make certain he does."

SIXTY-SIX

DOWNTOWN COLOMBO, SRI LANKA, SAME DAY, NOON

After a drive through mountainous backcountry, Angela and Ian arrived at the capital of Sri Lanka. Colombo, city of a million sprawled along the southwestern sea coast.

Angela gazed out on a startling mix of modern and ancient. Western-style skyscrapers erupting next to dome-topped topes and pagodas, gaudily painted Hindu temples, spired mosques and churches. She'd never seen the likes, an architectural hodgepodge from a half-dozen cultures.

The streets were thick with vehicles and pedestrians, keeping Ian on his toes as they pushed through.

Nearing the oceanfront they entered a kilometer-long stretch of palm-treed boulevard bordered by elegant, older buildings. One stood apart. White stone, four stories, sprawling and luxurious. Splayed on its façade was the name *Galle Face Hotel*.[24] The hotel from which Merton mailed his Ultimate Reality to Karl Barth and My Valentine many years ago.

Wearing caps and sunglasses, Angela and Ian entered from the hotel garage. They were by no means the only Westerners in the bustling lobby, Angela unsure if that was good or bad. English seemed the common language, a remnant of British colonialism, she assumed.

On the wall was a plaque declaring that the *Galle Face* had been established in 1864, having hosted such prominent guests as Richard Nixon, Indira Gandhi, and Emperor Hirohito. No mention of Thomas Merton.

They registered under fresh names, Ian acquiring suite 224—Merton's old room according to the receipt Frau Hummel had shown them.

"For good luck," he told Angela.

Though she felt uncomfortable with that at first, she quickly got over it. The suite was magnificent, no doubt refurbished several times since

Merton's stay. Four-poster king bed; twelve-foot ceiling; balcony overlooking pool, sand beach, and sparkling Indian Ocean.

As they unpacked, Angela wondered, "How could a poor monk like Merton afford all this?"

"He may have taken a vow of poverty," Ian said, "but he was a best-selling author who made a ton of money for the Church. And the Church knows how to treat its VIPs."

Showering, they ordered lunch, then feeling refreshed, they grabbed hats and sunglasses and slipped down to the lobby, Ian wanting to ask around about Merton's stay here.

"The hotel might still have records," he suggested. "And just maybe Merton left some notes behind."

They approached a clerk at the front desk, obviously born after Merton's time. She had no idea who the monk was, referring them to the manager, an older man with a brown complexion and British accent. He, too, was at a loss, but offered, "There is someone here who may be of help . . ."

He made a call, and moments later a small, slim, elderly woman appeared through a door behind the counter. Skin nutmeg brown, hair gray and tied back in a bun, glasses, orange shawl around her shoulders. She eyed Angela and Ian with shy curiosity.

The manager said, "This is Shanti, our bookkeeper—an employee here since a girl." He turned to her. "Shanti, Mr. and Mrs. Jones. They're asking about a guest who stayed at the Galle many years ago. I thought you might recall."

"Merton," Ian said. "Father Thomas Merton. A monk from America. A writer."

The woman's face went from inquisitive to surprised.

"Yes," she said, accent Indian, clasping her hands. "Father Merton. I was a chambermaid at the time."

Angela thought the woman looked uncomfortable.

The manager smiled and excused himself, and Ian continued, "We're great admirers of Father Merton. Did you have the good fortune to meet him?"

"We spoke several times. Very nice man. Very kind. Such a tragedy . . ."

"I spent time at his abbey in Kentucky," Ian said, "and I'd like to learn more about his trip here. His experiences. Do you happen to know if he had visitors during his stay?"

Again she seemed ill at ease. "We no longer have registry records from back then. But as I recall, he had no visitors. He spent little time here, always away. I regret I am no help."

Ian persisted, "In particular, I'm interested in a trip he made to Polonnaruwa. He had a vision there. I'd like to know what it was."

Angela watched Shanti's eyes move off Ian as if looking into the past, a faint smile creasing her face.

"Oh yes," she murmured, "his trip to the Dead City."

Ian's eyes lighted.

"I was late making up his room that day, I remember. Father returned before I finished, very excited, laughing, chattering. He was always cheerful, but especially so that afternoon. Beaming. He said a wonderful thing had happened at *Gal Vihara*. He said the world was about to change, forever, for the better—and he gave me a big hug. It startled me! And then he laughed and said not to worry with finishing his room, and he sent me off!"

Her smile faded. "He left for Singapore soon after, and . . . and then we got the news about Bangkok. Everyone here was very sad. We all liked Father Tom."

She paused, then asked Ian, "You visited Gethsemani? Where he wrote his books?"

"Yes. You know of it?"

"From his writings. I have read all his writings. He was a wise man."

"Wiser than any of us may ever know," Ian said softly. "Do you recall if he left anything behind when he checked out? Papers? A notebook? A package or letter?"

She gave him a sharp glance. "I know of nothing. And now if I have answered your questions, I must get back to my work. I am sorry I was no help."

Ian thanked her for her time and she disappeared back through the door behind the desk.

He sighed and placed his arm around Angela, escorting her away. "There for a minute . . ."

"Yes, I thought we were on to something, too. So what now, Singapore?"

Before he could answer, a voice called out to them.

Shanti, scurrying across the lobby, rueful look on her face. She caught up, hand to her heart.

"Forgive me," she panted. "I was not honest with you . . . There is a wrong I must make right. I *do* have something that belonged to Father Merton."

SIXTY-SEVEN

RUZYNE INTERNATIONAL AIRPORT, PRAGUE, CZECH REPUBLIC, SAME DAY, NOON

"*Ja,* it could not be more perfect," Quintus said, pulling back on the yoke, easing the powerful little jet off the runway into azure skies, heading for Rome. "Ponti's vife ist avay visiting grandchild. All you must do ist vait for my signal, den make contact vith him."

"I don't like it," Josef snapped, buckled into the copilot's seat, watching the Vltava River become a silver ribbon below as it wound through the city. He felt a pang, wishing he were down there strolling the Charles Bridge with his *matka,* a child again.

Quintus brought him back. "Do you know better vay to guarantee Ponti's cooperation?"

Josef was too tired to think. He'd spent the night in the catacomb where Cyril had left him, on his knees begging the martyred Gabčik, Saints Cyril and Methodius, and God, to make clear what he should do. But as dawn came he'd heard nothing, miserable, retreating to his flat, to bed.

Only to be awakened a while later by his Answer. A call from Cyril informing him that the man he'd once worked with and long admired, Antonio Ponti, had violated his vows. The honorable, incorruptible Antonio had broken Faith with his pope and his God!

At last it was clear. Baringer was indeed infected with Evil, and it was spreading. Now Ponti had to be stopped, too.

But Quintus's plan to handle Ponti gave Josef qualms. Even carried out in God's Name, it was heartless. Though he could think of no alternative.

Overhead, a speaker buzzed. Quintus punched a button.

"Ja?"

"We located the car Baringer and the girl took from Mayrhofen." Josef rec-

ognized the voice of a Swiss E&E. *"Bern. A couple matching their description hired a jet at the airport yesterday afternoon."*

"To vhere?"

"Anharapura, Sri Lanka. That's all we have now, but we've got E&E in that sector."

Signing off, Quintus grunted. "Sri Lanka? Vhat de hell dey doing dere?"

Josef closed his eyes. *Bern . . . Sri Lanka . . .*

And then it struck him.

"The Reality. They're after Merton's Reality again."

Quintus gave him a squint, and Josef explained, "Merton made two copies of the Reality—one he sent to Karl Barth in Bern, which we destroyed. Baringer must have gone looking for it, and when he came up empty he decided to focus on the second copy, following Merton's trail to Asia."

"Let him look. If *ve* couldn't find it all dese years."

Josef wasn't so sure. "How many *centuries* did we hunt Polycarpe's formula? Baringer has inside help from Ponti . . ." He snapped his fingers. "*That's* why Ponti was in the *Volta*. He's after Merton's journal—trying to get the original Reality for Baringer!"

Quintus appeared more confused. "But vhy ist de Reality important to dem? If ist de Knowledge of Good, how vill it help Baringer find his parents? Good has no place in Hell."

Josef didn't know, but the question nagged him.

"No matter," Quintus said. "Ve'll deal vith Ponti, den Baringer und his voman, und dis blasphemy vill be over."

Arriving at cruising altitude, he leveled off, setting the plane on autopilot. Then extending a large hand to Josef, he wiggled his fingers.

"Dossier . . ."

Josef reached beside him for a manila envelope, handing it over.

Quintus emptied a stack of papers and photos in his lap, thumbing through, selecting a color shot. A close-up of Baringer and his woman boarding a small jet, Rome terminal visible behind, she holding on to her cap in the wind.

"She ist *very* beautiful!"

"Not in the Eyes of God."

Quintus pointed to her hand and its ring, snorting. "Dey are engaged! Und he a *priest*? Little Jezebel!"

Josef watched a cruel leer form on the man's lips.

God help her if she falls into his clutches . . .

Another buzz from above, and Quintus punched a button. Josef recognized the voice of Cyril.

"We have a problem. Ponti is no longer in Rome."

SIXTY-EIGHT

GALLE FACE HOTEL, COLOMBO, SRI LANKA, SAME DAY, AFTERNOON

As the elderly bookkeeper led Angela and Ian to employee quarters behind the hotel, Angela felt her pulse race. Perhaps at last Merton's Reality was within reach.

"Shortly after Father Tom left for Singapore," Shanti told them, voice sheepish, "a letter arrived for him. We knew Father would be in Singapore only briefly, and to forward the letter risked missing him. So our manager mailed a delivery notice instead, asking instructions. But before he heard back, we got the news . . .

"I was brokenhearted. Father was so full of life and energy, such a good man. I couldn't believe he was gone. I saw the letter at the front desk, and I . . . I don't know why . . . I took it. A foolish young girl. I wanted something to remember him by. *I'm so ashamed . . .*"

Angela's hopes vanished. The letter wasn't *from* Merton, but *to* him. It couldn't be the Reality, after all.

She looked to Ian, seeing the fire in his eyes ebb.

Shanti continued, "A week later a man came to the hotel. A Catholic abbot, I can't recall his name, asking for any correspondence Father had left behind. I was too embarrassed, I said nothing. He was persistent, but finally left." She began to tear. "I kept the letter all these years, never opened it, never told anyone."

Stopping in front of her door, she faced Ian. "I want to clear my conscience and return it to the lady who sent it."

"Lady?"

"It's addressed in a woman's hand. Very elegant. Postmarked Paris, but no return address."

Angela saw the fire rekindle in Ian's eyes. No doubt he thought the letter from Merton's secret lover, Valentine, the only other person believed to have a copy of the Reality.

Shanti showed them into a single-room apartment, sparsely furnished, dominated by a large wood and glass bookcase. She went directly to the case, selecting from a shelf filled with Merton's books, withdrawing one.

Angela read its title with a wry smile.

Conjectures of a Guilty Bystander.

Opening it, Shanti removed a small, slim envelope. Faded, pastel blue, addressed in a free and florid hand. She surrendered it to Ian.

"Please, tell no one where you got it."

He promised. Then thanking her, assuring he'd do his best to find its sender, he and Angela left with their prize . . .

On the way to their room Angela could almost hear the gears grinding in Ian's head. And once inside, he locked the door, sitting on the bed, frowning down at the letter. But he made no move to open it, chewing his lip like a kid eyeing a forbidden cookie jar.

"Cold feet?" she asked.

"I feel like a peeping Tom."

She plopped next to him. "If you won't, *I* will."

It was postmarked airmail, *Paris France, 28 Nov 1968,* addressed to *Père Thomas Merton,* and marked *Privé.*

Angela gave Ian an elbow, and finally he exhaled and worked a fingernail into the flap. It gave way easily, without tearing, glue having long lost its cling, no doubt. He shook out a two-page letter. Beautiful longhand on stationery slightly less faded than the envelope. Angela was disappointed to see no inside address. She read aloud, " '*Cher Père*—Dear Father' "—the extent of her French.

Ian took it from there, " 'Another rainy night in Paris . . .' "

An account of a day in the life of an ordinary-sounding Parisian woman. A divorcee, it appeared, in a troubled relationship with an artist, Henri, who exhibited at a gallery, *Bruit d'Oeil.* The woman wanted to break off the relationship but hadn't the confidence, she said, complaining that little had changed in her life since last she wrote. Trusting Merton's trip was going well, she wished him luck in his *recherche grande,* hoping it brought him the answers he'd long sought. Ian finished the translation:

> *I pray you'll find time to visit me on your way home. Somehow I feel it's now or never. I don't expect we'll meet in Heaven, I'm bound for a*

different place. But never to see you for all eternity? Hell could hold no crueler a punishment!

All my heart,
Valerie

Sighing, he returned the letter to its envelope. "Quite the ladies' man."

"So you think Valerie is 'Valentine,' Merton playing off her name?"

"If she is, I don't see him loving her for her mind. I mean, she's not exactly in the same league as Karl Barth."

"Then why single her out for a copy of his Reality?"

Ian shrugged. "Maybe he really did love her. Or maybe she was just an old flame he'd dumped, and he was trying to ease a guilty conscience."

"Well he cared enough to give her his Asian itinerary. Should we assume she *is* Valentine, try to track her down in Paris?" Angela wouldn't have minded Paris.

"Not much to go on. I say we stay on Merton's trail for now, turn over a few more stones."

"Singapore, then?"

He shook his head. "Merton only spent the night there. But he was in Bangkok three days until his death. If we're lucky, the Bangkok police may still have his 'accident' report. Maybe even evidence from his room—notes, letters. And I'd like to check out the Red Cross conference center where he died, too. Maybe get a room."

She felt a chill. "The room Merton died in? *No way.*"

He gave her a look of mock surprise.

"But I thought you didn't believe in ghosts."

SIXTY-NINE

THE STREETS OF VATICAN CITY, ROME, SAME DAY, LATE NIGHT

Things were not going to plan. After leaving the *Volta Papale* yesterday morning, Antonio had gone straight to his office with the pope's envelope, intending to open it, find an inventory list with whereabouts of the secret Bull, reseal the envelope, and immediately return it to the vault.

Instead he'd been caught up in the urgency of an unscheduled papal trip. The pope's mother, ninety-six and living in Naples, had been hospitalized with a heart ailment, requiring Antonio and team to rush the pontiff to her bedside in the papal helicopter.

Antonio could only lock the unopened envelope in his desk before leaving, fretting about it the entire day, beset with guilt each time he looked at Papa. Nevertheless, he had no change of heart, the Bull his last hope to free his Church and friends from the curse of *Arma Christi.*

The pope's mother had improved by late evening, fortunately, Papa electing to return to the Vatican. Antonio had just delivered him to the papal palace and was now rushing back to his office across the desolate roads of the City. He planned to find the list in the pope's envelope, stay here the night, and return to the *Volta* in the morning while Papa said Mass. He wouldn't be missed at home, Carla was visiting their daughter and new grandson in Tivoli, a half-hour's drive to the east . . .

He pulled into his parking space to see himself the only car, *Governatorato* dark, seemingly deserted, as hoped. Entering with his passkey, he stopped at the receptionist's desk to check its garbage bin. Empty. *Good.* Janitorial had completed its rounds; there'd be no interruptions.

Hastening upstairs to his office, he left the lights off, locking the door behind, closing the drapes, switching on a gooseneck lamp at his desk. Then to the cabinet for a snifter of Courvoisier. He carried it to his chair and sat, downing it in one long pull, closing his eyes, waiting for the warmth to spread. And once it reached his hands to still them, he exhaled and unlocked his drawer.

The envelope was just as he'd left it, *thank God.* Fishing a penknife from his pocket he tested its sharpness on a thumbnail, set it aside, and put on reading glasses and latex gloves. Then removing the envelope, he placed it on his desk papal-seal-up, focused the lamp on the seal, and lowered the hood till it was scant inches above, allowing the heat of the bulb to do its job.

A delicate, stressful operation. Work the wax too soon, it would crack. Too late, it would run. But if the seal released properly, he'd have no problem covering his tracks. He'd simply heat the flap, reset the seal, and the hot paper would bind itself to the wax again, good as new.

He tested often with the knife, finally judging the wax pliable enough, and began to work the blade under the seal's edge, taking great care. His diligence was rewarded. The flap popped free cleanly, and he exhaled, crossed himself, and slid the envelope's contents onto his desk.

Two sets of documents, a half-dozen pages each. First, a letter in elegant Latin script, addressed to *Successor Meus,* "My Successor." Stamped across the front in bold red letters—

Illiciti Lectores Damnationi Aeternae Subjecti!

"Unauthorized Readers Subject To Eternal Damnation!"

Antonio froze. He hadn't anticipated this, the stakes much higher now. If he went no further he could yet salvage his oath—much more, *his soul.*

He took a long breath to calm himself.

In his heart he knew this was no betrayal of his Church. He was, with all good and loyal intentions, attempting to correct one of Her historic mistakes—and by the only means left to him now. There'd be no sin if he made swift, clean work of it. Thumb through this first letter, blind to all but an inventory list, seeking only the whereabouts of the Bull that gave *Arma Christi* its Frankenstein immortality.

Uttering a prayer for understanding and forgiveness, he began flipping . . . *No list.*

But it *had* to be here! Papa wouldn't fail to apprise his heir of the

Patrimonii's weighty secrets! If not in this letter, then surely in the pages of the second document.

A journal of some kind, he noted as he swept through. Hand-typed in English on ruled sheets of yellowed paper . . .

And still nothing!

He drummed his fingers anxiously on the desk. The only hope left now was that the pope's letter would at least mention the list, referring his heir to its whereabouts. Antonio had no choice but to search its lines more closely.

Beating back his conscience, wiping his brow, he skimmed.

The letter began with words of congratulation to Papa's successor, followed by advice on the many troubles besetting the Church—legal, financial, ideological . . .

Antonio sped on. Pet projects the pope wished to see finished, a plug for his favorite charities . . .

And then, three-quarters through, still no mention of an inventory, he met a passage he *could not* skim. A warning. So provocative, so unfamiliar to Antonio, as Security Director he *had* to know:

> *Of all the tribulations you may face, there is one unlike any other. An old and insidious threat, the existence of which you are no doubt unaware, though it has been with us since the earliest days of the Church. Gregory the Great was first to describe it, calling it* Sophisma Serpentis.

Antonio whispered, "The Serpent's Sophistry!"

> *It is a sleight-of-mind, an evil not unlike demonic possession, if far-rarer, thank God. It afflicts some who survive encounters with death—a near-drowning, heart failure, even suicide attempt—where the soul slips from life into death and miraculously back again.*

Antonio gasped, "NDE!"

> *During this brief journey into twilight the soul is vulnerable, like a lobster molted from its shell. Especially a soul whose Faith is weak. Forces of Darkness will sometimes intercept such souls and fill their minds with a false vision of Paradise—a sinister ruse to invalidate the Gospel of Matthew 16:18-19.*

Not knowing Matthew by heart, Antonio fumbled in a drawer for a copy of the Vulgate, reading:

> *And Jesus said, 'Thou art Peter, and upon this Rock I will build my Church; and the gates of Hell shall not prevail against it. And I will give unto thee the keys to the Kingdom of Heaven; and whatever thou shalt bind on Earth shall be bound in Heaven; and whatever thou shalt loose on Earth shall be loosed in Heaven.'*

The famous verse where Christ ceded His Earthly authority to Peter. Not found in the other three Gospels, the only such passage in the entire Bible. From these lines alone sprang the Church that continued to this day, two-thousand years and two-hundred-seventy-odd popes later. The Serpent's Sophistry, it seemed, was a devilish trick to undermine papal supremacy.

Antonio returned to the letter.

> *. . . The victims of such treachery, thinking their vision genuine, return to life with missionary zeal, spreading the blasphemy to other weak souls. The papacy has confronted these threats many times through the centuries, and failure to deal with them has led to crises—not the least of which, the Protestant Reformation.*
>
> *Written accounts of these sophistries survive in the* Patrimonii, *listed on the inventory sheet in my desk safe. I include one herewith, a journal of a more recent journey into death that well-illustrates the danger.*
>
> *Be warned, it is as beguiling as the serpent's temptation of Eve in the Garden. Yet once your eyes open to the deception, you will surely continue the safeguard I am about to mention—an unpleasant, if necessary legacy of this throne . . .*

"The inventory list is in his desk safe!" Antonio moaned, no possible hope of accessing it. And now adding to his worries, this ominous warning.

Ignoring for the moment the pope's "safeguard," he dropped the letter and went back to the journal, hoping to identify the source of this more recent threat. No title, merely a date in an upper corner. *12.5.68.* He skipped to the end looking for a signature, seeing none, eyes falling on the last lines:

. . . Next week marks the anniversary of the day I first entered Gethsemani, half a lifetime ago. The day I began my long, meandering search for Truth. A fitting day to complete the circle. To open the world's eyes to the Ultimate Reality.

"My God!" Antonio cried, realizing what he held. He could no longer restrain himself. Pulse racing, he read from beginning to end, feeling his eyes would burst . . .

Indeed, the journal posed a *grave* threat to the Church!

But the pope had a special safeguard.

Antonio picked up the papal letter once more, reading in disbelief. First his jaw dropped. Then his heart.

The pope's "safeguard," he discovered to his horror, was to underwrite the services of *Ordo Arma Christi.*

SEVENTY

BANGKOK, THAILAND, SAME DAY, MORNING

To make an 8:00 AM appointment in Bangkok, Angela and Ian had left Colombo in the middle of the night, flying three hours by private jet, leaping two time zones to arrive at Suvarnabhumi International by 7:00. Once through customs they grabbed a cab, schedule too tight to risk driving themselves, possibly getting lost.

Their destination was about twenty-five kilometers south. A Red Cross conference center where Merton had come decades before to unveil his Reality to the world, losing his life instead. Ian had been hoping the center might still hold clues to the Reality—if not a copy itself.

Yesterday online, however, he'd learned that the center, though still in existence, had been abandoned years ago. Undeterred, he'd shifted his attention to the Bangkok police, tracking down the inspector who'd originally investigated Merton's death, a Mr. Yin Nang, retired. And in an exchange of e-mails, he'd persuaded Nang to meet at the old center first thing this morning . . .

Angela anticipated a muggy day, the air already warm and thick as their cab exited the airport into heavy traffic. Cars, trucks, motorcycles, mopeds, and odd, tricycle-like passenger vehicles that reminded her of souped-up golf carts. All driving recklessly on the left-hand side.

Ian seemed oblivious. "I wonder if Mr. Nang knows the *true* cause of Merton's death."

Angela moaned. "For once, I'd like to think the Order wasn't involved."

"And I'm praying they were."

She looked at him.

"If Merton was murdered," he reasoned, "then I know it wasn't God's doing. God may allow men to commit murder, but He doesn't cause them to do it. He's incapable of Evil. So assuming the Order was responsible, that means God didn't punish Merton for stealing His Knowledge. Good news for me going into this next NDE."

That knot again. Tomorrow, barring a miracle, she and Ian would leave for Capetown and Ian's date with Death.

She stared out the window, watching their route go from crowded city to stretch of industrial plants and factories. Soon they arrived at a village overlooking a bend of the wide and murky Chao Phraya River. SAMUT PRAKAN, a sign read.

Zoning here seemed an afterthought, the area a mishmash of charming homes with steep-pitched curving roofs and elaborate eaves stuck next to shanty huts, storefronts, and vacant lots strewn with trash.

The cab slowed, driver hunting their address, stopping in front of a treed parcel of land thick with underbrush. To one side was a weatherworn, white stucco building, paint peeling to reveal cinderblocks. Faintly visible on its façade, a familiar Geneva cross in faded pink color, accompanied by the words SAWANG KANIWAT RED CROSS CENTRE.

Angela noticed another cab parked ahead. A white-haired man exited and approached. Eighty, perhaps, but sprightly. Asian, small build, pale skin, hair neatly parted. Spectacles, suit and tie. She and Ian went to meet him.

He smiled and bowed, speaking polished English. "Former Inspector Yin Nang. Pleased to make your acquaintance."

They returned the bow, Ian completing the introductions.

While their cabs waited, meters running, Nang ushered them down a path into the compound where they were quickly engulfed in deep shade beneath a canopy of trees. Angela's eyes wandered the derelict camp as the men chatted. Clusters of two-story bungalows to the right, larger buildings on the left—administration and meeting centers, she assumed. All stucco-covered cinderblock, finish flaking, roofs sagging like the backs of old mules. Windows on the lower levels were boarded shut; those higher, unprotected, the glass broken out.

Then rounding a bend, Angela suddenly felt her skin crawl—the sensation of eyes on her. She focused on the upper-story window of a building ahead. Too dark to see in, but she thought she detected movement; a shape coming forward, moving back into the gloom. She couldn't be certain, this ghost town lending itself to figments.

There it was again!

No . . . just a ragged curtain fluttering in the breeze . . .

Until she realized, *What breeze?*

SEVENTY-ONE

OFFICE OF THE DIRECTOR OF SECURITY, VATICAN CITY, ROME, SAME DAY, PREDAWN

"Merda, merda, merda!" Antonio moaned, bent over his desk in the glow of its lamp. He desperately needed to reach Ian, alert him to the magnitude of their problem.

Outside, the bells of St. Peter's Basilica tolled three times. Antonio had no idea where in the world Ian and Angela might be now, or what time zone, hours ahead or behind. Irrespective, he took out his cell and punched Ian's speed dial—only to be patched into voicemail. He left anxious word: "Ian! Call soon as you get this! Something's wrong! Something's *very* wrong—"

He broke off, astounded to see a tall shape materialize before him as if conjured from the darkness, face obscured in shadow. Dropping his phone to the desk, he lunged for a drawer, whipping out a handgun.

"Unnecessary," the shape said in Slavic-accented English, male. "I'm unarmed."

Familiar voice. Clothes dark, hands gloved and folded in front. Antonio swore. He'd been so caught up, the intruder had slipped in without him hearing, masked by the tolling of the hour.

"Wh-who are you?"

"You know. And you know why I'm here."

Antonio sprang to his feet, gun never leaving the man's chest, glancing around for an accomplice, seeing none.

The dark head inclined toward the envelope on the desk, papal seal open.

"I'm alone," he said. "And it appears, too late."

Christ! He knows!

"You signaled your intentions shutting off the *Volta*'s security camera.

We knew you'd fallen under Baringer's spell, but I would never have believed *so low.*"

Now Antonio recognized the voice, heart faltering.

"My God! Not *you,* Josef! You were a *son* to me! *I trusted you above all others!"*

The silhouette shifted its weight. "You speak of trust, Antonio, stealing from the *Patrimonii*? Violating your oath? God forgive me, I failed to stop this Evil before it destroyed your soul."

The director cocked his gun. "You expect to stop me *unarmed*?"

"Yes. And with your cooperation . . ."

Antonio's cell rang on his desk. He glanced down. No caller ID. *Ian?*

"Answer. Go to your video display."

Feeling icy fingers wrap his heart he snatched up the phone, seeing the softly lit image of a child sleeping in a crib. Then suddenly the view shifted to a man with long blond hair, pillow in hand.

"Bastardo!" Antonio cried, extending his gun point-blank at Josef's heart.

"Shoot, and you lose not only your grandson, but wife and daughter."

The director's eyes leaped from Josef to screen and back . . . No choice, he laid down his gun.

Josef pointed to the documents on the desk, and Antonio scraped them into the envelope, mind racing. Then as Josef reached out to receive it, Antonio held back, shielding his phone with the envelope, deftly snatching it up, angling its lens, pressing "video record."

Seemingly unaware, Josef leaned forward, face entering the halo of the desk lamp, demanding, "No games! Give it to me! *Now!*"

Antonio surrendered the envelope, and as Josef pulled back, he pressed his phone's speed dial.

SEVENTY-TWO

BANGKOK, THAILAND, SAME DAY, MORNING

Angela stood frozen on the path, detecting more movement behind the second-story window of the building ahead. Ragged curtains fluttering despite the still air—as Ian and the inspector continued toward it, unaware.

Before the cry in her lungs could escape, however, doves suddenly exploded out the window, vanishing into the trees.

She stood agape a moment longer, then swearing, hand to racing heart, she hurried to catch up with the men.

"The afternoon Merton died," Yin Nang was telling Ian, "there were over a hundred attendees and media at the conference." He pointed to the building that had just given Angela such a fright. "That's where he gave his last talk."

They passed what Angela assumed was once a garden, its small pond choked with water lilies. Then turning a corner, they arrived at a two-story cottage, roof tiles buried under fallen leaves, windows and doors boarded. Above the door was the outline of a numeral 2 left in grime.

"Here we are," Nang announced. "Merton's cabin. Shall we roust the ghosts?"

Ian needed no further invitation. Trying the door, finding it locked, he pried a board from its broken window and reached through to the latch inside. The door yielded to a shove, the shriek of rusty hinges causing Angela to cringe.

They picked their way through leaves and trash into a combination living room/dining room/kitchen. Stripped of furnishings; filthy. Air stale and dank. Floors dark terrazzo, walls a dismal brown print with splotches of mustard mildew. A hallway led to the back.

"Four bedrooms," Nang said. "Two up, two down, each with a bath. Merton's was on the first floor."

"You have an excellent memory," Ian told him.

"Not a case easily forgotten. Allow me to walk you through what I believe took place." He escorted them down the hall. At its end was a stairway up, preceded left and right by two closed doors with louvered top panels.

"There were two other gentlemen here the afternoon Merton died," Nang said, stopping at the doors. "The morning session had run late, well past lunch, and Merton was exhausted. It was hot, and he'd been going nonstop for days visiting shrines and temples. So he and a cabin mate decided to return to nap before the closing session that evening. Merton went to take a shower, his associate went upstairs, and that was the last Merton was seen alive."

Nang indicated the door to his left. "A monk from Manila roomed here. Around 2:45 he came back to brush his teeth, and about that time the man upstairs heard what he thought was a cry or shout, then the sound of an impact.

"He came down and knocked at Merton's door, got no reply, found it locked, and checked on the monk across the hall. But the monk had heard nothing, and knowing how tired Merton was, the men went back to their rooms.

"An hour later they both smelled something burning, and they rushed to Merton's room, pounding, calling in. Still no response. So they pried up a louver and saw him lying naked on the floor with a pole fan atop him."

Opening the door, Nang showed them into a small room with a closet, bath, and window. Angela hung back, all this too uncomfortable.

Nang pointed to a corner. "The fan's metal pole had burned a deep fissure across Merton, chest to leg, blades still turning in their cage. The monk rushed to grab the fan, but froze to it, and his associate had to pull the plug. The current here is very strong, 220 DC.

"According to the men, Merton was lying in a pool of urine—electric shock releases the bladder, you see—and there was much bleeding from the back of his head, his face was blue, eyes and mouth open, toes curled. Obviously dead.

"They fetched the conference director, a bishop who gave Merton Last Rites and had him cleaned up and dressed. All this before calling the police. By the time I arrived, the body was on the bed, Red Cross doctor examining it, evidence completely compromised."

Ian asked, "Could you determine cause of death?"

"Not conclusively. The head wound could have come from striking the floor after a shock from the fan, or just as easily from an assailant's blow.

"And it wasn't apparent whether the shock or the head injury caused death, or even which came first. The fan had a defective cord, but there were no burns on Merton's hands, which were said to be resting at his sides. If he'd touched the fan to switch it on or move it, his hand would have frozen to it the same as the monk's. Yet there were no burns beyond that lesion on his torso."

"Maybe he tripped on the cord and pulled the fan over, causing the short."

"Maybe. Though you'd expect him to be in a position other than on his back, arms at his sides. It's also possible he was knocked unconscious and the fan rigged. But without an autopsy, we were forced to rule it an accident."

"No autopsy?"

Nang spread his hands. "Red tape and politics. With Merton's fame, many agencies got involved. The Vatican, Merton's abbey, the U.S. Embassy and Air Force base here, International Red Cross, Thai government. Out of control. It took five days to get the body released, five more before it reached his abbey for burial. And there was never a post mortem."

The room grew quiet. Angela could feel Ian's tension, knowing he'd saved his most important question for last.

"Mr. Nang," he asked, "did you happen to find a journal with Merton at the time of his death? Possibly notes, letters he'd written? *Anything?*"

Nang paused. "A wallet, a watch, and a good camera—which seemed to rule out robbery. Clothing and other personal effects in drawers. But no journal or writings. Nor did anything turn up later, to my knowledge."

That was it then . . .

They made their way back outside, Ian looking like the air had been sucked out of him. He relocked the door, stuck the board back in place, and they returned along the path.

As they passed the conference center, Angela again felt the eerie sensation of eyes on her. She asked, pointing, "Mr. Nang, do you know what that room was used for?"

He followed her finger. "Odd you should ask. That was the only room with air conditioning. We kept Merton's body there while we sorted out custody."

Shivering, she picked up the pace.

At the cabs Ian opened his wallet and counted out a sizeable sum, handing it to Nang.

The man grinned. "Toward my grandson's education!"

Then thanking them, he shook hands, bowed, and left.

"So," Angela said as she and Ian turned to go, "was Merton's death accident or murder?"

He exhaled. "I suppose we'll never know. And I'm beginning to feel the same about the Reality."

SEVENTY-THREE

THE STREETS OF ROME, SAME DAY, MORNING

Head down, eyes alert, Josef hastened from the Vatican, having slipped out its walls the same way he'd entered, concealed in the cargo bay of a delivery truck. He strode south along the tree-lined *Rampa Aurelia,* all quiet save for the squawks of starlings in the branches above, a blush of dawn on the horizon.

This had been the most stressful mission of his life, and worse was yet to come. But after all the days of angst and soul searching, he at last felt right in his mind. He'd witnessed the Evil with his own eyes, seen the director he'd once held in such high esteem reduced to treason. Josef understood now the power of Ian's poison.

Nevertheless, while he finally grasped the Evil, he was no less baffled by Ian's actions. Why chase the Reality after already seeing proof of the Afterlife? Why descend into Hell knowing how grievously it would offend God?

Yes, Ian longed to see his parents again. But what sane man would flout his Maker and throw away his soul to do so? Did his parents mean more to him than his God? Was he possessed by Evil forces? There was something *else* going on here. Something very worrisome . . .

A noise behind—a dark-windowed sedan approaching, pulling alongside.

Josef opened the passenger door and slid in.

"Ist taken care of?" Quintus asked, alone in the car.

"Yes."

"Vhat vas it he took?"

"The pope's instructions to his successor."

Quintus grunted. "You returned it?"

"By way of a Curia cardinal."

The big man's face darkened. *"You involved others?"*

"I should hand it to the pope over breakfast?"

"Dere are better channels, Brother!"

"I wanted to be done with it. Surely a high cardinal will respect the Seal—even a broken one." Tired of the man lording his Whetstone, Josef snapped, "And *you*? Ponti's family is unharmed?"

"Dey never even suspected. Now let us finish dis."

Josef shared the urgency. Should Ian succeed in his mad plan, just souls would thereafter be denied their Heavenly Reward, consigned to no better than the eternal nothingness of Limbo. Not to forget Cyril's dire warning of worse consequences. The diabolical traps that awaited mortals in the Eternal Down Under, Ian possibly blundering into a mistake with cosmic repercussions . . .

He fell silent as they continued south toward the airport.

After a time, Quintus asked, "Vhat troubles you now? Still doubts about Baringer?"

"It's that he makes no sense. Why journey to Hell knowing it could mean his life and soul?"

"*Ja.* He vill join his parents soon enough anyvay—I vill see to dat."

"And this obsession of his with the Reality. He already has his proof of the Afterlife, why travel the globe searching for more? He has something up his sleeve."

Quintus shrugged. "He assumes de Reality's Secrets vill somehow aid him in Hell."

Suddenly the man's words made all the pieces fall into nightmarish place. Josef felt an ominous shadow pass over his soul. *"Oh my God . . ."*

"Vhat?"

"It's worse."

"Vorse dan costing us salvation?"

Josef's throat went so dry he could hardly speak. "He wants the Reality to help his parents, all right! He knows it's the Knowledge of Good—he intends to wed it back to the Knowledge of Evil *to open the Gates of Hell!*"

Quintus gasped. *"Vhat God hath put asunder, let no man join together!"*

"The fool will unleash the damned! A *second* Rebellion! *Judgment Day!*"

Quintus nearly ran off the road. "Ist he so stupid he vould risk Apocalypse!"

"Not stupid. Duped. *Think!* He couldn't hope to find his parents in Hell without help. He's struck a bargain with the Forces of Darkness. They're using him to free themselves, to strike back at God. For all we know, *Baringer is the antichrist!*"

A look came over Quintus unlike Josef had ever seen in him. *Fear.* He stomped the pedal and roared, "I be damned if I vait in Capetown! You go, Josef—*I track de bastard down!*"

SEVENTY-FOUR

ORIENTAL HOTEL, BANGKOK, THAILAND, NEXT DAY, PREDAWN

After their meeting with Inspector Nang, Angela and Ian had traveled back to Bangkok to overnight at its famous Oriental Hotel, a resort where Thomas Merton had stayed briefly before his fateful sojourn to the Red Cross Center. Another long shot that hadn't panned out. No hotel employees remained from the days of the monk's visit.

It was still dark outside their suite when Angela felt a warm hand on her arm.

"I got an e-mail from Yvette Garonne," Ian told her softly. "The third heart/lung bypass is in. I notified Emil."

Time had finally run out . . .

She rose with a heavy heart, packed her bag, and they left for the airport in a cab. Again, no signs of pursuit.

Earlier, Ian had chartered a sleek new jet for them, calling Angela's attention to it now as they boarded. A very fast, long-range Raytheon Hawker. As if she cared.

For the man in a hurry to die.

They departed to the west, jumping out ahead of the sun, heading for Mogadishu on the horn of Africa where they would refuel before turning south to Capetown.

Ian passed the time reading *Paradise Lost*. Angela, one of her psychology journals. But she couldn't concentrate, the dull siren in her head again. And it seemed they'd hardly lifted off when she looked out her window to see the tip of the Indian subcontinent below. The halfway point.

She could no longer hold back.

"I've got a *bad* feeling about Capetown."

He gave her arm a squeeze. "Trust me, I've spared no expense on equipment."

"Not just the lab. We've heard nothing from *Arma Christi* in four days."

"Not since that tracking device, thanks to you."

"It's too quiet. What if they know about Capetown? What if they're lying low waiting for us?"

He seemed undaunted. "I've taken extra precautions."

"What does Antonio think of your precautions?"

"We haven't discussed them."

Her siren grew louder. She realized they hadn't spoken to Antonio since leaving Bern, Ian reluctant to bother him, knowing the man's pressures.

"Call," she insisted. "You said he was working on another plan for us."

It being safe now to use his phone, Ian switched it on, and Angela saw several message alerts on his screen. Most from *Y. Garonne.* But also two from *V. Ponti.*

"Odd," Ian said. "He left a voicemail and a video."

Sticking the phone to his ear he listened to the voicemail, and Angela watched him frown. Then he held the screen for both to see. A murky, incomprehensible video clip accompanied by a man's voice—not Antonio's.

"No games! Give it to me! Now!"

Hurriedly Ian dialed the director's number. No answer. Redial. Nothing.

He recued the voicemail and held the phone to Angela's ear. Antonio's voice this time: *"Ian! Call soon as you get this! Something's wrong! Something's* very *wrong—"*

She gripped Ian's arm, and he lowered their window shade to replay the clip. Marginally clearer. A field of black with a patch of light glowing in the middle. This time Angela could make out a figure moving into the light, face indiscernible.

"No games! Give it to me! Now!"

Then it reached out to seize an envelope from another hand, withdrawing into darkness.

"Who is it?" she asked, anxious. "What's it mean?"

Ian shook his head. He dialed Antonio again, this time leaving a message, urging him to call.

Angela's siren was wailing. "The Order knows about the lab! Antonio's trying to warn us!"

Ian turned to his laptop. "Maybe he sent an e-mail . . ."

He opened on a bulletin, a Catholic news service he subscribed to. Angela read its headline, and the bottom fell out of her heart.

"Vatican Security Director Critically Wounded."

She felt Ian's arm tense beneath her fingers as he clicked a link to a TV newscast. File footage, it looked, Antonio at the Vatican standing next to the pope.

A voice-over declared, "Mr. Ponti remains on life support, suffering from what is said to be a self-inflicted gunshot to the head. He is not expected to survive . . ."

Ian swore, slamming his fist on the armrest, and Angela collapsed in tears.

SEVENTY-FIVE

THE SKIES ABOVE THE PERSIAN GULF, SAME DAY, MORNING

Quintus sat alone at the controls of his jet, one third into a grueling flight to Bangkok—last known whereabouts of Baringer and his seductive accomplice. Though up all night, he was no longer tired, mind in a boil over the calamity now unfolding. The threat of Baringer opening the Gates of Hell had sent the entire Brotherhood into a dither, the High Council into an emergency session.

A buzz from the loudspeaker, and he punched a button.

"Ja."

"Baringer left Bangkok—we picked up his cell over the Indian Ocean, heading west."

Quintus recognized the voice of an E&E in Jakarta. "Capetown," he replied. "His lab ist ready."

"Present course suggests the Horn. Possibly to refuel in Mogadishu, he can't make Capetown direct. But we've got no one in the area."

"Vhere ist Josef?"

"On his way to Capetown . . ." A pause, then, *"Over Chad, now. He's closer, shall I send him?"*

Checking his gauges, Quintus did a quick calculation.

"No, I vant Josef in Capetown."

"But Ernst and Yuri are already there."

"*Nein.* I can beat Baringer to Mogadishu."

"You should know, he uncovered something of Merton's at a hotel in Colombo."

"De Reality?"

"Unknown. We're investigating."

Swearing, Quintus pulled the plane's yoke sharply to starboard.

SEVENTY-SIX

THE SKIES OFF THE HORN OF AFRICA, SAME DAY, AFTERNOON

Angela gazed out the window, numb, as Ian placed calls to the Vatican. He was seeking details on Antonio's condition, getting nowhere, met by the Church's standard wall of secrecy.

"Scandals are controlled at the highest levels," he told Angela after another effort. "All anyone knows, Antonio is at a hospital, in surgery."

It was a bad time to raise another sensitive issue, but with their jet closing on Africa, Angela had no choice. She grabbed Ian's arm.

"Sweetheart, the Order . . . They're in Capetown. Antonio was trying to warn us."

Ian paused, giving her a strange look. Then sighing, he nodded. "Yes, I'm counting on it."

She thought she'd misunderstood, but he added, "They've known all along."

"What?"

"It turns out, we have our *own* mole . . ."

Angela felt her jaw drop.

"Down in St. Maarten, when the lab was wrecked and the team went back for the data, Emil caught Yvette in the stairwell on her cell, talking about Capetown. He assumed she was making arrangements, but she hung up when she saw him, claiming it was her stockbroker. She's been playing both sides. Emil didn't let on, not even to Luc Dow, only to me."

Angela was flabbergasted. "But if she's setting us up, *why are we flying into a trap*?"

"We're not. Once we refuel we're leaving for South America. Emil arranged a separate lab, under wraps. Capetown is a decoy. And by the time *Arma Christi* realizes it, we'll be an ocean away."

"You could have told me!" she snapped, hurt.

He took her hand. "I couldn't even tell Antonio. Emil was so paranoid after Yvette, he made me swear. And judging from Antonio's warning, the plan worked."

"But we don't know *what* his warning is. You've got to call it off!"

"No time. Yvette's already suspicious. When we don't show tomorrow, *Arma Christi* will know it's a shell game. They'll move Heaven and Earth to stop us. It could be my last chance to end this nightmare"—his voice softened—"and save my soul . . ."

She squinted at him, wondering what bizarre leap of logic he was taking this time.

"Save your soul?"

His eyes filled with anxiety.

"Sweetheart, if I don't go through with this, what happens to me at the end of my life? It won't matter where my soul goes, I'm damned either way! To know I had a chance to see my parents again, maybe help them—after they gave their lives and souls for me? Never to see them for all eternity? Surely Hell is no crueler a punishment!"

She pulled back, struck hard by a déjà vu. *"What?"*

"What?"

"What you said—'Never to see them for all eternity; Hell is no crueler a punishment'—where did we just hear that? *Same words?"*

The pilot's voice interrupted, announcing their descent into Mogadishu, and they were forced to table things.

But Ian's words kept playing in her head. Angela couldn't place where she'd heard them before, yet she sensed something important.

It continued to haunt her as they touched down, refueled, and took off, on course now for South America.

Ian suggested they get some rest, they reclined their seats, and soon Angela heard Ian's rhythmic breaths. But she couldn't relax, still kneading her memory as they soared over the grasslands of the Sudan.

And then suddenly she sat up.

"THE LETTER!"

"Wh-what, what?" he cried, bolting upright, fists raised.

"The letter Shanti gave us—Valerie's letter to Merton! *Where is it?"*

He gaped at her a moment, then frowning, grumbling, searched it out of a pocket.

"Open it," she told him. "Her last lines . . ."

Once again he translated: *" 'I don't expect we'll meet in Heaven, I'm bound for a different place. But never to see you for all eternity? Hell could hold no crueler a punishment!'* "

It was so clear! Angela grabbed Ian's arm, excited. "Valerie *isn't* Merton's lover. But she *is* My Valentine!"

His frown deepened, and she pointed to the letter's salutation. He read, " '*Cher Père.*' Dear Father. So . . . ?"

"Don't you see? Valerie isn't speaking to Merton the priest. She isn't his lover, or some infatuated fan. When she says 'Dear Father,' she means it *literally*. Valerie is Merton's daughter! A child longing for its parent. *Just like you!*"

He took back the letter, poring over it.

"Can't be. Mother and child died in the London Blitz. We don't even know the child's sex."

"It's *assumed* they died. Merton never confirmed it, you said. What if the child, a girl, survived, lost among thousands of war orphans? She would have been—what—seven, eight? Old enough to remember her father's name years later when she heard it."

"But this Valerie is *French*."

"Maybe French relatives took her in. Or she moved to Paris when older, I don't know. But trust my child psychology, this is a *daughter* speaking. A daughter in pain, appealing to her father."

She saw a light in Ian's eyes, and added, "Merton must have been carrying around huge guilt for abandoning them, thinking they'd been killed. Then one day, out of the blue—a letter! His daughter had survived the bombs." Angela tapped the pages in Ian's hand. "But with emotional scars."

Ian nodded slowly. "And Merton wouldn't acknowledge her. Not publically."

"Too ashamed, worried about his reputation. He kept her at arm's length, hushed her up. Even avoided her on his trip to Asia, taking the long route over the Pacific . . .

"But then, in the Dead City, in that cave, something happened to change him. He had an epiphany. How did he describe it in his letter to Sister Marjorie?"

"Knowledge to uplift the most despondent soul."

"Yes. Knowledge to heal his daughter's scars and redeem himself! The Ultimate Reality. The irony is, his need to hide her from the world may have saved her life. If it's true he burned her letters, maybe the Order never knew of her. Or if it did, not how to find her. Meaning she didn't meet the same fate as Karl Barth."

"Or poor Antonio . . ."

Angela took his hand. "If Valerie *is* still alive, seeing from her letter how much Merton meant to her, you have to believe she kept her copy of the Reality."

Ian pressed a button on his armrest, calling up to the pilot, ordering a change of course. Then he sent an e-mail to Emil, advising him of a temporary change in plans.

SEVENTY-SEVEN

THE SKIES ABOVE SOMALIA, AFRICA, SAME DAY, AFTERNOON

Like the lion whose prey escaped it on the savanna far below, Quintus was in a foul temper. He'd landed in Mogadishu less than an hour ago only to taxi right past his quarries, watching them take off—and in a jet faster than his. No hope to catch them now.

Then reporting in to headquarters, he'd learned that Baringer had filed a flight plan for Rome. Same old ruse. Quintus hadn't fallen for it, refueling, leaving immediately for Capetown, certain Baringer was headed to where Josef and two senior Swords were now waiting.

An end to this crisis at last—though Quintus was furious he wouldn't be in time for the finale, denied the pleasure himself.

His thoughts were interrupted by a phone call. Cyril.

"E&E just picked up Baringer's cell. He's over Ethiopia, on a northwest *heading!"*

"Northwest? *Scheiß!*"

The sly bastard was flying in the *opposite* direction of Capetown!

"We now know what he found in Colombo. Not the Reality, though it may lead him to it. An old letter from Merton's 'Valentine.' From Paris, no return address, contents unknown."

Swearing again, Quintus pulled the jet around, entering new coordinates into his flight computer.

SEVENTY-EIGHT

AN ALLEYWAY OFF BOULEVARD DE SÉBASTOPOL, LE MARAIS DISTRICT, PARIS, FRANCE, NEXT DAY, MORNING

"That's where it was, anyway," Ian told Angela, huddled inside a rental car in an alley, comparing the address of the café across the street with the paper in his hand. "Surely someone around here remembers it . . ."

Since landing at a small airport outside Paris last night and sleeping at a B&B, still with no new word on Antonio, they'd been trying to sniff out the whereabouts of Valerie, the mysterious writer of the letter they'd obtained in Colombo. They trusted she was still alive and living in the city, but with no address to go on, not even a last name, they faced a daunting task.

The letter mentioned an art gallery where Valerie's then-boyfriend, Henri, had exhibited. No current listing, but Ian found online an old address for La Galerie d'Art Bruit d'Oeil, leading them here. As he now saw, however, the gallery had been replaced by Edouard's, an upscale bistro sandwiched between posh retail stores.

"You take Edouard's," Angela said. "I'll try next door."

Pulling hats low, sunglasses on, they parted.

But reuniting a short time later at the car, Ian could tell from her face: "No luck?"

"All young salespeople. You?"

"Edouard was busy, and when I offered him money, he threw me out."

They widened their scope to more stores. Again, nothing.

Angela suggested, "Let's try calling art galleries."

"There must be a thousand in Paris—and you don't speak French."

Reflecting, she paid him a coy smile. "Wait here, I'll be right back . . ."

Before he could ask, she trotted over to Edouard's, stopping out front to remove hat and glasses and fluff her hair. Then unfastening a button of her blouse, she waltzed inside—emerging minutes later with a triumphant grin and a slip of paper.

She reported, "It so happens, Edouard ran Bruit d'Oeil before turning it into a restaurant. He remembered Henri."

Ian stared at the paper.

Henri D'Essoire. No phone number, but an address . . .

An hour later, assisted by Google Street View GPS, they made their way into Bobigny, a high-density, low-income suburb to the city's northeast.

Angela gazed out the window at an area bleak and unrecognizable as Paris. Tall, featureless concrete and steel apartment buildings, each its own affront to her aesthetics. Everywhere, graffiti, litter, and a general look of malaise—evident also in the blank stares of the locals. Black. Asian. Middle Eastern.

Ian pulled up to one apartment tower. Twenty stories, perhaps. Fifty years old at least. Balconies a jumble of drying laundry, bottles, and boxes. Anywhere there was metal, it was rusted.

"Not the best neighborhood to take a stroll," Ian noted as they conducted their standard surveillance.

"We've come too far to quit now . . ."

He reached over, fastening the button of her blouse, and they exited the car, picking their way around broken glass to a graffiti-marred entrance.

Inside, Angela removed her sunglasses to see a small lobby, elevators cordoned off by yellow tape reading HORS SERVICE.

Ian grunted. "D'Essoire is on the ninth floor. Can you handle the climb?"

She arched a brow at him. "After Mt. Grüblspitze?"

They found a stairwell and started up, Angela grimacing at the ripe scent of urine. She heard male voices above, and Ian took her hand.

Soon two toughs came into view, smoking on the landing between six and seven. Early twenties, heavily tattooed, piercings in their bristly faces; one dark-skinned with long dark hair; the other pale, shaved head.

At the sight of Ian they went silent. Then their eyes fixed on Angela, making her skin crawl.

"Pardon," Ian said as he guided her past, *"est-ce que vous connaissez Henri D'Essoire?"*

They ignored him, and Angela felt their leers, glancing back to see long-hair angle his head at her, slurring to his companion, *"Un belle cul . . ."*

Ian moved behind Angela, blocking their view, and in a voice soft yet conveying absolute resolve, he declared, *"Et je garde son belle cul . . ."*

The men went quiet, and Ian ushered Angela on to the ninth floor, through a door, into a dim, tunnel-like corridor.

Only one working light fixture, fluorescent bulb sputtering and winking. The flats were missing numbers, but from outlines left in the dark-green paint Ian located 929, and giving Angela a hopeful look, he knocked.

No answer. Again, louder. Then he banged, and the door suddenly popped open. Swearing, he went charging in—only to brake.

Angela saw a large man flopped on a couch, his back to them, snoring. Hair long, gray, and stringy, straggled over his shoulders; suspenders at his sides; holes in his socks. The room was a hovel. Empty liquor bottles and old magazines, art canvasses lying about in various stages of work, corners piled high with junk as if acquired from a lifetime gleaning dumpsters.

Ian started toward him, but Angela grabbed his arm.

"He'll find me less threatening . . ."

Looking hesitant, Ian allowed her past, hovering as she touched the man's shoulder.

"Mr. D'Essoire?" she cooed. "Excuse me, Mr. D'Essoire?"

The snoring ended in a snort, and the man raised his head, squinting. Bushy brows. Full beard, gray and wiry.

"Ce qui?" he said. Then focusing on Angela, his eyes went wide and he grunted. *"Merde!"*

She backed up. "Sorry! I didn't mean to startle you."

He appeared more confused than frightened.

"Américain?" he muttered, voice coarse and throaty. Seeing Ian, he swung his legs out, sitting, blinking at them with a look of anger and astonishment. "How you get in!"

"An accident," Ian explained. "The door came open when I knocked. Please, you *are* Henri D'Essoire?"

He regarded them suspiciously.

"What you want with heem?"

"Help in finding someone," Angela said.

Ian took out his wallet. "We'll pay . . ."

Looking more confused, if interested, the man scratched himself, studying them through bloodshot eyes.

"Who? And how much you pay?"

"A woman you knew in the late sixties," Ian said. "Fifty euros. All we know is her first name. Valerie."

Angela saw surprise in the man's eyes, which turned cagey as he extended a hand.

"One hundred euro. *Toute de suite!*"

Ian removed two one-hundred notes, keeping them.

"Now, *who are you?*"

"Henri D'Essoire," he admitted. "I know ze woman. We were lovers . . . once. Why you want her?"

"A personal matter."

He stared at Ian, then at the money, and groaning, he struggled to his feet. Hand on hip, he lumbered to a corner, Angela keeping his hands in sight.

She saw dozens of framed canvases resting against a dented metal cabinet, and D'Essoire stooped to thumb through. Grunting, he removed one, blew away dust, and held it up for them.

The portrait of a plain-looking, pale young woman with beaded necklace, daisy tucked behind an ear. Thirtyish. Uneasy blue eyes, blond hair, nose thick at the bridge. Lips thin and compressed. A definite resemblance to Thomas Merton. Angela exchanged a knowing glance with Ian.

"Her last name?" Ian asked, voice tense.

The man wiggled hungry fingers. Ian fed him one bill.

"Pardeau," he said. "Valerie Pardeau. We live together for a time. She leave one day, no word." He pointed to his head. *"Folle!"*

Angela asked, "What became of her? Where can we find her?"

Ian gave the last bill a snap.

"Eet was years ago. Last I hear, she was at *charité*. Not far."

Ian surrendered the bill. "Get me an address . . ."

A short time later they were back in the corridor, Ian clutching a slip of paper.

Angela asked, "Think he's telling the truth?"

"We'll know soon enough . . ."

They hurried to the stairwell, Ian opening the door for her. But as she stepped through, she suddenly felt her purse ripped away.

The two men from the landing—*one wielding a knife.*

Ian rushed forward, Angela grabbing him, holding tight.

"*No!* It's not worth it! Let them have it!"

They demanded Ian's wallet, too. Swearing, he gave it up and the men backed away, grinning like Cheshire cats. In a flash they were gone, scrambling down, footsteps and laughter echoing.

Ian took Angela in his arms. "Are you okay?"

She nodded, feeling his heart hammer against hers.

"My fault," he said bitterly. "I let my guard down!"

They'd both been negligent, caught up in their hopes of finding Merton's daughter. The thieves could just as easily have been *Arma Christi.*

"We've got spare IDs and passports," Angela noted.

"And thank God they didn't get these . . ."

Ian pulled from his pocket Merton's letter to Karl Barth, and Valerie's letter to Merton. "We're going to need them."

The stairwell silent now, they crept down, no further sign of their attackers.

SEVENTY-NINE

CLICHY-SOUS-BOIS, NORTHEAST PARIS, FRANCE, SAME DAY, LATE MORNING

Still shaken from their run-in, Angela and Ian navigated to yet another desolate ghetto.

Worse even than D'Essoire's, Angela thought. A ruin of old, ramshackle apartment buildings, boarded-up houses and stores—the last-known whereabouts of Valerie Pardeau. Ian parked next to a long, narrow, one-story cinderblock building with a rusted sign:

LES ANGES DES MALHEUREUX

"Angels of the Unfortunate," he read.

A soup kitchen. Graffiti-covered, but otherwise clean, a dozen destitute-looking individuals loitering out front.

Angela and Ian made sure they weren't followed, then entered to see many more such men and women at tables under fluorescent lights, eating what appeared to be stew. Others stood in line at a counter in back where several women served from large kettles.

Crewing one kettle was a thin, gray-haired woman, average height, simple blue dress and apron. Her face may have aged, but she remained recognizable as the subject of D'Essoire's painting.

Angela felt her heart skip, and she nudged Ian. But he was aware, seizing her hand, leading her into line. And as they drew near, his grip tightened.

Valerie wasn't what Angela had expected. Not that a person's nature can't change over time, but in light of the despondent letter the woman had sent Merton, Angela envisioned her lonely and maladjusted. Even neurotic.

All the same, this Valerie looked the epitome of contentment. Wretchedness of her clientele aside, she seemed to enjoy her work, greeting people cheerfully by name, sharing a comment or laugh. Her eyes had lost that edginess so evident in the painting. And when she smiled, it welled from the heart. The soul.

Angela and Ian dispensed with bowls, and when at last their turn came, Valerie found no place to unload her ladle, looking them up and down in puzzlement.

"Puis-je vous aider?"

Ian doffed his cap. *"Excusez-moi. Je suis* Ian Baringer, *et c'est* Angela Weber. *Pouvons-nous vous parler un instant, s'il vous plaît?"*

Smiling, the woman gestured to the long line and shook her head. *"Pardon, je suis très occupé en ce moment."*

Ian reached into his coat to produce a faded-blue envelope, holding it address-side out.

"I believe this belongs to you, *Mademoiselle . . .*"

The woman's face froze, and the ladle slipped from her fingers, disappearing into the pot. She backed away wiping her hands on her apron, removing it, passing it off to a fellow worker. Then making her way to an empty table, she sat in a huddle, head bowed, breathing heavily.

Ian and Angela took chairs opposite her.

She didn't look up. " 'Ow'd ya find me?"

"There were clues in this," Ian said, setting the envelope in front of her. "It was never delivered. No one else has read it, your secret's safe, we mean you no harm."

Then softly he asked, "You *are* Thomas Merton's daughter?"

She raised nervous eyes, searching their faces.

"In all me life," she said, voice breaking, "no un's ever asked me that. An' in all me life, I ne'er told a soul . . ." As if reclaiming a long-denied pride, she straightened her shoulders. "Yes . . . *Yes.* I'm Thomas Merton's daughter."

Then dimming, she added, "If ya've come to ask 'bout 'im, I can't 'elp ya. I ne'er met 'im. Ne'er so much as spoke on the phone."

Ian nodded. "A tragedy he died before that could happen."

" 'Is death 'ad nothin' ta do with it. I was just one of 'is mistakes, ya see, come back ta 'aunt 'im. 'E'd only speak ta me by letter."

"But he was planning to see you. On his way back from his trip to Asia."

She shook her head, eyes pained. " 'E was returnin' by the same route 'e came—'e sent me 'is itinerary so I could write 'im."

"He changed his plans," Ian said, reaching into his pocket again. "Do you remember a German theologian by the name of Karl Barth?"

"Rev'rend Barth—Father's friend. Yes, Father recommended 'is writin's ta me."

Ian opened Merton's letter and handed it to her.

She put on spectacles, seeming to recognize the handwriting, reading silently, lips moving.

When she finished she turned stunned eyes to Ian, then read again, aloud, voice trembling, "'*In light of the Reality, I am visiting Europe after all, tending to a personal matter in Paris. Very important and long-overdue! Afterwards, I will accept your invitation and visit you in Bern. I hope to bring a special companion with me. Together the three of us will celebrate the Reality . . .*'"

She trailed off, handing the letter back to Ian.

"Y-ya've no idea what this means ta me . . . All these years thinkin' . . . *thinkin' 'e didn't care!*"

Angela felt herself misting.

Ian leaned across the table to touch Valerie's hand.

"I understand. I've been separated from my parents since a child, too. I believe the Reality can help me reach them. I pray you still have it, and you'll share it with me."

She dabbed her eyes with a napkin. "Yes, I 'ave it. One thousand words strong . . ."

Angela felt Ian's hand like a vise under the table.

"It's got the Truth ta reach your parents, all right. Truth ta 'eal the world! But much as I wanted ta share its message all these years, I couldn't."

Incredulous, Angela blurted, "For God's sakes, *why?*"

"Father forbid it. In 'is last letter 'e told me ta keep 'is Secret till word was out. Too dangerous, 'e said, and I honored 'is request . . ."

Ian slumped as if the soul had been sucked out of him.

But Valerie patted his hand, adding, ". . . waitin' for this day. You've come. Word's out. Time for the world ta finally know the Reality!"

EIGHTY

AN ALLEYWAY IN AN IMPOVERISHED DISTRICT OF NORTHERN PARIS, FRANCE, SAME DAY, NOON

A late-model black sedan with tinted windows turned off Avenue Pierre Sémard into an alley bordered by old, concrete-sided buildings. It cruised slowly like a shark on the prowl, tires plowing through litter.

At the wheel, eyes hungry and alert, was Quintus. He'd gotten little sleep last night, canvassing the Paris airports with E&Es, searching in vain for these two. But now at last, they'd made a mistake. A *fatal* mistake . . .

He held a GPS locator in one hand, red dot flashing to indicate his quarries just ahead, around the next corner.

Pulling behind a dumpster, he switched off the engine and got out. He moved quickly, silently, pulling the brim of his hat low, tugging leather gloves over his thick fingers.

As he neared the corner, he hugged the building, slowing to peer around its edge into another seedy alleyway. Deserted but for two figures huddled together about fifteen meters away, sitting on steps.

He felt his blood heat, clenching his fists, crouching, rushing out. The two looked up, wide-eyed.

Not who he was after! *Punks!* One swarthy with dark hair, rifling through a purse. The other fair, shaved head, texting on a cell. They broke, but Quintus was faster, grabbing their collars, pivoting, hurling them hard into the building.

They collapsed, moaning, and he straddled shaved-head, grabbing his throat, demanding in French, "*The phone*—how you get it?"

The kid gaped up at him, shaking, silent.

Quintus squeezed the boy's neck till his eyes bulged red. Then relaxing, he snapped, "Last chance."

"St-stole it," he sputtered.

"American couple?"

He nodded.

"Where?"

"Tenement . . . down the block. *Let me go!*"

Quintus tightened his grip again, and the boy gasped, "An old drunk . . . Henri D'Essoire."

EIGHTY-ONE

CLICHY-SOUS-BOIS, NORTHEAST PARIS, FRANCE, SAME DAY, NOON

Ian and Angela accompanied Valerie Pardeau from the soup kitchen, down an alley toward her nearby flat.

Angela's heart raced, hopes high that Ian's long, circuitous quest for the Ultimate Reality was nearing an end. Still, she kept close watch on the abandoned houses and stores they passed, mindful after that attack in the stairwell earlier. Especially with Ian so absorbed in their new acquaintance, plying her with questions.

"How did you come by your last name, Mlle. Pardeau?"

"Please, *Valerie,*" she insisted. "Got it from me mum. She an' Father weren't together anymore when I 'appened, see. There was a cash settlement o' sorts an' 'e took off for the States. Mum din't talk 'bout 'im much, but she din't 'ide 'im from me, neither. I knew the gist."

"You lost your mother in the War?"

"Blitz of forty-one. 'Er sister took me in. Then she wed a French bloke an' we come 'ere after the War. 'E 'ad an eye for me, though, so I left for the streets at fourteen."

Ian's face darkened. "You've had a tough life."

She laughed. "That I 'ave! Popped 'round from chap ta chap after that, fell in ta drink an' pills. Finally got in a family way an' undid it meself—ended up in hospital. Ruined me innards, sterile as a mule!"

There wasn't an ounce of self-pity in her voice. But Angela felt deep sympathy. And anger at Merton.

"Then one day, I'm passin' this shop on the street, an' 'ere I see a book in the window with 'Thomas Merton' splashed on it. I'm thinkin' it's a fluke. But I go in, an' soon I sees 'is picture on the back, I knew. Same eyes. Knocked me over, 'im a priest an' all!

"So I nicked the book, an' just couldn't believe. All 'bout 'is life—but 'e din't mention Mum an' me! Talked 'round us. Stuff 'bout wastin' 'is youth in an 'ell of 'is own doin's—St. Augustine–like, sinner facin' 'is failin's. But 'e couldn't face what come of 'is failin's. I 'ated 'im!"

She laughed again, without bitterness.

Ian said, "So you contacted him."

"Took me years ta work up nerve. 'E was brilliant, educated. Me, ignorant an' crude. Finally I wrote. Din't let on me 'urt at first. Wasn't after money. Alls I wanted was 'im ta acknowledge me. Alls I wanted was a father.

"But not a word. Couldn't muck up 'is name with the likes of me. Still, I kept writin'. Bundled up me shames an' dumped 'em inside the walls of that abbey." She laughed again. "I was a sorry lot! Twenties, destitute, no will ta go on. When finally I wrote 'im that, *that's* when 'e wrote back. Saved me. Knowin' 'e put value on me life's what kept me from throwin' it away . . . 'E wouldn't claim me in public, though. Made me swear not ta tell."

"That must have hurt terribly," Angela said.

She shrugged. "Least we 'ad a relationship. 'E wrote such kind letters. Sent me l'il gifts. Cheese an' fudge from 'is abbey, 'is latest books. Give me advice on me problems, shared 'is thoughts 'bout religion an' society an' politics. So in 'is way, ya see, 'e was a father ta me . . ."

They arrived at a block of five-story tenements.

"And 'ere we are."

It looked little different from D'Essoire's building but for its height and worse state of repair. Windows broken and boarded up, graffiti and trash everywhere. Ragged children played soccer in the street as a stocky black woman on a balcony, cigarette dangling from her mouth, argued with two black men working on a car below.

Angela and Ian followed Valerie down a cracked sidewalk sticky with spent chewing gum, up a stairwell to her flat at the top. A combination kitchenette/living room with sleeper sofa, small desk, cabinet, and chair. Austere, neat, and spotless. On one wall, shelves laden with books, some Merton's. Angela saw no phone or TV.

Offered seats and tea, Angela took the chair, Ian the sofa. But they declined the tea, their thirst lying elsewhere.

Valerie went to the desk and opened a drawer, searching, removing items, setting them aside.

Ian looked astonished.

"You keep the Reality in an unlocked drawer?"

"Perfectly safe. Ever'one knows I've nothin' of material value."

And yet, Angela thought, if the Reality was the Great Clarification it was said to be, truly able to end hatred and strife around the world, it was priceless.

She found herself wanting to Believe . . .

The woman withdrew a large manila envelope, faded, rough-edged, its flap held shut by a simple string tie. Clasping it to her chest, she joined Ian on the sofa.

"This arrived the day Father died. See, I 'adn't 'eard 'bout the accident yet. I was workin' in a factory then, livin' with this artist bloke, 'Enri. I was expectin' somethin' in the post—Father said 'e was sendin' a special gift. An' when I got 'ome that night, this was waitin'."

She unfastened the flap, sliding out a handful of yellowed, standard-sized letter pages. "First, let me read ya 'is cover letter . . ."

Her voice grew hushed. *"Thursday, December 5, 1968. My Valentine."*

She broke away, smiling. " 'Is pet name for me.

"I tremble still as I write this! I am shaken to the soul! Dear Valentine, I have just witnessed something I believe no other man living has seen! An epiphany beyond anything I have ever experienced!

This morning, in the innocence of my heart, I stole through Heaven's back door to witness a Great Truth! A wonderful, irrefutable Truth that will transform the world! I don't know if what I've done is wrong, but I feel no shame. Indeed, the Vision is so perfect and compelling I must share it, whatever my risk!

I am entrusting it to you first—the most important Knowledge of my life!

The Ultimate Reality.

May it restore your wounded heart as it has mine. May it bring you the peace my weakness has cost you. All I ask is that you keep it in confidence till word of it is out. (Who Knows how the Almighty will react to having His Secrets told!)

Look for another surprise to arrive soon!

All my love,
Your father

Angela saw tears in the woman's eyes.

"Your father," Valerie repeated. "'E'd never called 'imself that afore. An' for all these years till today, I ne'er knew what 'is other 'surprise' was—

"'E was comin' to see me!"

Hands shaking, she passed the remaining pages to Ian, adding, "Whatever 'is failin's as a father, *this* saved me soul . . ."

EIGHTY-TWO

A SMALL FLAT IN CLICHY-SOUS-BOIS, NORTHEAST PARIS, FRANCE, SAME DAY, EARLY AFTERNOON

Heart pounding, Angela watched Ian accept five sheets of yellowed paper from Valerie Pardeau.

The account of a vision long hidden from the world. Not a divine vision, to be sure, but hopefully the answer to their problems all the same. If the Reality could inspire Thomas Merton to embrace his daughter, if it could transform Valerie from sinner to saint, maybe it could induce Ian to give up his NDEs. Maybe even sway *Arma Christi* to show mercy.

A slim hope. Slim as the faded pages in Ian's fingers . . .

From Angela's vantage point the text was upside down, but she could see that its lines had been composed on a manual typewriter. Lots of floating-cap letters, errors corrected by striking through. As if transcribed in haste.

Ian read silently, eyes intense. Until Angela could stand it no longer, protesting, and he explained, "So far, just a description of Gal Vihara. Hold on, I'm getting to the Cave . . ."

She watched his finger trace a few more paragraphs, and then inhaling, he read aloud:

At last I come to it—the Cave of the Spirits of Knowledge!

My guides wait outside and I enter alone. On the rear wall, a giant carving—another Great Buddha, seated in perfect meditation, surrounded by Disciples, all hewn out of granite. Ancient striations of color running through the stone, archives of time. Layers upon layers of history laid down like file folders over the eons.

Humbled, I sit, remembering the teachings, focusing on the practices of

Nyingma. I will myself. Mind over body. Spirit over matter. And slowly, clumsily the physical submits. Respiration. Heartbeat. Metabolism.

I go deeper into myself. The moment is right, I feel it! Deeper, deeper! Having never achieved bodhicitta, *I slip into it almost without realizing. A complete opening of the psyche; a seamless, inside-out unfolding! Liberated into nothingness! Mind transcending consciousness!*

I sense I should go no further. But the Knowledge I seek, I know lies deeper. I hear voices—the stone Disciples on the wall, crying out to me, warning me. I ignore them and push on. Deeper still. Deeper than ever I imagined!

My tired, aching shell slumps to the floor. My heart ceases its futile flailing. I wriggle and writhe, and suddenly I molt free. Separation! I am floating, ascending, looking down on the old self, bereft of its soul, gray of skin, pitiful.

I no longer care. Wisdom awaits, I sense it!

Above, a tunnel of cloud, and I enter, swimming toward the light. Then suddenly I burst free, radiance exploding over me! I can scarcely withstand the intensity! I raise my hands against it, but the brilliance shines through!

Voices call out to me, but I press on toward the light, eyes adjusting. I pass over golden fields of flowers to a golden forest, on to a vast mountain that sheds golden streams into a golden river and rises up in clouds, and I soar on!

Reaching a plateau, I find myself among throngs of glowing spirits, arms upraised in gratitude to God. One stands in my way but I pass straight through! Above and beyond lies a golden lake.

Then abruptly I slow. Not my will, outside of me. Like a leash tightening. I strain but cannot resist, I can rise no higher. No matter, I am high enough to See! I open myself to the brilliance that bathes me, letting it pour over my soul. Inundating! Saturating!

In front of me, gathered along the lakeshore and stretching out on every side, multitudes radiant with joy and fulfillment! Faces beaming golden in every shade! Black, brown, red, yellow, white—commingling in rapturous friendship and love!

And gazing into these glorious faces, suddenly a Knowledge fills me! It enters my consciousness whole and obvious, with acute clarity. I am witness to God's Ultimate Reality! These souls, I Know, are Christian, Muslim, Jew, and Protestant; Buddhist, Hindu, Shinto, and every other denomination, as far as the eye can see!

More than this, countless numbers who were Agnostic and Atheist in life; Heretic and Homosexual; Liberal, Conservative, and Moderate! What unites them all in Paradise, I Recognize, has nothing to do with religion or race, sexual persuasion or politics.

They are rewarded, each and every one, for the love and respect they gave in life to all God's creations. But mostly, for the love and respect they displayed toward their fellow beings. Before me, an endless outpouring of God's Blessed—and not a sanctimonious soul among them!

In light of this Reality, all the teachings and preachings of religion are muted. Doctrine and dogma, rites and rituals, Bulls and catechisms and excruciatingly fine points of theology—they all implode into one fundamental principle by which God values all Human conduct.

Compassion!

So clear to me now! Compassion is born into all Humanity. An innate part of us, in natural balance to our baser instincts. Yet throughout history Man has been distracted from this simple, guiding principle.

From birth we are conditioned to Believe religion is the only route to salvation, each faith claiming to be the one true path. But as revealed to me here, there are few popes and theologians in Heaven. Indeed, Matthew 16:18–19 is apocryphal, inserted by the early Church to validate itself!

Man has forever been subjected to spiritual intimidation, beset by endless, convoluted teachings. And however sincere and well-intentioned, they've led us far from the Truth. God's Signs have been ignored, misread, painted over until we lost our way entirely. Lost our compassion.

Instead we seek to remake others in our own self-righteous image. To think like us. Behave like us. Revere God in conformity with our own rigid Beliefs.

But now, let seekers of spiritual Truth brush aside the sermonizing middlemen and do as I have. Let them follow my path to gaze directly at the Source and confirm what I have seen: the Ultimate Reality—proof at last of God's Will for the world!

The implications for Humanity are enormous. Both wonderful and devastating. No longer is there need for priest or minister or rabbi or mullah to interpret God's Signs. Gone are the theologians splitting spiritual hairs. No pope to speak ex cathedra. Religion as we know it, with all its quibbling and confusion, divisiveness and bloodshed, passes forever into history . . .

As I revel in this vision, suddenly I feel the leash snap and pull, and I'm drawn back, against my will. I cry out in alarm—I cannot leave this bliss!

A spirit approaches. A majestic creature with golden curls and innocent eyes, neither male nor female, an adult child.

It says in a voice soothing as a breeze, "You are returning to life. You must not reveal what you have seen."

"What have I seen?" I ask as I slip away. And it calls after me, "Third of the Seven. Tempora. Heaven of the Spirit of Harmony."

I accelerate, reeling back into the tunnel, back down into my body, into the arms of my guides who are frantically working to revive me. I smile up at them, tears flowing. They cannot begin to imagine!

I've glimpsed the Mind of God!

For however long it lasted—minutes, seconds—I luxuriated in the glory that awaits those who love unconditionally.

God help me, if what I've witnessed is a Sacred Secret, I cannot keep it! This Knowledge will change the world! And when I think of the souls this Truth will save, the intolerance it will cure, the lives it will spare, how can I hold back?

Next week marks the anniversary of the day I first entered Gethsemani, half a lifetime ago. The day I began my long, meandering search for Truth. A fitting day to complete the circle. To open the world's eyes to the Ultimate Reality . . .

Ian's voice trailed off and he sat in a hush, bent over the pages, staring through them.

Valerie sat quietly, too, tears wetting her cheeks.

And Angela sat watching them both, stomach in a knot.

The Reality wasn't what she'd expected. Not that she'd known what to expect, but surely not *this*. Nothing so . . . so *secular*. Merton's Reality negated the teachings of *all* religions, rendering every one of them irrelevant!

At length she breathed, "No wonder the Church censored it."

Ian nodded soberly. He turned to Valerie. "How did you ever keep it secret all these years?"

She removed her spectacles, wiping her eyes. "Out a fear, knowin' 'ow God punished Father for disobeyin' the angel. But though I couldn't share its Truth, it was a wonderful blessin' to me. Changed me life. Changed me the moment I first read it . . ."

Her eyes looked into the past. "I was at the kitchen table in our flat at the time, 'oldin' the pages, tears drippin' down me face onto 'Enri's dirty lunch dishes. 'E was on the couch watchin' the telly, drinkin', oblivious. 'E knew nothin' 'bout me father, I never told 'im.

"Just as I finish it, the instant I read Father's last words, there comes news on the telly of 'is death. Strikes me like lightnin'. I'm shakin', goin' ta pieces. Then all of a sudden I feel this amazin' sensation. Passes through me like a ghost. A strange calm and peace.

"Somewhere apart from me pain, I realized Father 'ad finally found the Truth 'e'd been searchin' for all 'is life. 'E'd fulfilled 'is dream, free ta return ta that place of bliss 'e'd described, back ta where 'e longed ta be. That was a comfort. An' knowin' 'e'd entrusted me with 'is Secret gave me purpose. Gave me the strength ta go on . . .

"I packed me things an' left 'Enri that very hour. An' for the first time in me life, I did without the crutches I'd come ta lean on—alcohol, drugs, an' men. Done so ever since. If only Father could 'ave lived ta know . . ."

Standing, she offered Ian the envelope that had held the Reality, keeping her father's cover letter.

"I feel it in me soul," she told him. "God sent ya ta me. Take the Reality, use it ta bridge the gulf with your parents. Then please, spread its Truth ta the world."

Ian thanked her, slipping the pages back into the envelope. In turn, he handed her the letter Merton had sent Karl Barth about his plans to visit Paris.

Valerie clutched the letter to her heart, beaming. "Ya've no idea 'ow 'appy ya've made me," she told them. And wishing them Godspeed, giving them a hug and a kiss, she bid them adieu.

Ian was quiet as they headed down the stairs.

At length, Angela asked, "Well, what do you think?"

He looked at her as if she were joking.

"What do I think?" He raised the envelope in both hands, like Moses descending Mt. Sinai with the Ten Commandments. "Tell me this isn't real! Tell me you don't feel it, too!"

When she failed to answer, he cried, "Christ, Angela, *what will it take*?"

"If you're asking me to believe Merton saw Heaven, I can't. But I will admit, there's *something* to his message. Whether hallucination or dream, I applaud what he says."

Ian went quiet as they exited the building. Then out in the street, Angela asked, "What did Merton mean when he said 'Matthew is apocryphal'?"

"Matthew 16:18–19. 'Thou art Peter, and upon this rock I will build my

Church.' The only passage of gospel where Christ ever mentions establishing a Church. And according to Merton, a bogus verse inserted by the early Church to justify itself. Two thousand years of Catholicism nullified. A spiritual bombshell! And you think it a dream?"

She exhaled. "I think dreams can be inspiring. Mary Shelley's *Frankenstein* came to her in a dream. Paul McCartney's 'Yesterday.' But it's irrelevant what I think. The question now is, what will *Arma Christi* think?"

"It doesn't matter; others will Believe." He patted the envelope. "Once we go public with this, *Arma Christi* will be swamped with NDEs. That's the good news."

"There's bad news?"

"The angel that spoke to Merton told him he was at the Third Heaven. The Tree of the Knowledge of Good lies at the highest realm—the *Seventh* Heaven. Whatever you make of the Reality, it isn't the Knowledge of Good. Like Lucien said, Heaven holds many Secrets."

"So?"

"So, the Reality is no help to my parents. My only hope to free them now is to fight Evil with Evil. The Knowledge of Evil. And there's only one place I know to get it . . ."

A few blocks away, outside Valerie Pardeau's tenement, children playing soccer on the street scattered as a black car raced to the curb.

EIGHTY-THREE

ROCHAMBEAU INTERNATIONAL, CAYENNE, FRENCH GUYANA, SAME DAY, EVENING

Aboard a new jet with a new pilot, Ian and Angela arrived in South America at dusk, having leaped four time zones ahead in a seven-hour flight from Paris. Ian had carried the Reality on his person the entire way.

Before leaving Paris, however, he'd found a UPS store and faxed a copy to Charles Dunn at the TV station.

"An insurance policy," he'd told Angela, "just in case."

In case he didn't survive tomorrow's NDE, she knew . . .

They were met at Cayenne's small but modern airport by Emil Josten and two swarthy bodyguards, then ushered through customs and out to an SUV.

"Have you had supper?" Josten asked as they sped off.

Angela replied, "I ate on the plane, and Ian's fasting."

Ian was allowed no food the day before a "procedure."

Josten nodded and they continued down a two-lane road, the signs in French. From what Angela could tell in the twilight so far, Cayenne was much like St. Maarten. Mostly indigent blacks, shabby clothes, living in shacks.

Ian noticed, too, she saw, their eyes meeting.

"Divine Paradox," he muttered solemnly, and turning to Josten, he changed the subject. "Any signs of trouble?"

"Thankfully, no. I believe our strategy has worked. Everything is in place; we're set for first thing tomorrow."

The doctor seemed to have aged since last Angela saw him. Dark, deep-set eyes deeper now; bushy hair and beard grayer; frame lighter. He offered her a smile.

"You'll find your accommodations most comfortable," he said. "Ian insisted on the best."

Ian was often too extravagant for Angela's tastes, but there were times when she approved. Like earlier today after they'd left Valerie Pardeau's. He'd stopped by her soup kitchen to make a generous donation. And now, as they arrived at their destination, Angela was pleased to see he'd spared no expense on security. Before them were the grounds of a grand country estate, surrounded by a chain-link fence topped with glistening razor wire. Armed sentries stood guard—grave-faced black men in dark-green uniforms and berets, brandishing rifles.

"We were fortunate to find this place," Josten said. "The previous owner ran a gold strip mine in the rainforest, but international pressures closed him down."

Their car stopped at a guardhouse, its gate swung aside, and they proceeded up a winding drive through palms and flowering flora to a hacienda-style mansion. Three stories, multitiered white stucco, red pantile roof, large expanses of glass and balconies. The exterior was well lit. And everywhere, more guards patrolling.

They circled to a rear courtyard, pulling up to an automatic garage door that opened only long enough to swallow them. Inside was space for a dozen vehicles, several parked there. Including, Angela noted with disquiet, what looked to be a medical ambulance.

As they exited their car, Josten said, "I have some things to review in the lab. My men will show you to your quarters. After you freshen up, come to the basement and I'll introduce you to the team."

The men took the luggage and escorted Angela and Ian up an elevator to the top floor, doors opening into a foyer, then a suite that appeared to encompass the entire level. Airy, spacious, blond-wood floors, wall-length windows, and a garden terrace overlooking ocean and forested mountains in the distance. Fully furnished and luxuriously appointed—save for an office area that looked ransacked, suggesting the previous occupant had left in a hurry with his records.

"Straight out of *Architectural Digest*!" Angela marveled, taking it all in as the guards departed. But Ian's mind was elsewhere. She delayed him only long enough to wash up and change, and then they were back in the elevator, heading to the basement.

When the doors parted, Angela felt they'd been transported to another dimension. A large, empty, open chamber with hidden angles and high ceilings. It looked subterranean, no windows. And though spacious, its dim lighting, dark walls, and dark marble floor gave it a claustrophobic ambiance.

She heard voices echoing ahead, and they moved toward them, passing oil paintings on the walls. Each was haloed in a glow of track light. Ian pointed out several as superb copies of William Blake, Salvador Dalí, and Gustave Doré—if not the originals themselves. Angela noticed outline marks on the floor spotlighted from above, suggesting that sculptures may have also been on display. It seemed the room had once served as a private art gallery.

The space grew brighter, and as Angela rounded a turn she saw an operating arena gleaming under a bank of lights. Like that in St. Maarten, only three times the size—a large wall of equipment forming a solid U around a table. The equipment, she noted, was double-wired into both standard electric service and a back-up generator in a corner.

Josten stood talking with a woman and two men, turning as Angela and Ian approached.

"Outstanding, Emil!" Ian told him, pumping his hand.

Josten smiled and introduced his associates. Neurologists from Nagarjuna University, India, and Seoul National University, South Korea, and a cardiology researcher from Ankara University, Turkey. Early thirties, they looked, drawn here no doubt by urgent financial needs.

Angela hung back as Ian got acquainted, uneasy around these people who'd soon be putting him to death.

"If you like, Ian," Josten offered, "we can pre-op you now, and be that much ahead for tomorrow."

Ian thought that an excellent idea, and he and the Korean doctor adjourned to a back room.

No sooner had they left than Angela grabbed Josten, taking him aside, locking eyes.

"You can't go through with this, Emil!" she cried in a hushed voice. "An hour is insane!"

He remained composed. "I understand your concern, but I've every confidence in my team. Ian came through the first procedures well. With his layoff, I'm comfortable he'll do so again."

"*Layoff?* We've been running for our lives! He was nearly killed in an avalanche—he's stressed out, worn out!"

The doctor seemed taken aback, blinking.

"I'll check him myself . . . And you have my word, if I don't consider him fit, we'll postpone."

Snatching up his medical bag, he disappeared into the back room, leaving Angela a ray of hope.

She turned to the art gallery as she waited, wandering aimlessly, hearing the remaining doctors tap on keyboards and make adjustments to equipment. But outside the lights of the operating area, the somber atmosphere only added to her discomfort. Reminiscent of a museum after hours. And she found the tastes of the former owner disturbing.

The general theme of these paintings seemed to be the portrayal of human subjugation and affliction. Images of people bent and broken, emotionally and physically. Evocative of Hieronymus Bosch.

Finally unable to take any more, she approached the doctors.

"The fuses," she told them. "I want to see the fuses in everything—cardiac defibrillators on down."

They patiently obliged. And everything checked out. In fact, Angela could fault none of Josten's preparations. The security, the quality and redundancy of the equipment, the apparent competency of the team—all top-shelf. Yet that voice in her head was whistling again.

At last the door to the prep room opened and Josten emerged. But Angela could tell she'd be disappointed.

"Blood pressure up a trifle," he reported. "He's lost a few pounds, a bit hypoglycemic. But nothing serious. I gave him a shot to raise his blood sugar, and he should be fine tomorrow."

That was it then. Within hours Ian would undergo his longest NDE. Another pointless journey into illusion from which, Angela had a terrible feeling, he would not return.

Ian popped out of the room looking as determined as ever, and obeying Josten's orders to rest now, he took Angela's hand and they retired to their suite.

She prepared for bed while he stored the Reality in their room safe, making her memorize the combination. Then he went to check his laptop for updates on Antonio.

Moments later Angela heard him yell, and dropping her toothbrush, she rushed out to the living room to see him crouched over his computer.

"A miracle!" Ian gasped. *"Antonio's improving!"*

She crowded in and saw a bulletin on the screen. The director was nowhere out of danger, still in a coma. But his vitals had stabilized.

"Thank God!" Ian said, eyes ecstatic. *"Keep praying!"*

Angela hadn't been praying. Couldn't pray. But she kept that to herself—and also her doubts that Antonio could possibly recover from such an injury.

She offered her encouragement and stood for a time, hand on Ian's shoulder, watching him e-mail Charles Dunn to ask if the Reality fax had come through. Then unable to bear up any longer, she slipped off to bed as he shut down.

Ian soon joined her beneath the silken sheets, sliding into her arms in the dark, kissing her good night. She held on to him extra long and tight, so fearful this would be their last night together.

He nodded off while she lay awake in the glow of the rising moon, mind churning, watching him sleep as if he hadn't a care in the world.

The power of Faith.

It may have gotten him through a few brief skirmishes with Death. But tomorrow was the showdown. And Death was an adversary no mortal had ever defeated.

EIGHTY-FOUR

A PENTHOUSE IN THE OLD TOWN DISTRICT, PRAGUE, CZECH REPUBLIC, SAME DAY, LATE NIGHT

Cyril paced his office, glaring down the long angle of his nose at a speakerphone on his desk. Under his feet, Bavarian oak parquet creaked as flames from the fireplace cast his shadow against portraits of holy Roman emperors on the walls. Behind him, the lights of downtown Prague and Hradcany Castle glistened through lead-glass windows.

"How could you lose them?" he stormed. "You had them in your crosshairs!"

"Nein," the voice of Quintus replied. *"But I habe vorse news . . . Dey found de Reality."*

Cyril came to a halt. *"God help us!* How?"

"Merton's daughter. She survived de Blitz, hiding in Paris all dis time. She *vas Valentine."*

Slowly Cyril took his chair. That old time bomb, silent these many decades, was ticking again.

Quintus asked, *"I don't understand, how vill Baringer use such knowledge to open de Gates of Hell?"*

"Knowledge can open *all* doors. And if he uses it to free his parents, he'll unleash Hell on earth—a Second Rebellion God will surely not let stand. *Armageddon!"*

Heavy silence on the other end.

At length Cyril exhaled. "Where are you?"

"Beauvais. Ve found deir inbound iet, it leave vithout dem. Dey must use 'nother airport."

"Now that they have the Reality, they've left for Capetown, hopefully."

"I leave right avay."

"You're too late. And you haven't slept in days. Josef will have to handle it."

"I sleep vhen I see Baringer and Reality destroyed."

EIGHTY-FIVE

A PRIVATE ESTATE OUTSIDE CAYENNE, FRENCH GUYANA, NEXT DAY, EARLY MORNING

It seemed she'd just fallen asleep when Angela awoke with a start. Outside her window it was still night, but she could hear Ian swearing in the next room.

She rose and threw on clothes, hurrying to find him seated in the dark, dressed, mumbling to himself in the glow of his laptop.

"What are you doing?"

He raised anxious eyes. "I got an e-mail from Antonio."

Elated, incredulous, she rushed to his side to see two messages—the first not from Antonio, but Charles Dunn:

> Ian: Fax did not come through. What is the Ultimate Reality? And where the hell are you two? When you coming back? Please return my calls!
> Charles

The second message was but a single line:

> stop experiment. check cell phone. ponti

Angela whipsawed from Ian to e-mail and back. And then that whistle in her head turned to siren.

"You didn't check your phone, did you?"

"No, but I'm sorely tempted."

"It's a trick!"

"Maybe . . ."

She knelt facing him. "Ian, listen to me. *Antonio didn't send that.* He's in a coma, for God's sake!"

"Unless . . ." His eyes flashed hope. "What if the shooting was a *ruse*? What if Antonio staged it to lure out his spy—and now he's trying to warn us of something?"

"Then why didn't he put it in the e-mail?"

"That's what I've been asking myself."

He shook his head with confusion, and she found herself wavering, too. If this e-mail could halt his NDE . . .

They stared at each other. Then Ian shrugged and took out his phone.

"What the hell . . ."

She grabbed his arm in panic, but he stood, raising her to her feet.

"A lot of good it'll do them now," he said. "We'll be gone in little more than an hour, long before they can get here."

"And if they have a Sword in Cayenne?"

"It would take an army to get through these defenses."

"But you'll need time to recover!"

"That's what the ambulance downstairs is for. The team's coming with us, Emil has an EMS jet waiting. By the time the Order shows, we'll be in Miami, spilling our guts to CBS."

Angela moaned. Depending on what Antonio's message said, they could be leaving *now.*

She released his arm, tensing as he raised his phone so both could see. He flipped it on, the signal taking forever to sync. Then suddenly message alerts began popping. Most from Y. Garonne. But also V. Ponti. A digital photo.

Angela crowded close, holding her breath as Ian punched up the image—and her hopes dissolved in horror.

A man, sprawled across a desk in a pool of blood, pistol in hand. *Antonio.*

She felt the air empty out of her, stunned, nauseous.

Ian exploded, *"Those sonsofbitches!"* He stabbed a key, deleting the image, and an instant later his phone rang.

Y. Garonne.

"Don't answer!" Angela cried.

"Hell with it, they're on to us now!"

Her heart raced as Garonne's face materialized, smiling benignly. But Ian gave her no chance.

"You can tell those bastards you sold out to, it's over! I've got the Reality, I'm going to finish this, and there's not a goddamned thing they can do. *This one's for Antonio!"*

Before he could hang up, Angela heard shouts on the other end, seeing the image shake as if a struggle was underway. Then the terrified face of Luc Dow Hodaka jumped into view.

"Ian, watch out! Three of them, they—"

Suddenly hands wrested the phone from Luc Dow and a new face appeared. Familiar. Thirtyish. Hair thick, brown, and bushy. Features angular, eyes intense. He declared in Slavic-accented English, *"You mustn't go through with this, Ian! You don't know what you do!"*

The color drained from Ian's face. "No . . . no . . ."

"Antonio is dying. He won't last the hour. And neither will you if you don't listen."

Ian sank to his chair, Angela dropping beside him, frightened, confused.

"The Knowledge you seek will damn you. Damn us all. It defies God's Will!"

"You damn yourself," Ian replied hoarsely. "You were a *son* to Antonio. A *brother* to me. You risked your life for me! What happened to you, Josef?"

Angela was dumbstruck.

The man's jaw hardened. Eyes indignant, he breathed. *"I defend the Faith."*

Ian sneered, "Let God defend His own damned Faith!"

"I warn you, you mustn't *combine the Knowledges! It's mixing matter and antimatter! It will be the end of everything! Apocalypse!"*

"Watch me—on the six o'clock news tonight. The whole world will Know. It'll be the end, all right. The end of you and your goddamned Order!"

Josef's face went scarlet. *"God help me, I'll stop you!"*

"Go to Hell!" Ian roared back, hurling his phone against the wall, shattering it.

He buried his face in his hands, and Angela stroked his back, at a loss. But then he rose, the turmoil in his eyes giving over to resolve.

"No time to lose," he said, pulling her to her feet again, taking her hand, and they rushed to the elevator.

Inside, she held on to him tight. *"Oh God,* what if something happens to you? What'll I do?"

"The Reality is in the safe. If something happens, get it, take the jet, and fly straight to Charles. He never got the fax. Tell him everything, make CBS take it public—*not* you! Stay undercover till the horse is out of the barn, and this will all be over . . ."

He took a breath. "Have Faith, I'm coming back."

She pressed her face against his chest, wanting so badly to believe him. But she had no Faith.

EIGHTY-SIX

ROBERTS INTERNATIONAL AIRPORT, LIBERIA, WEST AFRICA, SAME DAY, PREDAWN

Reclined in his seat behind the controls, Quintus was catnapping as the tower prepared to clear him for his last leg to Capetown. He was exhausted, having just refueled after a four-and-a-half-hour flight from Paris, getting by on little sleep, about to rush off again. No matter, his fear and anger fueled him. He was full up with this damned Baringer, expecting word of the man's arrival in Capetown any minute. But Quintus would not be denied the pleasure of purging Baringer and his little temptress. He'd ordered Josef to hold them until he arrived.

Abruptly a buzzer jolted him awake. He punched a button, expecting the tower, instead hearing a frantic voice. *"Where are you?"*

He recognized Josef.

"Liberia," he replied, "five hours out. You habe dem?"

"More tricks! They're in Cayenne! A secret *lab! How fast can you get there?"*

Wide awake now, Quintus jumped to his flight computer, frantically altering his destination point, running a calculation. *4600 kilometers . . .*

"Four hours if I push, pending vinds."

"Nearest Sword is Mexico City. You're 800 kilometers closer."

"Not close enough!"

"You've got to try! I spoke to Baringer, he confirmed it—he intends to wed the Knowledges!"

"Gott in Himmel!"

"We have a retired E&E in Bogota—I'll have him meet you in Cayenne. It's best I can do."

"I go, but ist too late! *Think,* Josef, you are smart! *There must be 'nother vay . . .*"

Not waiting for clearance from the tower, Quintus powered up and roared down the runway.

EIGHTY-SEVEN

THE BASEMENT OF A PRIVATE ESTATE OUTSIDE CAYENNE, FRENCH GUYANA, SAME DAY, MORNING

As Ian prepped in a back room, Angela paced the lab. She strived to stay calm, not wanting to add to his stress, but the environment was working against her.

These bizarre paintings! Now, a work by someone she'd never heard of, Amos Nattini—a throng of naked, stampeding men and women fleeing some unknown terror.

And then she read its title.

Hell.

Moaning, she hurried past . . .

The door to the back room opened and Ian emerged in boxer shorts, his body tagged with electrodes, wires, and IV connectors. He looked so helpless.

She rushed to him, but with all his hookups she was afraid to touch. If only she'd hugged him harder when she'd had the chance. He took her hands and kissed her long and deep, and when they parted, he smiled.

"I'll be fine," he assured her, voice strong and confident. "You wait. Tonight we'll be drinking champagne on a beach in Miami, toasting an end to all this."

Forcing a smile, she kissed him a last time, he gave her hands a squeeze, and he pulled away.

She watched through blurry eyes as the team helped him onto the table, wrapping him in cooling pads, plugging him into the system, starting his transfusion. Fluids began to flow through tubes, instruments to whir and beep—Angela's heart louder than it all.

Soon the glow in his face waned, he gave her a faint smile and thumbs up, and then drifted off.

At 6:02 AM the last monitor flatlined, Josten cried, *"Time!"* and a digital clock began the count.

Angela resumed her pacing. She didn't know if she could endure the next hour, but of one thing she was certain. When this was over, whatever the outcome, she was going home. Ian's obsession and *Arma Christi* be damned.

EIGHTY-EIGHT

THE REALM OF THE DEAD, OUTSIDE OF TIME

Once more Ian traveled the ethereal tunnel, barreling down toward the mists of Limbo fast as his soul could go, mind racing ahead.

He'd put on a brave front for Angela, but in truth he was terrified. After all his forethought and research—Dante, Milton, St. Patrick's Purgatory, Bosch's paintings—he still had no idea what he was getting himself into. And no meaningful plan.

The thought of stealing Hell's Knowledge to snatch souls from its jaws sounded preposterous even to him. Perhaps the most foolish endeavor in the history of human folly. All the same, it was his only hope to help his poor parents. And though he had no plan, he at least had an opening gambit to spring on the demon, Zagan. Something so risky he hadn't bothered sharing it with Angela.

Beyond that, his strategy was simply to trust his instincts and overcome each obstacle as it presented itself, praying for the best, relying on his lifeline. And not forgetting that most important resource of all—*Faith.*

Ian had Faith that somehow he would prevail . . .

These thoughts roiling, he arrived in the Underworld once more, pulling up to peer again into Limbo's murk.

Deathly quiet. No sign of Zack Niemand's spirit. No movement but for the vast, orange-gray blanket of cloud whirling slowly across the surface. Cautiously Ian advanced, at last detecting a shadowy form in the haze.

The backlit hulk of a Dark Angel. *Zagan.*

Ian felt a shiver. The monster was alone and appeared impatient, shifting his massive body side to side, snorting, flexing his limbs like an athlete readying for a contest. Ian settled skittishly beside him, not too close, cloud parting under his feet. Finally he noticed Niemand at a distance.

"Don't do it!" Niemand called to him. "Don't go!"

But Zagan growled, and Niemand went silent. Then the demon turned to Ian, rumbling, "You've accepted the terms?"

"With . . . with one condition."

Zagan stiffened, fixing his crystal-black eyes on Ian. Steam jetted from his nostrils and he bared his fangs, hissing, *"No conditions!"*

The beast appeared to be in a foul mood already, and Ian worried how far he could push him, seeing only obstinacy in the nightmarish face.

Lumbering a step closer, Zagan angled his huge head, the horns of his brow poised like a bull about to charge.

Ian swallowed. "A *small* accommodation. While in the Pit, I, I want to see the Tree of the Knowledge of Evil."

Zagan curled his claws into fists and bellowed, "This is not some frivolous excursion, *soul*!"

"A simple request."

"More than you know! The journey is long and dangerous—the Tree most dangerous of all!"

Ian held his ground, folding his arms across his chest to hide his jittery hands, relying on Niemand's claim that devils had no powers in Limbo.

Zagan snorted louder, brooding, chomping his snaggled snout. But faced with Ian's resolve, he finally barked, "There is no guarantee you will survive even to reach the Pit. But if so, and you still desire to see the Tree, I will take you. Now we must go! *Every moment you delay, your soul hardens!"*

Niemand remained to one side, hands clasped in a plea, shaking his head. Ian wavered, eyeing the orange horizon, wondering what horrors must await, knowing this could well prove the greatest mistake of his life.

Zagan roared, "I go—*with or without you!"* and pivoting, he stamped off into the gloom.

Ian watched the massive frame recede. Then swearing, he leaped into the air and gave chase, looking back to see Niemand's anxious face dissolve in the mists.

He quickly caught up, gliding beside the demon at shoulder height, matching tempo. If Zagan noticed, he paid no heed, marching on, eyes front. Ian avoided cruising too close, fearing both treachery and the hot jets that shot from the devil's muzzle.

But after a time without incident, he settled, able to turn his attention to the forlorn landscape around him.

The carpet of whorling fog made him think of an inverted thundercloud. A great, orange-gray, churning plain. Oddly, the cloud parted in advance of Zagan's feet, as if averse to the monster's touch, revealing an inky-black surface. As if the demon walked on night.

Looking closer, however, Ian was astonished to realize that the cloud wasn't cloud at all, but *animate beings*. Millions upon millions of spirits—nether souls like Niemand, bunched tightly together in a vast bin of dirty, writhing cotton, stretching off into the foreverness . . .

Soon the atmospheric haze began to thin, and ahead Ian could make out what appeared to be a boundary, the spirit-cloud giving over entirely to dark substratum. As if a line had been drawn. And no sooner did Ian sail across than he tumbled, crashing hard to the blackness.

"Unnhh!" he grunted, Zagan never breaking stride. He scrambled to his feet, lurching after, rubbing his hip—useless, his hand passing through.

"What happened?"

"Your powers of levitation end at Limbo."

He would have appreciated a warning. But then, what should he expect from a devil? Forced on foot, he had to trot to keep Zagan's grueling pace, puffing as the temperature rose, sweat stinging his eyes, unable to wipe it away. They were on an increasingly downward slope, the orange glow brighter, and Ian heard the sound of dull droning. Like a distant hive of bees.

"Where are we?" he asked.

"Erebus. The in-between place."

The name held no meaning for Ian.

From behind came a soft, high-pitched whine that quickly developed into a loud cry, and Ian turned to see the dim shape of a soul skirt by. A man, the tone of his cries deepening as he passed. He streaked off to the horizon, followed periodically by more such cries and shapes, some close, some remote, all hurtling in the same direction.

Ahead, Ian could make out the edge of the night—an irregular precipice where steam and orange light emanated from below. The cliff stretched away right and left out of sight, nothing but black sky beyond.

Zagan slowed as they approached, horrible screams echoing up the other side. But unlike the previous cries, which seemed in terror, these sounded full of agony.

Ian hung back, fearful. "What's down there?"

"The Mill of Purgatory."

Behind, more screams, and Ian looked to see the soul of a young man in a gray robe tumbling toward them, quickly overtaken by an older man in a darker robe sliding feet-first on his stomach, clawing the ground with his fingers. And then zipping by both, a middle-aged woman in an even darker robe, screeching like a banshee.

One after the other they shot out over the precipice, squealing in panic as they fell from sight. More souls flew by as far as the eye could see, and Ian realized that the drone he'd been hearing was actually the cumulation of countless shrieks resonating in the vastness.

Another man—portly and goggle-eyed, curled in a fetal position, robe black as soot—zoomed within range of Zagan. The demon swiveled and lashed out with a foot like a soccer player, catching him neatly from behind, booting him far out over the edge as the poor soul yelped in pain.

Zagan sniggered. "He goes to join your parents in the Pit."

Before Ian could voice his anger, a sudden movement at the precipice locked the words in his throat. Fluttering up over the rim were delicate fingers seeking a handhold. Pale, battered, bruised, fingernails torn and bleeding. Then the contused, panting face of what Ian realized was once a pretty young woman. Cheeks bloodied, hair matted and straggled. Though surprisingly, her robe was pure white.

As if with her last strength she dragged herself atop—only to halt at the sight of Zagan's huge legs. Ian watched her gaze rise, her eyes widen with dread, and she moaned, "Oh no . . . *No!*"

Zagan silenced her with a foot to the face, shoving her back over the cliff, her wail fading.

Again Ian's anger flared—cut short by the demon reaching down, grabbing his arm, hoisting him in the air. He suddenly found himself planted on Zagan's shoulder, perched like a parrot on a pirate, head awhirl. Then, reacting to the monster's hot breath on his leg, he lurched, slashing his calf on a tusk.

"Hold fast!" Zagan ordered, and crouching, he launched out over the edge.

Ian yelled, clinging with both hands to one of Zagan's horns. The chasm seemed bottomless, and he shut his eyes. But it did no good, his lids were transparent. As they plummeted, he was astounded to see bat-like wings unfold from depressions in Zagan's back, spreading wide to brake their fall, nearly costing him his grip.

They settled into a glide, floating down past ledges that projected from the cliff face. Like giant steps, each ledge extended farther than the previous, reminding Ian of Dante's levels of Hell. And in the manner of that epic, the ledges exacted ever-harsher penalties on plunging souls.

The trajectory of a soul, Ian realized, corresponded to the darkness of its robe/weight of its sins. Those with lighter-colored robes, signifying slighter sins on their souls, moved at slower speeds, arcing closer to the cliff, landing on the upper levels, sustaining only bumps and bruises.

Heavier sinners, however, were propelled farther out, striking progressively deeper ledges, suffering harder impacts, heads smashing, bones cracking, entrails splaying.

Ian felt sickened. But as he saw, this was only the beginning. At each level the fallen souls were met by bizarre demons, hodgepodges of human, animal, vegetable, and mechanical parts, straight out of a Bosch painting.

Some creatures raked in the remains, dusting them with a white powder they dispersed from buckets. The victims then reconstituted and rose up shrieking, making frantic attempts to scale the cliff. Only to be snared and pulled down by more chimeras armed with gaffs and grappling irons, then tortured with an array of medieval-looking weapons that lay scattered about the ledges.

The tortures appeared to burlesque offenses the souls had committed in life. One man was being spanked with a flaming belt by a troll who ridiculed his intelligence. Another gnomish demon had a woman's tongue in a pair of red-hot tongs, chattering at her like a gossip, hot breath scorching her ears.

Ian recalled Niemand's claim that Dante and Bosch had never ventured past Purgatory, and he saw how they could have acquired their Hellish inspirations here, peeking over the cliff above. His heart went out to these poor wretches.

Zagan pointed to a bucket of white powder, shouting over the cries, "*Angel Dust* to bleach their robes. If a soul gains the top, it's free to make its way to Heaven . . ."

They continued their descent, down, down into the Abyss, following those souls with the blackest robes.

Eventually Zagan landed at the bottom with a thud, the impact cushioned by his powerful legs, sloughing Ian off. Other souls arriving here, however, experienced the full force of their falls from grace, walloping the surface at terrific speed, splattering into pulp.

Zagan used his wings to screen himself, but Ian suffered a bloody shower, shielding his eyes to no avail. If insensitive to the touch of other souls, he was obviously not impervious to their gore.

As his eyes cleared, Ian saw they'd arrived on a desertlike escarpment. A flat, barren stretch that continued for some distance, beyond which the orange light glowed brighter.

The air was stifling hot, and Ian asked nervously, "Is this Hell?"

The demon's answer was a scornful snort of steam.

Around them, more Bosch-esque creatures worked the grounds, some with squeegee-like appendages, scraping the mush and crumpled black robes into piles. The souls reassumed their bodily forms but Ian saw no bleach this time. And before they could fully recover, other demons arrived to drive them across the sands, flailing with arms that ended in barbs and cat-o'-nine-tails. The victims howled, staggering on, robes shredded, streaked with blood.

Zagan shook clean his wings, retracted them, and joined the grim procession. Ian followed—only to be stopped by a burning slash across his shoulder. One of the caretaker monstrosities had discovered him. A squat, pig-faced being with short arms and long, tentacled fingers that flailed down, cutting deep, raising nasty, stinging welts.

Ian cried out, recoiling, covering up, scrambling to get away. But the creature kept after him, scourging mercilessly, and in desperation Ian reached out and grabbed a bundle of tentacles. Ignoring their poison, he pulled the demon to the ground and pounced, venting his pent-up anger, loosing a barrage of punches, the beast squealing as Ian bloodied its snout and broke off a tusk. It felt wonderful.

But it was short-lived. The creature's cries roused its comrades, who descended in a rage. Ian was pulled off, about to be minced when he heard a voice thunder, "*Belay.* This soul is *mine . . .*"

Suddenly he was snatched up, shaken hard until his tormentors dropped off, then set back on his feet. Dizzy, bitten, beaten, whipped, stung, and clawed, he'd never known such pain.

But Zagan spared no sympathy, sending him along with a shove, snarling, "*Keep up!*"

Ian hobbled away, bloody slices of flesh hanging from his arms, demons yammering behind. He felt his courage ebb, tempted to turn back.

If this is only Purgatory, what must Hell be like?

It seemed Zagan read his mind, looking down to sneer, "You'll heal soon enough."

In fact, the cut on his leg from Zagan's tusk had already mended, though leaving a wicked scar. And to quit now might well cost him the monster's protection—or cause it to tear him apart in rage. Mustering his courage, he trudged on . . .

The heat continued to climb, and eventually Ian could make out an end to the escarpment. The sky beyond was like a fiery dawn, split by a towering mushroom of black clouds rent by lightning. The air rumbled, filled with sulfuric fumes that made him wheeze and cough.

Drawing closer, he saw the exhausted marchers being herded into queues—countless lines stretching off side by side. Souls slow to assemble were seized by demons with vicious, crablike claws and thrust in place. This time Ian stuck close to Zagan.

The purpose of the queues was soon evident. At the end of each stood three muscular, bug-eyed ogres. One would grab the next hapless person in line and tear away its robe, tossing the scrap onto a pile. Another would apply a white-hot branding iron to the left shoulder, marking it with Roman numerals from I to VII. Many shoulders, Ian saw, bore multiple brands. The last ogre would then impale the soul on a pike, loft it high in the air, and sling it naked into long, metal troughs of boiling oil.

The troughs were elevated slightly on trestles to allow for fires beneath, running like infernal aqueducts toward the edge of the escarpment. Demons straddled at intervals, using poles with hooks to snag the souls and move them along. No sooner could a mouth reach the surface for a gulp of air and a scream than it was thrust back into the cauldron. More devils attended the fires, fueling them with the discarded robes, which burned hot as sin.

The thought of his poor parents enduring this filled Ian with despair, and he stumbled along after Zagan in a daze.

They followed the bubbling flumes at length to the brink of the escarpment, where finally the souls were netted and cast onto the ground, parboiled and steaming, lobster red. Here they fell under the dominion of Dark Angels arriving via stairs from the orange brilliance below—now blazing like a minor sun.

These devils resembled Zagan, though Ian saw none as big, or with horns, teeth, or tail as long. They approached the fresh-cooked souls, snatched them in their talons, and dragged them teetering toward the cliff, each soul getting its own Dark Angel.

Ian trailed Zagan into the migration, sticking close, seeing some devils eye him and growl to one another. He suspected they took exception to his robe and the uncured state of his soul. But for now at least, Zagan's presence seemed to ward them off.

At the rim Ian felt a blast of hot wind, squinting out at an ominous sight. Far below was a vast, desolate crater with a giant volcano at its core in full eruption. Zagan announced, "The Valley of Gehenna."

Ian gasped. Hewn into the crater's walls were countless stairways spiraling down, funneling souls from every direction, creating a monstrous coliseum of the damned. At the bottom the stairs became trails, leading toward the volcano, which belched great plumes of gas, fire, and smoke. Lava erupted from the cone, heaving and seething down one slope, forming a molten flow that wrapped the mountain like a moat. Where it met itself again, the lava created a maelstrom, sucking and boiling and disappearing in a fiery vortex.

Zagan pointed. "The River Styx."

They joined the exodus, winding their way down under blazing sky. Ian cowered from the heat, ducking his face, and he noticed that unlike everyone else here, he cast no shadow. A welcomed sign his soul had yet to harden . . .

They marched on, and at length Ian could make out below what was absorbing all the traffic. Heat aside, he felt a shudder. There was an opening in one side of the volcano. A cave at its base, perhaps fifty feet high and three times as wide, gaping insatiably, black as pitch.

Ian needed no pronouncement from Zagan.

The Mouth of Hell.

It lay across the molten river, which was broad and without a bridge. Instead, passage was accomplished by bargelike ferryboats powered by oars. The ferries worked nonstop, overseen by Dark Angles that pressed souls into service as galley slaves. For the trip across, the boats were crammed to the gunnels with souls and devils. On the return, devils only.

But there were too few boats. Masses of terrified souls and short-tempered devils were backed up along the shore, jostled tightly together. In the dust, heat, frenzy, and confusion, some souls made the mistake of bumping into devils, incurring blasts of their steamy breath.

Ian trembled, gaping across the river to the source of the misery and mayhem. Above the Cave's crooked mouth he saw a message carved into the rock, repeated in many languages. And drawing nearer, he could make out its foreboding words:

GATE of the DAMNED
Abandon All Hope, Ye Who Enter Here

EIGHTY-NINE

THE RIVER STYX, SOMEWHERE IN THE NOTHINGNESS OF TIME

Ian came to a halt on the banks of the fiery stream, jammed among the frantic throngs like cattle at a slaughterhouse. He couldn't take his eyes off the Cave opposite, hearing the most haunting wails of despair echo from its blackness. And for the first time, he felt the full weight of his odyssey.

Hell.

The primordial Black Hole. The abyss from which, so far in eternity, no soul had ever escaped. How many billions had vanished down its throat? To Know his Fate could well be the same rattled Ian to the core. *Abandon All Hope.*

And yet, he alone among these desolate souls had hope to cling to. *A lifeline.* Albeit, that lifeline felt woefully slender and frail now measured against the great vacuum of the Void.

He gazed up at Zagan beside him. Was the monster plotting against him? The cold, blank eyes gave no clue.

Nearby, a despondent soul began the Lord's Prayer, others joining in. *Futile,* Ian thought with dismay; none had a prayer in Hell. And the Dark Angels quickly moved to confirm that. Already sour-tempered in the heat and congestion, they responded with vicious sprees of horn and tusk until the chorus ceased. No sounds now but sobs and moans, the damned made to stand and reflect upon their Doom, delay adding to the terror, stress unbearable.

Ian noticed next to him an elderly man, white hair, Van Dyke beard, whimpering, glancing around. Branded on his shoulder was the Roman numeral II. Whatever sin it stood for, the poor fellow surely regretted it now. His eyes met Ian's and he whispered, *"What mind could conceive such horror?"*

Ian remembered his catechism. Hell was the manifestation of God's righteous anger and vengeance, created to punish Evil. Heaven, an expression of God's Love, created to reward Good. Together they formed the Great Incentive that inspired Man to do God's Will.

He whispered back, "The same Mind that conceived Paradise. Divine carrot and stick."

The old man retorted, "What appeal has a carrot if you've never tasted one? What fear a stick if you've never felt its sting? I was a professor of literature in life. I saw the Bible in light of my profession, Heaven and Hell simply metaphors. *I never thought them real!*"

God's Incentive obviously hadn't proven effective for all these other souls, either. As Lucien had once pointed out, the Bible offered few details about the Afterlife. Even steeped in religion as Ian was, he'd never foreseen Hell to be this cruel. He had to wonder now, seeing how crucial an understanding of Heaven and Hell was to Man's salvation, why had God left it so vague?

To Ian's other side was a dark-haired, middle-aged man, listening in. He sniveled, "St. Thomas himself had doubts! An *apostle* who Knew Christ *personally*. Who received the Word *directly*. Still, he had to touch Christ's wounds to Believe! And here are we, two thousand years removed, nothing to go on but a book of ambiguous, secondhand Scripture?"

Ian gave Lucien's answer. "It's a test of Faith."

"*Which* Faith? Ten thousand religions in the world, each claiming to be right! How were we to Know?"

In light of the Reality, Ian suspected *no* religion had it right. Billions wandering through life spiritually off course. And yet as he was now seeing, God *did* hold Man accountable for getting His Message wrong. All these damned had in some way offended their Creator.

Why had God left His Word so open to interpretation? Which was it: *An eye for an eye,* or *Turn the other cheek?*

The old man with the Van Dyke put a finer edge on it.

"Why is God so aloof!"

Immediately Ian heard an uproar behind. The sharp ears of the old man's demon keeper had picked up on the *G* word, and it was howling, doubled over in convulsions.

The old man dropped to his knees, quaking, hands clasped in prayer—only making matters worse. The devil recovered in a frenzy, seized him in its claws, and tore him in two at the waist, guts spilling everywhere.

Ian was aghast. But there was no relief of death for the poor wretch.

He continued his horrid shrieks as the devil gnawed his pieces like legs of mutton, saving the head for last, poking it in with a long claw. The man's mouth kept screeching, muffled as it vanished down the beast's throat.

The demon gave out a bloody belch, wiped its muzzle on its arm, and resumed its wait.

Overcome, Ian cried to Zagan, *"Enough! I've had enough! Take me back!"*

He watched the creature's thick lips twist into a grin.

"No turning back. And you've seen *nothing* yet."

What glimmer of faith Ian had in Zagan flickered out, his knees going weak. For certain now he was in this to the end.

Numbed, he scarcely noticed the cries around him until they'd escalated to a roar. The Dark Angels had started driving his group toward an empty ferry, souls panicking, some trying to escape. But the devils were too quick, catching, smashing, dragging them forward. An elderly woman clutched at Ian and he reached out, hand passing through hers, watching helpless as she was dragged away.

Zagan moved, and Ian followed in a stupor, heart like lead in his chest.

Their ferry was moored along a stone wharf, a broad, flat-bottomed vessel with low sides, built of heavy planks that appeared wooden, yet defied the river's fire. Room for a thousand passengers, Ian guessed, propelled by dozens of oars along the sides, steered at the aft by a long rudder.

As Ian boarded behind Zagan, the demon rudder man stopped him, exposing yellow fangs.

"Why are you clad?" he barked, grabbing Ian by the neck, inspecting him. "You're not ripened, you bear no brand!"

Zagan intervened. "Nay, *Charon*, this soul has passage."

The creature turned to squint up at Zagan, who towered over him. No match, he snorted, "Piss off, then!" giving Ian a nasty heave.

Ian staggered aboard rubbing his throat—of no benefit, his fingers passing through. Quickly the ferry filled and pushed off, the heat and fumes of the river unbearable, sweat stinging Ian's eyes. Some souls swooned and lost their footing, toppling over the sides into the lava. Others the devils kicked overboard for inept rowing or out of sheer meanness, castaways left to make a frenetic slog back, bellowing in unimaginable torment.

The passage was tedious, but at length the boat made shore and the devils began to off-load. Again some souls balked, but no resistance was tolerated, sharp claws and tusks keeping the doomed in line, goading them on toward their infernal Fate.

NINETY

THE GATE OF HELL, SOMEWHERE IN ETERNITY

Driven up the riverbank by the Dark Angels, Ian and his procession of the damned came under the glower of Hell's black maw. In Ian's worst nightmare he'd never felt such terror, damning the stubbornness that brought him here—only to realize the irony.

The cries around him rose to a tumult, those not already sickened with fear now succumbing to the Cave's foul breath. Some souls made a last-gasp effort to flee, cut off by devils that beat, mauled, and forced them on. Many had to be dragged inside, hauled through a drool of sewage, vomiting, wetting, and soiling themselves, their screams burbling from the gloom as it swallowed them.

His time having come, Ian controlled his tremors, determined that Zagan not see his fear. Raising his eyes in silent prayer, he was distracted by a row of rusted metal teeth jutting from the Cave's upper jaw. Underside of a gate, he presumed, able to drop guillotine-fashion.

And then he was crossing, too late to pray . . .

The darkness engulfed him like a pestilence, the hysteria deafening, the stench insufferable. And all at once, a hot miasma swept through him. It invaded to the depths of his soul, sucking out what vestige of hope he had left, leaving him a husk of despair. In his heart of hearts, he now sensed he would never pass back out this Gate.

Dazed, panicked, he stumbled on, coughing, choking, eyes and lungs burning. He strained to orient himself, and as his vision adjusted to the murk, he saw he was in the throes of a stampede. Thousands of souls rushing madly by, some passing through him and one another. Pandemonium.

He looked up to see they were in a cavern, vast as a hundred Grand Central Terminals. Everywhere, giant stone fists protruded from the ceiling, forefingers pointed down in stalactites of accusation.

The sounds of growls and barking caught his attention, and he turned to see more wild-eyed souls rushing in his direction. As they passed, he saw behind them three massive hounds on leashes storming straight for him.

Not three—*one* huge hound, *three* heads. Ferocious, snapping, snarling, sinking fangs into foot-draggers. It was out of the control of its demon handler and it lunged for Ian. He barely had time to throw up his arms, sets of jaws biting deep into thigh, flank, forearm. He cried out and was pulled down, certain he'd be devoured.

But the mouths abruptly yelped and let go.

Ian risked a peek to see the animal suspended in the air by the scruffs of its necks, hearing Zagan order, "Away, *Cerberus*—or feel my teeth!"

Then releasing it, the devil gave it a boot and it retreated whining, tail between its legs. No further regard for Ian, Zagan moved on, and Ian struggled to his feet, limping after, his pain fierce.

The cavern eventually tapered into the bottleneck of a tunnel, wall-mounted torches lighting the way. The damned were squeezed into ever-tighter formation, and the devils began separating them into convoys of a thousand or so. Each soul was then made to pass single file in front of three large, dingy mirrors mounted side by side against a wall.

A sign above read:

GLASS of JUDGMENT

Below each mirror was a smaller sign. The first:

YE WHO FAILED TO RESPECT THY MAKER

Second:

YE WHO FAILED TO RESPECT THY BRETHREN

Third:

YE WHO FAILED TO RESPECT THYSELF

As the souls filed by, some appeared in one or two mirrors, others in all three. Ian understood. The glass reflected the three core offenses against

God from which all mortal sins sprang. Ian breathed a sigh not to see himself in any. Not for trespassing the Afterlife, surprisingly. Not even for his misdeed of stranding Niemand's soul after the man's execution. It seemed his remorse had indeed absolved him of that sin.

Past the mirrors Ian noticed writing on the walls. Ancient graffiti scratched into the rock by human fingernails, in different languages. Of those he could read, some inveighed against the Almighty, some against the parents who'd birthed them, others against those who'd allegedly led them into sin. Most simply pleaded for mercy.

And then Ian was stunned to spy three contemporary inscriptions signed by names he recognized, scrawled in English, in blood:

I erred in my Greed — Oral Roberts

I erred in my Self-Righteousness — Jerry Falwell

The Lord erred — Pat Robertson

Before Ian could search out more, he heard a disturbance ahead, the line slowing, souls screaming. Zagan swore and lashed out at those in front, and Ian could make out another large sign carved into the wall, bracketed by flickering torches. He felt his throat tighten.

I. HADES of the SEREB

The screams intensified as the line pushed forward, the tunnel expanding into a vast cavern, heat soaring. The floor fell away to the left, the main path continuing a milder descent against the right wall, and Ian could finally see the cause of the gridlock. Demons were seizing souls with the numeral I on their shoulders and hauling them howling down the slope as they resisted with all their might.

"What will happen to them?" Ian cried to Zagan.

The monster kicked a dawdling soul out of his way.

"They will be prepared for the mines. Sereb is the Realm of the Slothful. Those who wasted their lives will lament it here, forever."

The cavern opened wide, and Ian was appalled to behold the panorama of the first Hell's afflictions. Nearest him, souls were being tossed into the end of a long, cylindrical wire cage that hung lengthwise over a fire pit, hot as an oven. The cage rotated sideways like a clothes dryer, the victims made to run through, escaping the flames by staying as far up the arc as possible.

A difficult feat, Ian noted with pity. One heavyset man, gasping for breath, slipped and fell. It startled others behind him who also tripped, and they all tumbled together in an imbroglio of cursing, wailing, roasting flesh. The stench made Ian gag.

But as he saw, the horrors of this Hell were just beginning. Ever crueler obstacle courses awaited—hundreds more such contraptions suspended in the flames, each with its own insufferable challenges and disorienting motions.

A perverse fun house of the damned.

The Hell stretched on for miles, the souls eventually completing these ordeals to face worse. At the far end of the cavern Ian saw devils separating survivors into teams, manacling them to chains that stretched across the fires. Opposite were teams similarly shackled—countless souls facing off in an infernal tug-of-war. Losers were dragged through the coals to the winner's side, made to start anew as victors moved down a slot to continue the competition. On and on until at last graduating these gruesome games, the survivors were furnished picks and shovels and led away.

"To enlarge Hell," Zagan explained.

Making room for an ever-expanding population.

Ian reached the end of this Hellhole at last, escaping the cries of agony, if not the heat. But all too soon the cries rose anew, and Ian saw yet another torch-lit sign:

II. HADES of the INNER CHAMBER

Once again the tunnel broadened into a massive cavern, a wave of panic suddenly rocking the procession, howls of fear surpassing those before. In the dim light Ian watched devils snatch panicked souls from the line, shuddering to see the Fate that awaited.

The damned of this Hell were being subjected to the most vile and violent sexual assaults. Demons ravaged both men and women in every way imaginable and unimaginable, attacking in a wanton frenzy of grotesque, oversized appendages and all manner of sadistic devices. Horrifying shrieks echoed across the chamber as the victims begged for a mercy unknown here.

Shocked, disgusted, Ian averted his eyes, only to see an adjoining cavern. A smaller, inner chamber.

Zagan changed course toward it, sneering to Ian, "You were a priest, take special note—a place in Hell reserved for the most deserving of your kind . . ."

Ian saw before him endless rows of men bent over what looked like Communion rails, hands bound to ankles. They shrieked and pleaded hysterically, abused by devils with red-hot pokers the size of baseball bats and rimmed with spikes and barbs.

Revolted, Ian hurried past, hearing Zagan's snide laugh.

They soon left this Hell behind, continuing some distance before Ian had recovered enough to ask, "How . . . how did you know I was a priest?"

The demon halted under a torch.

"Do you know nothing? Observe your garment. *Close.*"

Ian lifted his arm to the light, examining the translucent sleeve of his robe. He was amazed to see that its gray color was actually the effect of tiny lines of writing. Statements woven into the clear fabric, telling all about him!

Some threads were white, some gray. White told of kindnesses and good works he'd performed—the very whitest, his generosity to the poor. Gray were minor sins. Small lies. Swearing. Insensitivities toward Angela.

And one black line, glaring among the rest—Ian's sin of stranding Zach Niemand's soul on Earth. Apparently forgiven him now.

The story of my life, written in good deeds and bad.

"If you saw through my eyes," Zagan said, directing his blank, bottomless globes at Ian, "you would need no words to read your sins. I see *all* in your soul."

Ian had the disturbing sensation of being turned inside out and back again.

They resumed their journey, following the tunnel as it made a sharp right, seeming to curve around and pass under itself. And once more came cries of despair, the route opening into yet another yawning cavern.

III. HADES of the SUB CHAMBER

Ian was surprised to detect savory aromas, feeling pangs of hunger and desperate thirst, throat parched from the incessant heat. He saw more souls being yanked from line, some corpulent, and he realized this was the Hell set aside for the gluttons of the world.

But as Zagan advised, "Not all gluttony involves food."

These damned were being led to a banquet table piled high. Sumptuous cuts of beef, poultry, pork, fish, lamb—every meat imaginable. Cornucopias of luscious produce. Mountains of desserts. And most irresistible—*beverages.* Even alcohol. Beer, wine, liquors of every kind. Other intoxicants, too—tobaccos, narcotics, on and on.

To Ian's amazement, the souls were allowed to help themselves, indulging whatever appetite they wished. How he envied them!

Until he saw their looks of frustration. None, he realized, could taste a single bite, drink a drop, inhale or inject anything. Every substance dissipated first. And now, worked into a frenzy, the tantalized souls were dragged off to pillories to have their heads locked in place.

Some of the demons approached with platters of rancid-looking food, prying open their jaws, cramming the matter in with ramrods as the souls choked and fought.

Zagan explained, "Their most despised dish, *that* is what they are fed. In putrid form."

Others had giant bellows thrust into their throats, devils pumping canisters of caustic fumes into their lungs. Still others had foul substances jammed up their noses or injected into their veins through giant needles.

The forced gorging continued, faces turning bright red, eyes bulging, gullets gagging, bodies writhing. And finally, skin stretched white and thin, the souls exploded, raining morsels, gas, fluids, and gore everywhere.

Then gnomish creatures scurried in from the shadows to mop the muddle back together, the souls reconstituted, and the process repeated.

Ian could stomach no more, unable to imagine a Hell any worse.

NINETY-ONE

THE BASEMENT OF A PRIVATE ESTATE, CAYENNE, FRENCH GUYANA, SAME DAY, MORNING

Angela continued her pacing, heels clacking the marble floor in an anxious metronome. Next to the operating table, a large LCD clock called out in scarlet:

0:26:07

Less than half an hour since Ian slipped into death. Less than half his allotted time. And Angela was suffering every interminable second. Could she hang on until 7:00 AM? Could *Ian*? Her eyes jumped to him again, as they had a hundred times before.

Unchanged. Still, gray, lifeless . . .

She yearned to flee this dungeon, to bolt outside into the sun, scream, burst into tears. But she kept her vigil, continuing her rounds of the basement.

Her eyes alighted on yet another bizarre painting. William Blake. A black-and-white etching of a six-footed dragon attacking a man as his lover looked on, helpless.

Swearing, Angela approached Josten once again, appealing for him to stop the madness.

And again, he refused.

NINETY-TWO

THE DEPTHS OF HELL, TIME IN PERPETUITY

The number of souls in Ian's convoy had thinned during the first three Hells, though hundreds remained. The weeping and wailing had also diminished, giving over to the mournful dirge of trudging feet.

But now, a strange new sound . . .

A horrid clamor unlike anything Ian had ever heard. Deep, booming bellows that he finally recognized as Dark Angels, howling in fear and warning!

Zagan came to a halt, hunkering, hissing, baring his fangs. Ian felt his hairs rise.

What could possibly panic such formidable creatures?

And then the howling resolved into words: *"Lay ho! Lay ho! Persefoni!"*

Zagan turned and dove for the ground. Ian felt the brunt of his tail and was sent sprawling. The yells were quickly drowned out by a roar, and Ian raised up to see a blaze of light approaching, glaring off the tunnel walls like a comet, demons and souls scrambling.

He lifted higher, two glowing white stallions thundering down. Behind was a two-wheeled chariot of gold and a warrior in golden armor, reins in one hand, bullwhip in the other. Female, by the mounds of her golden breastplate and smooth skin, face obscured by a gold helmet. Her flaxen hair billowed out, a bow and quiver over a shoulder, sword sheathed at her slim waist. She made no effort to avoid those in her way, running them over, whip lashing every demon in reach.

Ian rolled aside just in time, glancing up as she flew by. Short skirt of overlapping gold plates, muscular legs strapped in gold greaves. She stared back at him as she passed, and he could imagine how conspicuous he must look, the only human clothed here.

Then she was gone around a bend like a shooting star, leaving crushed and broken souls moaning in her wake.

Those demons unfortunate enough to have caught her lash rubbed their wounds, growling and gnashing their teeth after her. The agile Zagan, however, had escaped unscathed, rising, swearing, brushing off crud.

"Who *was* that?" Ian asked.

"Persefoni!" the demon spat. "Angel of Death. A She-Devil to us!"

"An Angel in Hell?"

"Her punishment for siding with the Rebellion."

The ancient Angelic War . . . Ian was still confused.

"But why isn't she like you?"

For a moment he thought he saw melancholy in the monster's huge eyes.

"Before the Great Battle," Zagan said, "Persefoni lost her nerve and stood down. She was therefore spared Damnation. But for all time she is made to ferry the names of the damned from Heaven to Hell. And to enforce upon us the Laws of Chaos."

Still cursing, he moved on, Ian following, realizing how little he understood this bizarre world.

They soon came to another torch-lit sign:

IV. HADES of the MESEN

If Zach Niemand had told him correctly, Ian believed this was the Realm where the jealous were punished. He was surprised then to find the air cooler—jealousy being such a hot-blooded sin. Indeed, the temperature continued to drop as the tunnel expanded into another sprawling cavern.

A mile across, Ian guessed, enclosing a canyon nearly as wide—and so deep the bottom was lost in darkness. The path narrowed to a ledge as it followed the rim, squeezing the procession into single file against the cave wall.

As Ian drew closer, he saw fog creeping out of the canyon and across the path. Souls slowed, the way slippery, and some lost their footing, plunging over the side, cries disappearing into God-Knew-where. But the demons with their clawed toes had no problem, bullying the laggards, causing more to fall.

Ian stepped into the fog to feel the temperature plummet, soon losing all sensation in his feet. He shivered so badly he feared he'd tumble over, too, and despite the risk of stepping on Zagan's tail, he moved closer to the demon's searing exhausts of breath. A mistake. The warmth was fleeting, offset by a coat of foul, brown ice that formed on his skin, making him even colder and stiffer.

He stole a glance into the chasm. Like a massive well shaft, perfectly vertical. Staircase cut into the sides, descending in a tight spiral like the threads of a screw, punctuated here and there by daggers of icicles.

Souls doomed to this Hellhole were being manhandled down the steps by demons, nothing to indicate their Fate but the sounds of cracking whips. Ian stretched to see openings in the walls far below, doorways into which the damned were being driven.

"What happens to them?" he asked Zagan.

The devil cast his eyes down, exhaling a noxious smog.

"To my kind, the greatest torment. They will be entombed and frozen in place—that part is not so bad. But throughout, their eyes will gaze upon visions of the first Heaven, where they will bear witness to the Joy of the Blessed, a Joy they themselves will never Know. And unable to look away, they will long for that which their envy has cost them." Under his breath he muttered, *"Worse times seven, those who Knew the highest Heaven."*

Of course. Once, long ago in the vastness of time, Zagan had been an angel . . .

They moved on, rounding the chasm, entering a tunnel on the other side. Ian trusted he was now but two levels removed from his parents. Yet despite all he'd seen and endured so far, he felt in no better position to help them, afraid he might soon share their fate, anxieties rising.

Not that he'd lost Faith. On occasion he felt a twitch from his thread of life. And there was still the Tree—if only Zagan would honor his word to take him there.

Looking up at that sullen face, however, Ian held out little hope of that. He sighed. Whatever the outcome with his parents, he *had* to survive and make it back for Angela. He dared not abandon her to the nightmare he'd left her in.

He glanced at his wrist, not thinking.

Dammit! No way to gauge time here! No idea how long he had left. It felt as if he'd been traveling for days. And assuming it was even possible for his soul to be retrieved from such a distance, he worried it might happen *before* he reached his parents.

He turned to Zagan. "How much farther to the Pit?"

The devil didn't answer, apparently still brooding over the last Hell.

Abruptly the tunnel angled and took a steep descent, the ground turning to steamy wet muck. Ian nearly lost his footing, holding on to the walls, slipping down into hot, fetid, yellow-brown smog. The air, already rank, grew unbearable, those in front choking and gagging as another torch-lit sign appeared:

V. HADES of the METEN

The odor got so foul souls began to retch, devils beating and berating them to move along. Ian sickened, too, struggling between bouts of heaving to keep up.

At last the source of the stench came into view, and Ian's shock overwhelmed his nausea. Stretching out ahead was a vast lake. Like none he'd ever seen. A quagmire of raw sewage, on fire. A burning, churning, boiling bog of effluvia, tossing with the flotsam of human souls.

He watched in horror as sinners marked for this Hell were seized by their demons, raised high, and hurled headlong into the gruel. They no sooner burbled to the surface, gasping, spitting, sputtering, than more devils in boats floated by to plunge them under again with oars and poles, doling out vicious whacks to any hand that reached out. Along the shore, hellhounds prowled, attacking those who gained the banks, driving them back into the mire.

"The Meten Sea," Zagan said. "Ocean of greed, selfishness, intolerance, and hypocrisy."

Ian made the connection. The place where the hard-hearted and hard-headed of the world were sent to soften, stewing in Hell's hot cesspool.

The sea absorbed at least a third of the remaining damned, and as Ian stared out at the breadth of humanity bobbing off to the horizon, he moaned with despair, *"Are there no souls in Heaven?"*

"None but Know Truth," Zagan replied.

Ian looked at him. "You mean Holy Scripture?"

The devil scoffed. "What passes for Scripture in your world is but an echo. The Truth was given to your ancients in visions, but its meaning diminished with each retelling. Now few understand."

He swept an arm across Hell's Ocean.

"Behold the Great Religions of the world, *all* well accounted for."

His point was clear. Over the ages, Scripture, like a tale passed through a crowded room, had lost its True meaning. No better understood now than the symbols in Bosch's paintings—which, relative to the Bible, had been created only yesterday.

Why then, Ian wondered, had God chosen to reveal Himself exclusively through archaic texts? Why such distance between Himself and His children when they yearned so desperately to Know Him?

God, the estranged Parent . . .

Ian thought back to the countless prayers of his life. Especially those of his childhood, pleading for adoption. He'd never felt God was listening. God never answered. Not in words anyway, not in ways he understood. In the days of the Bible, God spoke directly with Man. Today, only with those behind the walls of asylums.

Indeed Ian felt crazy himself seeking answers from a devil. Yet Zagan had once been an Angel. And demon or no, he surely Knew God's Truth. Frustrated, Ian pressed, "If Scripture is so muddled, how can Man ever hope to understand It? Must we all be theologians!"

The demon spat, "*Theologians.* They Know *least* of all. Quibblers. Manipulators. They bend Scripture to suit themselves."

Ian recalled a line of Shakespeare: *The Devil can cite Scripture for his purpose.*

Zagan directed a claw at the sea. "There," he said, indicating different souls. "*There* your Great Doctors of Divinity. Jerome. Augustine. Gregory. Adrift in their dogma, plying their teachings to the lemmings who followed them, peasant to pope."

Ian was stunned. "If not theologians, *who?* How can *any* man Know Truth!"

"You have a conscience, do you not? Why must you look to others to guide you? Preachers, proselytizers—whosoever thunders loudest. Sooner it rain in Hell than a Fundamentalist speak Truth!"

Then dismissing all with a wave of a hand, he snorted, "Bah! *Enough!*" and stomped off.

Ian hurried to catch up and they continued in silence for a time, Ian weighing all this, giving the demon's temper a rest. After what he hoped was a sufficient break, he dared, "Tell me about the Tree of the Knowledge of Evil."

The monster let out a huff, singeing Ian's arm. "Its Knowledge is of no value to undamned souls."

"Have you ever eaten its fruit?"

"None have tasted since the first man and woman—and look what it gained them. Even so, you cannot steal its fruit, the Tree is guarded." And growling, he barked, *"No more foolish questions!"* and picked up the pace.

They pushed on, no sound now save the drudging footsteps of the leftover damned. Soon, however, there arose cries and shouts ahead, and again Ian tensed. The sixth Hell, he presumed—hopefully the last stop before the Pit.

He soon saw what appeared to be a dungeon, its entrance sealed top-to-bottom by heavy bars about twelve feet high, continuing a great distance along one side of the tunnel. Iron, the bars looked, scarred on the lower half by odd indentations. Only one way in—a wide gate in the middle that bore an old-style key lock and a large, rusted sign:

VI. HADES of the METAL OBLONG GATE

According to Niemand, this was the Hell that harbored those whose anger had condemned them. Hearts filled with hatred, vengeance, and cruelty. Not surprisingly then, when the appointed damned were singled out by their demon tenders, they reacted with rage, digging in their heels, fighting furiously, swearing, biting, kicking.

Ian didn't blame them, seeing what lay on the other side of the bars. A carpet of souls stretched endlessly into the depths, each soul staked naked and spread-eagled on the ground, bloodied and shrieking, besieged by the vilest creatures. Spiders, flies, mosquitoes, scorpions, snakes, rats, and other vermin Ian couldn't identify. Including a brilliant-orange, wasp-like insect the size of a thumb, with nasty mandibles and a stinger.

One alighted on Ian's arm, and before he could brush it away, it stung and bit him. He howled, swatting it to the ground, crushing it with his heel as his arm began to swell.

Zagan took note, sniggering, "Hellfire fly."

Indeed, it itched and burned like Hell.

Inside the gate, countless more such insects were swarming the victims as other pests clawed, gnawed, and vied for their share of the ethereal flesh. The souls thrashed and screamed to no avail. Dark Angels patrolled with buckets, some tossing what looked like salt on the wounds, other's relieving themselves on their helpless prisoners, taunting, driving them to madness.

Except, as Ian recalled, madness was no option here, insanity a release granted only to the living . . .

A devil stepped up and rattled a key in the lock, swinging wide the gate, hinges screeching like harpies. The new prisoners were dragged through scratching and wailing, and as the last cleared, the gate clanged shut with resounding finality. Some souls broke free, rushing back to the bars, sobbing, gnashing their teeth against them—the source of the indentations, Ian realized. But there was no hope, demons seizing them in their claws, lugging them off to their miserable fates.

Zagan headed on and Ian stumbled after, arm swollen and dangling like a broken wing.

Next, Ian trusted, lay the final Realm. Culmination of his hopes and fears, most dreaded Damnation of all.

The Pit.

NINETY-THREE

THE BOWELS OF THE ABYSS, WHERE TIME DOES NOT EXIST

Eager to reach the last Hell, Ian was keeping abreast of Zagan when abruptly the demon reached down and pinched Ian's arm between two claws.

"Ow!" he hollered, the pain worse for it being his sore arm. *"What was that for?"*

"To see if you harden." The monster observed him closely. "Some souls ripen before others, but it appears you are not one." Then lengthening his stride, shoving souls aside, he called back, "Hasten, we near the Pit."

Ian broke into a trot, pain and exhaustion aside. If Zagan was to be believed, they were approaching the seventh and final Realm where prideful souls were sent to be humbled. Where his beloved parents were imprisoned.

And *still* he had no plan for them. He wasn't even sure what he would say, or what to expect in return. Would they be proud of him for his reckless odyssey? Or think him a fool? Would they have a way to help him help them? Or was he all on his own? Again he felt the old longings and loneliness, and filled with renewed vigor he pulled in front of Zagan, down another winding incline, around a bend to encounter one more torch-lit sign:

VII. HADES of the PIT

He trembled with anticipation and anxiety, his long-awaited reunion seemingly at hand. But then he saw his patience would continue to be tested. Ahead, souls were stumbling to a halt, plowing through one another and into demons, earning themselves vicious swipes.

As he drew closer, Ian was dumbfounded to see that the path ended. Beyond was nothingness. The tunnel simply terminated in a huge maw, gaping out onto empty space.

No, *not* empty . . . Straining, he could make out dim shapes in the night sky, hovering in the distance all around like will-o'-the-wisps. But before he could tell what they were, he was interrupted by horrid shrieks.

The remaining souls were being snatched up by the demons and hurled helter-skelter out into the blackness! Ian watched in terror as they sailed off in all directions, some falling far down to disappear, others soaring high, floating to a rest in the ether, cries dying in their throats. They simply dangled there, mouths moving, making no sound, hands waving over their eyes as if blind.

Advancing steadily to the brink, Ian was able to identify the dim shapes. Antecedent souls, he realized, some no doubt discarded from time immemorial. They held motionless, eyes and mouths open, faces blank as they vegetated in the void, ambient light reflecting silver off their naked skin.

Dim moons in a dead galaxy.

"What's happening?" he asked Zagan, his turn coming.

The devil nodded toward the outcasts. "Their sin is loftiness, therefore are they brought low to the Pit. As they once flaunted their egos to others, so now must they reflect solely upon themselves, each a universe unto itself for all Time, no stimulation of any kind."

A vast sensory-deprivation tank!

Ian was appalled. Pure psychological torture—worse by far than any of the previous Hells. Surely such isolation would drive a mind mad. Except, not here . . .

Knowing what his poor parents had endured these two decades shook Ian to his core.

He needed time to muster himself before facing them, but it was too late. He was at the precipice, Zagan grabbing him roughly in his huge hands, raising him up.

"Now," the demon declared, "you go to your parents."

And suddenly Ian realized—*I've been conned!*

Zagan was sending him to his parents, all right. Flashing in Ian's head was a vision of himself heaved out into the vacuum, landing blind, mute, and deaf beside his impassive parents, denied even the solace of their company, drifting derelict forever though the emptiness of eternity!

He felt petrified in the monster's grip, a scream welling in his lungs.

But before the last sound he would ever utter could reach his lips, he found himself planted once more on the giant's shoulder.

"Hold fast," Zagan ordered, launching out, wings unfolding, carrying them into the night . . .

Ian could only sit and shake, numb with relief. He clutched the devil's horn in both hands as they flew, working to regain his composure.

No wind, surprisingly. No sensation of movement at all. They soared as if weightless, a spaceship on an ethereal voyage, zooming down past countless hushed, spectral shapes. At length Ian found his voice.

"W-what suspends them in space?"

"They descend to the equilibrium of their sins."

Ian wasn't sure what that meant, except his parents' sins must have been great because he and Zagan continued to drop. On and on they fell.

Until at last, Ian sensed them. Far below in the stygian cosmos, a tiny glow!

He held his breath, watching the little nebula resolve into twin stars—then celestial bodies floating motionless, upright, heads bowed, arms out to the sides like drowning victims. A faint light from above revealed only heads, shoulders, arms . . .

He couldn't contain himself. *"Mom! Dad!"*

No response, not even an echo.

"They cannot hear you," Zagan said. "They cannot see, touch, or smell. Only think."

The demon slowed, gliding near. Ian marveled at the musculature of his father's back; his mother's smooth, delicate shoulders. And he grimaced to see the letters VII branded on their biceps.

Zagan dropped below them, and in the shadow Ian could make out their faces, beholding them again for the first time since age nine. Just as they'd looked that last day of their lives, twenty years ago . . .

Ian trembled, spellbound. His father, so familiar from photos, yet so surprising now. Ian's jaw, nose, brow, unruly hair. Seeing him face-to-face like this, Dad seemed more brother than father. And something else. In his eyes—a tiny dilation of the pupils!

Does he sense me?

Shaking, he turned to Mom. *So beautiful.* Elegant, slim. Hair long and flowing, black as the darkness that enveloped her. Complexion like platinum in the starlight, nose graceful and upturned, eyes bright, serious—the eyes she'd given him. Sweet, full lips that had smiled at him and kissed his face a thousand times . . .

Now more than ever he knew these angelic souls were undeserving of their Fate. Yet he had no clue how to help them. His hope of finding an answer along the way had netted him nothing, and he cursed himself, gazing back and forth between his parents, finally turning his rage on Zagan.

"The deal was, I could talk to them!"

"You *can* talk to them."

"You knew what I meant!"

The demon snorted and began to withdraw.

"Not yet!"

"We cannot linger. We have far to go, you've yet to be told your fare. And look at you—you're starting to turn."

Ian held his hand to the dim light. Indeed, it was losing its translucency, growing milky.

"Wait," he pleaded. "Let me say good-bye."

The monster growled and lowered his shoulder, bringing Ian even closer. Inches away, he was unable to resist, reaching out to caress Mom's face. As expected, his hand passed through. Yet he saw her pupils dilate, too! And her lips blossomed into a smile!

She feels me!

Zagan backed away and Ian had only an instant to reach out to Dad, brushing his cheek, receiving another smile!

As he retreated, Ian saw the light in their eyes fade, their brief respite from solitude over, and his soul ached for them now more than ever.

"Please," he begged Zagan. "I've got to help them! They don't belong here!"

"None belong here. Nevertheless, it is so . . ."

Tucking his wings, the demon began a free fall, and Ian turned to watch his parents recede.

"I love you!" he called out, deeply pained to lose them again, forever. But he did not leave empty-handed. The memory he carried away had in itself justified his journey. A memory he would cherish the rest of his life.

Assuming he still had a life.

NINETY-FOUR

SOMEWHERE IN THE SKIES ABOVE THE ATLANTIC, SAME DAY, MORNING

Quintus sat at the controls of his jet, studying his instruments, eyes bloodshot and scowling. The engines were running hot, pushed to capacity, fuel guzzling away. But he had no hope of reaching Cayenne in time to stop the catastrophe he suspected was now underway. He blamed himself that Baringer had snared the long-lost copy of Merton's Reality. And now it appeared the madman would soon acquire the Knowledge of Evil, if he hadn't already.

The marriage of Heaven and Hell.

What that unholy union would spawn—the end of Faith, if not the world! Quintus crossed himself.

"Let me reach him in time! Let *me* be the instrument of Your Justice . . ."

On the seat next to him sat a leather briefcase, open to reveal a pistol and a GPS locator. The GPS displayed a map of Cayenne, a red circle marking a suburb. A large briefcase for so few items. But awaiting Quintus at the airport would be an E&E with a fortune in euros to fill it.

NINETY-FIVE

THE PIT OF HELL, TIME ETERNAL

Ian hung tight to Zagan's horn as the Dark Angel continued to fall, leaving behind the galaxy of lost souls, entering a new zone of silent nothingness. No light save for the tip of the monster's muzzle, which glowed orange each time it exhaled.

"Where are you taking me?" Ian cried.

"To learn your fare."

They appeared to be plummeting in the opposite direction of Hell's Gate. Ian was able to feel the weight of his soul now as it solidified, no way to judge how much time he had left.

His journey through the Abyss seemed far longer than he'd anticipated. Alarmed, he asked, "How will you get me back before I harden? Can you fly faster than you fall?"

"To return the same route would take four times the descent. There is another way."

By the cord on my soul?

Ian felt its resistance on occasion, if weakly. No idea how well it had weathered the hardships. He imagined it was stretched to a fine strand by now.

Still strong enough to reel me in? With my soul growing heavier?

He had no idea either how much farther he could stretch Zagan's patience, but he wasn't finished.

"The Tree," he reminded. "You agreed to take me."

Zagan said nothing, nose flaring white.

Moments later, Ian detected a flush of rosy light far below in the blackness. Before he could even focus on it, it bloomed up large in a blur and they were upon it, Zagan extending his wings, swooping into a wide, banking turn as Ian strained to hang on. He was amazed to see them circling the summit of a huge, subterranean mountain—the leading edge of an even loftier range behind. It was bathed in an ambient orange light, its peak a cathedral-like formation of naked rock. Beneath was a desolate timberline, and below that, a primitive-looking city built into the slopes, wrapping the mountain all the way down to its base.

The city appeared ancient. Buildings of rough-hewn stone and wood, few taller than three stories, many crumbled to ruin. Windows without glass; streets narrow, cobblestone, lighted by torch lamps. Ian saw Dark Angels and other hellions trudging about by the thousands, no visible automation of any kind, nothing more sophisticated than hand-drawn carts. The pace of life appeared tedious and melancholy, no sounds of conversation or music.

"Where are we?" he asked in awe.

"Tartarus. Dwelling place of the Lords of the Abyss."

Flowing past the mountain at its base was a torrent of magma, source of the pale orange light. It slogged toward the range behind, disappearing into a cleft in the rock face.

"The River Lethe," Zagan said.

The glow reflected off the horizon—or what appeared to be horizon until Ian realized it was solid. Smooth, continuous, dark, extending up and out, disappearing into the blackness. He remembered what Niemand had told him. Golgotha. The terminus of Hell . . .

His attention was drawn to rhythmic sounds of metal striking metal, and he looked to see a large blacksmith's forge overhanging the river at the city's edge. Manning it were hulking, ox-faced brutes with muscular arms, some using tongs to immerse ingots in the lava flow. As the ingots heated, the beasts removed them to anvils, sparks flying as they wielded giant hammers to pound out swords, spears, and other tools of torture, fiery fumes pungent in the air.

Next to the forge, Ian saw a pier where a long line of squat, hunchbacked creatures fetched magma from the stream in buckets, lugging it up trails into the city.

"What's the lava for?"

"Mortar. Tartarus was destroyed during the Harrowing. It will be eons before it is rebuilt."

The Harrowing of Hell. Christ's descent into Limbo after His crucifixion, Ian recalled from his catechism, said to have shaken the Underworld to its foundations . . .

The demon soared on, passing over the city, aiming for the timberline below the mountaintop. Ian saw a clearing, and Zagan raised a claw to his leathery lips, commanding, *"Silence!"*

They glided in for a soft landing. Ian slid quietly from the demon's shoulder to stand before a wilderness of tall, leafless, skeletal trees bleached of their bark, long dead. Zagan pointed to a fog-strewn path leading into the darkness of the woods.

"The Tree is there," he whispered, "but you dare not enter . . . Now, I've done as agreed, let us leave."

He looked antsy, shifting his feet, scanning the forest.

If a creature of Zagan's prowess was nervous, Ian was nervous. But before he had a chance to ask Zagan's reason, it came slithering out of the gloom.

No monster of legend could have been more fearsome. Gigantic. Five times Zagan's size. Limbless, serpentine, head of a dragon. Fierce red eyes, pointed ears, crocodilian snout—open to expose saberlike fangs at the front.

"Leviathan!" Zagan cried.

Ian shuddered, recognizing the name of the biblical beast subdued by Jehovah at the beginning of Creation. Job 3:8 popped into his head.

Curse the day who awaken Leviathan!

The dragon spotted them, flames erupting from its mouth, smoke billowing from its nostrils. It gave out an explosive roar, dead branches shaking from the trees, crashing down.

"There is no worse pain in Hell," Zagan shouted, "than Leviathan's venom in your veins!"

He knelt, ordering Ian onto his back.

But Ian moved away.

"Not without the Knowledge . . ."

He still held hope for his parents, believing the Tree might yet yield a key to Hell's Gate.

"Fool!" Zagan stormed. "None has ever passed Leviathan! He will paralyze and eat us! We will lie in his gut in agony—*forever*!"

Ian paid no heed, turning to face the dragon as it snaked toward them.

High Noon in Hell.

Leviathan coiled, drawing up, hood expanding on the back of its neck. But Ian stood firm, calling out to Zagan, "Cover your ears!"

Then raising a hand to the beast, he cried, "In the Name of *God,* let me pass!"

As if struck by a thunderbolt, the great snake dropped to the ground convulsing, wrenching and writhing, turning in and out on itself in a ball. As Ian had trusted, no denizen of Hell could withstand the ineffable Sound . . .

His way cleared, he skirted by, shouting the Name again, racing down the path. He trusted Zagan would wait, the demon needing him to pay his fare, whatever terrible price that might be.

Slipping into the woods he slowed, no sounds or signs of life, nothing stirring. He found himself in the dismal atmosphere of a swamp, brushing through strands of Spanish moss that stung his skin. The trail wound past pools of yellow fluids and mist, ending at a patch of raised ground. In the middle stood a Tree, bent and broken. Gray, thick with age, branches gnarled against the sky like a doomed man fending off vultures.

Ian swallowed.

The Tree was split down its center, half missing, leaves withered. But among its branches Ian saw small, brown, desiccated fruits.

He approached and stopped beneath a limb, observing what appeared to be a mummified apple. Then, allowing himself no time to think, he plucked it, triggering a shower of leaves. He expected it to burn his fingers, presuming it no longer possessed its balance of Good. But to his surprise, it felt cool.

Trembling, he realized what he held. A Knowledge untasted by Humanity since Adam and Eve. Within this wrinkled rind, he prayed, lay the Secrets of Evil. The means to overcome Hell and save his parents.

If it didn't destroy him first . . .

Zagan's angry cries drifted from the clearing, ordering him back. Ian ignored him.

Raising the apple, holding his breath, he bit.

Immediately it ruptured, hot bilious liquid spilling into his mouth and down his throat before he could choke it back. The effects were instantaneous, heat shooting into his brain like a geyser, scalding his mind, dropping him gagging to his knees.

Poison!

He felt himself go numb, everything growing sluggish. In panic he watched the apple tumble slowly from his fingertips, throwing off droplets of black juice in a lazy pinwheel, rotating ever slower until it simply froze midair.

He was paralyzed!

Blinded, too, it seemed, consciousness turning inward. Though fully alert, he felt as if he'd been anesthetized—a patient awake in the middle of an operation.

Surgery of the soul!

He could sense something being implanted far inside him. Sinister, streaming into him like the downloading of a computer file, entering in merciless bits and bites. And he was powerless to stop it. The infusion surged on, how long he couldn't know, afraid that even if he survived there'd be no time to understand all this.

Then brusquely it ended. With a bang, the door slamming on his soul with such force it rocked him out of his spell—as the apple struck the ground. He watched it roll into a puddle, hissing and bubbling, stunned to realize that no time had elapsed at all. And incredibly, he still felt his lifeline . . .

Zagan beckoned furiously, and Ian struggled to his feet, wobbling back along the path, feeling strange pangs deep inside. He needed to make sense of them, and fast. Willing his head clear, he searched out that dark place within, found its door, and pried it back open.

Like bursting the hatch of a plane in a storm—turbulence sucking at his brain, a tornado in his head. Relentless bursts of lightning piercing his thoughts.

No, *not* lightning. *Images.* Countless moving images flashing in his mind! Abominable images. Scenes of malevolence, violence, cruelty. Visions, Ian realized, of every loathsome act of Man ever there had been, ever there would be. Odious as anything he'd witnessed in Hell.

And dare he pause an event to focus on it—a senile woman burned at the stake for witchcraft; Native Americans massacred by cavalry—it was as if he were recalling it *personally*, the Knowledge superimposed on him as vividly as if he'd lived it!

Revolted, overcome, he staggered to a tree, leaning against its bleached trunk. Zagan's cries were frantic. He hung there languid, panting, Knowing that he had indeed acquired the dark half of the Grand Equation. But he wasn't yet sure what it meant.

Was the Knowledge of Evil simply an amalgam of wickedness? He couldn't resolve its horrid scenes into a composite. He felt like a spectator in a stadium, his side flashing cards across the field, each a pixel in a giant, complex picture too close for him to pull into perspective. The Knowledge was inside him, yes, but seemingly beyond his comprehension.

"Be done with it," Zagan bellowed. *"Leviathan wakes!"*

He *was* done with it, the last hope for his parents eluding him. Nauseous, deflated, he stumbled back to the clearing.

Leviathan was stirring, all right, and fuming. It shook its horrible head, slinging venom, snapping its jaws. Beyond, Zagan was stamping and waving Ian on.

"Cover your ears!" Ian warned, giving the dragon another blast of the Sound and rushing past.

Zagan met him with a volley of curses, snatching him up, slamming him atop his shoulder.

"You son of a succubus!" he roared. "Speak that Word again, and I will devour you *whole*!"

Then, squatting, he sprang into the air, Ian looking back to see the dragon in a backwash of swirling dust and leaves.

As they sailed off, Zagan snarled, "If you think such a trick can save you from your fare, you are mistaken! Prayers do not leave this place! He to Whom you appeal does not hear!"

"He hears His Name wherever it's spoken."

"In the world above, perhaps. Take It in vain and you may be damned—as many here can attest. But in Hell where His Name is reviled, what more can He do to us? He spares Himself our insults, He shuts out all."

One by one Ian felt his hopes evaporate.

"I found the Knowledge," he grumbled, "but I don't understand it!"

The demon paid him a scoffing laugh.

"What did you expect? *You are a fool . . .*"

High above loomed the brooding brow of the mountain.

NINETY-SIX

MOUNT TARTARUS, THE PIT OF HELL, A MOMENT IN PERPETUITY

Perched on the shoulder of the demon Zagan, Ian soared over the dead forest, circling the mountaintop on his way to learn his fare.

Despite having just eaten from the Tree of the Knowledge of Evil, he had no more idea how to help his parents than before. And now he clearly felt the weight of his soul, his skin waxing ever more solid, surely little time left. Had he a living heart, it would have been pounding.

Each sweep of Zagan's wings brought them closer to the mountain's summit, a bleak, towering crest of granite thrust up like an angry fist against the blackness. They circled to the far side, where Ian saw a shelf of rock jutting from the cliff face some ninety meters below the peak. It projected out approximately twenty meters, twice that in length, and was illuminated in the middle by an Olympic-sized torch.

Zagan rose above the shelf, hovering, and Ian could make out two giant sculptures resting on its surface, carved into the cliff face on either side of the torch. Like the talons of some massive bird of prey.

Then abruptly Zagan banked, and when it seemed certain they'd crash into the mountainside, he pulled up and landed on the shelf, depositing Ian at its edge. Head spinning, Ian almost teetered off.

As his vision cleared, Ian realized the shelf was split lengthwise by a step of about a meter in height. He stood on the lower ledge, the upper holding the torch, under which sat an altar that appeared hewn from solid rock. Atop the altar was a large, ancient-looking chest. Lead, Ian thought. It featured on its front a bas-relief of two demons squatting, bowing to each other like mirror reflections, their batlike wings extended and touching at the tips.

Several meters to the right of the altar was a high-backed armchair, also cut from rock. In it sat a very old-looking man in a long black robe, with flowing white hair and beard, acutely prominent nose, eyes somber and deep-set, skin dark and wrinkled. His demeanor seemed thoughtful, composed, non-threatening. More dignified than demonic.

But then Ian heard Zagan growl low, "Do not speak unless addressed! *Show deference!*"

The old man rose. Tall, slim, poised despite his apparent age, greeting Ian with a slight nod. Ian responded in kind, sensing power in this ancient being, though seeing no resemblance to any satanic images of lore.

He beckoned Ian with a subtle move of a finger, and Ian advanced as far as the step, staring up into soulless eyes. Like Zagan's, lacking pupils. Even more disturbing in a human face. His lips were blistered and cracked, and when he parted them to speak, the words grated out in a rumble—tectonic plates grinding.

"I did not believe you would attempt this journey. Nor that your soul would endure if you did. Nevertheless, here you are, first of your kind to look upon Tartarus." He cocked his head. "Yet whatever gramarye has preserved your soul, by the looks of you, it's depleted. We must hurry, you'll need Life to pay your fare."

Folding his arms across his chest, he asked, "Are you satisfied Hell has fulfilled its bargain?"

Ian shifted his feet. "I saw my parents—but I couldn't speak with them."

"That was not the agreement."

"It was *implied.*"

Zagan snarled, but the old man raised a forefinger to silence him.

"You would have come regardless."

Ian lowered his eyes, and the old man declared, "Therefore, Hell has honored its contract, and you shall pay your fare. A simple one. All we require of you is to bear a message." The black eyes hardened. *"To He who damned us here."*

Ian took a step back. He'd had no idea what his fare would be, but surely not this—not to confront his Maker! And he'd promised Angela no more NDEs, he wouldn't survive another!

"I—I don't understand," he said. "The Creator Knows all. He already Knows your message."

"He Knows what He chooses to Know, and that does *not* include Hell! He has abandoned us."

Fearing the answer, Ian asked, *"What message?"*

The being's demeanor grew darker still. "There has been no word between Tartarus and Empyrean since the Rebellion. Persefoni refuses to speak for us."

Empyrean, highest Realm of Heaven, abode of God Himself. And Ian recalled Persefoni from his narrow brush with her chariot in Hell's Tunnel.

"We have suffered here for eons," the old man snapped, "exiled with no means to reconcile! Until now. Now *you* will carry our message. *An appeal for clemency . . .*"

Ian blinked, eyelids nearly opaque.

"Our labors here are no longer necessary! There are ample souls to take our places, let them preside over themselves, ancient subjugating new."

He pointed to the lead chest on the table.

"There, the Decalogue of Hell. *The Laws of Chaos.* Let Man obey them now!"

Ian pleaded, "I can't go to Empyrean—I'll be stopped!"

The black eyes noted his tarnished robe.

"Your sins are slight. The Dominions and Archangels may impede you—of the nine Choirs, *they* are overbearing. But none will use force. There is no violence in Heaven, all may travel the Seven Spheres even to Empyrean."

Surely this being should Know, having once been an eminent resident there.

"The journey will take you but a fraction as long as your trip here, and you will need no guide. Simply follow the light. Move always to the brightness."

"But I won't be allowed an audience with, with . . . *Him*. I'm *nobody*."

"In Heaven even the lowest are exalted. And prayers of supplication are coin of the Realm." Raising an angry fist, he thundered, "You *will* be heard! We have a *right* to be heard!"

Ian recoiled. "And if your appeal is denied?"

The black eyes flashed. "Knowing the Mind of He Who condemned us, we expect no better. Unlike souls, we Know He is not all-merciful. If therefore He denies us absolution—*we demand annihilation!*"

Ian's legs turned to rubber. The idea of facing God with such an insolent, outrageous demand was inconceivable.

The old man began to pace, and Ian heard clip-clopping and the rattle of metal on rock. Looking down, he was dumbfounded to see a heavy chain manacled to the man's left foot and secured to the base of the chair.

Not foot—*hoof!* The being walked on cloven hooves, a depression worn around his chair to the limits of his fetter!

He railed on, "None would have rebelled had we known the consequences! What purpose our further torment other than cruelty? If half an eternity here cannot atone our Sin, *return us to the emptiness whence we came!*"

Ian felt a tug on his heart. Not that he'd forgotten who this ranting creature was. The Great Dissembler. Master of Deception. Lord of Intrigue. But having just witnessed the plight of his parents, he could put himself in the old man's hooves. Still . . . to question God's judgment? *To His Face!*

He felt another tug. Not on his heart—his *soul.*

His medical team, attempting to retrieve him!

Another pull. And this one drew out an inspiration.

He turned to the old man. "You are lord and master here, are you not?"

"I am."

"Then I'll do what you ask. On *one* condition."

Behind, he heard Zagan growl. And at the back of the ledge he saw movement, accompanied by the sound of heavy chisels striking stone. He thought his eyes had deceived him, but the movements came again, and he gasped to see the talons of the giant sculpture drum-rolling against the ledge.

Raising his eyes, he stared in disbelief as a long, vertical fissure opened in the face of the cliff, like a drape parting. It fanned out, then arched into the air, and Ian was stunned to realize these were giant wings—batlike, similar to Zagan's, only of immense size!

The mountaintop was alive.

The wings unfurled to reveal a colossus beneath, tucked in on itself, squatting on mammoth, leathery haunches. Enormous arms stretched out, rippling with sinew, flexing spiderish fingers that ended in claws. The creature's terrible head rested on its knees, and it glared down at Ian.

It had the horns of a bull and a prominent brow, like Zagan, surly black globes for eyes, and pointed ears. But there the resemblance ended. The face was flat and wide with the muzzle of a gorilla and the scimitar fangs of a saber-toothed tiger. Snarling, it exposed a forked tongue that snaked out, flickered, and retracted.

The old man raised a palm to the giant, his fathomless gaze never leaving Ian.

"Belay, *Churnabog,*" he ordered.

The behemoth settled; Zagan, too.

Then in a voice controlled but with a hard edge, the man told Ian, "You cannot change the terms, the deal is struck."

"I'm *un*-striking it," Ian replied, emboldened by the tension on his soul. "I'll do as you say, but only if you free my parents first."

The toes of Churnabog rolled another angry tattoo, and the old man hissed, "No soul damned has *ever* escaped Hell. Nor would Heaven accept souls tainted with damnation!"

"Where will *you* go if pardoned?"

"Limbo. The absence of misery is Heaven enough."

"Very well then, release my parents to Limbo. In return, I swear I'll deliver your message."

"Nay, we cannot break the *Laws of Chaos*! If Persefoni learns, we shall feel her arrows, tipped in Leviathan's venom—and she will cast your parents back into the Pit!"

"You wouldn't risk her arrows to be free of that chain? Besides, she has no powers in Limbo—no Angels, White or Dark, have powers there."

He'd learned a thing or two in the Underworld.

The old man held immobile on the ledge, black eyes staving a hole in Ian as Zagan and Churnabog rumbled. But at length, exhaling a dark vapor, he pointed to Zagan and snapped, "Fly now, take his parents back the way you came, far as the boundary between Erebus and Limbo—and hold them there."

Gesturing to the colossus, he added, *"Churnabog!* Carry this soul to Limbo by way of Lethe. Quickly, before he hardens."

And then he turned his foreboding finger on Ian.

"Go back, replenish your life, and *pay your fare.* Do so by the time your parents reach Erebus and they will be released to Limbo. Fail, and they return to the Pit."

"But how will you know if I paid my fare?"

"We will Know."

Ian felt Churnabog's huge claws encircle him as the old man leveled a final warning.

"There are souls on Earth you love?"

"Yes," Ian said, whisked up in the grasp of the giant.

"Fail us," the old man hissed, eyes blazing as he faded into the gloom, *"and you will know the sorrows Hell can visit on the living!"*

NINETY-SEVEN

THE BASEMENT OF A PRIVATE ESTATE OUTSIDE CAYENNE, FRENCH GUYANA, SAME DAY, MORNING

"Nothing!" one of the doctor's cried as Angela stood trembling over Ian's gray body, his heart unresponsive after another jolt of cardiac paddles, monitor lines flat.

Her heart was beating hard enough for the both of them.

"Five more amps," Josten ordered.

An eternity for the light to turn green, then, *"Clear!"*

Angela pulled back, grimacing as Ian's body heaved, despairing as it came to a deathly rest again. The stack of monitor lines continued flat, like the bars of an empty musical staff.

She grabbed his hand, frantic.

Please! Please!

The time clock ticked on.

1:04:58, 1:04:59, 1:05:00 . . .

Five minutes since they'd begun resuscitation—and still no signs of life.

NINETY-EIGHT

THE PIT OF HELL, TIMELESS

Held fast in the grip of the giant, Churnabog, Ian peered out over its knuckles as it flew across the subterranean mountainside. Its wings beat a hurricane on Tartarus below, snuffing out streetlamps as the city's denizens scrambled for cover.

Ian was expecting the monster to make an upward turn. Instead, it tucked its wings and headed down.

"Where—what—?"

Picking up speed, it angled in the direction of the mountain range behind the city, aiming for the cleft of rock into which the molten River Lethe disappeared. Before Ian could question, Churnabog raised its thumb and stuffed him inside its fist, and an instant later—jarring impact.

Ian panicked, unable to budge, heat rising, no idea what was happening, his only solace the twitching tether on his soul and the belief his parents were on their way to freedom.

An eternity later, surely only moments, he felt the behemoth burst free of the heat. It loosened its grip and Ian poked his head out, gasping, amazed to see the Valley of Gehenna and its erupting volcano far below.

Shaking lava from its wings, the monster flew on as Ian gathered his wits.

Zagan had said that for Ian's parents to return from Hell via its seven Realms would take four times as long as Ian's descent. The equivalent of roughly four Earth hours, Ian presumed, before his parents reached the boundary of Erebus and Limbo. Four hours in real time for him to pay his fare before Mom and Dad were doomed to the Pit again. Plenty of time for another NDE—assuming he survived this one.

Peering out from Churnabog's fist, Ian watched as they passed over the cliffs of Purgatory. Then abruptly the giant banked and swooped to a landing on Erebus's slippery plains, skidding to a halt at the boundary of Limbo.

The demon lowered him to the ground, but no sooner did it open its fist than Ian felt himself snatched away, propelled into Limbo by his lifeline. Last he saw of Churnabog, the colossus was squatted on its haunches, simian brow bunched in a frown, glowering after him.

Ahead, Ian spied Zack Niemand, arms raised, waving.

Ian waved back, accelerating toward him, the entrance to the tunnel coming into view. He could feel the rush of life returning. Feel his body again, heart beating, sweet air filling his lungs!

NINETY-NINE

THE BASEMENT OF A PRIVATE ESTATE OUTSIDE CAYENNE, FRENCH GUYANA, SAME DAY, MORNING

Through her tears Angela thought she saw a blip on the heart monitor. She rubbed her eyes, looking harder.

There! Again! Accompanied by a soft beep!

The room hushed, four doctors staring with her. A pause. Then another blip and beep.

And another, if weak.

Angela cried out, squeezing Ian's cold hand in both of hers as the doctors hustled to nurture their patient's fragile flame. They added stimulants to the IVs, adjusted oxygen levels, temperature controls, as the blips and beeps continued, more frequent, stronger.

Josten set down the cardio paddles and Angela rested her head against Ian's chest, numb. An hour and seven minutes of unrelenting tension. She couldn't have taken a second more. And then . . .

Silence.

The heartbeats ceased, monitors flatlining once more.

Josten sprang for the paddles.

"Clear!"

Angela moaned and pulled away, releasing Ian's hand, joy turned back to panic.

ONE HUNDRED

THE NETHER REGIONS OF LIMBO, SOMEWHERE BEYOND TIME

Ian hurtled toward Zack Niemand, seeing the spirit wave his arms wildly in the air.

"Stop!" Niemand called up, sounding hysterical. *"Look out!"*

But there was nothing Ian could do, he had no control now.

He zipped by, several feet overhead, Niemand's anxious eyes following, the entrance to the tunnel glowing ahead.

And then he spied the objects of Niemand's concern.

Standing between Ian and the tunnel were three dark shapes. Souls, robes filthy black. One carried a battle-ax and gaff; another, a mace and grappling iron; the last, a sword.

As Ian flew over, he saw the grapple swing toward him on the end of a rope, feeling a sharp pang in his shoulder. Then the gaff reached up and sank its hook deep in his flank, and he was yanked from the air like a fish from an inverted sea.

He hit the ground hard, coming to rest on his back, the fog of Nether souls billowing out of his way. Dazed, he saw three large men looming; one tall and bald, one broad and bearded—neither he'd ever seen before. But the third he recognized, with despair. Rugged, angular features, dark brushy hair, eyes fierce with self-righteous resolve.

And suddenly Ian realized how they'd gotten here—the Capetown lab and its three sets of equipment!

For a moment he feared he'd lost his lifeline, but thank God he could still feel it, painfully lurching against the barbs in his flesh, inching him toward the tunnel.

"Stop him!" Josef ordered.

His men dropped their weapons to grab at Ian's arms and legs, and Ian took heart to see their hands pass through. But then they went back to gaff and grapple, digging in their heels in a tug of war for Ian's soul. He resisted, too weak to break free, stretched, torn, bleeding, and in agony.

The bald man leaned close.

"Did you gain the Knowledges? Did you wed them?"

Josef answered, "He's failed, or the damned would be set free by now. All that remains is to hold him here until his body dies, and whatever he Knows dies with him."

The henchmen bore down. Yet they couldn't keep traction on the mud-like surface, Ian's lifeline continuing to budge his mangled form toward the tunnel. In the midst of his misery he felt a flicker of hope.

Until Josef came forward with his sword.

Somber, eyes cold, he told Ian, "I gave you your life once. And now, by God, *I reclaim it . . .*"

Ian watched helpless as Josef took the weapon in both fists, point down, raised it high, and plunged it into Ian's breastbone, throwing his weight behind it. The pain was unlike any Ian had ever felt, a lightning bolt to the heart. He moaned, body shocked rigid as the blade drove all the way through, cutting off his breath, nailing him fast to the firmament. Fatal without death.

Josef glared down. "You've failed, Ian! A Brother is now on his way to put an end to your woman and your accomplices. Your sacrilege is over!"

Ian glared back, unable to voice the oaths in his throat. Though he could still feel the pull of his lifeline, he was stuck like a bug under a collector's pin.

The two men were able to remove their hooks, Nether souls rising from the fog to gather around, joined by a few curious Dark Angels, huge arms folded across their chests.

But they made no attempt to intervene.

From somewhere behind, Ian heard a remorseful voice whistle, "Sorry, Ian, I couldn't stop 'em. They went to Purgatory and stole weapons . . ."

Ian tried to look, the pain too much; tried to answer, couldn't. He heard the bald assassin say, "He's finished. Let's get back to the tunnel of light, I want to be inside when we're revived."

"Not till his soul is as pale as these others," Josef told him.

"Let it be soon," said the bearded man. "Look, our skin grows pale, too!"

Pain aside, Ian twisted to see the three drooping under the burden of their sins, their complexions as pallid as his. Though they'd arrived after him, he suspected they'd undergone their NDEs hastily, without the benefit of fasting and red-cell packing to help weather the stress. If he could just outlast them and free himself. If only Angela and Josten wouldn't give up.

He grabbed the sword's blade in both hands and shoved, giving it everything he had left. All he managed was to slice fingers and palms to the bone. The flesh hung off him milk white, and he knew the end was but moments away now, the tugs of his lifeline growing infrequent, feeble.

Still, the assassins were faring no better. Ian watched them strain to keep their footing, the bearded man staggering. And out of the corner of his eye, he noticed movement in the crowd. Nether souls parting as someone strode rapidly in his direction. Male. Face obscured, but by the looks of his translucent feet, newly molted, robe nearly white.

Then suddenly the newcomer snatched up the discarded mace and, without a word, pivoted and leveled a ferocious blow to the head of the bearded man! The assassin shot off toward Hell and kept going, Nether souls scrambling out of his way. Before Josef and accomplice could react, the stranger stepped, turned, and laid his club hard into the bald man, catching him in the gut, doubling him up, sending him on his way, too.

Ian couldn't believe it! He wrenched against the blade in his chest, seeing Josef take up the battle-ax. Josef appeared in better condition than his henchmen had been, rolling the weapon in his hands with a look of confidence, squaring off against his challenger.

And then the new soul turned, and Ian saw his face—

Antonio!

"Come!" Josef called out defiantly, waving the director on. "I'll finish what I started."

Antonio needed no coaxing. He attacked with a vengeance, the two charging each other like medieval knights, weapons clanging and jarring in the stillness, Nether souls scattering.

Ian struggled to keep the battle in sight, twisting against the ache in his chest, silently rooting his friend on.

He saw with worry, Josef was a skilled fighter, deftly fending off Antonio's blows, landing several of his own. But the director fought like a man possessed, and Josef was tiring under the weight of his sins.

At last Antonio gained the advantage, driving Josef to his knees, blasting the ax from his grip. Then, like a golfer teeing off, he measured his target, planted his feet, and drew back his club.

Josef gasped, "He mustn't escape, Antonio! It will be the end of Faith! End of the world! *Armageddon!*"

The director puffed, "To Hell with you, you sanctimonious sonofabitch—" And he delivered a stroke that sent Josef rocketing off into the mists.

The crowd cheered and Ian tried to applaud, exhausted, his flayed hands not making contact.

Antonio dropped his weapon and hurried to Ian's side. "You're in pitiful shape, my friend," he said, shaking his head, eyes anxious. "I only hope I'm not too late!"

Ian felt both gratitude and sadness, knowing Antonio's presence meant he'd lost his battle for life. Unable to express his thanks, his chest pierced by the sword, Ian offered a weak smile instead.

Until Antonio grabbed the hilt and began to pull.

The pain was excruciating, a hot poker through the heart. But the blade broke free at last, and Ian released a pent-up howl into the void. Antonio extended a hand to assist him, unable to make contact, and Ian raised up on his elbows.

"It's my fault you're here," he wheezed. "Can you ever forgive me?"

The director shook off the apology. "It was my job to deal with *Arma Christi* and I was blind to them. I just wish I could join you in the fight—assuming you make it back."

Ian felt a meager tug, moving again, sluggishly.

"How can I ever repay you?"

"Watch over my family," Antonio said, and he raised the sword in a solemn salute.

Ian gave his word, seeing Zack Niemand come forward to wave farewell. Ian could scarcely lift his hand in return.

Picking up speed, he entered the tunnel, the two men disappearing into the fog. He called back to Antonio, "Hang on to that sword, it'll speed your trip through Purgatory."

Antonio replied, "Take what you Know to the pope—he's the key to ending *Arma Christi*."

ONE HUNDRED ONE

THE BASEMENT OF A PRIVATE ESTATE OUTSIDE CAYENNE, FRENCH GUYANA, SAME DAY, MORNING

"Clear!" Josten yelled, slapping the cardio paddles to Ian's gray chest once more.

Angela released Ian's hand again, closing her eyes, nerves frayed raw. She refused to give up, insisting Josten continue past all hope, screaming silently at Ian, *Don't you* dare *leave me!*

She blamed herself for not stopping him. For not taking a club to this damned equipment, not taking a club to *him*—

A bleep from the monitor . . .

Her eyes popped open. Did she imagine it?

Another bleep! Another! Continuous! Regular!

"By God, I think we've got him!" an assistant said.

"Hold on to him this time!" Josten ordered, keeping everyone to their posts.

Angela watched Ian's chest rise and fall, respiration steady, color improving, vitals charging back strong. She collapsed to her knees, laying a shaky hand on his forehead.

"Please," she begged, *"let your mind be here, too!"*

ONE HUNDRED TWO

A PRIVATE ESTATE ON THE OUTSKIRTS OF CAYENNE, FRENCH GUYANA, SAME DAY, MORNING

Ian awoke with a start, a stinging in his nose.

Hovering over him with smelling salts was Josten, and behind the doctor, the anxious faces of Angela and the medical team. Ian was in bed, back in his top-floor suite, propped up on pillows. His head throbbed as he blinked away the fog, body still trembling from the terrors of Hell.

How long have I been out? How long before Mom and Dad reach Erebus?

A clock on the dresser read 9:47 AM.

Mind thick, he tried to do the math. He'd begun his NDE at 6:00. Assuming it had lasted the planned hour, then he'd been asleep nearly three. Zagan had said that to ascend Hell by its seven levels would take four times as long as the descent—four earthly hours to carry his parents to Erebus. Meaning Ian had until 11:00 to fulfill his pact with the Devil. An hour and thirteen minutes. Not much time, but hopefully enough . . .

Angela bent to embrace him, tears in her eyes, and he strained to return her hug, achy, numb, tingly. Over her shoulder he saw their packed suitcases by the door.

"Talk to me," she said, voice worried. "Tell me you're still in there!"

He managed a positive-sounding mumble, and she surrendered him to Josten, who shined a light in his eyes.

"Can you tell me who you are?"

"One very blessed guy," he said, flinching as another doctor roamed his chest with a cold stethoscope. Ian could feel his senses slowly returning. "Trust me, I'm all here."

Josten put him through a few more drills all the same, asking history questions, testing his reflexes. Then sounding relieved, he announced, "I think we got you back in one piece."

There was a round of congratulations, but the doctor with the stethoscope held back.

"Listen," he told Josten.

The room went quiet as Josten checked. After a moment he nodded soberly to Ian.

"Arrhythmia. Irregular heartbeat. Not unexpected after what you've been through. But nothing time and rest won't heal. We'll need to keep an eye on it, put you on some meds."

Angela asked, "Is it safe for him to travel?"

"I think so, if we keep him off his feet."

She took Ian's hand, squeezing. "I e-mailed Charles. He's meeting us in Miami tonight at the CBS affiliate. And afterward, you and I going to disappear for a while."

Ian felt a palpitation unrelated to his arrhythmia.

"Sweetheart, I, I'm sorry. Not just yet. I've got to go back—" She let go, pulling away, gaping at him. "One last time . . ."

The hurt in her eyes ran clear to her soul, as if he'd struck her.

"Please," he tried, "let me explain—"

Too late. He watched her lips curl into a snarl of seismic magnitude, and she retreated, doctors darting out of her way. Ripping Ian's ring from her finger, she hurled it at him, stormed to her suitcase, snatched it, and stalked out.

"Angela, *no*!" Ian called weakly, answered by the front door slamming.

He rolled out of bed, legs failing, Josten and team rushing to support him. They helped him to a chair, exchanging uncomfortable glances.

"Get me our two best guards," Ian told one of the men. "Have them follow her wherever she goes—they're never to leave her unprotected. But she mustn't know."

Wide-eyed, the man nodded and withdrew.

Ian looked to Josten. "Ready the lab for a short run. Fifteen minutes should do."

The doctor's face paled. *"You can't be serious."*

"I'll double your fee again. Triple it. And all the equipment, it's yours."

Josten stared at him, then shook his head.

"No, Ian . . . I won't be party to your suicide."

Ian turned to the two remaining doctors.

"One million each, wired directly to your accounts. Half up front, half when it's over."

ONE HUNDRED THREE

ROCHAMBEAU INTERNATIONAL AIRPORT, CAYENNE, FRENCH GUYANA, SAME DAY, MORNING

Quintus left his jet ticking on the tarmac, engines overheated, in sore need of service. He slipped into the shadows of a hangar, briefcase light in his hands, met briefly with a dark-skinned man, then exited through a security door, briefcase heavy now. Skirting customs as the official looked the other way, he headed through a hall to the terminal and outside toward a waiting car.

But as he passed a taxi stand he stopped, seeing a cab pull up, door open, young woman step out. *Gorgeous.* Tousled dark hair, casual skirt and blouse. She appeared upset, cheeks tear-streaked, lips compressed, body posture tight, clenched.

A lithe, svelte body.

More beautiful even than her pictures. His blood stirred.

He watched her hand the driver a large bill, no engagement ring on her finger. She didn't wait for change, grabbing her suitcase, marching into the terminal.

His base instincts urged him to follow. But Quintus deferred to duty. For now . . .

ONE HUNDRED FOUR

THE BASEMENT OF A PRIVATE MANSION NEAR CAYENNE, FRENCH GUYANA, SAME DAY, LATE MORNING

Half an hour after Angela left, Ian was back in the lab on the table, body prepped as he pushed his two remaining doctors to hurry. Like Josten, the third had bowed out.

A physical and emotional wreck, Ian would nevertheless soon depart this life for yet another engagement in the next. This time, intending to meet his Maker and deliver a demand so brazen it could well send his soul back to Hell, permanently. Not that he had a choice. The Fate of his parents *and* Angela hung in the balance, the Devil threatening both.

But he was having second thoughts about the deal he'd struck. It meant presenting Hell's petition to God while blindly trusting the Devil to free his parents. The very being who'd once set up Eve for the Fall of Man.

And even assuming the Devil kept his bargain, Ian would feel cheated. Limbo, after all, wasn't Heaven. There'd be no true happiness for his parents there. Simply a numb, twilight existence in a realm of the in-between.

Nor could he now hope to be reunited with them. Only briefly in passing on his way to and from Purgatory, perhaps. Or, God forbid, on a one-way trip to Hell. Ian wanted so much more for them. But to dare raise their case to God might well lose them the gains he'd accomplished.

He winced as a doctor inserted a tube in his leg.

Even if he managed to survive this NDE, a long shot he knew, he'd still have to cope with *Arma Christi.* No doubt Swords were on their way, as Josef had claimed, and Ian was now all alone in the fight. Without Antonio. Without Angela at his side—though he'd still need to protect her somehow.

And also get the Reality safely to Charles—Angela had rushed off without it. The guards he'd assigned to her had reported back that she was at the airport, booked on the next flight to the States. He'd paid them well to watch over her until he could make other arrangements. Assuming he lived to do so—

A doctor interrupted, drawing Ian's attention to the array of monitors. "Heart rate, blood pressure, respiration—everything sky high! Try to relax, we're starting."

He nodded, feeling his body chill, mind growing numb. And as he slipped away, his last conscious thoughts were filled with misgivings. He saw himself as some perverse Daniel Webster, about to plead the Devil's case before the Court of the Almighty.

ONE HUNDRED FIVE

THE PAPAL APARTMENTS, APOSTOLIC PALACE, VATICAN CITY, SAME DAY, EARLY HOURS OF THE MORNING

Pietro Cardinal della Roca panted as he approached the door of the pope's private study, Swiss Guards snapping to attention and stepping aside. In his four decades of devoted service to Mother Church—indeed in his entire life—he'd never felt so distraught.

Two days ago in the predawn hours, a specter had appeared to him. A specter bearing revelations that had challenged his Faith and rocked his soul. Ever since, he'd been in shambles, there being only one person who could restore him.

But Pope Julius had been consumed by back-to-back tragedies, and Pietro had hesitated to impose, especially with such sensitive matters. Tonight however, unable to sleep, taking a walk on St. Peter's square, he'd looked up to see a light in the pope's study. Papa, too, was restless it seemed. So Pietro chanced a visit.

He rapped softly on the pope's door.

"Entri," a hushed voice responded.

The pope wasn't at his desk where Pietro was accustomed to finding him, but at a window in a high-back armchair, chin cupped in hand, gazing out into the night.

"Apologies for intruding, Papa, my deepest sympathies."

The pope nodded, eyes glistening. "She plays canasta with the angels now," he said. "And she will beat them, too—provided they overlook her cheating."

Pietro chuckled, then assumed an awkward silence.

Finally Julius offered, "Forgive me, I'm sure you have pressing business to make so late a call, unannounced."

Unsure whether this might be a bit of an admonishment, the cardinal swallowed and pressed on. "Sorry, Papa, but yes. I . . . I have a most difficult story to share. I'll be brief." The pope motioned him to a chair, but he remained standing. "The night of Direttore Ponti's . . . accident. I was asleep in my bed when I was awakened by a hand pressed to my mouth. A gloved hand."

Julius turned, eyes widening.

"The lamp came on, and I looked into a masked face. The intruder held a finger to his lips and said, 'Make no sound and I will release you.' I nodded, and he said, 'The Papal Vault has been violated.' "

The pope looked stunned.

"I asked, 'You?' He said, 'No. The thief has been dealt with and the materials recovered. And now you must guard their confidentiality and return them.' "

Pietro removed a large envelope from his crimson cape. It bore the papal seal, detached.

"Antonio?" The pope's voice sounded broken.

"Apparently so. This stranger, whoever he was, said he'd caught Antonio in the act of reading the contents, but was in time to stop him from disclosing what he saw."

"Antonio betrayed me? *But why?"*

"Do you recall the American couple he sheltered here—our renegade priest, Ian Baringer?"

"The couple whose lives we nearly lost . . ."

"According to this man, it was Baringer who led Antonio astray. He said Baringer has been traveling to the Underworld consorting with demons—and had spread his corruption to Antonio."

Julius crossed himself. *"God help us!* Your visitor—he was an Angel?"

"I suspect not. He spoke with a Slavic accent."

The pope accepted the envelope, turning it to read its inscription—*A successore meo confestim aperiri—To be opened immediately by my successor.*

He sat staring at it. But as the silence expanded, he suddenly raised his gaze to Pietro, eyes darkening.

"First my Director of Security! *Now* my Prefect of Faith! *Is there no loyalty under Heaven!"*

Pietro lowered his eyes. "Forgive me, Papa, I had to know. I had to know what is worth the cost of a man's life. The cost of the Church's treasures."

"And now that you've meddled in the affairs of popes, what is it you know?"

"Things better left *un*known . . ."

The pope stood and tossed the envelope in his chair, moving to the window, glaring out. Rain started to fall. "Is it so surprising," he said, "to learn the Church engages in *realpolitik*?"

Pietro was astounded. "In God's Name, Papa! *We sponsor a secret police force.* A deadly force we have no control over!"

"You do not understand—precisely why these matters are left to popes!" He turned to face Pietro. "The Church has many enemies. *Powerful* enemies. Once we had an empire behind us, an army to defend us. Now Europe is given over to seculars, the rest of the world to Muslims and Evangelicals. Mother Church is left with a hundred paltry acres and as many Swiss Guard. Why, we can't even identify all the threats, much less defend against them!"

"But spies and assassins, Papa? Millions of lire over the centuries paid to this—this 'Fund for the Defense of the Faith'? No one to account for it?"

Julius snapped, "*History* is our accounting! In times past if popes reneged on the Fund, the Church was vulnerable. It led to Protestantism, the loss of the Papal States, the—"

"And the *moral* accounting?"

"How do I make you see? Outside these walls, turning one's cheek only invites a harder blow. We must strike back to survive. As Christ said, Matthew 10:34: *Think not that I am come to send peace: I come to send a* Sword!"

The cardinal said nothing, and Julius calmed, sighing. "There are few things a man knows for certain in this life, Pietro, but I will share one with you . . . In the endless battle between Good and Evil, *Evil* holds sway. Good fights openly in the light, Evil in darkness, stabbing in the back. Against such tactics, what chance have we? To survive, the Church must fight Evil on Evil's terms, distasteful as that may be."

"But how can we be party to such things and not be sullied?"

"By keeping our distance, leaving these matters to those who wield Christ's Sword. We perform God's Work in our way, they in theirs, trusting in a Greater Wisdom."

Pietro licked his lips. "There is *another* matter that troubles me. These longstanding accounts of Heavenly visions—not the least of which, Merton's Reality."

The pope snorted. "Those tales from the Dark Ages—the by-products of mold-tainted ale! And Merton's Reality, the culmination of Buddhist practices and superstitions. Do you really Believe God's Truths derive from such sources?"

"There'd been rumors of the Reality in the Curia for years. Of an, an *awkward* Revelation. What if verses of Matthew *were* fabricated? It wouldn't be our first forgery."

Pietro didn't have to mention that the Church had a long history of falsifying documents. The *Donation of Constantine*, a purported fourth century decree by the Emperor transferring his territories to the pope—actually forged in 752. Many more such ploys. The *False Decretals of Isidore*—a hundred missives claiming to grant special powers to the early Church, all counterfeited centuries later.

Julius looked stricken. "My own Prefect of the Faith, questioning doctrine! Has the Serpent's Sophistry spread even to *you*?"

The room fell quiet, no sound but the rain pelting the windows. At length the pope exhaled. "Kneel," he said with an air of forbearance, motioning Pietro forward. "I will grant you absolution—but you must swear *never* to speak of this again!"

Pietro wavered, his nagging doubts pitted against a lifetime of Belief, the gravitas of his career, the infallibility of St. Peter's successor . . .

Counterweights that finally buckled his knees.

ONE HUNDRED SIX

THE REALM OF THE AFTERLIFE, OUT OF PLACE AND TIME

Again Ian left his body, a veteran at this now, speeding directly for the tunnel of light. He'd allowed himself fifteen temporal minutes—an hour by Afterlife reckoning, he trusted. If the Devil was correct, sufficient. And hopefully time enough for a peek into Limbo afterward to ensure his parents were safely there . . .

Entering the tunnel at full speed, he veered hard to the right, careening up toward the brilliance. It shined with such intensity he had to avert his eyes. And just when he thought he could endure it no longer, he shot out the tunnel's end, sucking a contrail of vapor after him.

He slowed to find himself in a celestial white-out. Dazzling haze surfeited by radiance from above, glow wafting over him. *Through* him. Warm, soothing currents of peace and tranquility. He felt strangely alert, filled with heightened awareness. As if awakened from a long and restful sleep, acutely conscious, more so than ever in life.

Not the reaction you'd expect from an expiring brain!

Recalling his visit to the Swiss Neurology Center, he wondered how Angela might explain this inconsistency. And to his amazement, just thinking about her now in his enlightened state, he could detect her presence back in the material world. Actually *feel* her life force! She was safe for the moment, he was relieved to Know. But he could sense danger looming, and he hastened back to business.

Head always toward the light, the Devil had advised, and he did so, hearing a most glorious choir on high.

The haze soon dissolved and he saw before him a breathtaking panorama. An immense pastoral valley at the height of spring. Resplendent in wildflowers of every hue, scent of bouquets on the air, souls strolling the meadows hand in hand, rolling hills behind.

"The Elysian Fields!" he realized as he flew over, awestruck. A river of gold wandered through, sparkling in noonday brilliance. Beyond, a verdant forest, trees filled with blossoms, birds darting in the foliage as souls mingled beneath with exotic animals of every kind.

"Paradise!"

Past the forest, an enormous mountain, peak obscured by cloud. Golden streams cascaded down its sides, eventually merging to form the valley's river. The light and celestial choir seemed to emanate from the summit, and Ian hastened toward it, entering the layer of cloud.

He soon emerged over a forested plateau. Not unlike the forest in the valley, except here the season was summer—trees, bushes, and flowers in full bloom, laden with ripe fruit, wonderful fragrances in the air. The plateau curved off right and left, girdling the mountain, it appeared.

A heavenly ring of Saturn!

Under the trees, souls socialized by the thousands, attended by young, pale-skinned, red-haired, sylphlike beings of wondrous grace and beauty, attired in sarongs. Ian approached one gathering blossoms in a basket, and she looked up, eyes green as emeralds, face sweet and innocent.

"What is this place?" he asked.

"Corpus," she replied melodically. "First Sphere. Heaven of the Spirit of Love."

"And what are you?"

She smiled coyly, tossing her hair. "Seraph." And she returned to her task.

Ian noticed transparent wings on her back, like a dragonfly's but in sets of three pairs. Seraphim, he realized. In Christian lore, the highest angelic hierarchy of the nine Choirs. Except here, it appeared Seraphim occupied the lowest rung. He recalled Matthew, 20:16: "The last shall be first, and the first shall be last."

Glancing about, he saw several clearings crowded with souls. At their centers were people he recognized. Mother Theresa surrounded by children. Muhammad Ali shadowboxing and working magic. George Harrison serenading on a guitar. Roberto Clemente coaching baseball.

Ian grinned, longing to linger. But the light came from above, and he pushed on, skirting the mountainside, ascending through yet another layer of clouds.

The brightness intensified, and he emerged above a pasture. Similar to the Elysian Fields but populated by countless more souls. Some gathered flowers, others sat in circles on pillowed divans, communing, their every whim for food and drink catered by naked, chubby, childlike little angels with golden curls and large blue eyes.

Cherubs, Ian recognized. One came buzzing by on gossamer wings, ferrying a basket of pastries.

"What Heaven is this?" Ian asked.

The cupid hovered, angling its head, regarding him with impish eyes.

"*Insula,* of course," he chirped. "Heaven of the Spirit of Peace. *Everybody* knows that!" And he flitted off.

Ian laughed. Looking around, he recognized the faces of Will Rogers, Mahatma Gandhi, Anwar Sadat, Martin Luther King, Jr., Malcolm X, Nelson Mandela . . .

So far, a quick and easy journey, just as the Devil had promised. But Ian was growing anxious again. It appeared the Third Heaven was next. The highest point Thomas Merton—or even St. Paul himself—had reached in their lifetimes. Man's celestial high-water mark. Ian felt presumptuous thinking he could exceed that. And yet he had no choice but to try.

He rose into cloud again, slowing as it broke to reveal a Heaven even more breathtaking than the last. Before him, a golden mountain lake, the far end adorned by a rainbow, waves rippling and sparkling, reflecting glorious colors.

Souls by the thousands bathed in the waters. Many more reclined on blankets along the shore or sat in groups under large, spreading trees, conversing. Every nationality and age, it seemed.

Like a picnic at the UN!

Tending them were majestic creatures with long, golden curls. Adolescent, naked, neither male nor female, complexions milky white.

Thrones, Ian guessed. Third Choir.

One walked near, and Ian asked, "Pardon, can you tell me where I am?"

It smiled at him, face serene, eyes a mesmerizing hazel. "You are in *Tempora,*" it said, voice airy, soothing. "Heaven of the Spirit of Harmony."

Ian thanked it, and it strode gracefully away.

Nearby, a group of wise-looking men in long robes were conversing, surrounded by throngs of admirers. Seized by his enhanced intuition, Ian realized—Moses, Abraham, Isaac, Jacob, Elijah, Siddhartha, Mohammed, Shankara—*and Christ Himself!*

Awestruck, Ian was filled with esteem and affection. As he now Understood, the souls of this Heaven were of every ethnic, religious, and political stripe, and both heterosexual and gay. All convening in a spirit of camaraderie, celebrating the joy of unconditional goodwill.

Ian grasped this implicitly. What elevated a soul to Heaven, he saw, wasn't the religion one practiced in life, nor the amount of time spent in church, temple, or mosque. Not the quantity of prayers said, or the praise and adulation one heaped upon God as if He lacked self-esteem. And certainly not, God forbid, acts of proselytizing.

What earned one a place here was nothing less than the quality of love bestowed upon others in life. Not selectively. Not by singling out only those deemed worthy. But love given unconditionally to all. Family, friends, strangers, enemies alike.

Ian sighed to think of the thousands of world religions promoting their separate beliefs, each claiming to have the Answer. One man's Faith, another's Heresy. And *all* missing the point. Salvation wasn't about the process—the rites and rituals and grinding of scripture—all irrelevant in the grand scheme of things. It was about what a person did to bring happiness to others.

That was the Ultimate Reality of this Heaven.

Seeing the masses gathered here, Ian Knew that many had been agnostics and atheists in life, understanding that salvation didn't even require Belief. People who loved and cherished one another, by default loved and cherished God, even if oblivious.

And like Thomas Merton, Ian recognized that revealing the Secrets of this Heaven could well end the World's most tenacious hostilities. The Reality could at last free Man from the self-righteous purveyors of dogma—those preachers, priests, rabbis, and mullahs who laid privileged claim to God's Truth.

As he cast his eyes across the joyous inhabitants of Tempora, Ian was thrilled to spy Merton himself, standing not forty feet away! The monk was in discussion with others Ian recognized—the fourteenth Dalai Lama, Karl Barth, Richard Dawkins, Jon Stewart. But Ian was dumbfounded to see him with his arm around the waist of a young blonde.

Merton and his women!

The monk happened to look up, somehow recognizing Ian, and he spoke to the woman at his side. She turned, too, face lighting, waving.

A familiar face, though it took Ian a second to place it. And when he did, he felt confused—it was the girl in the portrait Henri D'Essoire had painted long ago. Merton's daughter, Valerie Pardeau, restored to her father now as her young self . . .

Oh my God! I led the Order straight to her!

Devastated, Ian pleaded for forgiveness with his eyes. But if Valerie harbored ill feelings, it didn't show. By her glow, she'd finally found the paternal bond she'd always longed for.

Ian wanted to stop, let them know that their vision for the Reality might yet see the light of day. But he had no time, not even halfway to Empyrean yet.

A wave and a rueful smile, and he soared on.

ONE HUNDRED SEVEN

ROCHAMBEAU INTERNATIONAL AIRPORT, CAYENNE, FRENCH GUYANA, SAME DAY, LATE MORNING

Boarding Air France for Caracas, first leg of her trip home, Angela was in a stupor, trying to shut out the thoughts crowding her. At this very moment, not far away, Ian was likely lying dead, victim of a mania from which she, with all her efforts, had been unable to save him. She couldn't bear to let him go, but he'd given her no choice.

Nor had she a choice what to do with her life now. She couldn't return to her career. Even if she could escape her emptiness, she had no hope of escaping *Arma Christi*. In her anger and haste, she'd rushed off without the Ultimate Reality, leaving it in the safe of their suite, no stomach to go back for it, no confidence it could protect her, anyway. Her immediate plan was to stop home long enough to see her mom and sisters, transfer her savings to a Swiss bank, and disappear. To where, she had no idea yet.

She grabbed an aisle seat up front, masking her swollen eyes behind an issue of *Neurology* . . .

Two burly men boarded after her, giving her guarded glances, finding seats farther back. In turn, they were followed by another man—tall, broad-shouldered, long blond hair, carrying a briefcase and brimmed hat. He also gave Angela a sly look, taking her in head to toe, selecting an aisle seat behind the two men.

While the flight attendants prepared for takeoff, a late-arriving family bustled aboard. A couple with twin babies, stroller, diaper bag, and other carry-ons. They took seats just behind Angela, struggling to install themselves, a baby dropping a teddy bear in the aisle.

Angela stretched to retrieve it and lost her place in her magazine. When she resettled, flipping open to a new page, her eyes fell upon an illustration. The human brain. Large, full-color, all the major parts labeled.

She felt an odd sensation. There was something strange about the image. Something *evocative.* She couldn't make the connection, poring over it . . .

And suddenly the pieces fused into critical mass—

"OH MY GOD!" she shouted. *"I was right!* It *is* all in his head!"

The plane went still, passengers gawking as she threw off her seat belt and dashed for the exit. A steward was moving to close the door, but like a fullback finding a hole in the defense, Angela squeezed past, rushing into the gangway, angry cries echoing after her.

In the back of the plane Quintus sat alone, exhausted, eyes closed, briefcase stowed under the seat in front of him. It was empty now but for a half-dozen yellowed, hand-typed pages of paper.

He couldn't restrain a smirk. He'd accomplished a seemingly impossible mission, having ended the blasphemy that was Ian Baringer, in the process recovering this profane Reality from a safe in the man's hideaway. But there was still one last, pretty, loose end to tie down . . .

His musings were interrupted by a disturbance, and he looked up to see that pretty, loose end disappear out the hatch of the plane. Swearing, he grabbed his briefcase and sprang into the aisle—only to find his way blocked by two husky men and a family stowing gear.

Flight attendants converged on the fracas, ordering everyone to their seats while Quintus stood seething, watching the steward lock the door.

ONE HUNDRED EIGHT

THE FOURTH SPHERE OF HEAVEN, AT SOME POINT IN ETERNITY

Ian emerged from another layer of cloud into ever-brighter brilliance. Eyes adjusting, he found himself above golden grasslands—a vast steppe wrapping the mountain. Down its middle wandered a golden stream. On each side, souls sat in small groups listening to lectures. Some speakers Ian recognized—Sigmund Freud, Dorothy Day, Margaret Sanger, Susan B. Anthony, W.E.B. Du Bois . . .

The groups were attended by tall, dignified beings in long vestments who served trays of beverages and exotic-looking hors d'oeuvres. Ian took them to be *Dominions,* fourth Order of angels. Male and female, dark hair, pale complexions, males bearded, females with their hair up.

A pair spotted Ian and made for him, sapphirine eyes taking in his robe.

"You are not consecrated to be here!" the male said.

"Where am I?"

"*Occi!* Heaven of the Spirit of Counsel!"

The female raised a brow. "You are not purified!"

Ian assured them, "I'm just passing through," and he began to move away.

"You cannot ascend," the male snapped. "*Go back.*"

Embarrassed, Ian apologized but pushed ahead anyway, relieved to hear their grumbles fade as he escaped up into more cloud.

The light continued to intensify, and Ian could hear the sound of warbling water. He arrived at the next Sphere through a cascade of golden waterfalls—thousands stair-stepping off the mountainside, feeding a stream. The spray felt cool, refreshing, and to Ian's surprise, he wasn't wet.

At the falls were multitudes of golden-haired, golden-skinned angels catching the liquid in gilded goblets. The fifth Choir, Ian assumed. *Virtues.*

Dressed in silken white robes, they carried the goblets to countless banquet tables where souls feasted on all manner of fine food. Ian recognized Abraham Lincoln, Harriet Tubman, Raoul Wallenberg, Chiune Sugihara, and many others engaged in warm conversation and laughter.

A male Virtue passed with a tray of berries and cream, and Ian asked, "What Heaven is this?"

"Parieta," he said with a welcoming smile. "Spirit of Contentment."

All seemed to be having a wonderful time, and Ian felt such a spirit of friendship and camaraderie, he was tempted to stop. But presuming two Heavens to go, he couldn't allow the time, and wistfully hastened on . . .

He rose through the next layer of cloud to emerge beside a golden spring. One of thousands bubbling up across field and forest to the eye's limit. Fountainheads of the waterfalls below, surely. Alongside were multitudes of souls reclined on divans, hammocks, and golden-fleece blankets, reading. At their service were muscular angels in togas, operating ostrich-feather fans and fetching refreshments.

Two angels passed between Ian and the spring, male and female, excusing themselves. They were impressively built, golden locks and skin, and they bore across their broad shoulders a large wooden chest lashed to poles. Ian assumed them *Powers,* the sixth Choir.

"What's in the chest?" he asked the male.

"Scrolls and codices from the ancient world."

"And where I am?"

The female replied, *"Fronta,* Heaven of the Spirit of Inspiration."

Curious, Ian watched as they delivered the chest to several men, three of whom he recognized as Albert Einstein, Carl Sagan, and Stephen Jay Gould. Another man ran up to them, thin, beaming, declaring in a British accent, "Dibs on Archimedes' *Spheres in Motion*!"

He looked startlingly familiar, but Ian had to search his mind before finally placing him.

Stephen Hawking . . .

Ian grinned and flew on.

But as he entered the next layer of cloud, he sobered . . .

Beyond, presumably, lay the seventh and final Realm, and the thought filled him with a dread not even the tranquility of Heaven could dispel.

Dwelling place of God.

ONE HUNDRED NINE

THE SEVENTH HEAVEN, WHERE TIME DOES NOT EXIST

The brightness became almost unbearable, the angelic chorus ever louder, and Ian burst through the haze blinded and trembling, floating down to feel a hard, cool surface beneath his feet . . .

As his eyes adjusted, he was spellbound to see before him a great golden wall with tall turrets and battlements and a wide, golden gate. Inside was a vast, gleaming, bustling metropolis spread over the entire mountaintop, rising up in terraces to disappear into blazing cloud.

Architecture in the classic Greek style. Palaces, towers, mansions, arenas, courtyards, and public squares all built of white marble, embellished with gold and silver. Parks, fountains, sculptures, gardens, and flowers; scents of blossoms in the fresh, balmy air. The streets teemed with souls of every age and race, all attired in pure-white robes, talking, laughing, reveling in an atmosphere of uninhibited joy and celebration. Ian saw no mechanical devices, as if the City were frozen in some idyllic time warp.

The gate stood open and unguarded, spanned by an arching sign:

EMPYREAN
Cerebrum Dei

Godhead. Source of all Knowledge.

After so many hardships, at last Ian had come to the pinnacle of everything. Stretching out before him now, rising to the sky, the utmost expression of the Supreme Being Himself—quintessential tribute to worthy souls.

Yet *his* soul was far from worthy, Ian knew. He felt conspicuous and embarrassed in his dirty robe. All the more distressed knowing he must try to face God like this. But there was no choice. He wouldn't desert his parents or Angela. Whatever the cost, he had to finish. And not only for them, for *himself.* For all the unanswered questions he carried, reaching back to his childhood . . .

The angel choir was close, if not yet visible, and temporal time wasting, Ian hastened to soar on.

Only to find himself grounded.

Puzzled, he tried again, unable. Indeed, everyone inside the gates was also on foot. Empyrean, it appeared, was a no-fly zone!

Ian felt a wave of anxiety. He had no idea how much farther he had to go, how much time he had left. Taking a deep breath of perfumed air, he hurried through the gates.

No one tried to stop him, to his relief. He slipped into the crowd, up a street of gold cobblestone. Not that he went unnoticed. Nothing judgmental or reproachful, simply curious glances—his tainted tunic a unique sight here, surely. Avoiding eye contact, he pushed on.

Every soul he passed, it seemed, was accompanied by a host angel. Male or female, with stunning Hellenic looks. Alabaster complexions, large dark eyes, long hair of differing shades, graceful physiques and flowing robes. Most were the opposite sex of their soul mates and attended them with great tenderness. *Principalities,* Ian figured, seventh of the nine hierarchies.

Whenever he came to an intersection or fork he took the high road, increasingly steeper as he pressed toward the mountaintop, imminent now, too dazzling to look upon. Ahead, souls were slowing, forming queues.

Waiting turns to meet their Maker.

Here their escort angels parted company to enter a huge amphitheater—composing the glorious choir that echoed across the Heavens.

Ian dared a look at the summit, shielding his eyes with a hand—before remembering it a useless gesture. Except, *it no longer was.* Astonished, he saw shadow! His skin had lost its translucence. It was nearly as pale as the marble buildings, and he could feel himself heavier.

A chill came over him. He'd underestimated his body's resilience. *He was dying.* And at the pace the queue was moving, he knew he'd never make it. His soul would solidify, its weight dragging him down to Purgatory before he could deliver his message.

I have to jump the line!

If ever he needed to rely on the kindness of strangers, this was the place . . .

He pushed forward, meeting no resistance. His soul simply passed through those ahead, no objections, only an occasional gasp of surprise. The luminosity was so intense now he had to avert his eyes. And when finally he broke through the line, he crashed headlong into something hard.

Stunned, he bounced back, squinting down at two powerful male legs in golden sandals. Then to the hem of a white tunic cinched by golden belt and scabbard. And at eye level, a broad chest and two muscular arms—one wielding a sword of fire, tapping it into a large, open palm.

Ian swallowed, staring up into the scowl of an *Archangel,* no doubt, one of God's soldier/messengers.

The creature regarded him through fierce blue eyes, face stern and boldly sculpted, hair golden and flowing. In a gruff voice, he demanded, *"Who goes before the Throne of Divinity?"*

"A, a humble soul—with an urgent message!"

"Speak."

"For God's Ears only."

Ian tried to skirt by, but the angel lowered his sword like a flaming toll gate. Ian recalled the Devil's words that no violence was allowed in Heaven—and surely not within the aura of the Almighty Himself. But then he also recalled that a great battle had once been fought here against the rebellious angels . . .

He was beginning to despair when an aged voice intervened.

"This is a soul in distress," it said, crackling with authority. "He may pass."

Over the flame Ian saw another angel. Tall, slim, in a floor-length white robe. Ancient-looking—long white hair and beard, eyes pale, skin wan and wrinkled. But his withered appearance belied his grace as he approached. Ian presumed him of the highest angelic order, one of God's personal servants, known simply as *Angels.*

"Come," he said, motioning Ian forward.

The Archangel grumbled but raised his sword, and the old spirit took Ian's arm, leading him toward the light.

As they walked, the Angel regarded Ian's many scars.

"My, you've suffered."

"You've no idea . . ."

They proceeded up a path, and as they neared the crest Ian slowed.

"My robe," he said. "Will God be offended?"

The Angel looked him up and down, then shrugged.

"It depends on His Mood."

Ian blinked. "God has *moods*? Like people?"

"No," the old spirit said matter-of-factly. "People have moods, *like God*."

As Ian mulled this they arrived at a tall steeple of rock, steps carved into it, spiraling upward, disappearing into the brightness. The old man halted.

"All must meet their Maker alone."

Ian nodded, feeling a surge of trepidation. He wasn't prepared. But then, was *anyone* ever prepared for this moment? He felt the Angel's hand on his shoulder.

"I pray you find what you've come for, my son."

Ian thanked him, watching his thin frame melt back into the haze . . .

Never had he felt so alone or afraid. Despite having devoted most of his life to the Supreme Being he was about to meet, Ian really didn't Know Him. He had no idea what to expect. All the years he'd talked to God, it was always a monologue. He'd never felt his prayers were heard, never heard an Answer. Then in later years, frustrations and doubts mounting, the tone of his prayers had grown sullen. Until finally, not long ago, he'd renounced God altogether. Waged a campaign against Him. Like the Fallen Angels!

And now he was to bare his spiteful soul to that God?

His nerve deserted him, panic clawing. Yet from somewhere within, he Understood that the strange, convoluted course of his life had led him inexorably here . . .

He took a breath and started up the stairs, the brilliance so searing now he could scarcely see. With each step he felt himself weaken, his soul taxed beyond limits, mind reeling.

Then all too soon the peak tapered and he arrived at a flat table of rock, falling to his knees, the Moment at hand.

ONE HUNDRED TEN

A PRIVATE ESTATE OUTSIDE CAYENNE, FRENCH GUYANA, SAME DAY, LATE MORNING

Having bribed her cabbie to hurry, Angela sped back to the mansion, screeching up to its guardhouse. She expected armed sentries—instead, disturbing quiet, gate wide open.

"Go! Go!" she cried, siren screaming in her head.

The driver pushed on, no movement on the grounds, no guards. House dark and desolate. Angela knew what it meant for Ian if the power was off.

"Flashlight!" she begged. "Matches! Lighter!"

The cabbie fished a flashlight from the glove box.

"Don't you dare leave!" she ordered, leaping out without paying.

The front door was ajar and she entered, heart pounding. No answer to her calls, light switches dead. She snapped on the flashlight, spotting a large envelope on the floor.

Valerie's envelope!

Torn open, the Reality gone.

"Ian!" she screamed, bolting to the elevator. Not working, precious seconds lost. She searched out a stairway, down to the basement, dark as her fears. Around a corner, casting her light beam on the table—

And there he lay, pale and motionless, abandoned . . .

She rushed to him, heart hammering, placing a hand to his cheek. *Cold.* She felt for a pulse in his neck. *None.*

He was still hooked to the equipment—as if a wind from the Devil's Triangle had swept away the living. How long he'd lain neglected she had no idea, the coolant pads that wrapped him barely cool to the touch.

Overcome, she lost it, dropping to her knees, letting out a wail that echoed through the mansion.

ONE HUNDRED ELEVEN

THE PINNACLE OF HEAVEN, TIME EVERLASTING

Ian hunkered atop the table of rock, petrified, engulfed in an aura so brilliant it was all but tangible. He could feel God's Presence, if not see Him. From below, the invisible angel chorus blazoned up as Ian rehearsed the message he was sworn to deliver.

It seemed like hours he'd been here, surely only moments. Then the choir softened, the light surged, and suddenly the atmosphere abounded with a resonance beyond anything Ian had ever experienced. As much in mind as ears, reverberating inside and out, existing everywhere at once.

"ASK AND YOU SHALL RECEIVE," came a Voice ancient, powerful, and eternal, fatherly and commanding, loving and intimidating.

"KNOCK AND IT SHALL BE OPENED."

Ian shrank back, quaking. But he gathered his courage and sputtered, "Lord, I—I ask nothing for myself. I come on behalf of others. I bear a message from, from Your angels in Hell—"

No sooner did the last word leave his lips than the singing ceased, all Heaven lapsing into a Silence unlike anything Ian had ever not heard. Then a murmur began to build. The consternation of countless anxious spirits.

Fearing his message would be drowned out, Ian rushed to finish, blurting, "Lord, Your fallen servants seek Your Forgiveness, but if in Your Wisdom You choose to deny them, they ask to be turned back to the nothingness from which You—"

A fierce wind cut him short, all Heaven cowering. The brilliance flashed and the Almighty Voice bellowed, *"SPEAK NOT OF THE DAMNED!"*

Ian cringed, expecting to be hurled into the Abyss. He begged, "Forgive me, Lord—I was only trying to help them, they suffer so . . ." Trailing off, he realized in panic, *I just ignored a direct command from God!*

The flashing ebbed, the wind died, and there was more Silence. Ian felt suddenly naked. Mind and soul laid bare, penetrated to the deepest recesses.

The Voice said, *"THERE IS TURMOIL IN YOUR HEART. YOU KNOW OF EVIL."*

Ian swallowed. God Knew all.

"YOU SEE BUT YOU DO NOT UNDERSTAND."

"Yes, Lord," he admitted, "I don't Understand. I want to Know You. All Humanity wants to Know You. But the harder we try, the more confused we get."

There was perfect quiet, then God said, *"HAVE I NOT SENT COMMANDMENTS TO GUIDE YOU? PROPHETS TO INSTRUCT YOU? HOW DO YOU NOT UNDERSTAND?"*

"We've done a poor job preserving Your Words, Lord," Ian confessed. "The Bible is riddled with contradictions, we have *three* versions of Your Commandments, and no one can agree on Your Will. We've built ourselves another Tower of Babel."

There came a sigh of infinite indignation.

"I SENT YOU MY SON, WHAT MORE MUST I GIVE?"

Two thousand years was perhaps a blink of God's Eye, but in the time since Man last heard from Christ, it seemed the world needed a refresher course. Ian hung his head.

"You surely Know, we've muddled *His* Message, too. Christianity is splintered into hundreds of sects, each with a different take on Who You are and what You want of us. And all across the world, Christian is fighting Muslim, is fighting Jew, Hindu against Buddhist, on and on. All killing in Your Name. All gone terribly wrong."

The sigh rolled into thunder—*"CURSE THE DAY WHO DO VIOLENCE IN MY NAME!"*

Ian cowered. "We need Your Clarity, Lord. If only Man Knew the Reality of salvation, surely the hatred and bloodshed would end."

"YOU WOULD REMOVE THE TEST OF FAITH BY WHICH MAN IS JUDGED?"

How impudent—*presuming to advise God!*

From somewhere below came the anxious voice of the elderly Angel. *"Enough! You try God's Patience! Others wait!"*

Still, a last question . . . What had his parents done to deserve damnation? Yet Ian dared not ask. Should God learn of his deal with the Devil, his parents would be cast back into the Pit.

But Ian forgot, God could read thoughts!

"SO SHALL YOU KNOW YOUR PARENTS' SIN!"

Was it surprise or anger he heard in God's Voice? Either, it was terrifying!

"IN LIFE, YOUR PARENTS WERE WELL BLESSED. YET IN THEIR HOUR OF TRIAL DID THEY ABANDON FAITH IN ME, YIELDING TO DESPAIR, CURSING MY NAME. THEREFORE DID THEY EARN THE ABYSS."

Ian was reminded of the story of Job. His parents had failed the Test. Regardless, Ian still found their punishment extreme. How could one desperate mistake made under the most stressful circumstances outweigh a lifetime of good works? How could an all-Good, all-Loving God act so unGodly? Was He perhaps in a foul mood that fateful day?

The Almighty's Voice came booming back, *"MUST YOU KNOW THE MIND OF GOD?"*

Ian didn't say, but he thought it. And no sooner had he than there came a brilliance to surpass all before.

God exhaled a tempest, declaring in a Voice that shook the Heavens, *"BEHOLD! SO SHALL IT BE . . ."*

ONE HUNDRED TWELVE

THE BASEMENT OF A PRIVATE ESTATE OUTSIDE CAYENNE, FRENCH GUYANA, SAME DAY, LATE MORNING

With Ian lying pale and cold before her, for how long she had no idea, Angela didn't bother to call an ambulance. No EMS crew in the world would do anything but pronounce him dead.

She was on her own.

Rushing to the backup generator in a corner, telling herself it wasn't sabotaged, she flipped the ignition switch and fired its starter. It churned to life, the room lights winking on.

"Thank God! Thank God!"

Doubts crowding, she switched on the equipment. She was a psychologist, not a physician.

"You worked in a hospital once," she reminded herself, sidestepping that it had been a psychiatric ward. "You're trained in CPR. And you've seen this procedure—twice!"

She had in fact watched closely. Little comfort now as she faced the wall of intimidating machinery.

"Cardio-bypass first," she recalled, anxiously studying its many dials and gauges.

But as she racked her memory for the steps, she was interrupted by a strange echoing over the hums and beeps. A calm, unhurried clip-clop on the marble floor behind.

As if some skeletal finger tapped her shoulder, she turned to see a large man in a brimmed hat rounding a corner. Hair blond and long, face as placid as if he were strolling a park on a summer day.

But eyes cold as winter.

She'd never seen him before, though she knew who—*what*—he was.

"Vell, vell, little *Kaninchen,*" he said, voice deep, cavalier, "you got whole airport after me. Now I must find 'nother vay home."

Numb, she retreated, backing into the wall of equipment, frantically glancing around for a weapon. Scalpel, hypodermic needle—anything.

Nothing.

He removed his hat and tossed it aside like a man home from a day at the office.

"How I vait for dis moment," he sighed, and he unfastened his belt.

Horrified, Angela watched him remove it and loop the end back into its buckle, holding it like a lasso, lips curling in a wet grin. She flattened against the machinery.

"You don't have to do this! You have the Reality!"

"Ja. Reality ist bits of litter on road now. I habe new reality for you, pretty one."

He made a move and she ducked, but he was too quick and strong, slinging the noose round her neck, hauling her upright, slamming her against the equipment. Her cry died in her throat as he snugged the garrote tight with one fist, forcing her to look up at him, eyes feral, breath hot.

"So sad," he cooed. "You find lover dead und hang yourself fur grief . . ."

She flailed at him, fists mere nuisance against his bulk. Tried to knee him, but he'd pinned her legs apart.

And to her disgust she realized—*he was aroused.*

Her lungs burned, face on fire, tears squeezing out as if her eyes would explode.

Then in a final indignity, the monster slathered his thick lips over hers, his free hand fondling.

Not like this! she screamed silently. *Don't let me end like this!*

But she was weakening, growing faint, vision blurring.

ONE HUNDRED THIRTEEN

THE PRESENCE OF GOD IN THE FOREVER OF TIME

About to be granted a glimpse into the Mind of God, Ian trembled, no idea what he'd gotten himself into.

Beware what you ask for.

But it was too late. The aura of brilliance around him was dimming as, a short distance away, a large halo of light materialized. Ian could make out a tree inside. *Half* a tree—split down the middle. Ancient-looking, thick trunk, long, spreading limbs.

Was he to be the first man since Adam to Know Good and Evil? The prospect was both thrilling and terrifying.

The Tree appeared healthy despite its injury. Bushy with leaves, branches full of blossoms and ripe fruit—golden apples. One hung low, glistening, gleaming.

God's voice boomed again. *"TAKE AND EAT, AND ALL THINGS OF THE SPIRIT SHALL YOU KNOW."*

Ian wasn't sure he wanted to Know all things of the spirit. But the fruit beckoned like a siren, mesmerizing.

Slowly he rose, legs weak, moving closer—if only for a better look.

God warned, *"SUCH KNOWLEDGE IS NOT FOR MORTALS. FIRST MUST YOU CAST OFF THE CORD THAT BINDS YOU TO LIFE."*

The Divine Catch.

Ian halted inches away, hunger pangs rumbling deep. Before him, Answers. Secrets of Eternity. The Meaning of Everything. And all he had to do was die . . .

Another great wind swept the Heavens and Ian felt a vacuum in his soul, realizing God had departed. The spirits below cried out in disappointment and frustration. Had God left in anger? Or merely so Ian might wrestle his decision alone?

He eyed the luscious fruit, so beguiling.

No, he couldn't. He wouldn't desert Angela. Who would protect her now from the Evil he'd brought upon her? Even if he had lost her love, *his* love endured. And it transcended his desire for this Knowledge.

Just thinking of Angela now, he sensed her—and he felt a dreadful shudder. To his horror, he realized she was dying! He could feel the very life force draining from her! Feel her panic and desperation! She had but seconds!

"God help her!" he begged into the vastness.

But God was no longer listening. No more than He'd listened to Ian's prayers in the past. Angela was losing her life as Antonio and Valerie had lost theirs, Ian responsible and powerless. He felt cursed. Cursed in Heaven.

With no hope for her now, in his anger and desperation he chose to join her. Life without Angela held nothing. Here, he had an eternity to win her back . . .

He reached up and snatched the apple.

Instantly he felt the tether on his soul snap, a great tension releasing. He raised the fruit to his eyes, seeing his anguish and despair reflected in its golden skin. How could *any* Knowledge make sense of his confusion?

Whatever the apple's Secrets, Ian was no longer afraid. He sank his teeth into it. Crisp, cool, sweet. Delicious beyond anything he'd ever tasted.

But to his surprise, a bitter aftertaste.

He waited in the stillness. All Heaven waited, it seemed.

And then, he could *feel* It. The Knowledge slowly entering . . . Subtle, drifting in, stealing into his awareness. He could actually *see* It. Like a galaxy forming around him. A golden, spiraling nebula folding in on him, silken strands circling his consciousness, growing in size and clarity and brilliance. Countless shining stars in a breathtaking array of colors. Astonishingly beautiful!

No, *not* stars, he realized. As the points of light drew closer, they resolved into four-dimensional dioramas—moving images, playing out scenes of love and sacrifice and nobility. He stared, mesmerized.

A threadbare Cambodian boy carrying his grandfather on his back, fleeing the Khmer Rouge . . . A politician sacrificing reelection to vote his conscience . . . A teenage girl defying her peer group to befriend an outcast . . .

Ian *lived* the experiences. These star-images orbiting him, they were

Eternal Records, he Knew. Living archives of every act of human kindness, integrity, and selflessness ever there was, ever there would be.

Overcome, he felt filled with hope for Humankind.

But then abruptly he felt a harsh pang from somewhere deep within. Reminder that there was yet *another* Knowledge present at his core. A Black Hole, awakening. Expanding. Swirling in the opposite direction.

The Golden Nebula continued to circle him, closing on the Black Hole, two forces spinning faster as the distance narrowed. Cosmic hurricanes roaring to a showdown—irresistible Good converging on immovable Evil.

Ian watched spellbound as the collision impended, wisps of Knowledge stretching ever closer to the event horizon. And when at last a scintilla of Everlasting Light brushed the edge of Infinite Darkness, there came a suspension of Everything, the entire Universe at a standstill . . .

Followed by an explosion so prodigious and apocalyptic, Ian thought God Himself was screaming.

Simultaneously the forces burst to infinity and imploded into a single point, each absorbing the other, consuming even the emptiness of space, sucking in all until *nothing* remained.

ONE HUNDRED FOURTEEN

THE BASEMENT OF A PRIVATE ESTATE OUTSIDE CAYENNE, FRENCH GUYANA, SAME DAY, LATE MORNING

Angela stood crushed against the wall of medical machinery, in the foul embrace of the assassin, noose clamped tight around her neck. She felt her life ebbing, fight drained out of her, eyes blurring, arms sinking to her sides. As she slumped toward oblivion, her hand brushed the equipment behind, and she latched on in a death grip. Only to realize—

A cardiac paddle.

Its mate was right there, inches away! She stretched for it, straining against her attacker's bulk, fingertip touching . . .

No good. Her strength was gone, she couldn't reach it.

Everything was now starting to go white, and she could feel herself fading, dissolving, slipping into a merciful glow of peace and tranquility. It was seductive, and she was too weary to resist any longer. With thoughts of Ian, she surrendered to it . . .

And then suddenly from nowhere and everywhere, she was rocked out of her stupor by an unworldly resonance. Unlike anything she'd ever heard. A harrowing, bellowing wail of pain and anger and indignation—louder, *louder*!

So piercing it jolted her back to consciousness. She lurched out for the paddle again, this time grabbing hold, and in a last muster of will and resilience, she swung her arms up, slapped the plates to the brute's head, and fired.

Bang!

He whipped back, cried out, and released her.

She dropped the paddles and collapsed, clawing the strap at her neck, gulping air. She couldn't move, it was all she could do to regain her breath, drooped against the equipment in a daze. Her inner voice, it seemed, had saved her . . .

But slowly, as her senses returned, she raised her eyes. Through fog she saw the man on his knees next to her, head hanging as he shook it.

Oh God! Oh God!

Somehow she summoned the strength to reach for the defibrillator dial, swiping at it, spinning it to full power. Then reeling in the paddles by their cords, she fumbled for the handles, turning to find him eye-to-eye, and glaring.

"*Schlampe!*" he roared.

She screamed and slammed the paddles to his temples once more, firing. His eyes rolled back in their sockets and he heaved up, hurling backward, his head striking the table corner with a sickening thud. He slumped to the floor, a grunt escaped his lips, and he went still.

Angela sat horrified, panting. He wasn't moving, didn't appear to be breathing. She inched toward him, reaching out with shaky fingers, feeling for a pulse in his wrist as if touching plague.

Nothing.

If she'd had time to break down, she would have. But with Ian lifeless on the table, precious time wasting, she wiped her eyes and struggled to her feet.

"Cardio-bypass," she began again, hands trembling such that she could scarcely work the controls. She flipped a switch to send blood coursing through Ian's veins, reset the clock, opened IV valves to start stimulants dripping. Other steps for which she had no understanding, she was forced to skip.

The jobs of three, but she persevered, steadily raising his temperature, having to guess the proper rate.

Fifteen Celsius, slowly climbing . . . sixteen, seventeen. Slight color returning to his cheeks—a hopeful sign!

Please! Please! Please!

She switched on the ventilator, filling his lungs with oxygen. As his temperature approached target, she applied lubricant to the area of his heart like she'd seen the doctors do, preparing for the defibrillator, excited to feel his skin warm, see his chest rise and fall with artificial breath.

The critical moment neared, time for the paddles—

And then she froze, siren blaring.

The assassin! Focused on Ian, she'd ignored him, and now she could feel him rising up behind her like some B-movie monster, noose in hand.

Cringing, she turned . . .

To see him on his back as before, motionless, arms at his sides, eyes wide and staring. A pool of blood had formed under his head and the front of his pants were wet dark.

She gasped with relief, and fighting a wave of nausea, she stepped past him to collect the paddles, certain he'd reach for her.

He didn't. Now if only her luck would hold . . .

She adjusted the defibrillator to its first setting and placed one paddle over Ian's heart, the other on his side. And the instant the temperature gage ticked to twenty-nine, she closed her eyes, held her breath, and fired.

Boom!

He bucked, and she shrieked, jumping back. But then he fell still again, monitors impassive.

She upped the amps and repositioned the paddles, waiting for the light, clenching her teeth, giving him another shock. Again he convulsed, again she shrieked.

Again, no pulse.

"Please God, please don't take him!"

She moved the dial another click and jolted him again. Nothing. Raised it again, jolted him again—over and over, fast as the paddles could recharge. Until at last she was at maximum, his chest blistering. The clock showed twenty minutes elapsed, temperature normal. And no sign of life.

Drawing back his lids, she searched for the blueness she so loved, seeing his irises dull, pupils fixed. All around, the monitors were dormant.

She could contain herself no longer. Despair striking like a mallet to her heart, she hurled the paddles to the floor, buried her face in his smoldering chest, and sobbed.

ONE HUNDRED FIFTEEN

PARADISE IN A MOMENT OF FOREVER

Ian awoke to find himself beside the golden waters of a brook, lying braced against the trunk of a tree. As his eyes cleared he realized it wasn't the Tree of Knowledge, but very old nonetheless, branches long and bent low, heavy with clusters of golden cherries and blossoms.

Beneath him was a soft bed of golden petals, more floating down on a gentle, fragrant breeze, sleepy, dreamlike. Nearby, songbirds trilled. In the distance, a comforting chorus of angels.

And then he realized he was not alone. Seated barefoot and cross-legged to his left were a man and woman he'd never seen. Handsome couple. Middle-aged, skin ebony. The woman wore a simple white tunic, gold earrings, necklace, bracelets, and rings. Her hair was dark and plaited, wrapping her head in an intricate design, adorned with golden bangles. The man's hair was dark and close-cropped, and he was bare-chested, wearing a white sarong, no jewelry.

Several yards beyond, Ian saw a tall, broad-shouldered Archangel with golden hair, back to them, flaming sword in hand, as if standing guard.

The man and woman smiled, eyes questioning. Ian tried to sit, too weak. And then he recalled with a start—

Angela!

Just the thought of her brought the awareness that she was alive! To his great astonishment and relief, somehow she'd survived, thank God!

His mind jumped again.

"My parents!"

"They are safe," the man answered, his voice a soothing baritone, no discernable accent. "They reside in Limbo now. First ever to escape Damnation."

Ian realized this was true. He *felt* them there.

Excited, he tried to rise, still feeble.

"I have to see them . . ."

The man placed a warm hand on his arm.

"You cannot. Persefoni will not allow it." His smile expanded to reveal perfect white teeth. "She is *furious.*"

Ian sank back, mind reeling.

The woman asked, "How do you feel, my son?"

"I-I don't know . . . *Confused.*"

"What did you see atop Mt. Empyrean?"

He rubbed his eyes, surprised to feel skin beneath his fingers. In Heaven, it appeared, death brought tangibility to the soul. And, he noticed, a pure whiteness to his robe.

"I saw God," he said. "At least, I *think* I saw Him. I saw into His Mind. But It wasn't what I expected. I found Goodness and Love, yes, great, boundless Love." He sighed. "But also *Darkness.* Infinite, unbearable Darkness."

The man nodded. "You found Good, and you found Evil. That is the True Nature of God. That is the Knowledge you came for."

Ian forced himself upright. "*Impossible.* God is perfect."

"Yes. Perfectly Good and perfectly Evil, in perfect measure."

The woman added, "It is Man who equates perfection with the absence of Evil. The image of an all-Good God comes from Man, not God."

"It comes from the Bible!" Ian insisted, stunned. "It's the foundation of Faith!"

The man smiled gently. "God's Darkness is as evident in the Bible as His Light. Does not the Lord giveth with one Hand and taketh away with the Other? Is He not loving and kind one moment, wrathful, vengeful, and jealous the next? Look to Lamentations, 3:38: *'Out of the mouth of the Most High doth not there proceed Evil and Good?'* "

The woman said, "Nothing is beyond God. He is the embodiment of All. Highest Good, basest Evil, whichever serves His Great Purpose. Why else would Man fear Him?"

Ian was appalled. This violated everything Faith stood for! No, this man and woman, whoever they were, they were wrong!

"God may *allow* Evil," he was willing to concede, feeling a desperate need to defend the Almighty, "but God Himself, He does not *create* Evil!"

"In the Lord's Own Words," the man said, "Isaiah, 45:7: *'I form the*

Light and create the Darkness: I make Peace and create Evil: I, the Lord, do all these things . . .'"

Ian fell back against the tree. How could it be stated any clearer? A declaration of divine duplicity from God's Own Mouth, plucked straight from the Bible! God as Jekyll and Hyde!

The Paradox, resolved!

Seen in this light, Ian realized, Scripture was indeed *filled* with examples of God's Iniquity. The collateral damage alone from His piques of anger—women, children, elderly, and infirm put to the sword, enslaved, burned, crushed, stoned, starved, and drowned. Even defenseless animals, Noah's ark being only three hundred by fifty cubits.

"Apart from the Bible," the woman said, "the Truth of God's Nature is all around, if Man would but see. Everywhere in the world are Signs."

Ian was amazed to Know she was right. God's True Nature was and always had been on display, apparent in the natural calamities that befell Mankind. Earthquakes, hurricanes, plagues, volcanoes, floods, droughts. Acts of God, were they not?

The man offered, "Man himself is a Sign. A Metaphor. Look to Genesis 1:26."

Ian recalled the passage, a straightforward statement from the very first chapter of the Bible: *And God created Man in His Own image and likeness.*

Indeed, Man was a reflection of his Maker. Not in the physical sense, as so often interpreted. *Spiritually.*

Good *and* Evil.

"Unfortunately," the woman explained, "Man hasn't yet the Wisdom to balance his nature."

Ian wondered now how he could have gotten God so wrong. How the world could have gotten Him so wrong. Or perhaps, refused to see.

Lucien is right, he realized. *God's Truths are clarifications of things we should already Know—conspicuous in the countless Signs we see in the universe. Light/darkness; order/chaos; creation/destruction; life/death. On and on. All born of the same thinking that gave us Heaven/Hell. Insights into the Mind of God!*

Ian felt his last breath of Faith leak out of him like the air from an overpatched inner tube. He no longer Believed. He *Knew.* And he Knew now why his life had always felt so bereft of God. Why the *world* felt so bereft of God . . .

Once, long ago, God walked among us. Spoke to us. Listened to us. If we faced adversity, we could appeal directly to Him through prayer and sacrifice, and God could be moved to intervene. Showering manna from Heaven. Dividing seas. Smiting our enemies with fire and brimstone. Overt displays of His Presence.

No longer. No such miracles anymore. God had distanced Himself. It's something we all suspected—more so any parent who'd ever lost a child—the fear that God wasn't listening. A fear no manner of theological apologia could ease . . .

As if reading his mind, the woman said, "God's patience ended not long after the death of His Son. Christ came to free Man, not enslave him. Yet many abused Christ's Words to control the minds of others, wielding Scripture for power and gain. When God saw, He turned away in disgust. Now His only contact with Man is in Heaven. You are the first living soul to speak with Him since."

Ian Understood, but couldn't accept. "How can God just abandon us? His Own Creation!"

"In His Wisdom, God did not leave the world helpless. Within Man's limitless mind and universe is everything needed for him to succeed. Even to heal the Rift with God."

"But Man *isn't* succeeding! He's destroying himself—and the Earth along with him!"

Ian saw clearly, Man was a child still. An orphan searching for his missing Parent, afraid to face the world alone, clinging to the security blanket of religion. Even as religion obscured God's Signs—or worse, smothered Man's innate compassion with self-righteous intolerance.

Frightened for the world, Ian pleaded, "How does Man heal the Rift?"

The man and woman exchanged long glances. Then the man turned to Ian. "God no longer endures the pleas of the world. But He is not insensitive to the prayers of Heaven. There may still be a way—if you are willing."

"Me?"

Patting Ian's arm, he reached to pluck a cluster of golden cherries from the tree. As he did, Ian noticed a scar stretching across his flank, a rib missing.

The man handed Ian the fruit.

"You are the first soul ever to attain both the Pit of Hell and Pinnacle of Heaven. Perhaps there is hope yet for the Family of Man. Eat . . ."

Ian accepted the cherries, confused, staring into the eyes of the only other beings ever to taste the Knowledge of Good and Evil.

Raising a cherry to his lips, he bit into sweet ripeness. And he began to feel sleepy again.

"Rest now, my son," the woman told him.

He lay back, fading.

And last he saw were their perfect white smiles . . .

ONE HUNDRED SIXTEEN

SOMEWHERE IN THE VAST HEAVENS

Black, starlit sky. Perfectly clear, intense, surreal. Below, a billowy landscape of cloud undulating away to the horizon, accompanied by a lulling, droning sound . . .

Ian blinked, lying on his side, stiff and achy. He rolled onto his back, feeling a sharp pain in his upper leg. Then a warm hand touched his arm and he looked up, stunned.

Ecstatic!

Angela!

They were in a small jet, he saw, the only passengers. He was reclined in a window seat under a blanket, having awakened on the night sky—and now, an angel!

A tattered angel. Angela looked anxious and exhausted, eyes red-rimmed, blouse torn, nasty welt encircling her neck. As if she herself had been through Hell.

She leaned into him, giving him a big hug, crying, *"Please tell me you're still in there."*

He winced, needing a second to unstick his tongue. "Yes . . . all here."

Pulling back she searched his eyes, looking hopeful, if wary. "You've been talking in your sleep—I told myself it was a good sign . . . Count backwards from a hundred."

"Trust me, I could count backwards from infinity now."

He tried to sit, sore everywhere. She helped him raise his seat, and he took her hand.

"I don't understand," he said. *"What happened?"*

Her face clouded. "The Order. They found the lab and drove everyone off. They left you to die. When I got there it was deserted, everything shut down.

"And then a Sword came back . . ." He could feel her pulse pounding through her fingers. "It's okay; I took care of him. He crossed wires with the wrong girl."

Ian couldn't imagine. It seemed Angela had proven again that the Order wasn't the invincible force they'd once thought. More than ever now, he was convinced they would somehow prevail—as long as they had each other.

"I worked on you twenty minutes," Angela continued. "I was sure you were dead. Then—I don't know how—your heart just started beating again! I was afraid more Swords would come, so once you were stable I bundled you up and got you to the plane. A cabbie helped."

She paused. "I'm sorry, the Reality is gone. The Sword destroyed it."

All Ian cared about now was that he had Angela back.

He sighed. "I never thought I'd hear from you again."

There was a flash of hurt in her eyes and she retorted, "And you wouldn't have, either. But after I left you this morning, waiting on the plane to take off, I saw something. Something I think will open your mind to these NDEs . . ."

She withdrew a psychology journal from her purse.

"I was hiding behind this when suddenly—there it was, staring me right in the face!"

Opening, she held up a color image of the human brain, bisected to expose its many components, each labeled.[25]

"A brain? I don't get it."

"Read these," she said, indicating the names for the regions of the lower brain.

Mumbling through, he was none the wiser.

"Look closer. Remember your names for the Realms of Hell?"

She pointed to a walnut-shaped structure near the brain stem, inflecting her voice, "*Cereb*ellum—'Hades of the *Sereb* . . .' "

Moving to an almondlike organ in the center: "Thalamus. I looked it up, Greek—*Inner Chamber* . . ."

And just beneath that: "Hypothalamus—*Sub Chamber.*"

Ian was incredulous.

"They're all here. Medulla oblongata—*Metal Oblong Gate*. Pituitary—the *Pit* of Hell . . ."

Ian traced an unsteady finger across the gray matter of the upper brain, also seeing its parts reflect the names the angels had ascribed to the Heavenly Realms.

He felt his chest tighten.

Angela closed the journal.

"Your subconscious had been signaling you from the start. The NDEs were all in your head. Literally. A bastardized blend of old memories—biology, scripture, movies, who-knows-what?—cobbled together into your own private Hell."

Dumbfounded, Ian sank in his seat.

The logic seemed overwhelming. The lower brain—the primitive half—was the recognized source of Man's base instincts and emotions. *Evil.* Which clashed endlessly with the upper brain, source of reason and rational thought. *Good.* Had his subconscious simply played off his awareness of that? If so, why did he feel so *different* now? These strange thoughts! And he recalled something the woman under the Tree had said: "God's Signs are all around, if Man would but see."

Could it be the human brain was *itself* a Sign? A Metaphor? The Afterlife in microcosm?

But Angela wasn't finished.

"When you lost your parents, you felt abandoned. A common reaction in children too young to understand death. Subconsciously you blamed them for your pain and loneliness, and you carried that your entire life.

"Until the idea of seeing them again brought it to the surface during your NDEs. *That's* why you imagined your parents in Hell—to punish them for leaving you. At the same time, you felt responsible for their deaths and duty-bound to rescue them . . ."

Ian saw empathy in her eyes, her hand tightening on his.

"Sweetheart, you've been through a terrible ordeal. But now that you've faced your demons, it'll be cathartic. You'll finally be able to lay your nightmares to rest."

Cathartic? That wasn't how it felt. The Knowledge, real or imagined, still lingered in his soul, filling him with anxiety.

Angela opened her purse again. "By the way, after that business with your scapular, I want to check something with you . . ."

His mind raced. If his NDEs *were* real, it meant his return to life wasn't merely good fortune and Angela's heroics. It meant he'd been *sent* back. Man was being given another chance—and *he*, Ian, was that chance! Except that was preposterous. If Christ Himself was unable to save Mankind, what absurd hope had *he*?

Angela continued her rooting. "I almost threw them away . . ."

Ian felt a great weight descending on his shoulders like a monstrous vulture. This Knowledge, he wanted nothing more to do with it! Angela was right, it *was* all in his head. Another delusion. Another expression of that manic, lifelong, obsessive-compulsive neurosis inside him.

A neurosis that was now trying to manifest itself in a messiah complex!

Enough! It's over!

"Aha," she said, turning back to him. "Look what I pried out of your fist in the lab . . ."

His weary eyes fell on her open palm.

Cherries. Golden cherries.

LIST OF IMAGES

(Available for viewing at: kleier.com/images)